Enchanting the CEO
Layla Hagen

Copyright ©2024 Layla Hagen

All rights reserved. No part of this book may be reproduced or transmitted in any form, including

electronic or mechanical, without written permission from the author, except in the case

of brief quotations embodied in critical articles or reviews. This is a work of fiction. Names,

characters, businesses, places, events and incidents are either the products of the author's

imagination or used in fictitious manner. Any resemblance to actual persons, living or dead,

or actual events is purely coincidental.

Contents

1. Chapter One — 1
2. Chapter Two — 11
3. Chapter Three — 20
4. Chapter Four — 32
5. Chapter Five — 42
6. Chapter Six — 49
7. Chapter Seven — 64
8. Chapter Eight — 74
9. Chapter Nine — 81
10. Chapter Ten — 88
11. Chapter Eleven — 101
12. Chapter Twelve — 105
13. Chapter Thirteen — 113
14. Chapter Fourteen — 119
15. Chapter Fifteen — 125
16. Chapter Sixteen — 134
17. Chapter Seventeen — 143
18. Chapter Eighteen — 149

19.	Chapter Nineteen	170
20.	Chapter Twenty	185
21.	Chapter Twenty-One	195
22.	Chapter Twenty-Two	201
23.	Chapter Twenty-Three	212
24.	Chapter Twenty-Four	222
25.	Chapter Twenty-Five	237
26.	Chapter Twenty-Six	242
27.	Chapter Twenty-Seven	252
28.	Chapter Twenty-Eight	263
29.	Epilogue	268

Chapter One
Gabe

"All right, we're done for the day. I'm heading to the bar," I told my assistant, Betty, while arranging my cuff links.

"Working overtime again?" she teased. It was a running joke between us. I wasn't a workaholic, unlike my brothers. But I'd only opened the bar a few months ago, and I made it a habit to stop by after the workday was over.

"Whatever's necessary. All right, see you tomorrow," I said before strolling down the corridor.

I wasn't the last to leave by a long shot. Even though I made it clear when I hired them that I didn't expect them to be here around the clock, everyone worked at their own pace. I rarely stayed in the office past six. My office was in the building just next to the distillery. The bar was in front of it all. It was my pride and joy, my own contribution to the Whitley legacy. Whitley Bar & Distillery was now one of the most popular bars in Boston.

There were already customers inside when I stepped in, as expected. Happy hour was very busy around here. All three bartenders were here tonight, thank fuck. There was a flu going around, so I'd jumped behind the bar on many evenings to help fill in when needed. I considered my employees part of my family. I paid them well and treated them the same; I genuinely wanted people to be happy at their workplace, and

I felt it was my responsibility to provide a decent work environment for them.

I was about to head behind the counter when I noticed that one of my bartenders, Celia, was engaged in conversation.

Celia was one of my favorite people. She was an exceptionally hard worker. She was also insanely attractive, which sometimes got her into trouble. Not with me—I didn't date my employees—but customers started hitting on her after one too many drinks. The guys and I were very protective of her and always made sure no one bothered her. But Celia didn't need our help. She could handle her own battles.

Zeroing in on Celia, I noticed that the woman she was talking to resembled her. She was exceptionally attractive, too, with long blond hair. It reached her elbows and lay in a perfect line across her back. As I continued to the bar, I saw she was eating a burger. We'd introduced some finger foods and other bar staples a while ago, and they were a hit.

"Who's that?" I asked Ron, one of the bartenders.

"That's Diane, Celia's sister. She actually said she wanted to introduce you to her. Hey, Celia," he called to her.

Celia whipped her head in our direction. She smiled when she saw me and gestured for me to come over.

I walked down, and Celia's sister offered me her hand. "Hi, I'm Diane."

"Gabe Whitley," I said, shaking her hand. Up close, I noticed her eyes were blue and gorgeous, and her full lips were a perfect shade of pink. She wasn't wearing any kind of makeup as far as I could tell, and she was hands down one of the most beautiful women I'd ever met.

"So glad you came by tonight. I didn't know if you would," Celia said. "I've wanted to introduce you to my sister ever since... well, since everything went down with Mom."

"How is she feeling?" I asked. Last year, their mother needed help paying off some medical bills. I'd offered to pay them up front, but Celia had flatly refused, so she'd taken a loan of sorts against her salary.

"Much better. Thanks for saving the day."

"I didn't."

Celia looked at me sharply. "Oh yes, you did. I won't let you downplay it."

"Celia, when have you known me not to brag when I get the chance to?"

She grinned. "Anyway, Diane just stopped by to..." She bit her lip, darting her gaze away. That was unlike Celia. She usually didn't mince words and spoke her mind. "Oh crap. A customer needs me."

Did she change the subject on purpose?

"I'll let you get back to work. I need to get going anyway. Just want to finish my burger," Diane said, dangling a set of keys in her hands.

"Bye, sis," Celia added hurriedly before taking the customer's order.

Diane turned to me. "You know, I've been wanting to meet my sister's knight in shining armor for a while."

I grinned. "I really didn't do as much as I'd wanted to, but I'll take that nickname."

She tilted her head. "Wait, you wanted to help more? You've done a lot."

I shook my head. "I wanted to outright pay the bills rather than giving Celia a loan, but she refused."

Diane rolled her shoulders back. "Good thing she did, because that's not right, taking your money like that. Even if you can afford it."

She smiled, leaning forward. She was wearing a tight white dress with thin straps. It cut a straight line over her breasts. I couldn't see her cleavage, but my pulse quickened anyway. I hadn't had this sort of reaction to someone in a long while. I exhaled sharply, maintaining eye contact.

"Anyway," she said, "my sister always talks about you and how great of a boss you are, so I might already have a biased opinion of you."

I grinned, clapping my hands once. "A *good* biased opinion? That's excellent. A change for once."

She tilted her head, smiling. "Wait, so people's opinion of you is usually bad?"

"You did *not* hear me say that," I replied.

She straightened up after she finished her burger. "But you did. Now I can't unhear it."

"Do you want a drink?" I asked.

She frowned. "No. I shouldn't be keeping you from work." She immediately got up from the chair. "I got what I needed, so I should go. By the way, the burger was fantastic."

It was on the tip of my tongue to ask what exactly she needed from her sister, but it was none of my business.

"Are you sure I can't tempt you with anything?" I insisted.

She shook her head. "No, no, I've got lots to do. But it was really great meeting you, Gabe."

I stepped from behind the bar, shaking her hand again. Her eyes fell on my cuff links for a split second before she lifted her gaze. My brothers and I got into the habit of wearing them, which was a bit unusual, especially for a guy filling in as a bartender. They were out of place here.

"And you too," I said. I was tempted to ask her again if she wanted a drink, anything to find an excuse for her to stay, but I couldn't flirt with her. She was Celia's sister, for God's sake.

I inhaled Diane's perfume as she passed me, a mix of roses and something else. I loved it. I'd never smelled that fragrance combination before.

After she left, I went back behind the counter, checking on my bartenders.

"All good?" I asked.

"Yeah, boss," Celia, who was nearest to me, replied. "You don't have to be on duty tonight. We have everything under control."

"All right, then I'm going to head out. See you tomorrow."

My family thought I might be stretched thin because I spent a few hours a week at the bar, but I enjoyed it. It was a welcome change from being stuck in my office all day. I liked being the CEO of my own company, but I also enjoyed bartending and being among people.

But I was glad there was no need for me to stay tonight. I was meeting my family, and I didn't want to cancel on them at the last minute. My brothers and I were getting together at our grandparents' house. Lately, our half brothers, Nick, Leo, and Maddox, would join us, but they couldn't make it tonight.

The Whitley family had a complicated history, to say the least. Our father, Ryan Whitley, had led a double life, resulting in our three half brothers. My second-oldest brother, Jake, had discovered Dad's infidelity, and it was as if a bomb had detonated in our family. My mother became ill soon after and passed away, and my father had lived in Sydney ever since, abandoning everything. We were lucky as hell that our grandparents stepped in and raised us. Well, mostly Cade, Spencer, and me. I was the youngest. Colton and Jake were already adults, though our grandparents offered them stability.

I had always had a great relationship with Nick, Leo, and Maddox. Grandmother said I liked to put a positive spin on things, and it was true. I still remember the day I found out about Dad and our half brothers. I was devastated, of course, and I felt deeply betrayed, but I'd also been curious about meeting them as soon as I knew about them. Jake and Colton hadn't been as interested. I think they'd blamed them somehow and had been at odds with them for years. All that was different now that the two of them had come around, and we all got together regularly.

Ryan Whitley didn't just abandon his family when he left. He'd also abandoned Whitley Industries, the company he'd taken over from our grandfather. As we reached adulthood, each of us kids took over a branch of the business. Unfortunately, Dad left them in dire financial condition, but we were able to turn them around. I was proud to continue the legacy of our family. All of us kids were different from our father. None of us were as self-absorbed as he was.

I arrived at our grandparents' home in the Dorchester neighborhood half an hour later. Spencer's and Jake's cars were already in the driveway.

Grandfather opened the door. "Come in, come in," he said.

I gave him a hug, taking him in. He looked good, but both of our grandparents were in their nineties and had some health scares over the past few years. We all stayed on alert to make sure they had what they needed.

We went to the dining room, where Jake was seated with his wife, Natalie, and Cade with his fiancée, Meredith. My brothers all had better halves, which was perplexing because only two years ago, I would have bet my company that we Whitley boys would remain bachelors forever. Even though they'd succumbed to marital bliss, I certainly intended to stay single—though Grandmother thought she could persuade me otherwise. She told everyone she knew that she'd helped matchmake the rest of my brothers. And in a way, she had, which was scary as shit.

"All right, everyone. Colton and Spencer said they're gonna be late and we should start without them. Dinner is served," Grandmother said dismissively. This was so unlike her, and I glanced at my brothers to see if I could get them to tell me what was going on.

"She's not happy with us because we insisted on ordering in," Cade said in an uncharacteristically serious tone; he was usually laid-back like me. But now I understood her brusqueness.

"I've got to give it to you and Jake. You were quite convincing," she huffed.

Grandmother *always* insisted on cooking. I chose my battles, and although I could convince her of many things, giving up cooking was not one of them. My older brothers were so much better at it. I had a hunch that their better halves had a lot to do with it as well. For some reason, Grandmother was more receptive to their suggestions than to ours. But a win was a win. I didn't care how we achieved it. At their ages, we needed to cater to our grandparents, not vice versa.

As we sat down at the table, Grandmother said, "Gabe, darling, I have a bridge session with some friends on Saturday. Do you mind driving me there?"

I stopped putting mashed potatoes on my plate, contemplating her odd request.

"Isn't Cal available?" Jake asked, unsuccessfully suppressing laughter. Cal was Jake's driver, but he ran errands for the whole family.

Natalie grinned. "Oh, Jeannie."

Meredith was smiling too. "I'm not surprised."

Grandmother looked sternly at Jake. I was obviously missing something.

"I can take you. I don't mind," I said.

She looked at me triumphantly. "Excellent."

"Oh, dude, come on," Cade said. "She wants to introduce you to some of her friends' granddaughters."

"Cade," Grandmother admonished. "Did you have to give me away?"

I started to laugh. "Grandmother, please stop trying to matchmake me. It's not going to happen."

"It will. I simply haven't introduced you to enough young women."

"Right. Because that's the problem," Jake said. "Meeting women."

I must have been exhausted—that was why I didn't see through the ruse. For the past few months, she'd made up reasons for me to drive her to several meetings with her friends, and without fail, she'd always introduce me to a woman. I'd been polite about it all, of course, but I had no intention of settling down, and I hated that Grandmother was going through all of this for nothing.

"But you didn't even take any of them on a date," she added.

"Jeannie, leave the boy alone. Let's change the subject," Grandfather said. "How is the construction on your new home progressing?"

"Slow, but it's going to be faster now that I'm living in the area. I can go there every day," I replied.

Jake rolled his eyes. "Why would you want to oversee construction? It's a nightmare."

I shrugged. "I know, but it's going to be my house. I don't mind putting in the effort."

"You didn't have to literally move in across the street, though," Cade added.

"Yes, I did," I replied.

I might be laid-back, but when I cared about something, I wanted to oversee it personally. That was why I'd rented a house in the same neighborhood. It was a huge villa, and I'd been surprised that it had been available at all. Then I found out that it was two separate units. Unfortunately, the current occupant of the upstairs one was a nightmare.

"Are things going better with the neighbor?" Natalie asked, as if reading my thoughts. My sister-in-law was very good at reading people.

"No," I said. "But I'm going to take care of that."

"Have you offered to pay rent for the whole house?" Jake asked.

"Yes, of course. That was one of the first things I did. But the owner insists that she prefers having two tenants, so if one of them leaves, she still has an income."

"That is a fair point," Meredith said.

Maybe, but the entrance to the attic rental was through the main house. So really, it wasn't a separate unit at all. I didn't have a neighbor, I had a roommate, and it was fucking annoying. But it was the only house available in that area, so I'd taken it anyway. I'd solve the problem of my annoying roommate too. But one thing at a time.

"Well, I, for one, think it's a good thing that you're overseeing the construction closely. It's going to be such a wonderful home. Big enough for a family," Grandmother said.

Grandfather just shook his head while my brothers grinned.

I finished loading my plate with mashed potatoes and turkey breast, then regarded at my grandmother calmly. " I know you have my best interests at heart, but it isn't going to happen. Not on your terms, anyway."

"Huh," she said. "All right, then. If you want to make it happen on your own, I'm good with that." Suddenly her smile encapsulated her entire face. "Oh, Gabe, this is such wonderful news!"

I barely bit down a groan. Crap!

I looked up in time to see Jake and Natalie exchange a glance. Cade was staring straight at me. I knew he couldn't wait to share this with Spencer. They had a bond that I sometimes envied, although all of us were close.

"Oh, just wait until Nick, Maddox, and Leo hear of this," Cade said. "They'll be thrilled that Grandmother can now focus on them, since you're clearly taking matters into your own hands."

"Oh, please. I've been keeping my eye out for suitable companions for them all the while. Now I just have to ramp up my efforts," Grandmother said, making us all laugh.

That was life in the Whitley family. We all looked out for one another, whether we wanted it or not.

Chapter Two

Diane

If I didn't have bad luck, I'd have no luck at all. But right now, the corners of my lips tilted up in a smile as I knocked my elbow on my sister's bedroom door.

"I'm awake," she said.

I walked in carefully, putting a tray with breakfast on her bed.

Celia yawned. "What's this?"

"I want to spoil you a bit. What's the use of having an unwanted house guest if they don't bring you breakfast?" I said in a teasing tone, though I was half serious.

"You're my sister. You're not unwanted."

I was usually such an optimistic person, but over the past six months, my life had taken a complete nosedive.

First, my boyfriend broke my heart. Then my work started downsizing. At least I got lucky and wasn't fired, but they reduced my hours to part-time, and unfortunately, that wasn't nearly enough to pay rent. Shortly after, my landlord evicted me. He probably thought I was a huge risk, and... he was right. I'd debated taking legal recourse, but I didn't have any money for that.

Bottom line was, I had to see the positive in all this. One, I still had a job, and two, I had a roof over my head, even though I was living with my sister. Honestly, I'd missed being this close to her. Growing up, we'd always been real tight.

"You're eating with me?" she asked.

"Obviously. You think I broke my back just so you can eat all these goodies by yourself?"

"I can't believe you did this. Thank you. When did you wake up?"

"About an hour ago."

Her jaw dropped as she checked and saw it was now just six o'clock in the morning. "Why would you wake up so early?"

"I couldn't sleep well," I admitted. "The better question is why are *you* up? You came home late."

Celia yawned. "You know I have a weird sleep schedule."

She had a waitressing job during breakfast hours between nine o'clock and twelve o'clock. She usually slept in the afternoon before waitressing at the bar. She was a damn hard worker. I was determined not to be in her hair for too long.

I'd made an omelet with a side of bacon and toast, plus pancakes with blueberries and a dip that I mixed from honey and a dash of vanilla extract, all topped with whip cream.

"Oh my God. If you spoil me like this every morning, I'm going to get used to it."

"Well, as long as I'm in your hair, you will definitely get spoiled," I said.

I loved cooking, and my sister appreciated it. She always had. My mom had been sickly even when we were kids, so both of us had been on cooking duty for as long as I could remember. Celia disliked being in the kitchen, but I relished it. Creating something from scratch with my own hands was truly my thing.

She yawned, then asked me, "What are you doing today?"

"I have a tour in an hour. Then in the afternoon, I'll unpack and apply for some jobs, but I'm also thinking about tutoring French. I found some online platforms where you can set up a profile and schedule sessions."

Her eyes widened. "You're a genius."

I smiled. "I just want to make the best use of my skills. I can tutor as a freelancer—and the best part is, I'd get the money right away."

"I can lend you some money, sis."

I shook my head. "Don't even say it, okay?"

She bit the inside of her lip. "But I want to help. You're family."

"You're doing enough by letting me stay here."

We both fell silent as we devoured the breakfast.

"What did you think of Gabe?" she asked after a while.

It was on the tip of my tongue to say, *"Why did you never tell me that he's basically the hottest man alive?"*

"He seems friendly enough," I said instead, trying to keep my voice neutral.

"I know, right? I can't believe I'm lucky enough to work for him. Most of the time it feels like I'm working *with* him."

I simply nodded, finishing off the pancakes. Mentioning how hot Gabe was would be akin to opening Pandora's box. My sister would berate me and tell me to stay away from him.

As if.

I had enough on my plate as it was, and my heart was still covered in scars from the breakup.

After breakfast, Celia left for her job, and I left for mine as a tour guide with Boston Guided Tours. I'd been working here ever since I moved to the city.

I was heartbroken that they'd cut back my hours and I could only do it part-time. Soon enough, I wouldn't be able to do it at all if I found another full-time job. Though maybe I could squeeze a few tours in during the weekends.

As I got on the bus, my phone lit up with a notification. My entire body tightened when I saw it was from my ex, Chuck.

Chuck: Did you take anything out of my storage?

I stared at the phone. *Is he for real? He went off the grid for months, and now this? No "Hi, how are you?"*

I wasn't even going to dignify his text with a response. My body was completely wound up, and I hated that he still had this effect on me. Every time I saw his name or thought about him, that wound opened up again.

I managed to shove Chuck Forrester to the back of my mind during the tour. Afterward, I spent my afternoon unpacking my boxes. Yesterday, I'd only opened one with kitchen utensils—my sister had next to nothing, and I needed them to prepare meals while I was here. I didn't have many belongings, which was a sad state of affairs for someone who was now the ripe old age of twenty-six.

I moved to Boston *for* Chuck, who'd promised me the moon and delivered nothing. I'd thought we were in love and marriage was in the future. I was wrong. But I didn't regret moving here. I was happy to be closer to my sister and mom too. Our mom lived in Baltimore, less than a day's drive away. But right now, my life was a mess.

Thank heavens Celia could help me out with her spare bedroom. It was tiny, but I was very happy with it. If she could have only put me up on the couch in the living room, I probably wouldn't have taken her offer. I knew she valued her alone time, and I wanted her to have her space.

After unpacking, I created an account on the tutoring platform, which took up the entire afternoon. I was beyond grateful that I'd taken accredited tests for my French because they qualified me for this job.

I'd done that primarily so I could advertise it on my résumé, but it had benefited me in many different ways, and I was nothing if not flexible. *"Richardsons don't give up"* had always been our mother's motto, and it served me well.

After I set up the account, I wasn't sure what to do with myself. I felt restless, so I got dressed and went outside. It was a sunny April day, but I also grabbed a jacket because the weather was finnicky.

I loved Boston and couldn't be too mad at Chuck for jerking me around, as I probably would have never moved here otherwise. For better or for worse, I was glad that my journey had led me here, though I had hoped I'd be at a more stable point in my life by now.

I passed a small delicatessen shop that sold pancetta, not just regular ham. That gave me an idea, but I wanted to check with my sister first.

Diane: Hey, sorry to disturb you at work. Do you like spaghetti carbonara?

She replied a few seconds later. I thought that was a good thing, as it meant she wasn't too busy. But her message proved the opposite.

Celia: You know I eat anything. Love you for wanting to spoil me. I'm up to my eyeballs in work. Two bartenders are sick. I can't wait for the flu season to be over.

I had no idea the flu was still around. It *was* April already.

Diane: Holy shit, that is not good.

Diane: You want me to come help? I'm good behind the counter.

Celia: You don't mind? You'll get paid, of course.

Diane: Of course. I'm on my way.

We lived quite a ways from the bar, but I immediately looked up the route online. Even though I'd been there yesterday, I didn't remember the name of the subway station. The public transportation system in Boston was so efficient that I'd already put my car up for sale online and was sure I'd sell it any day now.

On the way there, I browsed Craigslist, looking for a shared accommodation because I couldn't afford anything else.

Part of me wanted to ask Celia if she was tempted to move into something bigger with me. But even though she loved me dearly, she liked living alone, and I respected that.

After getting off from the subway, I hurried to the bar. Stepping inside, I glanced around, wondering if Gabe was here too. My heart was beating a bit quicker at the thought, but I told myself it was simply a knee-jerk reaction to the fact that he was so absolutely, impossibly handsome.

Celia should have warned me, and I would have braced myself. Still, it didn't matter. I was certain that I wouldn't see him again.

Five seconds later, I was proven wrong, as Gabe was with my sister behind the bar.

Gabe looked in my direction as I joined them. Sweet Lord, those blue eyes were far too sinful. And his light brown hair... how could it be so thick and shiny?

"Thanks for saving our butts. I'm in your debt," he said somewhat theatrically.

I couldn't get a good read on him. Celia had mentioned that he owned the distillery and wasn't a fancy-ass CEO. But judging by his suit, he was. Yesterday, his cuff links were pretty extravagant, engraved with his initials. On instinct, I lowered my eyes to his wrists, wanting to check if he was wearing a pair today.

Then my knees weakened because Gabe had rolled his sleeves up to the elbows, revealing ink that crisscrossed both his forearms. I didn't recognize the pattern, but it was damn sexy. Swallowing hard, I looked back up.

"All right. What do I have to do?" I asked. My voice was a bit on edge, but I didn't think he could tell. The bar was already quite busy and loud.

"I have a list with run-of-the-mill cocktails that are easy to make," he said. "Why don't you take those over, and Celia and I will do the house creations."

Celia told me that when they'd first opened, they only offered surprise cocktails but gradually added a normal menu of drinks.

"Do you have any experience bartending?" he asked.

I nodded feverishly. "Yeah, I did this a few years back. I'm good at it, though it's best if I stick to the simple drinks. Otherwise, I'll just slow everyone down."

I took in the details. It looked straightforward enough: ice, lime, alcohol, fresh fruit juices. There were also bottles of wine in the fridge underneath the bar. I was ready to go.

Gabe was the one who took the actual orders, and then he passed the easy ones on to me, like Bloody Marys, margaritas, and mojitos. I couldn't help but glance at him every now and again. He looked so at ease talking with customers, making drinks, and slicing lemons and other garnishes.

"Are you deaf?" a male voice asked.

I looked up, one eyebrow raised. "Excuse me?"

"I've been trying to get your attention for ten minutes."

"I've been preparing cocktails," I replied coolly.

"Yeah, but I'm a customer, and I want to order."

"They'll take your order, sir. I just mix them."

He snorted. "Now listen to me. I'm not going to wait until one of—"

"What's going on here?" Gabe said in that strong, sexy voice. I didn't realize he'd moved next to me. "Someone giving you trouble?"

I pointed at the guy. "This man would like a drink."

"If you'd come to the register, we can take your order. Diane's just helping us out for the night," Gabe explained.

"I'm not waiting in that long line. Get me a bourbon on the rocks." It was shocking how rude this guy was, even to Gabe.

I leaned over to Gabe and said, "He seems to think that he can skip the line by intimidating us into making him a drink."

Gabe nodded, then looked at the customer. "I'm going to have to ask you to leave."

The guy snorted, and I wondered if he'd already had one drink too many. "Yeah, right."

"I'm serious. We have security outside. If you don't leave, I'll ask him to escort you."

"You've got some nerve. I'm not going to let a... I want to talk to the owner."

"I *am* the owner," Gabe said without missing a beat.

The guy narrowed his eyes, and Gabe gestured to someone at the far end of the room. "Security is coming to help you find your way out."

"Now, wait a second," he protested. But he barely got the words out before a tall, strong guy I hadn't even seen until now stepped right next to him.

"I'm here to escort you outside," he boomed.

The guy glared at me, then at Gabe. "This is unbelievable. Fuck your shitty establishment."

"By all means, do us all a favor and leave it," Gabe retorted.

He put an arm around my shoulders, and the contact singed me. I wasn't expecting it. I glanced sideways at Gabe, who was still looking between the guy and the bodyguard. Then he tilted his head downward to me and our eyes connected for a brief second.

I immediately shifted and looked to his throat. For some reason, I couldn't hold his gaze. Heat coursed through me, starting from the point where he had splayed his fingers on my shoulder.

He leaned forward, and I realized he was bringing his lips to my ear. "Are you all right? Do you need a break, or do you want to go home?"

I shook my head and accidentally brushed my earlobe against his lips. I sucked in a breath as goose bumps erupted on my skin.

"No, I'm fine, really. He was just annoying."

He straightened up. "I'm really sorry about that. If anything else happens, tell me immediately, okay?" He stepped back.

"Sure. Don't worry about me."

He looked me in the eyes, and this time I did my best to keep his gaze. I wasn't one to melt, but Gabe had supernatural powers.

For the rest of the evening, I stayed focused on the job at hand. Fortunately, no one else gave me grief—except for Gabe, but that was a different kind. Every time he came closer to me to tell me what to make, I had to brace myself.

The man exuded trouble, but I wasn't too worried. I knew I wouldn't see him after tonight. I just had to make it until the end of the shift.

But as I counted the money I got from tips and the cash Gabe gave me once we'd closed, I heard Celia tell Darren, one of our busboys, that we needed help the next day moving a huge bookcase from my room into the living room to give me more space.

"No can do," Darren said apologetically. "I come here straight from my other job."

"I'll drop by," Gabe said from behind me.

Celia whipped her head in his direction, looking at him like he'd hung the moon.

"Thank you so much! You're a lifesaver. Again."

Sweet Lord. I'd better brace myself for tomorrow.

Chapter Three
Gabe

"I can't believe we're breaking yet another record," my assistant, Betty, said.

I looked at the article on my phone, grinning. "That's what we do."

"All right. I'll let you get back to work."

I shook my head. "No, I'm taking off early today."

I felt victorious. We'd made it into the Michelin Guide.

That was a fantastic milestone, even though we were already listed on various other top ten websites. But I knew a ton of tourists relied on printed city guides, so the more accolades we could acquire, the better.

"Good for you. Or wait, are you going to the bar tonight?"

"No, it's been a busy week, and I want the night off. Besides, I have stuff to do tonight." I was meeting my half brothers, and before that, I had to stop by Celia's place to help with the bookcase.

I bid everyone goodbye before leaving. I trusted people to do their job without me hovering over them. And they didn't think I was slacking just because I didn't burn the midnight oil every night. I had a great team.

Maybe it wasn't fair, but I had to admit, I was more proud of the success of the bar than the distillery. Probably because it was my brainchild—I'd come up with the idea and set it up. Ultimately, I'd envisioned this as a franchise with a bar in each major city, and maybe in

Europe too. The world was at my fingertips, and the possibilities were endless.

And to think there was a time when our grandfather wasn't sure his legacy would survive.

I didn't remember many things from when Dad left, but I did remember him telling Grandfather that the empire would go to waste without him running it. We'd proved him wrong. I didn't wish my father any ill will, but I never understood how he could turn out to be such a two-faced bastard.

Grandfather and Grandmother were two of the kindest people I knew, and for Dad to do what he did just made no sense whatsoever. But it didn't matter anymore now.

I was determined to build on to my legacy, and I'd been looking to expand the distillery for a while now. I couldn't keep up with demand within the space we had, and there wasn't enough room on the property to grow. I needed space for adding another production line, and we'd have to move the operation before that could happen. I also wanted to venture into hotels and planned to open the first one next to the distillery.

My half brother Leo could help me find the right property. He ran the top real estate agency in the country and was absolutely the best. I called him on my way to the car; even though I was meeting him later, we wouldn't have time to talk shop then.

"Hey, Gabe. Change your mind about joining us for tennis?" he asked.

"No. I told you I want to give it another try. I was actually calling because I'd like your help with a project."

"I'm listening."

"I want to look for a huge property in Stockbridge. I want to build a distillery there and also a hotel."

"Cool. But Stockbridge? That's oddly specific."

I had my reasons, but I didn't feel like sharing them with him. Yet.

"It's mostly because that's where I want the hotel to be," I explained.

"Sure, I'm on it. That's going to take a while, though."

"I assumed so."

Leo was excellent at what he did, but this was a challenge. Stockbridge was tiny. There wouldn't be many properties that fit my requirements and didn't have any zoning restrictions.

"I'm on it."

"Thanks."

We'd often vacationed with Mom in Stockbridge in the summer, and some of my happiest memories were from that village, especially the botanical garden.

She even confessed during our last summer there that maybe after we were grown and out of the house, she'd open a hotel there, but she never got the chance to do it. I liked the idea of fulfilling that wish of hers.

After ending the call, I got into my Mercedes SUV and headed straight to Celia's place.

I'd never been in this neighborhood before and didn't realize it was so far away from the bar. How the hell did she get home after work? I didn't know if she had a car or not, and I didn't like the idea of her taking public transportation that late in the night.

When I arrived at the address, I found a parking spot opposite her building. I buzzed Celia on the intercom, and she let me in.

She lived on the second floor. When I reached her door, I rang the bell and then glanced around, noting that there were four other units on the floor.

Suddenly the door opened, and although I'd expected to see Celia, I came face-to-face with Diane.

Her eyes widened in surprise. She was wearing short pants and a yellow pinstriped top and looked adorable.

"Gabe!" she exclaimed.

Fuck! I couldn't stop imagining those long legs wrapped around my torso.

I cleared my throat and asked, "Celia didn't tell you I was coming?"

"She did but didn't specify to me when."

"Gabe, hi, come in," Celia said, walking up behind Diane. "Thank you so much for coming. Right this way."

The place looked welcoming, but it was tiny.

"Celia, how do you get home after work?" I asked.

"Oh, there's a T-station about five minutes away. It's perfect."

I groaned. "Why didn't you tell me? From now on you can take an Uber and expense it to me."

Diane's mouth fell open.

"You are the most generous boss I've ever met," Diane said.

Celia shrugged. "That's very kind, Gabe. But not necessary. Nothing's ever happened. And anyway, I have Mace with me."

Diane whipped around to look at her. "You're carrying Mace? You didn't tell me that."

Celia shrugged. "Why do you think I was so blasé last night when that drunk guy was loitering around us?"

Diane shook her head. "Oh, Celia."

"You expense it to the company. And yes, before you ask, this is what I offer all my employees when they work late."

"Yeah, for a manager," Celia countered.

"*All* employees. I offered that to the guys, too, but they all drive to work." I found it easier to ignore my dirty imagination if I focused on Celia instead of Diane. I'd never, not once, had the impulse to flirt with Celia, but it was taking all my self-restraint to behave around Diane.

"All right, what's with the bookcase?" I asked. "Where is it?"

"It's in the small bedroom," Diane said.

"Show me."

We walked from the living room down the corridor. One door was open to something that looked like a master bedroom, and another door opened to what I thought was a small closet at first glance.

Wait, is this the other bedroom? There was a single bed inside it and a huge bookcase.

"Someone's sleeping in here?" I asked.

"Hey, don't sound so shocked or judgy," Diane said. "This is my bedroom for now."

No fucking way! No one could live here. There wasn't enough space to breathe. I didn't say it out loud, though. I didn't want to sound like a snobbish ass.

But why the hell was she living with her sister anyway? And if they had to share an apartment, why were they living in this matchbox?

"All right, let's do it. You two grab that end, and I'll take this one."

I made a concerted effort to keep my eyes on the shelf, especially when Diane leaned forward and grabbed the lower part, giving me a direct view of her cleavage. She wasn't wearing a bra, and I drew in a deep breath at the sight. I had a visceral reaction to this woman unlike anything I'd ever experienced. I was a flirt, that was true, but I'd never had trouble keeping myself in check. Something about her just caught me completely off guard.

"One, two, three, now," I said.

We lifted at the same time. It wasn't that heavy, but I couldn't see the two of them being able to do it on their own.

We carefully got it through the door, then down the narrow hallway, and all the way to the living room. Celia gestured to put it near the TV.

Once we set it down, Diane put her hands on her hips, stretching backward. "All right, that's going to give me a backache."

"I'll give you a massage," Celia said, and my brain went straight to the gutter again.

Diane straightened up. "So listen, Gabe," she started, pressing her palms together, "I've prepped a delicious afternoon snack. Do you want to join us?"

"Please say yes," Celia added.

"Sure, why not? Need my help setting the table?" I offered.

"Not at all."

Diane waved her hand. "Well, my sister feels the need to be polite because she works for you. But you're not the boss of me, so I'd love it if you could help me bring some plates from the kitchen."

"Diane!" Celia said with a grin.

I liked Diane's sass. And when she walked in front of me, I had to keep my eyes up so as not to check her out. As soon as we stepped in the kitchen, she handed me three plates and cutlery while she took two bowls of food.

"You made fried chicken wings," I said appreciatively.

"They're my sister's favorite, and I love cooking." The other bowl contained a delicious-looking salad. "She's not much of a cook, but now that I'm here, I can take care of her for a bit."

Ah, so Diane only moved here recently.

We sat down at the table, and Celia smiled. "You're spoiling me, sister."

Diane nodded. "Yep, that's exactly what I intend to do before I get out of your hair."

I looked at Diane. "You plan to move?"

"Yes. I certainly didn't plan to move in here in the first place, but life is full of surprises."

"What happened?" I asked while we passed the food around. I put three wings on my plate along with salad.

Diane sighed. "My company downsized, so they've reduced my hours to only part-time. I couldn't really afford my rent, and my landlord was quick to ask me to leave. He didn't even give me proper notice. I had to move in a week."

"That's illegal," I said.

She shrugged. "It is what it is. Anyway, I'm searching for a shared apartment or something, but in the meantime, I'm crashing here with my sister."

"You know I love having you here," Celia countered.

A dangerous idea formed in my mind, and I put down my fork. My brothers often teased me for being impulsive, and they were right. Sometimes it got me into trouble, but I didn't care one bit. I followed my instincts.

"I have a proposition." I looked at Celia. "As you know, I'm currently living in a rented house that has an unwanted guest." I said the last two words through gritted teeth.

Diane jerked her head back. "Meaning?"

Celia laughed softly. "Gabe's building his new house in the Seaport District, and because he's a bit of a control freak—"

"I am not. I just like to *oversee* some things."

"Anyway, Gabe wants to monitor the construction crew more closely, so he's rented a house on the same street. And the landlady insists on renting the attic apartment to someone else."

"And it's not really separate from the rest of the house," I added. "That guy goes up and down the stairs at least fifty times a day, which wouldn't be a problem if he wasn't so obnoxious."

"And you can't get the house all for yourself?" Diane asked.

I couldn't help but smile. "No. Believe it or not, Diane, I'm not all-powerful."

"Hmm," she said, looking at Celia. "Not according to my sister." She laughed, then locked eyes with me again. "So, what's your proposition?"

"How would you feel about moving in to replace him?"

Diane's jaw dropped, and Celia frowned.

"Is that even possible? You said you couldn't get rid of him before," Celia said.

"I wanted to take over the entire lease so I could live there by myself. The landlady said she prefers having two tenants so she still has at least a bit of an income even if one leaves. But I'm sure she won't be opposed to switching tenants. As far as I remember, the guy wants to move out but couldn't find a replacement to break his portion of the lease."

"But I don't think I can afford it," Diane said in a very small voice.

I shook my head. "The rent is really not a lot. That's why the whole thing is frustrating."

"How much is it?" she asked me. I told her the amount, and she nodded, narrowing her eyes. "All right, that really isn't that bad."

"The attic is basically one room, but it's bigger than what you have here and is fully furnished with its own bathroom."

"It would be an improvement over this tiny bedroom," Celia said.

What was I thinking? Living with Diane would be challenging. I could barely keep myself from flirting with her when her sister was around. I stood no chance when we were alone.

"This actually does sound like a good offer," Celia added.

"I agree," Diane said. "Can I think about it?"

I nodded. "Sure."

"Do you need my bio to check me out or something? I can give you recommendations from my boss."

I chuckled. "There's no need for that. I'll ask the landlady if she does, though."

"I can't believe you'd just ask a perfect stranger to move in with you."

Celia laughed. "Nope, that's normal for Gabe. He does things differently."

"I'm already living with a stranger," I pointed out. "And I don't like him one bit."

"And you're so sure you'll like me?" Diane asked. A smile played on her lips as her eyes flashed.

"I like my chances," I countered, and she blushed. I immediately looked at Celia, but she was too busy devouring yet another chicken wing.

After that, Celia rose from her chair. "All right, well, I have to go. My shift starts in half an hour. I'll barely get there in time."

"I can drive you."

"Nonsense. You stay here and enjoy the wings. Besides, you said you're meeting your half brothers later on."

"I am. I'm trying my hand at tennis." I wiggled my eyebrows. "And failing spectacularly."

Celia laughed, taking her plate into the kitchen before grabbing her purse. The sisters said their goodbyes, and after Celia left, I could swear I heard Diane draw in a deep breath.

I turned to look at her. "Did you go to culinary school?"

She smiled brilliantly, straightening up in her chair. "Actually, I was only there for a semester before focusing on my business major, but I picked up a lot of valuable skills."

"These are delicious. I've only eaten fried chicken this good in Louisiana."

"Thanks."

"So, what do you do for work?"

"I'm a tour guide. And before you say it, I know you don't need a college education for that. I used to work in hotel management. I started doing tours when I moved to Boston from Portland. The move here was quick, and I needed a job. Turns out I quite enjoy it."

Once again, I tried to focus on the wings, but without Celia here as a buffer, it was becoming increasingly difficult. Something drew me to Diane.

"Why did you move here?" I asked her. She averted her gaze, which made me think it was a sensitive topic. "That's an intrusive question, sorry. Don't feel like you have to answer it. I was just curious."

"No, that's fine, I mean, if we're going to live in the same house, maybe it's not a bad idea if we know each other a bit."

She put her fork down and pushed her chair back a bit, crossing her legs. "I moved here with my ex-boyfriend. Well, he got a job here, and..." She looked at the ceiling, and I realized her eyes had become glassy. "Well, I suppose I misinterpreted his wanting me to move here with him as a marriage proposal or at least that he had long-term intentions." She forced a smile and then focused those gorgeous blue eyes on me. "Turned out I was completely wrong. But hey, I'm happy to be here. I'm closer to my sister for the first time in ten years."

"So you're committed to staying here?" I questioned.

"Definitely. But Boston is expensive, so it will take me a bit to get back on my feet. Tell me about the house."

She crossed her legs again. Was I making her nervous? Excited? Both?

I took out my phone. "I've got some pictures here from the original email the landlady sent me." I tapped the screen, finding it in seconds, and opened the email before handing it to her.

Her jaw dropped as she scrolled through the photos. "This looks fantastic. But there aren't any with the upstairs apartment."

"I've never seen it, actually. I can't vouch for the condition, but the specs are noted farther down in the email."

She looked up, shrugging. "Honestly, anything's better than my sister's room. I don't want to sound ungrateful, but I'm super cramped, and I know Celia also likes to have her space. I mean, who doesn't? And I never in a million years thought I'd break up with my ex..."

"Your ex doesn't sound like a prize," I said. "I'm sorry you had to go through that."

She shook her head, running her hand through her hair. "We all have our journey, right? I guess it brought me here, so there's a good side to it." I liked that she focused on the positive—it was something we had in common. She frowned and looked me in the eye. "Listen, Gabe, you don't have to feel obligated just because my sister works for you."

"That's not why I'm doing it at all. You have a need. And honestly, so do I." The corners of her mouth twitched. Hell yeah, that was definitely an innuendo, and I didn't even mean it as one. "This sounds like it could solve both of our problems."

"What a coincidence, right?" Her flirty smile was back, egging me on like nothing else.

I moved my chair closer to her, almost involuntarily. She didn't even attempt to lean back.

"I like to seize opportunities when I see them," I said.

"Clearly," she murmured. "Thank you for the offer, though I will need to think about it for a bit. Is it okay if I give you an answer later this week?"

"Sure. Give me your phone number."

She typed her number into my cell, and then I called her. It rang somewhere in the room.

"Thanks," she said. "I'll save it later."

"Want me to help you clean up?" I offered.

"You really are something," she replied as we both stood, grabbing dishes and cutlery.

"Why, because I want to help? I don't mind doing housework," I said as I watched her load the dishwasher while I moved everything within her reach. "When I'm at my grandparents' house, I help every time. My brothers and I split tasks. Grandmother likes to cook up a storm when we visit, but at least she accepts us helping with the cleanup. We always have to choose our battles with her. Lately, though, she's accepted ordering takeout. Her doctors told her to slow down."

Diane looked at me with a strange expression, then smiled as if she was having a conversation with herself. She started the dishwasher. "All right. Do you want a glass of wine or something?"

"No, I need to leave. Let me know about the place, okay? Because then I'll have to let the landlady know, and it might take some time until she figures out how to manage it all."

"Sure." She sounded on edge as she walked me to the door.

I turned to face her and said, "I think you and I would have a really great time."

She raised a brow. "Ah, that's your sales pitch, huh?"

I wiggled my eyebrows. "This entire evening has been a sales pitch."

"I knew it. This was too good to be true."

"You think I'm too good to be true?"

She grinned. "Have a good evening, Gabe."

"I'll be waiting for your call."

"I won't leave you hanging, I promise."

I exhaled sharply as she closed the door. I'd always enjoyed playing with fire, but even for my standards, this might be too much.

Chapter Four

Diane

The next morning, I was on pins and needles waiting for Celia to wake up. I'd brought her breakfast, but she didn't even stir when I sat at the edge of the bed. I surmised that meant she simply needed to sleep more, so I came back to the living room.

I'd barely slept a wink. After Gabe left, I looked up apartment listings. My options were slim, and his offer sounded more attractive by the minute. But I didn't want to tell him anything before I discussed this extensively with my sister. I wasn't sure whether she'd agreed with everything last night just because she didn't want to be rude in front of Gabe or if she really thought this was a good idea.

I jumped from the couch when I heard her moving around. "Good morning," I called from the living room.

"Morning. You've got your 'I've prepped something delicious' voice."

"I do," I admitted with a laugh.

God, I'd missed being with my sister. But though living together was cozy and brought us even closer, it wasn't feasible in the long term.

I went to the kitchen and pressed the button on the coffee machine as she came into the living room, yawning. "This is for you," I said, taking the cup from the machine and handing it to her.

"You've got good instincts." She took a sip and then sat down, admiring the food. "You don't have to prepare breakfast every day," she said, but I knew she loved it. "You're not going to join me?"

"I already ate."

She took two spoonfuls of the oatmeal topped with nuts and honey and then looked up at me. "You're nervous. Did you sleep badly or something?"

"That obvious, huh? Listen, I wanted to talk to you about Gabe's offer."

"All right."

"Did you mean it last night? You think it's a good idea?"

She shrugged. "Well, I mean, he *is* my boss. I've known him for a while. He's a decent person. Between you living with a perfect stranger or Gabe, I'd take Gabe every time." She bit the inside of her cheek. "I just don't know how actually living with him might be."

"What do you mean?" I asked.

"Maybe he has a deep, dark secret."

That should have scared me, right? But I found myself yearning to know what that might be.

"I don't know him personally. Though I will say he likes to hook up," Celia continued.

I stilled. "But you two haven't...?"

"No, for God's sake. He's my boss, for one, and he's never even *tried* anything. He's very professional. He's got a reputation, but he never gets involved with anyone he works with. So I can't really say if it's hearsay or not. Maybe people just assume that because he's hot."

I smiled. If he was a womanizer, even better. It would completely cut off my... appetite. "So you really wouldn't mind?"

"No, of course not." She smirked. "You want to take him up on his offer, don't you?"

"The rent his landlady wants is a bit higher than I was hoping for. But the location is so amazing that she could easily charge three times more."

She rolled her eyes. "It's just the attic, okay? Don't get your hopes up."

It was hard not to. I longed to have a little corner of my own. The past few months had felt like a roller coaster, and I needed someplace I could call home.

"And it'll be temporary. Once I have a good job, I can afford a place of my own."

"You have my blessing."

I love my sister.

"Then I'm going to call Gabe today and tell him the good news. He said it might take a while for the landlady to process it all."

She nodded. "Great. I'm gonna get in the shower. Thanks for breakfast!"

Once my sister left for the bathroom, I dialed Gabe's number. It was nine o'clock in the morning, and I couldn't remember if Celia mentioned if he's an early riser or not, but this seemed like a decent hour.

"Good morning."

Ah, his voice was just as sexy on the phone as it was in person.

"Hi, Gabe. This is Diane, Celia's sister."

"I know who you are. I saved your number."

Duh. "Of course. So listen, I told you I need more time to think, but I've made up my mind. I'd love to take you up on your offer. But I'd like to see it first."

"Excellent. I'll set everything in motion with my landlady, and I'll keep you posted, okay? It might take a few days to convince my 'roommate' to let us look around."

I laughed. "You strike me as a man who can convince anyone to do what you want."

"Believe it or not, some people manage to resist my charm."

Oh yeah, I was definitely not one of them. I felt charmed already and the man wasn't even trying.

"I'm easy to live with, I promise," he continued.

"Do you get visitors?" I wondered.

"I see my family often. They haven't been here yet, but they'll make an appearance at some point."

What I meant was female overnight visitors, but I couldn't ask that. It wasn't any of my business anyway. As far as I understood, the only thing I had to worry about was that staircase, as it was the only adjoining area where we'd possibly meet. Judging by the layout of the house, it was right next to the entrance, so we shouldn't cross paths too often.

"All right, then, I'll leave you to it," I said. "Have a great day."

"You too. Diane, this is going to work out great for both of us."

I grinned. "Oh, I hope so."

I wasn't expecting to hear from Gabe at all for another few days, but I was surprised when he called me four hours later. I was with a group of tourists, but I didn't want to ignore the call.

I glanced at my group. They were taking pictures in front of the Boston Common, so I picked up.

"Hi, Gabe."

"Diane, hi." His voice was tight.

"Uh-oh. What happened?"

"Listen, I actually convinced my roommate to let me see the attic." His voice sounded ominous, and I had a sinking in my stomach.

"And?"

"You should see it before deciding to move in."

"It's that bad?" I asked.

"Let's just say it's nowhere near as fancy as the rest of the home."

That could mean a lot of things. Still, it was better to see it. "When could I drop by?"

"Do you have time right now?"

"Not for another ninety minutes. I'm doing a tour."

"That's fine. I'm going to tell him that you're coming so he's aware and lets you in."

"Listen, Gabe, I honestly don't have high expectations. I'm sure it's going to be fine."

"Wait and see," he said.

Gabe struck me like an optimistic guy, but if he thought it was unacceptable, then maybe it really was. Though I didn't think it could be much worse than everything else I'd seen online.

I finished the tour on time and then headed to the subway. There was a station about fifteen minutes on foot from Gabe's house.

I arrived a few minutes earlier, so I walked through the neighborhood at a leisurely pace. The brick homes simply dripped with wealth. It was a mix of colonial style and modern architecture, but somehow they all fit together.

I recognized Gabe's house from six feet away from the pictures he'd shown me. Checking the address, I confirmed it was his building. It was an older construction, colonial style with a tiled roof. The facade looked a bit run-down, even more so than in the photographs, and suddenly I had an uneasy feeling.

I walked up the front steps and knocked on the door. A few seconds later, I heard footsteps, and then Gabe opened it. He was wearing comfortable clothing—a white T-shirt that showcased his muscles, paired with jeans.

"Hey," I said.

"Come in." His eyes were missing the twinkle I'd gotten used to.

"Stop scaring me," I teased him.

"Let's go up. The guy went out and said we should look around while he's gone."

"Wow, that's nice of him."

"By the way, all the furniture you'll see will be yours. It belongs to the landlady."

"That's even better."

I didn't even get to look into the main living space because the spiral staircase was right next to the door leading up to the attic apartment. It was wide enough to carry up furniture, but I imagined it was terribly difficult. Hopefully I wouldn't have to buy much.

"This is good. It's almost like a separate entrance," I said, determined to focus on the positive. My breath came out in pants as we went higher and higher up. "You have your own staircase for getting to the upper floors?"

"Yes," he said.

I have a good feeling about this. It can't be too bad...

Not five minutes later, I changed my mind. It was...not good.

"Well, at least there's no mold that I can see," I said. There were a lot of downsides. For one, the main window appeared drafty and old, and there were several cracks along the walls and the ceiling. But the bathroom was decent.

There was a single bed against the wall. The dresser was rather small, but I had one of those mobile racks that I could easily set up next to it.

By far, the worst part was the kitchen area. It had no oven and only one electrical socket.

"I don't know how to spin this into a positive thing," I said, looking at the appliances and their obvious wear. "I like to cook, but I can't do much here."

"It also explains why the guy's always bringing up take-out food." Gabe sighed. "Listen, Diane, if this is your only deal-breaker, you can always use the kitchen downstairs. I don't mind. I don't cook at all, so it's not like you'd be in my way or anything."

He was right behind me. I *almost* felt his body—the heat of it, the strength of it. I was certain that if I touched his abs and arms, they'd be rock hard.

"But that's more of a roommate situation, not a separate unit," I countered. I didn't want to intrude on his space, though I definitely would like to use the appliances.

He laughed softly, and his breath tickled my ear. "I would take you over this guy any day."

"And he actually wants to move?"

"Fuck yes. He just couldn't find anyone to take over the lease."

I turned around. "Hmmm... This place could be cozy. I can put up lights by the window, and I can pad all the windowsills with something so there's no draft." I glanced around again. Fortunately, the floor was wood and easy to clean. "I can work with this. I've lived in far worse places. Honestly, I can't believe people would turn up their nose at this."

"I don't know how hard he looked for someone to take over the lease."

"I like the energy of this place," I said with a grin. "Oh, where are the washer and dryer?"

"Nothing up here, but you can absolutely use mine. They are downstairs."

"Thank you. Really, Gabe. This isn't a dump. Not at all."

I had to admit I'd been shocked when I first stepped in, but it grew on me.

He shrugged. "Didn't want you to get your hopes up."

I thought about the one-bedroom apartment Celia and I grew up in. Mom couldn't afford to rent anything bigger until I turned fifteen and Celia was twelve. It was probably one of the main reasons both of us preferred to live alone—we liked to have our space after having to share for so long.

"If you're sure about the kitchen thing, then I'll take it," I stated firmly.

Gabe nodded. "Come on downstairs and I'll show you the kitchen, washer and dryer."

He gestured for me to walk in front of him, and I accidentally brushed his chest with my arm on the way out. Oh yeah, his pecs were even harder than I'd imagined.

But why was I even checking him out? Gabe was completely out of the question. My sister worked for him, and I would never want to put her in a bad position.

I went down the stairs quickly, and Gabe pointed through the double doors connecting the entrance to the living room. I stepped inside, looking around. It dripped of old luxury: high ceilings, chandeliers.

"This looks amazing," I told him. "But somehow I imagined you'd prefer a modern setting."

"This isn't my style at all. My house will be completely different, but this was the best I could get."

The kitchen was in the back and separate from the living room, which was even better. That meant I wouldn't be bothering him at all.

"This is *gorgeous*," I said.

The appliances were surprisingly new. The floors were old-school with intricate inlays, though they must have been polished recently based on the shine.

"I can do so much in here," I mumbled.

"All right, then, be my guest." A huge smile lit up his face. "And this door leads to the washer and dryer. Feel free to use anything you need. The detergent and dryer sheets are in the cabinet here." Gabe moved over to show me everything. "It's all standard."

"This will be great. I'll finally be able to reevaluate everything and get my feet back on the ground."

He stepped closer. "You've had a rough few months, huh?" The concern in his voice warmed my heart.

"Yeah, but it's going to be fine." I didn't want to delve into that again. "So, did your roommate tell you how long it'll take before he can vacate?"

"He's moving in with his girlfriend, so he said he can be out of here by the end of the week."

"That's great! Oh, I have another question. How long is your lease?"

"I intend to stay here less than six months."

I nodded. "That gives me enough time to get a decent job and look for another place."

My stomach rumbled.

"Want to order dinner?" he asked.

I shook my head. "No, thank you. I want to start packing."

And besides, I wasn't quite ready to spend more time alone with him, which was silly, since I was going to move in with him. Well, not *with* him—above him.

An image flashed in my mind—of the dirty variety. Damn it, this was not going well. But I knew that after some time passed, and he brought home female guests, I'd be singing another tune.

"I'll drop you off at home," he offered.

I shook my head. "Gabe, that's really not necessary."

"I insist," he said as we walked to the front door.

"I appreciate your concern, but it's all right." I turned to him just before I headed out. "I'm going to spend some time in the city before going home. I need to buy a few things."

"Do you have Mace?" he asked abruptly. It was barely dusk out, and I had plenty of time to do my errands before I got back to Celia's.

"I do. Thanks for your concern."

He was far too overprotective. To be honest, I wasn't used to it. I'd always been the one to care for my sister and myself.

"What day do you want to move in?"

"Is Saturday okay?"

He nodded. "Sure. I'll give Celia a key as soon as the guy moves. On Saturday, I'll be here to help you carry up boxes."

"That's not—"

"Diane, I'll be here."

I laughed, smiling coyly. "Thanks. Then I'll see you on Saturday."

Chapter Five
Gabe

On Saturday morning, I went by my grandparents' house. I was picking up Grandmother to drive her to the bridge session.

Despite our conversation at dinner the previous week, she stuck to her guns when she had an idea. I was thirty-one and in charge of my life, but I didn't mind Grandmother's inquisitions, as they gave me a chance to catch up with her and find out how she was really doing. When all of us were together, she put up a brave front, making it difficult to know if everything was okay. She especially didn't like to admit to not feeling well in front of Grandfather.

I sent her a text to let her know I was here and waited for her on the front porch.

She came out a few minutes later. "Darling, you're early. Do you want to come in and drink a coffee?"

"No thanks, Grandmother. Are you ready to go? We can drop by my new house first. I'd like to show it to you."

"What a wonderful idea. I've been curious to see it." I'd shown her pictures, but she hadn't been there. "Let's go."

I took her arm, and we walked together to the car. I opened the door for her and had to actually assist her in because it was a bit too high for her. After making sure she was situated, I went around the front and climbed into the driver's seat.

"So, tell me a bit about your house," Grandmother said as I pulled onto the street. "Can we go inside?"

"No. The workmen leave too much stuff lying around, so we'll see it from outside."

"I couldn't believe it when you said you're buying that big house for yourself."

I shrugged. "Why not? It's perfect. It's got plenty of space."

Grandmother chuckled, "It's definitely a sign."

"Of what?" I asked, bewildered.

"Oh, don't mind me."

This was typical for Grandmother. I thought that if I got her alone, I could check out how she was, but she'd already changed it up. But I was determined to find out if she'd been having any more dizzy spells. She'd scared us all a few months ago with a trip to the hospital because she'd been severely dehydrated.

"How are you feeling lately?" I asked her.

"I'm good, I'm good. No more headaches or dizzy spells. I'm religiously using that drinking bottle that Zoey gave me. And your grandfather is on my case all the time too."

"Good for him, and for Zoey." Colton's fiancée bought grandmother a water bottle that kept track of how much she drank. I was very grateful to her. If any of us boys would have given her that, Grandmother would have shut us down. But she didn't mind it coming from Zoey.

We arrived in front of the house twenty minutes later. I helped Grandmother out of the car, and we walked around the yard, looking at the house from all angles. There were three construction workers here today doing some of the detailing on the windows.

"This is a thing of beauty," she exclaimed.

"Thanks, Grandmother. I agree. I'll go talk to Mateo." He was overseeing everything. "Be careful where you step."

"You don't have to baby me," she said in a belligerent voice.

I absolutely had to, but I chose my battles.

I kept an eye on Grandmother while I spoke to the head of the construction site. They'd found some issues in the basement that required more work than we anticipated.

"Just do what you have to do, okay?" I told him.

Mateo nodded. "Sure. But we hit a roadblock, so we'll have to pause the work until we get all the materials we need."

I ran my hand through my hair. "Right, then we'll pause it."

When I first started this project, I was annoyed whenever something like this came up, but now I was just rolling with the punches. These were the risks of building on the bones of an old house. And since I was living nearby, I didn't mind. It didn't matter if I had to wait a few more months. The lease on the current house was for one year. I aimed to move in six months, but I was adaptable.

Once we agreed that the crew should focus their efforts on another part of the project until the materials came, I got Grandmother back into the car. I started to drive away, then stopped in front of my rental. Diane had arrived earlier than we'd agreed.

"What's happening over there?" she asked.

"Ah, that is my new neighbor," I said.

She turned to face me. "You didn't tell me the old one was moving out."

"He wanted to move in with his girlfriend, but the landlady would only let him out of the lease if he found a replacement. And I found one for him."

"Oh, that's nice, dear. So who is it?"

"It's the sister of one of my bartenders."

Grandmother beamed. "Lovely. I'd like to meet her."

I frowned. "Why?"

"Indulge your old grandmother, would you?"

"Won't you be late for bridge?"

She waved her hand. "It's still early. Besides, there are enough of us old hags that they can start a game without me."

"All right, then, let's go."

I got out first, then opened the door for Grandmother and helped her out of the car.

"Good morning, Diane!" I greeted. She was leaning over the trunk of a battered old Honda.

She straightened up, turning around. "Gabe, hi." Then her eyes fell on Grandmother. "Hello, I'm Diane."

"I'm Jeannie Whitley, Gabe's grandmother. He tells me you're his new neighbor."

Diane nodded. " Yes, and I'm super happy this worked out. I'm very lucky that my sister knew Gabe. Anyway, I'm not going to keep you. I just want to bring all this stuff up."

"Gabe, you help the young lady. She doesn't have to carry it all by herself."

I cocked a brow. "Grandmother."

Diane smiled. "Gabe did offer to help, but I showed up earlier than planned. I thought it would be best to just get started." She looked like she was about to burst with happiness. "I already have a buyer for my car. I can't believe it. Things are finally starting to look up! But I need to get all the boxes out first."

I pointed at the one labeled Books. "That's got to be heavy. I'll help you with it."

"You know what?" Grandmother said. "Why don't you stay at home and help Diane unload? I can get a cab to my friend's house. It's our bridge meeting today," she informed Diane.

I narrowed my eyes at her. "You said you wanted me to drive you there."

She waved her hand. "There's no need. If you order an Uber, then you can also follow the trip."

Grandmother knew me well. I disliked calling cabs for her, but Uber was different because I could see where she was on the app.

"Are you sure?" I asked.

"Of course. I'm not a hundred yet. I like to be independent."

Something was off. She'd been dead set on introducing me to her friend's granddaughter, and I was getting downright suspicious. Why had she changed her mind? Then again, I didn't need to look a gift horse in the mouth. I was glad I didn't have to pretend to be excited about being introduced to yet another of her friends' granddaughters. Not that I really minded. Even though grandmother could be a bit meddling, I really didn't mind, as she'd done so much for me and my brothers. But I was glad that I was off the hook today.

I ordered her a luxury version of Uber, and it arrived right away.

"You two have fun," she told me and Diane as I helped her get into the car.

After she left, I turned to Diane. She had her hair in a tight bun at the base of her neck. A single curly strand came out over her right ear, and she kept pushing it back.

Fuck, she's sexy.

"Your grandmother is very thoughtful. Does she have a bridge session with friends every weekend?" Diane asked.

"No, just from time to time. Now, put me to work."

"If you insist."

I grinned. "I do."

"The boxes labeled Books are the heaviest."

"Got it."

She took a suitcase, and I grabbed two of the boxes labeled Books, putting them one atop the other.

She stared at me, mouth agape. "You're strong."

"They don't weigh that much. I'm good. Lead the way."

It was a big mistake to ask her to walk in front of me. I couldn't take my eyes off her ass; she was wearing shorts again, and since she was a few steps higher on the staircase than me, I had a great view. I forced my gaze away, looking down at the stairs to the side.

"Why are you selling your car?" I asked, trying to get my mind off how hot she was.

"This old thing barely moves. I'm not getting a lot of money for it, but I don't want to be stuck making car payments, especially since I'll be living here. I checked and the public transportation in this neighborhood is great."

"There's no subway around here," I countered.

"It's about fifteen minutes away. The walk will do me good. I typically only do tours in the city center, and the connections are great. Anyway, once I'm back on my feet, I'll consider buying another car."

I didn't say anything, just kept focusing on my steps and not looking at that gorgeous ass, no matter how lusciously it was displayed in front of me.

Once we got upstairs, she said, "Just stack everything there in the corner."

I looked around, taking it all in. "This is in better shape than the last time I was up here. Did he clean up after himself?" I asked.

She smiled sheepishly. "No. Since you gave Celia the key, I came right after he left and did a deep clean."

"I didn't know that."

"Well, you were at the office." She avoided my gaze.

She'd purposefully scheduled her visits here when I wasn't home? What was I missing? Did my presence make her uncomfortable? That was the last thing I wanted.

"Ready to go down again?" she asked.

"At your service."

A smile played on her lips. "Really?"

"Oh yeah. Just put me to work."

"If you don't mind, I am more than happy to use your muscles." She sucked in her breath and again pushed that one strand behind her ear. "I didn't mean that. That's to say... I wasn't hitting on you."

I burst out laughing. "I didn't think you were, but it's interesting that your mind went there."

She turned beet red instantly. I'd never seen anyone blush like this in my whole life. She was utterly beautiful.

"Let's move, then," I said.

Chapter Six

Gabe

An hour later, we'd managed to get all the boxes into her room.

After setting the final one off to the side, Diane stretched her arms over her head. "I can't believe it only took an hour to lug all this inside."

I chuckled. "See? It's a good thing I was here."

"True. I don't know what I would have done without you." She glanced at me over her shoulder. She was standing near the sea of boxes, looking around. "I'm going to tackle opening them after I sell the car." She bit the inside of her cheek, obviously thinking of all the things she needed to take care of. "I'm going to need to buy plates too. Otherwise, I've got the rest of my dishes…"

I was good at reading people's worries from their body language and the way they spoke, and it was easy to conclude that she was worried about money.

"Listen," I said. "You're going to use the kitchen to cook anyway. There are plates, pans, utensils, and all that crap in there too. You're more than welcome to use them."

Her eyes widened. "Are you sure? What if you're entertaining or something?"

"I rarely entertain, and if I do, I'm sure we can coordinate."

"Okay. Thanks." She looked around again, then startled as a beeping sound filled the air. "Oh, that's my phone." She took it out from her back pocket. "My buyer is already here. I really hope he won't change his mind. All right, I'll see you later."

"I'll come with you."

"Why?"

"To make sure everything's okay and that the dude isn't trying to intimidate you into lowering your price or something."

Her face opened up in a gorgeous smile. "Gabe, I can't be intimidated easily. You'll learn that about me soon enough. I can fight my own battles. Except, of course, when a predatory landlord throws me out without proper notice," she said through gritted teeth. "But you look a bit intimidating, so you might help just by being there. In case the guy *does* try anything."

She took the stairs two at a time as I followed her down and then out the front door.

An elderly man stood outside the gate, staring at the house. She would have been much better off selling the car when it was parked in front of Celia's apartment. I could practically see the guy thinking she was loaded simply because she lived here. That never helped in these situations.

The Whitley name had cost me in negotiations over the years. Everyone assumed the money was endless. That was true right now, but there had been enough times in the company's history when we weren't sure one branch or the other could be salvaged.

"Hi, I'm Diane," she greeted.

The guy looked at her, then at me, and said, "I'm Dawson. This is the car?"

"Yes. Do you want to take it for a test drive?"

"I will later," he said. "I just want to take a look at it for now."

"It's a bit battered, but I did say that on the sales page."

"Yes, you did." After circling the car once, he stopped again, looking from Diane to the house as if he couldn't quite figure out why someone who lived here had this decrepit old thing. "Why are you selling it?"

"I honestly can't afford owning a car right now," she replied.

He jerked his head back. "And you can afford living here?"

"That's none of your concern. For all you know, I could just be making this my meeting point. Anyway, you said you were very interested in buying it today. Cash."

"True, but there are more scratches on it than I saw online. I'm going to have to fix them. That'll probably cost about five hundred. I want that taken off from the overall price."

I opened my mouth, then closed it again. Diane wouldn't want me to step in right now.

She straightened her shoulders, putting her hands on her hips. "I've posted specific photographs of these three scratches, and I also explicitly wrote about them in the description, so no, I will not be accepting any attempts to negotiate. As it said online, the price is final. If you don't want to buy it, that's your decision."

He scoffed. "You just said you can't afford making car payments."

"I've got other people interested. Two are scheduled for tomorrow morning."

"I don't believe you."

She shrugged. "Believe what you want."

I had to admit, she definitely knew how to negotiate.

"Fine, I'll take it for a test drive."

"I'll need something to hold on to while you do." She smiled sweetly. "Just so I know you're coming back."

"You think I'd steal it?"

She quirked an eyebrow at him. "Dawson, you're a perfect stranger."

"Fine, here you go." He handed her his credit card before getting into the car, starting it up, and heading down the street.

"I'm impressed," I said, stepping closer to her.

She looked at me over her shoulder. "I told you I'm good, and I was expecting him to try and wheel and deal. He already did online. It was his right to ask and mine to decline."

"If he doesn't want to take it, you've got those other sellers lined up anyway."

She grinned. "No, that was a negotiation tactic."

I whistled. "Damn, you're good. You fooled me."

On instinct, I leaned in even closer.

Why couldn't I keep my distance from her? She was my neighbor and Celia's sister. There was a line in the sand, and I absolutely didn't want to cross it.

"Told you," Diane said triumphantly, then sighed. "Today feels like I'm starting a new life. I'm so excited about it. Maybe it's a sign that my bad luck is gone."

I wanted details, but decided not to push. Despite knowing Celia for close to two years, I didn't really know anything about her family situation aside from the fact that their mother had been sick. Celia wasn't one to share personal details.

I couldn't explain my infatuation with Diane. It wasn't my usual approach, and despite my grandmother's best intentions, I only casually dated, nothing more. Once, a few years back, I had a so-called girlfriend for about two months before we moved on, but I'd never been serious about anyone.

Why my sudden interest in Diane?

Just then, the guy returned with the car and stepped out of it. "Rides good. I'm taking it."

"Perfect," Diane said.

Despite her confident answer, I saw her shoulders relax a little in relief. Clearly she needed that money. Was she *that* cash-strapped?

"All right."

She didn't seem like she needed my involvement anymore, and I didn't want to be overbearing. So as they exchanged documents, I made to step back inside the house. But then I heard the dude say, "Why don't you throw in a perk and go for a beer with me or something?"

What the fuck?

"I don't think so."

"Oh, come on. Don't be like that. You're getting paid well enough for this."

"What the fuck?" she exclaimed.

I turned around and walked straight back to him. "Give her the money, take the car, and fucking leave."

"Who are you to have any say in this?"

"Fuck off," I sneered. I was having none of this. This guy needed to get the hell out of here.

Diane crossed her arms over her chest, looking down at her feet. Then she glanced back up at him. After he gave her the money, she immediately shoved it into her pocket.

"Fine, whatever," the guy said, cowering quickly.

"You got the keys. The rest of the documents are on the passenger seat, as you probably saw."

"Yeah, yeah." He got into the car.

The second he drove off, she let out a huge breath. Then she turned to me. "Mischief managed."

"Hmm?"

"Not a *Harry Potter* fan?"

"I've seen some of the movies," I said.

"Never mind. Anyway, thanks for making that moron finally leave." She shook her head. "I'll never get over the fact that when a woman tells a guy no, he just thinks she means *maybe*. But when another guy tells him to fuck off, he takes it seriously."

"I've never thought about it like that."

"Probably because you've never had to." She waved it off. "It doesn't matter. I've got the money and got rid of the car. Now I can focus on making my space all cozy. And as a thank-you for helping me today, I'd like to cook dinner tonight for both of us after I unpack—if you don't have plans, that is."

"You don't have to do that. I can order something."

She shook her head vehemently. "No. You helped me with my boxes and that idiot, and I want to return the favor by cooking something delicious."

"All right. I won't say no."

"And thanks a lot for being here. He was a creep, and I should have realized that online when he asked all of those dumb questions. Here I thought he just wanted to lower the price."

"No problem. Glad I could be of service. Are you sure you don't need any help unpacking?"

"No, I need to do it myself. Feel the energy and all that."

I stared at her. *Energy?*

She smiled sheepishly. "You think I'm a weirdo, huh?"

"No, I just think you're different than anyone else I've ever met." And I liked it.

She laughed. "I happen to think different is good."

"It is," I said. "It definitely is."

She went past me on her way back inside the house. Her arm almost brushed my chest, which she seemed to realize at the last second, because she took a step to the side. Was she avoiding me on purpose? Was it because I made her uncomfortable or because she was attracted to me? I needed to know, and I was going to find out.

Once Diane went inside, I returned to my construction site across the road, but I only spent half an hour there, since there really wasn't much I could do. I had no clue about construction in general, but one thing I realized was that the crew was much more productive if they knew I stopped by regularly. I didn't believe in micromanaging, but some things needed more attention than others, and my house was important to me.

I headed to my half-brother Nick's gym afterward. I always asked if he was around when I was here, but today he wasn't. I did my usual routine at the weight section and then my cardio exercises. Some people preferred to jog outside, and I could definitely do it in my neighborhood—it was quiet, and there wasn't a lot of traffic—but I wanted to focus on my workouts, and I did that best at the gym. But I also had an entire workout room at home for the days when I couldn't make it here.

After finishing the workout, I saw a missed call from Maddox and immediately called back.

"Hey!" I said when he answered. "I've been training. Are you at Nick's gym too?"

"No. Need to blow off steam in the middle of the day?"

"Something like that."

"Right."

I frowned. He wasn't being his usual self. Usually by now he would have already cracked a joke or given me shit about something.

"Brother, why do you have a stick up your ass?" We didn't do subtle in our family.

"Is it that obvious?"

"Yes. What happened?" I asked, going into the juice bar.

"I heard through the grapevine that Dad wants to return to Boston and open up a business here."

Every muscle in my body tightened. "Fuck no!" I exclaimed.

"My thoughts exactly," Maddox replied in a clipped tone.

"Define *grapevine*."

"After we bought him out of the company, I started keeping track of his moves."

Dad had held minority stock in Whitley Industries until recently. We bought him out—at his request. We figured it would get him out of our lives for good. He'd claimed he needed the money to settle some debts, but apparently there was plenty left for him to start a new business.

"Do you have details?"

"Not yet."

"Let's not share with the whole family until we know more."

"Sure," Maddox replied. "But Nick and Leo know. I asked them to help me keep an eye out for him."

"Thanks for staying on top of this. I have to admit, I never thought it was necessary."

"I had a hunch it was." His voice was uncharacteristically dry.

He made it sound like it wasn't a big deal, but I was starting to think he'd just been placating us. That was very unlike Maddox.

"All right, keep me up-to-date."

"That's the plan."

After hanging up, I decided to run another thirty minutes on the treadmill. I needed to blow off steam even more than before.

When I returned home, I was surprised by the delicious aromas permeating the house. Putting my gym bag down, I called "Diane?"

"Hi. I'm in the kitchen," she replied. "I wasn't sure when you were coming back, but I thought I'd get started on making lasagna."

I went straight to the kitchen. She was wearing a dress now. Was she trying to kill me? She looked absolutely mouthwatering. It was short but not tight. Thank fuck, because then I wouldn't be able to keep my eyes off her. I was fighting to be on my best behavior as it was.

"It won't take long for it to be ready," she said. "I made the sauce already." She was now frying the meat.

"Can I do something to help?"

"No, I'm used to cooking by myself. I'm not even sure how to delegate in the kitchen."

"You went grocery shopping?" I asked, looking at all the ingredients on the counter.

She smiled sheepishly. "There was nothing in the fridge, and I wanted to cook us something. You really live on takeout, huh?"

"Honestly, yes."

"Cooking is one of my favorite things. And lasagna is my comfort food. I used to be in charge of all the cooking duties growing up."

"What about your mom?"

She sighed. "She'd been sick for years, so she couldn't always do it, but she taught me well. Whenever she felt better, I took advantage and asked her to show me as many recipes as possible."

"You had a lot of responsibilities on your shoulders growing up."

"Yeah, but it worked out. My sister and I split tasks. Celia hates cooking, but I never minded it. She went grocery shopping when she was old enough, and I had to be strict with her about the budget and everything."

She spoke about this as if it was the most natural thing in the world for kids to manage household budgets and do the brunt of the cooking and chores.

"Your dad?"

She shrugged. "Not in the picture."

So we had that in common. Shitty dads.

"So, you don't cook because you don't have time?" she asked. "Or because you don't know how to?"

"Caught me there." I grabbed a Coke and stepped next to her. I seemed to naturally gravitate toward her when we were in the same room. Frankly, it was disconcerting. "I've maybe cooked three whole meals my entire life."

"That can't be true."

"And I'm pretty sure two of those were making ramen noodles in college."

She laughed. "Gabe, how do you even survive?"

"I get by. Don't know why I never learned. Mom was a good cook, actually."

"Oh, is she in Boston too?"

It felt as if someone pressed down on my shoulders. I cleared my throat. "She passed away many years ago."

She turned to look at me, her expression sad. "I'm so sorry. I didn't know."

"You don't have to apologize."

"Celia and I have never talked about your family. Honestly, the only thing I know about you is that you're a great boss, and the part where you helped us with Mom. Didn't want to bring up bad memories or anything."

"No worries. Her death was unexpected," I said.

She bit her lip and took the meat off the stove, arranging it in the dish where she'd already put the lasagna. "Was it an accident?"

"No, she got sick. It just felt unexpected because it happened soon after we all found out that our father had another family."

A loud clank startled both of us. Diane had dropped the pan on the stove. "That sounds horrifying. I totally understand if you want to change the subject."

"There's not much to say. Dad had two families. He abandoned them both. Mom was devastated. Shortly after, the doctors discovered she had melanoma. She passed away quickly. Needless to say, it was a challenging time for the family. Our grandparents didn't miss a beat, though. I always thought the bright side was finding out we had three additional brothers."

"Are you on good terms with them?"

"They're my best friends. I don't differentiate between my actual brothers and my half brothers, even though we didn't grow up together."

"That's honestly amazing. I don't know many people who would take that in stride."

"Some of my older brothers definitely didn't. But we all have a good relationship now."

We fell silent after that as she poured the meat and the sauce in between lasagna sheets. Then she shoved everything into the oven.

"It only needs twenty minutes. I'll use that time to set the table."

"I'll do it, since you're cooking."

She looked at me playfully. "But you're the one who put in all those muscles to help me today."

She wasn't averting her gaze because she was uncomfortable with me; she felt this inexplicable attraction just as much as I did. What the hell had I been thinking, asking her to move in? I'd noticed from our first interaction that there were sparks between us. But we were adults, and I was certain we'd be able to handle it.

I opened the overhead cabinet at the same time as her. Diane turned slightly to me, pressing her soft breast against my chest. She wasn't wearing a bra.

Fuck, I was wrong. I definitely can't handle this.

"I've got the plates," I said, fighting to keep my voice even. It was low and gruff, which was completely ridiculous. No one had ever had an impact like this on me.

"O-Okay," she stuttered. "I'll check on the lasagna." She glanced inside the oven. "Looks good."

I noticed a slight change in her voice too. She was just as rattled as I was.

I brought the plates to the table, as well as forks and knives. "Want a bottle of wine?"

"No. But I won't say no to a Coke."

"One Coke it is." I took a bottle from the fridge and opened it for her.

I liked that Diane didn't know much about me and my family. Usually the Whitley name preceded me. Most people had already made up their mind about me before we even met, women included. More than once I'd had the impression that a woman had read every article available about my family history before we even went on a first date. They knew where I'd lived growing up and where I'd gone to school.

It put me off completely. For whatever reason, they thought I was some fixer-upper they needed to put together.

Nothing was further from the truth.

Diane

We sat down opposite each other at the dining room table and immediately dug in.

"This is delicious," Gabe exclaimed, and I smiled. I loved when people complimented my food.

I took a mouthful, chewing slowly. "Yep, I nailed it. The sauce, the meat—I'm happy with it."

Gabe laughed. "You're analyzing it like a business proposal."

"Food is important to me. I want to get it right even if it's not what I do for a living."

"Speaking of, do you ever want to go back to the hotel business, or do you prefer being a tour guide?"

"I actually love doing tours, but objectively speaking, working in the hotel has better pay, better opportunities. Career ladder and all that. Besides, I'd like to have a stable income. It would put my mind at ease, with Mom's medication and all."

Gabe stopped moving his spoon to his mouth and put it back down. "Your mom still needs help? Celia didn't say anything."

I shook my head. "It's not like before. It's not an emergency situation, but her regular medicine is not cheap. Mom's been a diabetic all her life. The dialysis and her prescriptions are very expensive, and unfortunately, insurance doesn't cover that much."

"I can help."

"No, Gabe. You've done more than enough."

I couldn't believe he was offering help again. Chuck, my ex, had been very cagey with his money. Not that I ever asked him for help, but he certainly never offered.

"What happened?" Gabe asked.

"What do you mean?"

"You're frowning."

"Just wondering... why are you offering to help strangers?"

"The people who work for me aren't strangers."

"I was just thinking about my ex. He never helped, and I never asked him. When things were a bit rough, I needed him to cover a portion of my rent some months so that I could help Mom. He flat-out told me that he didn't have enough funds to pitch in. And then he bought a Harley. Obviously everyone is free to do whatever they want with their money, but why lie? I'm glad things are over between us."

Reflecting on those times definitely made me sad. If two people truly loved each other, wouldn't they be there to help no matter what? At least that's what I'd always thought. Of course, the men in my life—my ex, my dad—never did that.

"You know, the more I hear about that ex of yours, the more I realize what a moron he is."

I laughed. "He is. There's no mistake about that. Back when we lived in Portland, I worked at the hotel full-time and supported him through grad school. Then he got this good-paying job here in Boston. When I didn't find a marketing position in a hotel, he pressured me into finding something else. He insisted we needed another income because he couldn't support me and pay the rent."

"After you put him through fucking grad school?" Gabe asked through gritted teeth.

"Yeah! That was a red flag right there, but I overlooked it. Anyway, after a while, he was promoted and started looking down on me." I sighed. "God, I'm so happy it's all over. Let's not talk about him anymore."

"As you wish."

After we finished the lasagna, I leaned back to relax in my chair when it suddenly dawned on me that this wasn't part of the deal. I could use the kitchen but not lounge in the living room for hours. I immediately straightened up, taking the plates.

"That's on me," Gabe said.

"All right, that means I can get out of your hair quicker."

"I don't mind if you want to stick around."

"I've still got a ton to do upstairs."

He pinned me with his gaze. It was so unnerving that I needed to do something with my hands, so I grabbed our empty glasses and took them to the kitchen, moving right in front of him. The kitchen was a mess, which was no surprise, as I always left it in a state of disarray after cooking. I typically only bothered to clean up after I'd eaten.

I started to open the dishwasher, but Gabe caught my wrist, and the contact was almost too much. I almost gasped but managed to pass it off as a hiccup.

"I insist." He said the words in a low voice, his tone brooking no argument.

The kitchen was small, and there were far too many opportunities to brush against each other if we both cleaned up at the same time, so I threw in the towel. I was very susceptible to his touch.

"All right, thanks. But just because I've got a ton to unpack. I always leave a disaster in the kitchen until after I eat, and you can't always clean it up."

"We'll work out a system, and things will become easier to navigate, roomie."

"Neighbor," I said on reflex. The distinction made me feel better.

He lifted one corner of his mouth, and though he didn't say anything back, I knew exactly what he was thinking.

The truth was, we were obviously *not* just neighbors.

Chapter Seven
Diane

Things truly were starting to work in my favor. On Tuesday morning, before I left for my first tour, I received a request on the tutoring platform. I immediately replied—I wasn't going to turn down any money that came my way.

I was giddy as I dressed, putting on my name tag and grabbing the yellow umbrella I used for larger groups, which made me easy to spot. I had thirty people today, so I'd most definitely need it.

The day was unexpectedly windy and cloudy, yet I put on my best smile as I walked with the tourists on the Freedom Trail. This was my most popular tour. I'd done it more than a hundred times already, but I was still excited.

Celia asked me once how I could keep my enthusiasm while reciting the same thing for the hundredth time. But each group reacted differently, so the experience was fresh for me every time.

I had three back-to-back groups. Usually, I invited them to ask as many questions as possible at the end of the tour, but after the last one, I needed to hurry home in time for my tutoring class. I bid everyone goodbye after they handed me their tips.

Once I arrived home, I was surprised to see Gabe's car. It was six o'clock, but I figured CEOs stayed later at the office. My stomach somersaulted at the sight.

Good gracious, I can't react like this every time I come home.

I sprinted up the staircase and opened my laptop. I'd made it with ten minutes to spare.

I immediately plugged in my password and login data on the platform. As I checked my phone for the onetime passcode for double security, I realized I had a message from Gabe. My stomach somersaulted again. Smiling, I opened the app.

Gabe: Hey, I heard you come up the stairs. Are you free this evening?

Hmm. What does he have in mind?

Diane: Later, yes. But I have a tutoring class starting in a few minutes.

Gabe: Good luck. Come downstairs afterward.

Ha, that sounded a bit like an order, but I didn't have time to properly tease him back.

I focused on the screen, and my client connected a few seconds later. It was a French lady in her fifties named Antoinette. She was starting a new job in the US in three months and wanted to improve her English as much as possible. I'd signed up as both a French and English tutor.

"Hi, Antoinette. Nice to meet you."

"Hi, Diane."

We started right away. I had specifically requested to work with adults because I didn't have any experience with kids. Antoinette's English was decent, but I knew we could do even better. Three months was a long time. I dearly hoped she wanted to meet up regularly.

I kept glancing at my phone now and again. I was trying to check if Gabe had explained what he had in mind for tonight, but I didn't want to be unprofessional; I had my camera on, and it was easy to notice any movement.

One hour later, Antoinette said, "Oh, I believe we're up."

"Yes, we are. Do you want to meet weekly?"

"I don't think that's going to be enough. I really want to be able to converse in English more often. Do you have time twice a week?"

Did I have time? Goodness, I did. "Yes, of course," I said, trying to keep it together and not burst out in a happy dance.

"Good. Then I'll book through the website."

"Great. See you, Antoinette."

"Wait, are you sure you don't want me to do any homework?"

I shook my head. "No, not yet. I think that would definitely take the fun out of it. And I honestly don't think you need it."

"All right, then. See you later this week."

"Yes," I said before closing my laptop.

I looked around, sighing. I had yet to buy my twinkle lights and drapes. The plan was to make this place cozy, make it mine. I was warming up to it. All the cracks just meant the house was old and had character.

Then I remembered I was going to meet Gabe downstairs. Grabbing the phone, I checked my messages and completely deflated when I realized he hadn't written anything back. What exactly was I expecting? That he'd want to throw a party together? Maybe he just wanted to go through some rules regarding cohabitating.

I went downstairs, shoving the phone into my back pocket. The staircase creaked under every step, but I liked it. It wasn't creepy, just old. I wondered who lived here before and what their stories were. Why did they move out?

A strange smell snapped me out of my thoughts. Someone was cooking, but Gabe told me he wasn't any good at that. I sniffed the air. It smelled like burned food.

I jumped down the last four steps, nearly breaking my ankle because I skidded on the floor, then went into the living room. The door to the kitchen was open. Wafts of black smoke were coming out of it.

"For fuck's sake," Gabe exclaimed.

His voice had come from inside, so I hurried that way, trying to ignore my pulse going up.

The smoke was even darker in there, and I wondered how the detector hadn't gone off. I looked up at the ceiling and saw Gabe had removed it. He'd also opened the window.

"Can I help?" I asked.

He looked in my direction. "Great. You weren't supposed to see this part."

I grinned. "What's this?"

"I wanted to return the favor for dinner," he said, pointing to the scorched pan in the sink.

"That's probably going to need about a year or two to soften up," I remarked.

"If it's salvageable at all."

"It is. I've saved a few pans after Celia tried to cook."

I stepped past him, making sure not to accidentally touch him, and inspected the pan. It looked absolutely dreadful. Had he fried peas? There was no way to tell.

Gabe moved close enough for me to feel the heat of his body.

I straightened up, carefully turning, and took stock of him. He'd rolled up his sleeves and was wearing an apron. Fuck me, the only way he'd be sexier was if he took off his clothes and went commando.

You never know. Maybe I'll have the chance to spy on him naked while I live here.

Great, we'd been in the same room for almost two minutes, and my thoughts were already spinning out of control.

"You didn't have to cook. My dinner was to thank you for your help, remember? We're roommates. We could share tasks. I don't mind cooking."

"We're back to roommates territory, huh? You were very insistent on the term *neighbor* before," he said with a chuckle. "Anyway, I've got it covered. I'd only put half the ingredients in that pan."

There was another one on the stove.

"What are you cooking?" I asked.

"It's a surprise," he said.

I peeked in the pan, but he moved in front of me. I narrowed my eyes. "Really? I can't help, then?"

"*I'm* preparing dinner."

In our tango to get to the pan, we'd ended up far closer than I intended. Now my heart rate was completely haywire.

I stepped back and said, "Okay. So what do you want me to do?"

His eyes flashed. "Wait in the living room."

"I'll open windows in the living room to get rid of the smoke."

"Perfect."

I took one last look at him before leaving the kitchen. *Yum*. Even with an apron covering the front of his body, he was incredibly appealing. I'd never thought a shirt with cuff links went with an apron, but he'd proved me wrong.

I opened one window, then realized I had to open them all to get the smoke out.

Once I'd done that, I inspected my outfit. I was still wearing jeans and my company-mandated polo shirt in the same shade of yellow as our umbrellas. I suddenly felt completely underdressed, even though that was nonsense considering we were at home.

Would it be terribly ridiculous if I went back upstairs to change?

Oh, I didn't care if it was. I wanted to look my best.

I scooted up the stairs a little faster than usual and could barely draw my breath when I reached the top. The staircase was a good workout. It was going to give me a kickass butt. Even more points for this place.

I decided on a cute, simple dress, light blue with wide straps. I had a thing for straps. I didn't know why, but I had several dresses like that. This one was tight around my waist and ass, but it didn't show any cleavage. I walked back down the stairs slowly because if I made my steps too wide, I risked tearing it.

To my surprise, Gabe had already set the table and brought out two platters with food.

"Gabe?" I called out, but he didn't answer.

On one platter was clearly steak. Next to it was a heap of veggies. They weren't burned, but they looked both overcooked and undercooked. That was just my first impression, of course. Some things tasted better than they looked.

"You're fast. I went to change too," Gabe said. "I reeked."

I turned around and nearly swallowed my tongue. He'd put on a T-shirt with short sleeves, and it was the first time I realized his ink extended up his arms. God, it was so damn sexy.

"Yeah, I figured it was better to get out of those clothes," I said, happy to come up with a perfectly good reason for changing that wasn't because I wanted to doll up.

This is not a date. Damn, don't forget that.

"Shall we?"

"Yes, please."

"I'll do the honors." He put a steak on my plate and one on his as I served the veggies.

The first bad sign was that I gave my arm a workout trying to cut the steak.

"Oh, for fuck's sake. This is beyond well done. It's scorched," he said.

I shoved it into my mouth anyway, not wanting to be rude, but I could barely chew it.

Hoping the veggies would compensate, I ate a spoonful and had to fight my gag reflex. I could only taste soy sauce and honey or sugar, possibly lime. It was a combination I usually loved, but something was terribly off.

I didn't have to say anything, though, because Gabe tasted it and then spit it back out in a napkin. I did the same.

"Right. That was my last attempt at cooking." And then he started laughing.

"Let me just look in the fridge, okay? I'm sure I can whip up something from there."

His laughter subsided. "No. *I* wanted to treat *you* to dinner."

"Then let's order something in. You know what's good in the neighborhood? I haven't looked yet."

Gabe straightened and moved slightly toward me. "I'll do one better. Let's go out. I know some great restaurants."

"I'm sure everywhere is booked."

He lifted one corner of his mouth in a smirk. "I'll get us a table."

"All right, let's see you try." Boston restaurants were very hard to get into during the tourist season, especially at the last minute.

"What do you like to eat?" he asked me.

"Seafood or mac and cheese. Actually, no. Steak."

"I know just the spot," he exclaimed, then grabbed his phone from his pocket, tapping the screen before putting it to his ear. "Hello. Gabe Whitley here. I'd like a table for two for tonight. Yes, I'll wait." A few seconds later, he added, "Excellent, thank you."

After disconnecting the call, he glanced at me. "We've got a table at Rare."

I stilled in my seat. "Wait, what?" Rare was hands down the most expensive restaurant in the city. As a tour guide—it was literally my job to know about these things. "No, Gabe, you cannot take me to Rare."

"Yes, I can. I'm doing it."

I cleared my throat. "That's very expensive."

"You wanted steak. It's the best steak place I know."

I grinned. "I can recite ten more off the top of my head that are delicious."

He smiled. "But could we get into any of them without reservations?"

"Well, you got us into Rare," I said. My voice was hoarse. "I bet you can get us in anywhere."

He shook his head. "No, that's the thing. I've got a contingency at several restaurants where I eat regularly, one of which is Rare."

I'd never get used to the difference in our tax brackets. Then again, why should I? I was simply renting the attic.

He came closer. "If you think you won't like it, or that you won't be comfortable, I'll cancel it and we can figure out something else. But if the only reason you don't want to go is—"

"Because it costs an arm and a leg—"

"Because it's more expensive than usual, then leave that to me, all right? I'll take care of everything."

I considered his words. I was curious, and Gabe seemed to want to go there.

"Fine, but we do need to change, right?"

He laughed. "Yes, they have a very strict dress code."

"What do you mean, strict? Long gowns or something?"

"No, they want business attire. Men are required to wear a suit."

"I can work with that," I said. My dress was cute but would not be good enough for Rare. "I'm going upstairs."

We rose from the table at the same time.

"You do that. I'll throw these away and start the dishwasher, then put on a suit."

As I stepped past him, I accidentally tripped on the hardwood floor. I caught the edge of the table, but my butt collided with his crotch.

My face was on fire. Hell, my entire body was.

Gabe groaned, and I looked up at him. "Are you hurt?"

He pinched his eyes closed.

"Gabe?" I asked.

"I'm good."

"God, I'm so sorry. I can't believe I'm such a klutz. How can I make it up to you?"

He smiled, but it was strained. He probably was in pain. I sucked in a deep breath.

"Let's hurry up so we don't miss the reservation," he choked out.

"I'll go change really quick."

I walked away, looking over my shoulder just before I left. Gabe's face was stuck in a grimace.

Oh good Lord. Should I suggest he put ice on it?

No, just mind your own business. He probably knows how to take care of his own dick.

I hope I didn't break it.

I went upstairs with careful steps. The way this evening was going, I wouldn't put it past me to rip my dress.

By the time I reached the attic, I already knew what I wanted to wear. It was in one of the garbage bags I hadn't opened, but I had a steamer, so I could smooth it out in no time.

I took out the dress I wore at my graduation dinner. It was pink silk and went all the way to the floor. I hadn't worn it since then because I didn't often go to fancy restaurants. But tonight was the night.

I was going to knock Gabe's socks off. It was the least I could do after I'd demolished his dick.

Chapter Eight
Gabe

I wasn't used to failing. Generally, when I put my mind to something, I succeeded. But clearly I had my limits. Still, tonight was a win. I was going to have a nice dinner with Diane, and we'd actually enjoy some delicious food instead of trying to pass mine off as edible.

I changed into a suit quickly, then walked out to the living room and closed all the windows. The smell was gone, thank God.

While I waited, I paced the entrance hall, glancing up when I heard footsteps. My breath caught at the sight before me. Diane was absolutely stunning. The fabric of her dress shimmered, molding against her body with every step she took. She'd pinned her hair to one side, and her neck was delectable.

"Do you think this will pass as acceptable?"

"You look amazing," I said with a growl.

Her eyes widened, and she stopped moving.

I cleared my throat. "I think it's perfect."

"I don't get many chances to doll myself up, so I thought I'd take this one."

I'd been attracted to her since the first time I saw her, but this was on another level altogether. Suddenly, I wanted to find an excuse to stay home and order in, just so I didn't have to share her with anybody. But clearly she was looking forward to this. And I wanted to give her many, many opportunities to doll herself up if that's what made her happy.

"I ordered an Uber for us."

"How come?"

"If I have a glass of wine or two, I don't like to drive."

She nodded. "Good thinking."

She also had a light jacket on. It seemed almost flimsy, but I could always give her mine if she was cold when we came out of the restaurant.

I took in a deep breath as she stepped off the last stair and stood next to me. She was petite. I wouldn't even need both my arms to lift her up. And she smelled *amazing*.

"Gabe? Anything wrong?"

Oh, for fuck's sake. I cleared my throat, pulling my thoughts together.

"Let's go," I said.

I offered her an arm, but she must not have seen it because she walked in front of me. The way her hips moved drove me crazy, and I looked away for my own sanity.

The Uber was already waiting in front of the gate when we stepped out. I opened the car door for Diane, and she slipped in. I climbed in on the other side. We were both silent during the ride. I looked at her out of the corner of my eye as she skimmed her hands on her thighs. The impulse to reach out and touch her was overpowering.

We arrived at the restaurant fifteen minutes later.

"Wait for me. I'll open your door," I said.

"Oh, thank you. I'm honestly not even used to walking in such long dresses. I don't want to trip in it."

An image flashed in my mind—of her dress completely undone, pooled at her feet. I wondered what kind of lingerie she liked to wear.

I shook myself out of it as I opened the door for Diane. She stepped out, one long leg peeking from under the fabric, fueling my thoughts. I offered her my arm again, and this time she took it.

"Small secret: I'm also not used to wearing such high heels."

She fell completely silent as we walked up to the entrance. Two doormen opened the double doors for us, and we went inside, straight to the host.

"Mr. Whitley," he said. Since I was a regular, I didn't even need to introduce myself. "Your table is ready."

He glanced at Diane curiously but had the good sense not to say anything. I usually came here with my brothers or on my own, and I was sure the host noticed.

Diane looked around as we walked to our table, mouth slightly open, eyes wide.

"This place is so elegant," she said once we sat down. "I like that they space everything out to give guests more privacy."

I nodded. "I like that too."

I hated restaurants that were so crowded, you could hear every conversation around you. This felt intimate.

"And they obviously knew who you were," she said. "I can't believe you have your own table here."

I shrugged. "It's not really my table. I'm just here very often. Out of courtesy, they told me once that I can even call on short notice and they'll find me a spot."

She pressed her lips together, looking around again.

"Are you feeling uncomfortable?" I asked.

She lowered her gaze and then raised it back up. "Is it that obvious?"

"Listen, the last thing I want is for you to feel that way. I wanted to do something nice."

"This *is* nice," she said. "I'm just out of my comfort zone." She smoothed the top of her hair with a palm even though not even a single hair was out of place. "But I promise I'm going to enjoy this."

"Great, that's all I want."

The waiter came to us just then. "May I recommend the daily specials?" he said after handing us the menus.

"Sure."

"We have Argentinian steak with extra foie gras."

Diane wrinkled her nose. I wasn't a fan myself.

"There's also a flank steak with pepper sauce and duck breast," he continued.

"I already know what I'd like," Diane said. "I want a medium-cooked steak with roasted potatoes."

"And I want a rib eye with sweet potato fries," I added.

The waiter also recommended a Rioja red wine.

"Why don't you bring a glass for the lady? If she likes it, we'll take a bottle," I said. The second he was out of earshot, I grinned.

She raised a brow. "A whole bottle? You want to get me drunk?"

I laughed. "No, not at all. Are you a lightweight?"

"I can hold my liquor," she said. "And red wine isn't that strong anyway."

The waiter came back almost immediately with a bottle, uncorking it in front of us and pouring just a bit into Diane's glass. She grabbed it with shaky fingers and clumsily twirled it around, then took a sip. She blinked her eyes wide open and exclaimed, "This is fantastic."

The waiter poured wine into both our glasses. Once he left, she said, "I take it back. Cheap carton red wine isn't strong, but this has a bit of a kick."

"It's Rioja," I explained. "Definitely more potent."

"It's delicious. Good thing I grabbed a few bites at the house so I don't drink on an empty stomach."

I snorted. "You cannot call that a bite."

"Yes, I can. You get a lot of points for trying."

"I'm not used to trying. I usually succeed at what I do."

"I see." She leaned back in her chair and shifted her body in a way that made me think she crossed and uncrossed her legs. "I can't decide if you're serious or not."

"I am."

"You never fail at anything?"

I hesitated, taking another sip, wondering if I should share this with her, but why not? Somehow, I felt at ease with her. "When I first took over the distillery, I almost did fail."

Her mouth formed an O. "My sister said it's always done well."

"The profits weren't up to par in the early years. My father," I said, carefully weighing the word, "had an empire-building problem."

"What's that?" she asked.

"He wanted to grow the company, so he opened new businesses under Whitley Industries, shifting money from one venture to another. But he wasn't focused on profits, so naturally after he left, things were up in the air. The distillery wasn't in such dreadful shape as some of the other companies, but it wasn't the slam dunk people thought it was."

"What made you decide to take it over instead of, I don't know, opening something else?"

"I take pride in the Whitley name, no matter our past. Once Dad was out of the picture, I knew it was up to us boys to regain our status, rebuild our name. My brothers were already in charge of other branches, and I wanted to make my mark. Not just for my ego, but I knew it would make our grandparents extremely happy. It was all they ever wanted, for us to be owners of the business and legacy."

She flashed a huge smile, revealing dimples at the corners of her mouth. "That's very considerate of you. So that means you're close to your grandparents."

"Yeah, I am. Very."

"I still don't understand why your grandmother just up and left on Saturday."

I chuckled. I might be digging my own grave if I voiced my thoughts, but what the hell? It relaxed me. I genuinely liked being around Diane. "First you need to know some background info. Grandmother likes to play matchmaker."

"Really? Is she any good?" Diane asked. "Can I ask her to find me someone?"

My entire body tightened at her words. I was physically rejecting the idea of Grandmother setting her up with someone. What the hell was up with that? The idea of a guy coming to the house, waiting around to take her out on dates or even going up to her room, was unacceptable. My own reaction was shocking.

"Gabe?"

"She's good," I said, ignoring her other question. "She's been successful with four of my brothers, though her involvement varied from one case to the next."

She laughed, seeming even more relaxed than usual.

"Anyway, lately she's been asking me to drive her to meet all sorts of friends and then carefully introduces me to her friends' granddaughters or nieces or what have you. At first she tried to pass it off as accidental, but then she just told me the truth to my face."

"So she had plans for you on Saturday?"

I nodded. "Yes."

"And yet she changed her mind. I wonder why."

I had a hunch that I knew what changed Grandmother's mind, but I didn't voice that.

Our dinner arrived just then.

"This looks amazing," she said as soon as the waiter set hers down.

"Glad you think so, ma'am."

After he left, she looked up at me. "Do I look old?" she asked.

"No. Why?"

"He called me 'ma'am.' That's unexpected."

I laughed. "You don't look old. If you looked any more gorgeous, I'd have to fight off people asking you out."

She snorted. "Don't worry, I can fight them off myself. I think I have a built-in man-repellent anyway."

I fixed my gaze on her. She seemed to feel that I was looking at her because she glanced up from her steak.

"I'm not very lucky in the dating department. I mean, this is by far the best dinner I've ever had, and it's not even a date. So who's a winner? Me."

"You really like to see the good in every situation."

She nodded. "It's how I keep going, no matter what."

"I'm the same," I replied. "At least that's what people say about me."

She took another sip of wine and said, "This is going to my head."

"I'll take care of you, don't worry."

She winked. "Lucky you know where I live."

Yeah. Though I wasn't sure if I was lucky or screwed.

Chapter Nine

Gabe

"You were so adorable tonight, trying to cook. Hmm, this wine is definitely working some magic. I never use the word *adorable*," Diane said.

"I'm not sure how I feel about it either," I confirmed.

She sighed. "Tell me the truth. Is this where you bring your dates to impress them?"

"Why? Are you impressed?" I asked with a smug smile. "And if yes, then will you consider this a date?"

She shifted in her seat, but her gaze never wavered.

"You answer first," she said. Her voice was more uneven than before.

"I used to," I admitted. "A few years ago. But lately I only come here by myself or with my brothers or a business partner. I brought Grandmother a few times, but she's not a fan of steak."

I tilted my head and shifted closer to the edge of my seat. My left leg collided with hers, and she exhaled sharply. Then she focused her eyes on her plate, carefully slicing her steak, putting her fork through it and then into one of the potatoes. She didn't make eye contact.

Did she feel the current that passed between us too? Was she used to it? Because I sure as hell wasn't. Another thing about Diane that took me by surprise.

She looked up a few seconds later and asked, "Can I have one of your fries?"

I burst out laughing. That was not where I thought she was going, but I got the message loud and clear—she wanted us to change the subject. "Sure, but only if I can have one of your potatoes."

"Obviously. Sharing is caring." Then she laughed nervously, avoiding my gaze again. After munching on a fry, she added, "I like sweet potato fries better than regular ones."

"So do I. I haven't had them in a while."

"Mom loves sweet potato fries too," Diane added.

"Do you see her often?" I asked.

"Not really. Whenever I want to visit, she insists I use the money for something else. Still, I'm closer to her now than before. One of the reasons I really don't mind that I moved to Boston. Maybe that's why it was meant to be, you know?"

Her tone was optimistic, but her expression had changed. The light in her eyes went out. I felt an inexplicable surge of hate for that guy for taking her joy away. She was clearly trying to be nonchalant about it, but it was obvious that it still hurt.

I couldn't pretend to understand what she was going through. I'd never had a relationship that was significant enough that severing it caused me pain. I'd glided through life by engaging in hookups whenever I felt like it. It hadn't even been a conscious choice; it was simply what I did. I'd never felt the need for anything more.

"I'm so full," she said after taking the last bite of steak. She drank the final sip of wine, then dried her lips with the napkin.

The waiter had refilled our glasses a few times, and even I was starting to feel the effects of the Rioja. I didn't want this evening to end.

Damn it, Gabe. She's Celia's sister. You live together.

Not together, I corrected myself. *She's your neighbor.*

Things were starting to blur in my mind. But one thing was clear: I hadn't had nearly enough of her.

"Do you want dessert?" I asked.

"No, I can't possibly eat anything more. It was truly exquisite," she said. "Also, I'm dehydrated. I'm going to drink a lot of water once we get home."

"Do you want to order something nonalcoholic?"

She giggled, leaning over the table. "Honestly, I want to go home and get out of this dress." Then she giggled again. "Whoops, I can't believe I told you that. It's just that, well, it's a few years old, and I've put on a pound or two. It's a little bit tight. I feel like it's squeezing my boobs and my ribs." She glanced at the bottle. "Yeah, remind me to never again think that I can hold my wine. Clearly I can't."

I chuckled. "Come on, let's go. You'll drink plenty of water, and you'll be fine tomorrow."

We both got up at the same time. She wasn't swaying, so she wasn't inebriated.

"Don't you have to ask for the bill?" She sounded shy.

"No, they have my credit card on file."

She jerked her head back. "I think I've only ever heard that expression in movies. I wasn't sure it was real."

"It's convenient," I said.

"Are you going to offer me that super-muscular arm again?"

"My pleasure."

I stand corrected. She was a bit tipsy, because she clung tightly to my arm.

We walked slower than before. Once we stepped outside, Diane started shivering despite putting on her jacket. Then I draped mine over her shoulders.

She slid her arms into the sleeves, then arched her shoulders back into me and bared the back of her neck. It was unbelievably seductive.

She looked at me over her shoulder. "Thank you. I was feeling a bit chilly."

"I thought you were. You had goose bumps."

She laughed nervously.

"Everything okay?" I asked.

"Yeah. I totally had goose bumps because it's chilly," she said.

By the time we arrived home fifteen minutes later, my head had cleared up somewhat. As we walked up the stairs to the house, I realized the same wasn't true for her. She swayed a bit on the front steps.

When she reached the staircase leading to the attic, she groaned. "Oh, screw it. No way can I make this staircase in these heels right now." She took off her shoes, holding them in her right hand, then turned around. "Thank you for this evening, Gabe."

"I'll walk you up."

She smiled sheepishly. "I'd fight you on it, but I don't think that's such a bad idea. My balance isn't great."

"Walk in front of me."

"Uh-huh," she said, putting one hand on the banister.

I held my hands behind her at enough distance that I wasn't touching her but was prepared in case she fell. I was trying extremely hard not to look at her ass.

But I *should* have looked. That way, when she stumbled on the second to last step and fell backward, I would have placed my hands on a more appropriate side of her body, like her back. But I barely had time to register her yelp before feeling her soft ass in my hands.

"Oh my God," she said, then straightened up.

Pulling herself up and gripping the banister, she put one leg forward, and a ripping sound echoed through the stairwell. She'd stepped on her dress, and it tore around her waist.

"Nooo!" She took one of her hands from the banister but lost her balance again.

This time I acted more appropriately, putting one hand on her back. With the other, I kept her dress together. My thumb was brushing her rib cage. Her skin was so damn soft that I couldn't even think straight.

"I've got you," I said.

"I dropped my shoes."

Looking back, I saw them a few steps down. "I'll get them for you."

"Thank you." She put her hand where mine was before. The heel of her palm brushed the back of my hand in the process, and she gasped lightly.

Did she feel this small contact as intensely as I did? Did she want more?

I went back and grabbed her shoes, bringing them to her as she unlocked the door to her room.

"I'm sorry for that," she said as we went inside. "I'm really not that inebriated, but I lost my balance."

"The spiral staircase is tricky," I said, looking determinedly away from where she was holding her dress together.

"So much for that one pound I gained. I think it was more like ten. Maybe the dress was old. It shouldn't have ripped all the way to my freaking bra."

She turned around, facing me. She'd only turned on the small lamp above her mirror. I couldn't resist moving closer to her. In fact, I preferred that, because if I was right in front of her, then I couldn't see her skin beneath the ripped fabric.

I was wrong. As soon as I stepped forward, she turned sideways to the mirror, and I had a fantastic view of her cleavage.

I groaned at the sight.

"Oh my God, can I embarrass myself any more in front of you? I put on a dress that clearly didn't fit me because I'm a whale."

"You're beautiful. Don't say anything to the contrary in front of me."

She snapped her head up, parting her lips. "Oh."

"I was barely keeping myself from kissing you all night."

"You wanted to kiss me?" she whispered.

"Yes. Fuck yes."

"Then kiss me."

Her voice was even softer than before. In fact, it was so soft that for a brief second, I wondered if I'd imagined it.

I cupped her face the next second, tilting her head up and brushing my lips against hers before capturing them. They were perfect. Plump and soft and so damn inviting.

I ran my hands through her hair. It was just as silky and thick as I'd imagined. Everything about her was magnificent: the way she sighed against my mouth, the way she pressed her chest to mine. Then she let go of her dress and wrapped both hands around my neck, tugging me even farther down.

I immediately gripped the dress, intending to keep it together. Instead, I ran my hand down her rib cage, all the way to the hip. My cock turned semihard when my fingers touched the elastic band of her panties. I brushed them back up, my thumb reaching the fabric of her bra. I wanted to yank everything down, to have her completely naked and at my mercy. I needed to work her with my fingers and mouth.

I deepened the kiss. Every moan reverberated through my chest. I kept my hands splayed wide on her rib cage, but then she pressed herself against me even more and groaned.

My cock was now rock-hard, and she'd felt it. I moved my hand farther down, cupping her buttocks. Goose bumps broke out on her skin, just as they had before at the restaurant. And that cut through the brain fog.

Fuck, what am I doing?

She'd had a few drinks, and her dress ripped. True, she told me to kiss her. She clearly wanted me. But I wasn't going to take advantage.

"Diane," I murmured, stepping back.

She clasped a hand over her mouth, the other on her dress. "Oh my goodness, I'm so embarrassed right now."

And cue the regrets.

Fuck, I shouldn't have kissed her. I was an opportunistic bastard.

"Wow. Tonight was a bit insane. I don't think you anticipated that you'd be flashed like this and then I'd jump your bones."

"*I* kissed *you*," I reminded her.

"Right! I should change."

I had to leave. "I don't want to intrude. Just wanted to make sure you got to your room safely. See you tomorrow."

She laughed, and then it turned into a hiccup before she said, "Good night," in a high-pitched voice.

I closed the door, turning around and taking a deep breath.

What the hell did I just do?

Asking her to move in was one of my worst ideas.

And yet, I didn't regret it.

Chapter Ten

Diane

The next morning, I gave myself a pep talk as I finished putting on my makeup.

"Come on, Diane. Don't be a chicken. Go downstairs, have breakfast. If Gabe is there, just play it by ear."

But I didn't know how to play it by ear. I could still feel his lips on mine and his hands slipping under my dress. I'd enjoyed it so much that for a few seconds, I lost myself in the memory, smiling at my reflection in the mirror. Then I shook my head. I had no idea how last night ended the way it did, but I didn't regret one bit.

I descended with quick steps, stopping when I was on the last one, listening intently. There was no sign of Gabe, even though it was nine o'clock. Still, I entered the living room cautiously, looking around. Everything was completely silent. I sighed with relief.

I stepped into the kitchen and smiled. There was a small tray with a glass of orange juice on the counter, as well as toast and sunny-side ups. There was also a note.

Diane,

Last night was unexpected. And delicious. My cooking skills suck, but I make a mean breakfast. Enjoy.

My face exploded in a huge smile. *So he wined and dined me last night, then kissed the panties off me, and now he's left me breakfast? Who is Gabe Whitley? Is he an alien or something?*

I ate the food, then downed the juice, still trying to figure out how to handle the situation. He said it was delicious, so clearly he was still in a flirty mood.

Then my smile fell. I couldn't do this. I had to shut it down. Celia would seriously be pissed off if I got involved with her boss. Besides, she'd told me that Gabe was a bit of a womanizer.

My stomach constricted at the reminder. *Oh, that's why he's such a good kisser. That's why he knew how to charm me.*

But still, this had been a nice gesture, so I took out my phone to text him.

Diane: Gabe, thanks a lot for breakfast. It's a great way to start a day.

He didn't reply. He was probably in a meeting or something. Then again, I didn't know how to have this conversation with him, so it was likely a blessing in disguise. Maybe I'd have an idea or two by tonight.

However, I never got the chance. Gabe didn't arrive home at his usual time that night, and I texted Celia, asking her how things were at the bar.

Celia: It's madness. One of our bartenders quit, but Gabe's here, thank God.

I bit my lip. Maybe this would give things a chance to cool off a bit.
Who am I kidding? Gabe probably isn't even thinking about me.

Turned out I was wrong. I got a text message from him a bit later in the evening.

Gabe: Probably Celia told you, but I'm going to be trapped at the bar this whole week.

Diane: Do you need any help? I can jump in.

Crap, so much for things cooling down. I was already looking for any opportunity to be close to him.

Gabe: No. It was great of you to do it that one time, but I've got this covered.

Diane: I'm going to cook myself a delicious dinner. You can have leftovers if you want.

Gabe: I won't say no to that. Thanks.

Oh yeah, that just gave me a good reason to make a kick-ass dinner. It seemed like a waste of time to cook for one, so I always made more portions, but I couldn't eat the same thing four days in a row.

I was grinning from ear to ear as I thought about what to make. *Why am I so giddy, for goodness' sake?*

Looking at it objectively, we'd made it through an entire conversation without any awkwardness. I suspected it might have gone a bit differently if he was standing before me in all his glory. But still, a victory was a victory.

For dinner, I'd made a huge portion of chili con carne that would last us for two meals. When I woke up the following morning, I was happy to see Gabe had eaten a portion.

I ate breakfast hurriedly, tiptoeing around the house, suspecting he was asleep. But when I stepped out, his car wasn't there.

Holy shit, he's gone to the office already?

That wasn't right. He couldn't work until late into the evening and be at the office again six hours later.

I didn't know what possessed me to do it, but I took out my phone and messaged him.

Diane: You're at work already?

He answered a few minutes later.

Gabe: No rest for the wicked.

Diane: Hmm, I disagree. Even the wicked need some sort of pampering now and then.

Gabe: You volunteering to do that?

I sucked in a breath. Ah, I'd declared victory too soon last night.

Diane: I can certainly cook dinner. I'm not in the mood for chili again.

To my astonishment, Gabe replied again right away. How did he have time for that?

Gabe: Diane, I'm grateful that you cooked last night, but it's really not necessary. I can eat at the bar.

Diane: I know for a fact you can't. Celia said it's almost impossible once the place is full. She sometimes forgets to even drink water, and her lips are dry at the end of the night.

Gabe: My lips are certainly dry. So if you wanted to help with that, I wouldn't say no.

Oh, that was way more direct than I expected. Does he mean kissing? Or... well, silly me, what else could he mean?

I grinned, shaking my head. My sister would so hand me my ass.

Diane: I'm going to keep cooking dinner for myself. You are more than welcome to help yourself to it.

Gabe: I know what you're doing. But this is a conversation we'll have face-to-face.

I started laughing for no reason at all. I could imagine Gabe saying that in that semi-flirty voice he always used, like he didn't have an off button when it came to charming everyone. My sister had warned me he was a shameless flirt, and I could attest to that. I mean, I'd only been living here for a short while, and we'd already kissed. But I was certain that by the time I saw him, he'd probably have forgotten all about it. Hell, maybe he'd even hooked up with someone else in the meantime.

An unexpected pang of jealousy shot through my chest as I hurried to the subway station. Yep, I intended to ignore that completely. It wasn't warranted and was probably just an instinct, though I was nothing if not excellent at disregarding those.

I called my mom as I walked at a rapid pace, putting in my earbuds.

"Darling, good morning," she said.

"Hey, Mom. I thought I'd check on you before my first tour. How are you?"

"I'm good. You girls, will you ever stop worrying about me?"

The honest answer was "No, Mom. We will always worry about you." That was as true as it was that the sky was blue and the grass was green. Instead, I said, "I just wanted to check in, that's all. I cooked a fantastic chili con carne last night."

"Ah, what did Gabe say about it?"

I told Mom that he'd appreciated my lasagna, so I wasn't surprised when she asked.

"He wasn't home. He needs to be at the bar this week."

"Oh, good gracious. That man works so much."

I smiled at the protective tone in Mom's voice. She'd never met Gabe, but she'd worshiped him ever since he helped with the bills.

"Yeah, I agree. Anyway, Mom, I was thinking of paying you a visit this weekend."

"Nonsense. I'm fit as a fiddle, and I know you're busy."

I sighed. "That's true."

"I'll tell you what. We can FaceTime," she said proudly, pronouncing the words slowly. She tried hard to keep up with technology.

"Sure, let's do that."

I talked to her more about my tutoring sessions. Mom was always my champion. She'd never chastised me or made me feel bad about myself, even when I made the mistake of giving up my job at the hotel in Portland to chase a man to Boston.

Celia said I got my positivity from her. She was probably right, not that we knew anything about our dad. Mom never spoke of him, and we never pressed.

For the rest of the week, I felt a bit like I was living alone. I was sure Gabe came home to sleep, but our paths didn't cross. In fact, I'd gotten so used to it that I didn't even think about him when I went into the living room on Saturday morning. And then I stopped in my tracks when I noticed him doing... chin-ups?

He was in the doorway of what I'd assumed was his bedroom but was actually a workout room. He'd installed a pull-up bar in the doorway and was currently lifting himself up.

Wowzer, the man was strong. I had no idea how many he'd done, but the grunts he let out indicated he was putting in a lot of effort. Damn it, those grunts were too sexy. I had to make my presence known, so I cleared my throat.

"Good morning," I said.

Gabe immediately stopped and lowered himself to the floor. Then he turned around. I checked him out before I even realized it. His chest was a bit sweaty, but he was the sexiest man I'd ever seen in my life. His eyes were wide, and his muscles... yummm. I finally slid my gaze back up.

"Good morning," he said with a half smile.

"How come you're up so early?" My voice was high-pitched, but I hoped he'd let it slide. I mean, he had to expect this reaction, right? He was so damn sexy, I was surprised I could even remember how to talk.

"I always wake up at seven during the week, so I can't turn it off on weekends."

"It's been a long week, huh?"

"Yeah."

"I almost forgot I had a neighbor."

"Nope, still here, not going anywhere. By the way, I meant to talk to you about something, but I never got the chance because I was barely home. My brothers are stopping by today."

"Are you having a housewarming party? Should I make myself scarce?"

He came closer, and I folded my arms over my chest so I wasn't accidentally tempted to reach out for... oh, I don't know. I was sure I could find an excuse. Maybe I'd lose my balance again.

"They're just coming to hang around. And you don't have to make yourself scarce. In fact, you're invited. I'd like for you to meet them. They'll show up here often, and it's best if you know them."

"Oh, okay," I said. "So when is that exactly?"

"They're coming in about two hours. I was just going to shower and check how the construction is going at the house. I haven't been there in a week." After a beat, he added, "Want to come with me and see it?"

I bit the inside of my cheek, hesitating for a split second.

Oh, what the hell? The best way for things to return to normal was for me to *act* normal. Besides, I was curious.

"I'd love to."

Gabe

Fifteen minutes later, we left the house.

"So, how's the bar been?"

"Nightmare. But we found a good replacement. How was your week?"

"I've booked a few more tutoring clients, so that's going well."

Diane was avoiding my gaze, yet she clearly wanted to spend time with me. The feeling was entirely mutual.

When we arrived at the house, Mateo, the construction site manager, waved at me.

"Wow, this place is huge. Amazing," she gushed.

"Let me check with Mateo to see if it's safe to go inside."

"Perfect, because I'd love, love, love a tour." She glanced around with a warm and curious smile. I didn't detect one ounce of envy in her eyes.

I left her to her perusal and went over to Mateo. "How are things going?"

"Oh, good, good. We've made a lot of progress."

"Can I go inside?"

He nodded at Diane. "Want to show this to the missus?"

How had he concluded that she was my partner? I certainly hadn't introduced her, yet the idea didn't scare me away. Quite the contrary, I found the idea appealing.

What the hell?

"She's my neighbor," I clarified.

"Oh, okay. Yes, you can go inside. The guys and I are preparing to leave anyway. We need to buy some materials, and it's best to do it before all the DIY people line up."

That was one thing I hated about building my own house. I couldn't understand why construction crews couldn't get the hang of things;

how would they not know what they would need and buy it the day before?

"Right. You don't need to lock up because Diane and I will be inside."

He nodded. "Thank you, boss. Boys?" He turned, looking at the two other workers. "Come on, let's go."

"We both need to come?" one of them asked.

"Yeah, we can't carry all we need with just two people."

I didn't bother asking what "all" was. Mateo was working at his own pace, but he knew what he was doing.

Diane stood on the front porch. Her smile was even wider.

"What did he say?" she asked as I walked back over to join her.

"We can go inside and explore."

"Yes." She clapped her hands once, grinning.

"But we need to be careful where we step."

We headed up the stairs. I instinctively put an arm around her shoulders.

"I can keep my own balance now that I'm completely sober," she said in a teasing tone.

I leaned in, whispering in her ear, "It's for your own safety. The floor isn't very stable."

"I see." She laughed nervously.

As we stepped inside, she looked around. The ceiling was high with an intricate post-war molding around the corners.

"Before we begin, I have to say that most of this will be stripped away."

She turned her head to me abruptly. "What do you mean? The house isn't in such a bad shape."

"It's old as dirt."

"But it's so beautiful," she murmured.

"If you like old buildings."

"Well, I do. Though I also like modern ones. But why buy it if you plan to change all of it?" she asked as we proceeded farther inside.

"Because I like the location. And it needs a thorough renovation because all the walls were infested with mold."

She winced. "Yikes. Okay, well, that's tough. You can't take that crap out properly no matter how much you try."

"I agree. That's why I prefer to rebuild. Here I'm going to have an open space that will serve as living room, dining room, and kitchen. The living area is going to have three couches."

"Wow," she exclaimed.

"What can I say? I have a big family, and we like visiting one another."

I pointed at the left. "It's going to be here, and the TV is going to be hidden in the ceiling and only lowered when someone watches it. I don't like TVs hanging around like pieces of art. The kitchen is going to have an island that adjusts to the height of the cook because Grandmother insists she wants to spend time here, too, and she can't help herself from cooking."

She tightened her arm around mine. "It's cute that you want to build this so it fits your family too."

"Why not?"

"Indeed," she murmured.

"Want to go upstairs?"

"Sure. You'll have a basement too?"

"Yes, but only for storage. And there's going to be a gym upstairs."

The staircase was wide enough that we could walk side by side.

"This is the most unstable part," I informed her.

"All right."

Two steps later, the wood creaked. We both stopped moving, and I tightened my grip on her waist.

She swallowed audibly. "It's fine. My foot didn't sink in or anything."

We went up the rest of the stairs to the second floor without any other suspicious sounds.

"There are currently five rooms here, but I'm going to tear down some walls and make it three instead: my bedroom, a workout room, and an office. And then on the next level will be three en suite guest rooms."

"This is going to be quite the home!" she exclaimed.

"I've always wanted to have a proper home office," I said excitedly, leading her into the room where it was going to be. "I'm actually going to bring in my mom's old desk. I've liked it since I was a kid. It's one of those ancient things. My designer is struggling to fit it into the modern design, but he'll work it out. I'm going to put it right here." I pointed at the spot in front of the window.

"This home is going to make you happy, I can just feel it. Although I probably would have set it up completely different."

"How would you set it up?" I asked. "I'm genuinely curious."

"Well, I don't actually need a home gym, just a mat to do my yoga. I'd prefer actually joining a gym. I'll do that, you know, once I've gotten my life together." She avoided looking at me. "I think I'd probably use all these rooms for the bazillion kids I'd have."

I swallowed hard. My breath was trapped in my throat, which took me by complete surprise. I hadn't expected her to speak about this so openly.

"You want a big family?" I asked her.

"Don't you, with all the brothers and half-brothers you have?"

I shrugged. "I didn't buy the house with that purpose in mind. It's not something I ever planned for."

"Well, I'm not really planning for it either. But this house is inspiring."

I raised a brow. "So you don't, in fact, want a gazillion kids?"

She looked as if she was fighting herself. "Well, I did, some time ago... Doesn't matter. Anyway, no matter the setup, this is a gorgeous home."

"I agree. I'm glad I snapped it up."

"I'm so happy for you, Gabe. It's so good when you're finally able to fulfill your own dream." She walked closer to the window, and I followed her.

"What do you dream about?"

"Oh, well, that depends on what stage in life I'm currently at... or how I feel in the moment. Right now I feel like teasing my neighbor," she said, looking over her shoulder.

"Neighbor or roommate?" I teased right back.

I stood behind her, inhaling the scent of her hair. It smelled like cherries today. Did she keep changing her shampoos, or was it perfume? Was it the smell of her skin? Was that even possible?

"Both," she whispered.

"That night was fantastic," I said. I hadn't meant to bring it up, but I couldn't help myself; I needed her to know that I'd enjoyed it, that it wasn't just a fluke. I definitely didn't want to forget about it.

She turned around, looking straight into my eyes. "I know, right? I thought maybe I'd hyped it up in my mind, but no... it was delicious. The dinner and the kiss."

I grinned, loving that she took it in stride. "I like you, Diane."

She sucked in a deep breath. "Don't say that, Gabe, because I'm so attracted to you that I can't even think straight."

"Why are you saying that like it's a problem?" I all but growled.

"Because I think Celia would kick my ass if she knew."

I stilled. "Why?"

Diane laughed and ran her hand through her hair. "Because you're her boss, and, well... you know, things can be weird. Anyway, I thought I was doing such a great job behaving, and then I went and flashed you."

"I didn't see too much. Though I wanted to."

I tilted closer, kissing one corner of her mouth. She shuddered.

"Do you like this?" I asked. When she nodded, I moved to the other corner of her mouth and kissed it too. "How about this?"

She gripped the hem of my T-shirt; I took that as a yes.

I put a hand on her back, drawing a straight line from the base of her spine up to the back of her neck. "You want me to touch you, Diane?"

"Yes. God yes, I do. I want you."

Chapter Eleven
Gabe

I moved my mouth down her jaw and the front of her neck, tilting her slightly backward. She completely trusted me. It was a huge turn-on. Then I kissed back up her throat and drew her lower lip in my mouth before kissing her. She moaned against my mouth instantly, curling her arms around my neck and plastering the front of her body against mine.

I felt a light thrum through her. She needed more than a kiss; she wanted to come, and I was going to give her everything she craved. I wanted to see her come apart in my arms and feel the pleasure unraveling inside her.

I moved us deeper into the room without breaking the kiss, finally resting her against one of the exposed brick walls. It was a nook of sorts.

I started by kissing her slow and deep, savoring the way her body vibrated. She moaned, her tongue moving against mine without restraint. I wrapped one hand in her hair and moved the other one down her back, circling her tailbone. She shuddered at the contact, and I nearly lost it.

I raised her dress slowly, giving her all the time in the world to stop me, but she didn't. In fact, she grabbed at her dress, bringing it around her waist herself, as if she needed me to thrust faster.

I ran my hand down the front of her body, pressing my palm on her navel before reaching down, tortuously slow.

"Oh God, I want you so much," she whispered.

Hanging on to my last threads of self-control, I moved my hand farther down over her panties. I slipped it between her thighs, pressing against her pussy. She moaned even harder than before, spasming against me. I lowered my hand down her right thigh. Her legs were perfectly toned, and her skin was soft. I could touch her forever. I wanted to lick every inch of her before focusing on her pussy and giving her relief. But we didn't have time for that, and she was too on edge to withstand that sort of teasing and taunting.

I inched my hand back up between her thighs and instantly turned hard when I realized she'd drenched her panties. Fuck, the way this woman responded to me was absolutely delicious. Needing to touch her bare skin, I pushed her panties down to her knees. She groaned against my mouth.

"I want you to feel my tongue and fingers at the same time," I whispered before kissing her again as I slid my fingers inside her, first one and then another.

She pulled her head back, closing her eyes, like she couldn't take my tongue and my fingers at the same time. Good to know. I didn't want to overwhelm her; I wanted her to feel everything I was doing to her.

I rubbed my thumb over her clit, keeping my eyes on her face. Fuck, I wanted to give her my cock, but this wasn't the moment. Right now it was all about pleasing her. My needs didn't matter even though I was so hard I could barely keep it together.

I watched her carefully. She was so expressive that it was only too easy to read on her face what she liked and what she loved. I gave her more of the latter, moving the hand I'd buried in her hair down to her chest, teasing her nipples over her dress. They were both tight nubs. She wasn't wearing a bra. How the hell didn't I notice that before?

I was lost in her: inhaling her scent, absorbing her moans, feeling her shudders. This moment here was absolute perfection—the way she opened her eyes with a start, looking absolutely lost, as if she didn't even know what day it was or what her name was. She put one hand on the wall next to us and the other behind her, bracing herself. "Gabe... Oh my God, Gabe."

I covered her mouth, giving her my tongue at the same time I pressed my thumb on her clit and curled two fingers inside her. Her inner muscles went so damn tight around my fingers that I couldn't help imagining how she'd feel around my cock.

I felt the sheer force of her orgasm as it swept through her. Her entire body tightened up, then just as quickly loosened. Her muscles relaxed, and she pulled back from the kiss, resting her head on the brick wall and giving me a completely sated smile. This image of her would be imprinted in my brain forever. And at the same time, I instinctively knew I wouldn't be satisfied with this image alone. I needed to make her come again and again.

And I would, just not right now.

I took my hand away, letting her dress drop, then kissed the corner of her mouth again. "Back here with me?"

"I don't know." Her voice was still teasing. "I might be lost in a dream. A very sexy one." She opened one eye and then the other. "Oh, would you look at that? It's not a dream. We really are up here, and your hand was under my skirt, doing things to me." Then she straightened up, sucking in a deep breath. "Gabe! Do you think the crew is back?"

"No, but we should go down. My family will stop by soon. They want to see this place."

"Wow, that was... I kind of lost track of where... Um, do you have a working bathroom here?" she asked.

"No, just a sink. I'll wash my hands there. They have a makeshift toilet downstairs, but trust me, you're better off going back to the house to clean up."

"Oh yeah. That's exactly what I'm going to do."

Chapter Twelve

Diane

I hurried home and headed straight in the shower. Right then I was on cloud nine, and not even all the worries thumping around my mind could keep the happiness at bay. I was going to indulge in this one day of joy before I pulled myself together and behaved the way I should.

I didn't want to make things awkward between Gabe and me, yet resisting this man proved to be impossible.

The new construction had been pretty dusty, so I ended up washing my hair too. After blow-drying it, I put on fresh panties and another dress, and then I opened my door. A lot of voices were coming from downstairs. His family had already arrived.

I looked over my shoulder. What if I just stayed here? I could read. Or I could leave the house.

But he'd told me that he'd love for me to meet them. But that was before we'd gotten down and dirty. What if he'd changed his mind? What if this would be awkward?

Oh, pull yourself together, Diane. The only way to make this truly awkward is to leave. That's not your style. You face difficult situations head-on.

When my ex started behaving like he didn't actually like having me around, I didn't beat around the bush. We'd only been here for three months, and he was acting like I should be grateful to be with him. He thought I couldn't afford living on my own with my new tour job, which was true. He kept picking on me about anything and everything, so I confronted him about it, and we broke up.

I couldn't understand why he'd changed so much after we moved to Boston. Then I watched some therapy videos on YouTube because I couldn't actually afford to go to a therapist, and I discovered that some people completely changed their attitude when you were dependent on them. I'd vowed never to let that happen again. Yet somehow, I'd gotten myself in this situation.

It's not the same thing, Diane. You are renting from Gabe's landlady. It's not even remotely the same situation.

I took a deep breath and headed downstairs, then listened for a few beats at the foot of the staircase. There was laughter, and I heard two distinctive female voices.

I stepped into the living room, and the sight simply demolished my defenses. Gabe was holding a toddler, and he looked adorable.

Good gracious, a girl needs warning.

It was a boy, or at least I thought so. He was wearing a blue outfit that was absolutely adorable. His pants mimicked jeans, and they had suspenders. Gabe turned him around, and again I melted for entirely different reasons.

"Hi, you must be Diane," one of the women said. She was tall and slender, and she offered me her hand to shake. "I'm Natalie, Jake's wife."

One of the guys rose from the couch, coming to me. "Jake," he said, giving me his hand, and I shook it too.

"Come on, everyone, you don't all have to shake hands with her. Don't overwhelm her right now. Diane, I'll introduce you to my brothers in the order of how I like them best."

Everyone laughed, me included.

"Okay, let's hear it," I said.

He moved to the couch, putting a hand on one of the men's shoulders. "This is Cade and his gorgeous fiancée, Meredith."

Meredith waved to me from the couch.

Then Gabe patted the shoulder of the brother sitting next to Cade. "This is Spencer, Cade's twin brother and Ben's dad." He kissed the baby's head when he mentioned Ben. "And this is Penny."

He pointed at the man sitting next to Penny. "This is Colton."

Then he looked at the three men sitting in the chairs at the table. "And these are my half brothers, Maddox, Leo, and Nick."

That would explain the subtle difference between the two groups of men. The trio had darker hair and their eyes weren't blue, whereas the guys sitting on the couch had the exact same shade of magnetic blue as Gabe.

I smiled. "I'm pleased to meet everyone."

"By the way, you just went in chronological order for everyone except me," Colton pointed out.

"Yeah, that *was* lazy of you," Spencer said and then looked at me. "Which, by the way, does describe my brother pretty well."

"How do you know I didn't do it on purpose?" Gabe asked.

"Because I refuse to believe you like us less than Colton," Maddox said.

Colton grinned. "Yeah, I actually don't buy it either."

Gabe laughed. "Man, your sense of humor improved drastically since you've met Zoey."

I surmised Zoey was his girlfriend.

"I agree. She's upset that she couldn't come today," Colton went on. "But I promised to pass on any... gossip."

Gabe rolled his eyes. "Let's move on to something else. I don't actually have favorites. Diane, do you like pizza? I'm ordering in for everyone.

I don't want to subject them to my cooking and make a mess of things like last week."

I smiled sheepishly, though I felt a blush. "It wasn't that bad."

"What happened last week?" Cade asked.

Gabe opened his mouth, but I started to speak before him. "He tried to cook as a thank-you that I'd cooked the night before. It didn't work out, so we ended up having dinner in the city."

I felt a shift in the room, although I couldn't explain it at all.

Spencer got up. "You cooked? You never do that. Not ever."

"No, he did once, but he almost burned down his loft, so he gave up," Cade said and then stared at me. "But he wanted to make an effort for you. Good for him."

The silence became strange somehow. Natalie and Meredith looked like they were suppressing laughter.

"Okay, you called it," Jake said as Cade gave Gabe a thumbs-up.

"Called what?" I said.

"Please ignore my family," Gabe replied.

"It's impossible," Maddox said.

"Honestly, I think we should tell her, just so she's not caught by surprise," Leo said. Or was that Nick? I couldn't tell them apart.

"What is everyone talking about?" I asked.

Gabe returned Ben to Spencer and said, "Way to make this awkward. Remind me never to invite you here again."

"We're a handful," Spencer said, "but just the first time. You'll get used to us eventually."

"Want to do the honors or should I?" Cade asked Gabe.

Gabe looked straight at me. "Grandmother told these bozos that she thinks you and I have a spark. That's why she didn't want me to go with her that morning when I was supposed to drive her to her bridge meeting."

"Your grandmother... huh?" I mumbled. Maybe I misunderstood.

"Don't take it personally," Meredith said. "She usually makes statements like that. Though I have to say, she was correct with all of us."

I did remember Gabe telling me that she'd had a hand in matchmaking his brothers.

"Anyone know if she's ever been wrong?" Natalie leaned forward, looking at the trio.

Maddox put his hands in the air. "Not that we know of."

"She's failed to introduce me to any friend of hers who I actually found interesting," Gabe said.

Spencer pointed at him. "That still doesn't mean that she had a bad hunch. She never said that you'd make a good pair with any of them."

"I wonder why she was introducing him to all those women anyway," Meredith said.

My jaw went slack. I couldn't believe this conversation was actually happening. They were talking about this with the same nonchalance as if they were debating the weather.

Gabe grinned. "Diane, pizza?" he asked, looking at me with a bemused smile.

"Sure."

"What type?"

"I eat everything, honestly."

"Okay! I'm on it," he said, tapping on the screen.

"Did you go over to the house?" Meredith asked me.

"Yes, this morning." I blushed at the memory of what we'd gotten up to while there.

"We saw it today too. It's going to be so amazing," Meredith exclaimed. "

When did they have time to go? Although, to be fair, it took me a long-ass time to wash and blow-dry my hair.

"I liked the second floor best," Natalie said. "I especially liked that cute nook with the brick wall."

I stood completely still, afraid that if I said even one word, I'd give us away, but I couldn't stop the vortex of thoughts. Was my face super red? Did I look embarrassed? Guilty?

I stole a glance at Gabe. He was staring straight at me intently.

"Yes, that nook does have a je ne sais quoi, doesn't it?" he asked.

Oh sweet Lord. The man was going to be the death of me.

"Do you guys want something to drink?" I asked, looking around.

Gabe seemed to snap out of it then. "Diane, you're my guest just as much as them. Just because you live here doesn't mean you have to help me entertain, especially not these bozos."

"But I don't mind," I said. I felt I needed to do something with my hands. But Gabe pinned me with his gaze, so instead of finding an excuse to head into the kitchen, I sat down in the empty armchair.

Jake turned to me. "So, Gabe tells me you're renting the attic apartment?"

I nodded. "Yes. Honestly, I couldn't believe my luck when this opportunity came up. Thank goodness Celia knew Gabe was moving."

"Who's Celia?" Meredith asked.

"My sister. She works for Gabe."

He hasn't told them anything about me, huh?

Why was I feeling disappointed? He didn't have to talk with his family about me.

"Oh, so you don't work for Gabe? I had my story all wrong," Meredith said.

Wait, so he did talk to them?

"No. My sister is a bartender at his bar. So, you all work at Whitley Industries, right?" I glanced around the room.

"Well, I don't," Meredith said, glancing at Cade. "I still work for the competition."

"Yeah, she's playing hard to get," Cade said playfully. "But I'm going to win her over to the dark side sooner rather than later."

"What do you do?" Jake asked.

Suddenly, all eyes were trained on me.

I thought it was lovely that they all worked together. Well, it wasn't together-together, but they were involved in the family business.

I spoke about my job as a tour guide for a bit, and then the pizza arrived. When the doorbell rang, I jumped from the armchair immediately.

"I'll get it," I said, darting to the door.

I felt Gabe come up behind me. "You can't carry ten pizzas all on your own, Diane." He tipped the delivery guy, taking the entire stack.

"I can help," I said. But clearly he didn't need it, because he was only holding them with one hand.

He put his other hand on my arm, and the contact singed me. "Diane, do you feel uncomfortable with us?"

I licked my lips. "No, just on edge."

"Listen, we can talk about this later, okay? Once we're alone. If you enjoy spending time with me and my family, then I'm glad. But if you don't, then don't feel obligated to stay, okay? I'd love for you to get to know them, but it's up to you."

It was on the tip of my tongue to ask why he wanted me to get to know them. Just because we were roommates?

"Let's get back to the dining room," I said. "I'm starving and need some sustenance."

"Yes, I agree," Meredith called.

Crap, had she heard the whole conversation? Didn't seem likely. And I'd said that last sentence louder, after all.

Gabe walked in front of me, and I couldn't take my eyes off his ass as everyone filed in around us. The man was incredibly delicious.

As we ate at the dining table, I listened more than I talked. The dynamics were absolutely fascinating and completely hilarious. I felt Gabe's gaze on me the entire time we were eating, and even afterward, when we moved back to the couch area.

"All right. I think we've lingered here long enough," Colton said after a while, and I frowned.

"No, man, I can stay longer—" Maddox said but stopped abruptly when Leo glanced at him.

What's happening?

"Oh, yeah, sure. Okay. Cool," Maddox finished awkwardly.

"It was nice meeting you, Diane," Jake said, and then everyone bid us goodbye.

Gabe closed the door after they left and chuckled.

"What was that?" I asked. "They just... up and left."

He turned around, giving me a wry smile. "I bet one of them noticed the way I was looking at you and spread the word."

"You mean they know?"

"One thing you can assume about my family is that everyone knows everything."

"Wow," I murmured.

"But they were right about one thing: I want you."

Chapter Thirteen
Gabe

I kissed her the next second. I couldn't think straight anymore. In fact, I couldn't think, period. I was acting out of instinct. I needed Diane right now. By the way she kissed me back, I knew the feeling was mutual.

What happened back at the house wasn't a mistake, and this wasn't either. I savored her mouth, tilting her head to one side and deepening the kiss. I didn't just want a distraction but a connection. This was something entirely new to me, and I wanted to pursue whatever it was.

My bedroom was on the second floor, and I had to get her there. Earlier, we'd improvised everything, but now I wanted to take care of her the way I'd meant to all morning.

My cock twitched. Fuck, I craved relief. I lowered one hand to find hers already at the zipper of my jeans, and I nearly exploded.

Damn it, Pace yourself.

I craved her touch, but I planned to make her come first, so I swatted her hand away before undoing the button myself. She groaned in protest, but I didn't give her a chance to voice it. I kissed her harder, then hoisted her up by her ass, holding her under each buttock. She relaxed her legs and planted her arms on my shoulders, pulling back after I took the first step to look over her shoulder.

"I wouldn't mind going upstairs." Her voice was huskier than I was used to. "Let's make sure we don't accidentally trip on something."

"I wouldn't drop you," I assured her.

She turned back to face me. "That means I'm not driving you *that* crazy."

"You have no idea," I said. "You've been on my mind every day since you moved in."

Her eyes widened, and she dug her nails into my back.

When I reached the second floor, I headed directly to the master bedroom and lowered her onto the bed. She kneeled on the mattress, her eyes dark, looking me up and down. She bit her lower lip as she reached for the fly of my jeans. Since it was already open, all she had to do was undo the zipper. She lowered it, then pushed my jeans past my ass.

I tilted my head back, groaning. Fuck yes. I needed exactly this. Then she tugged at my shirt, and I pulled it over my head, throwing it across the room. Before pushing my jeans down completely, she made a move to tug at my boxers, too, but I grabbed her by the wrist and said, "No."

She jerked her hand back in surprise.

I wanted her lips on my cock, but I knew that if her mouth came anywhere close, I wasn't going to be able to stick to any plan.

"You first" was all I said.

"I don't understand," she replied.

"You will soon."

I lifted her dress, drawing my fingers from her knees up to the apex of her thighs. When I heard her swallow, I couldn't suppress a smile. I moved my fingers farther up, gathering the fabric on the side of her body, then started to pull her dress over her head. She was wearing black lingerie. It looked amazing against her skin, and I couldn't wait to take it off.

Her wrists got tangled in the straps before I completely removed her dress, and that gave me an idea.

Hell yes, this will be perfect.

"Lie down," I said, putting one knee on the bed. "On your back. Hands at the headboard."

"Why?" she whispered.

"I want to tie you up." I moved until my lips were only inches away from hers. "Anything against that?"

"No." She sounded breathless.

"Good. Then lie down."

She lowered herself onto the bed, first sitting down on her ass, then lying on her back, putting her hands above her head. I wrapped the dress around her wrists, careful not to make the knots too tight as I fastened it to the headboard. I reached between her legs, drawing my fingers over the fabric of her panties. She was completely wet. I smiled and took them off, and she sighed in relief, as if she couldn't possibly bear feeling them against her skin a second longer.

Then I leaned over her, tracing a line with my mouth from her clavicle down to her navel. I went farther down her pubic bone, stopping just short of her clit. She rolled her hips, clearly attempting to press her pussy against my face, but I moved back up before she could. A groan of despair rocked through her. I liked feeling her lose control and exploring her body slowly.

"Gabe," she whispered.

I traced my mouth back up her chest, drawing circles around her nipple. At the same time, I circled her clit with my fingers. I moved them slowly at first but then faster and faster as I directed my attention to her other nipple.

The way she shifted her hips on the mattress was exquisite. Then she planted her feet on it for more support as her body writhed in sync with my mouth and fingers.

Needing to kiss more of her, I moved away from her breasts even though I knew they were a sweet spot for her. I positioned myself between her thighs, kissing one leg and then the other. But she needed to come. I felt it in the way her muscles tightened and her breath quickened. I could draw this out, but this wasn't the moment to tease her further. After the first orgasm, yes, but not right now.

I put my mouth on her pussy without any notice and dipped my tongue inside of her. She bucked her hips off the bed. I was so hard that I could barely take the friction of the mattress against my cock. But it would be a while until I'd bury myself in her. I pushed my tongue in and out, pressing my thumb on her clit. She exploded at the sensations, and it was even better than I'd imagined. I pulled both my hand and mouth back. This wasn't the moment to give her more pleasure. No, I needed to let her ride the wave first.

As her body calmed down, her breathing slowed, and she tugged at her wrists. She trained her eyes on me. "Gabe," she muttered, "I want more."

"I'm going to give exactly that," I assured her.

I kissed up her belly and then reached for the nightstand, ready to put on a condom.

I got rid of my clothes, slid on the condom, then kissed her again unexpectedly. I liked taking her by surprise. The kiss was different than before; she was soft and even more open to me after her orgasm.

I parted her thighs wider, but I wasn't going to give her my cock yet. I pressed two fingers on her clit. She groaned deeply, and I knew it wouldn't take long to make her come again. Her body shook and the kiss became wetter. She twisted and turned. I liked having her body under mine. I could even faintly feel her heartbeat against my chest. Yet I was still hungry for more closeness.

Her second climax took both of us by surprise. She widened her eyes, opening her mouth in a delicious O while tugging hard at the headboard. I was lost in watching her cry out. She surrendered even more than the first time, maybe because she couldn't brace herself for it. It was absolutely amazing to watch her come apart. Her breaths were quick and shallow, her eyes unfocused, and then the tremor in her body intensified.

I kept my hand over her pussy, moving it lightly above her clit. I knew she was ready because she was completely drenched, and I pushed in, intending to thrust inside inch by inch, but I slid until my cock was all the way in. My vision blurred. My breath caught.

For a few seconds, I was completely lost. I didn't know where up and down were. The pleasure was too intense, too all-consuming. And I knew, deep in my bones, this woman would be my undoing in every way possible. Nothing would be the same after this.

I straightened up, sitting on my knees and keeping her legs draped over my arms. I slid in even deeper at this angle. I watched her as she tugged once more at the headboard.

"Want me to untie you?" I asked.

"Yes, please." She sounded shy.

I reached over, pulling at the knot. It came undone quickly, and she immediately put her hands on her breasts, pinching her nipples between her thumbs and forefingers. I almost exploded right then and there at the sight, but I managed to rein myself in.

I thrust faster, needing to bury myself in her as much as possible. I didn't want to hurt her, so I kept watching her face for any sign that this was uncomfortable.

"You're so big," she murmured.

I was chasing my release already; I'd been on edge all day, and watching her come twice fueled me even more. I was losing myself in her completely: her scent, her sounds, the way her body moved to meet my thrusts. It was glorious and all I needed.

Her pussy tightened around my cock. Her moans turned to gasps. She swallowed hard. My own body was strung so tight that I was barely keeping my climax at bay. I felt her come once more, and I exploded seconds later.

I succumbed to the pleasure, riding out the wave. I couldn't even make out my groans from hers. I'd never felt relief like this. My body was surrendering completely, and I didn't fight it. It felt so good.

In fact, it felt perfect, glorious. My body went from being completely wound up to 100 percent relaxed, as if all my muscles had turned to mush at the same time.

I pulled out, sitting on the edge of the bed, knowing that if I lay down, I wouldn't get up any time soon. I took off the condom, and we both went to the bathroom, cleaning up at the sink.

Once we returned to bed, she yawned. "Oh, man, all those stairs."

"What are you talking about?" I asked.

"Well, I have to go down the stairs to the first floor, then up the spiral staircase to the attic. Not sure how I'll climb them. My legs feel like rubber."

"Here's a thought—don't. Stay here with me."

She gave me a small smile, but then it grew wider until it was a full-on grin. "Yeah?"

"Fuck yes. You're not going anywhere tonight."

Chapter Fourteen
Diane

A beeping sound filled the air. I put a pillow over my head and tried to go back to sleep, but I could still hear it. A few seconds later, it stopped. I faintly heard a man's voice, and after that, silence. But I couldn't fall back asleep.

I took the pillow off, opening my eyes and looking at the ceiling. I smiled. Ah, I was in Gabe's bedroom. I'd spent the night here. I was still half asleep and wondered what time it was.

Then I heard footsteps outside the door, and I glanced in that direction. Gabe stepped in. He was butt naked, holding his phone.

"I woke you. Damn it," he said.

I yawned. "What time is it?"

"Six o'clock in the morning."

"And you're up voluntarily?"

"No. I got a call from the distillery we have in Texas."

"What happened?" I asked. He was clearly worried, or was it annoyed? It was too early in the morning for me; I couldn't properly assess the situation.

"A storm rolled in. We had a blackout at the factory and issues with the generators. Anyway, I'm heading there."

I rubbed my eyes, feeling them bulge. "To Texas? Now?"

He nodded. "Yes. Whenever there's a crisis, I prefer to be there versus trying to coordinate everything over the phone. People seem more motivated if I'm present."

His voice was tight. This was the first time I was seeing the CEO side of Gabe. He was no longer laid-back and ready for fun. Now he was all business.

"Okay."

"I'm going to pack some things."

I made to get out of bed. "I'll just go up to my room."

"There's no need for that," he said, putting two suits on the foot of the bed before coming closer and sitting at the edge of the mattress. "You look like you're about to fall asleep any second now."

I chuckled. "You're not wrong. I can barely keep my eyes open." I yawned. "But still, this is your room."

"Diane," he said, leaning forward to me. Did I mention he was naked? Even though I was half asleep, my hormones went to overdrive.

I splayed my fingers on his chest. I could clearly feel that he was tense. His muscles were taut, and a few veins were popping along his neck. I pressed my thumbs in two spots just on the side of his clavicle.

"Hmm. I can't let you leave like this. You need a massage. You're so stressed," I said. Licking my lips, I kissed down the front of his neck until I reached his Adam's apple. "How about a little de-stressing session beforehand?"

He groaned and fisted my hair. "Don't tempt me, Diane. The plane's leaving in two hours."

I fell back on my pillow. "You coordinated a flight already? You're very efficient."

He groaned again, and I realized I'd dropped my sheet, so he had a full view of my breasts and my nipples. "I'm so good at tempting you, huh?" I asked.

"Damn. Yes, you are," he said, lowering his head, taking one nipple into his mouth and then moving to the other one.

I arched my back as a spasm of pleasure ricocheted through me. It was so unexpected that I didn't have time to brace myself. Then he straightened up and rose from the bed.

I pouted. "No, you can't leave me like this."

He grinned. "We can pick up from right there once I return."

I smiled lazily. "That works."

Through a haze I watched him pack his bag. I was getting sleepier by the second, although I did manage to focus on watching him get dressed. He was just as sexy putting his clothes on as he was taking them off.

He put on suit pants and a shirt, then a belt. He added cuff links too. *Of course.*

I felt a pang in my stomach. I didn't want him to leave, but I knew he'd be back soon.

"Come on, sleepyhead, go back to bed. I can see you want to sleep," he said as he moved his suitcase by the door.

"I am definitely going to sleep like the dead after you're gone, but I didn't want to waste a single minute of watching you dress up. It was delicious."

He smiled and rolled his suitcase out. I thought he'd leave without giving me a goodbye kiss, but he came right back and put a knee on the mattress. Leaning over me, he kissed the side of my neck and said, "Be good while I'm gone."

"Huh? What do you mean?"

He just winked.

"How long are you staying?"

"Probably the whole week."

"Oh." Yeah, the pang in my stomach was definitely one of disappointment. He was going to be gone for a full week? I wanted to tell him to call or text me, but that sounded needy even in my mind. He was just my housemate, after all, even though we'd slept together and been on a date. Now things were confusing.

I smiled at him and said, "I hope everything works out."

This time, he did leave the room. Hugging his pillow under my head, inhaling his delicious masculine scent, I fell back asleep the next second.

When I opened my eyes again, the light outside was much brighter.

Did I dream that Gabe went away?

I looked to my left and then my right.

No, the bed was empty. It definitely wasn't a dream.

I checked my phone. It was eight o'clock. My alarm was set for eight fifteen. I paused it, but instead of getting out of bed, I stayed in, propping the pillow against the headboard and sitting upright, glancing around.

The sheets weren't just soft, they were luxurious. Maybe silk or Egyptian cotton or something. I tried to replay the morning in my mind. I remembered spying on him while he dressed. His scent lingered all around.

I got out of bed, dashing out of the bedroom and heading to the attic. I didn't want to use Gabe's shower. It felt like I'd be intruding in his personal space. After all, maybe this was just a onetime thing.

Oh God, that would be so awkward.

I washed my hair quickly and then dressed, not really caring about what I was wearing. I didn't have any tours today, but I'd scheduled four back-to-back tutoring lessons.

Going down to the kitchen, prepared to forage for food, I stilled when I saw a glass of orange juice. There was a note next to it too.

Morning! I didn't have time to prep breakfast but figured you'd enjoy this.

I put a hand on my chest. Smiling, I leaned closer, inspecting the note. It was handwritten, with splashes of juice on it. I couldn't believe it. He had to leave on an emergency trip, yet he not only remembered that I liked orange juice but had poured a glass for me. This was so unexpected. I didn't even know what to do except, of course, thank him.

I downed the juice quickly. Today, it seemed to give me extra energy. Was it because a certain sexy man made it? I thought so.

After finishing it, I texted him.

Diane: Thank you for the juice. It really is the best way to start the morning.

I assumed Gabe was flying or something because the message wasn't even marked as seen. Setting the phone down, I made myself some sunny-side up eggs and ate breakfast standing.

As I glanced around, my chest became a bit heavy. *Crap, what did I do? Why did I fall for Gabe's charms?* I was living with the man, and I currently had zero prospects for an apartment. Why did I have to go and mess things up? I had to get a grip on myself for the both of us. Otherwise, things between us could get complicated and living with him would be awkward. Not to mention, I really didn't want to put my sister in an uncomfortable position.

I had so much energy from breakfast and my juice that I decided to use the time to work out. But since Gabe wasn't home, I didn't have to stay in the attic. I went upstairs to change into my sports bra and jogging pants, then came back down with my mat and set up in the living room.

I'd been down here so often that it felt like a common space, although it obviously wasn't. But I was getting cabin fever in the attic.

I worked out using the barre method, which I'd discovered when I was in high school. It worked for my body. It resembled Pilates a lot, mixed with ballet moves. Typically, I needed some piece of furniture to hold on to. A stool and a table were just what I was looking for. I was in the midst of a plié when my phone beeped. I usually ignored messages or calls when I worked out, but I saw Gabe's name on the screen. I immediately reached for it and lost my balance, crashing to the floor.

"Ow!" I'd hit my elbow and my knee. My eyes watered. *Damn it!* I swallowed hard, rising to my feet as I sighed, rubbing the sore spots. I checked my phone even though my eyes were still watering.

Gabe: My pleasure. Thought you'd like to start your day on a good note.

Diane: Thanks. I love surprises, and this is the best. How was your flight?

Gabe: Uneventful. There is a shit show going on down here. I guessed right. What are your plans today?

Diane: Tutoring and nothing much else.

Gabe: So you're working from home?

That was an odd question.

Diane: I am, yep. It's going to be pajama day all day. Well, right now it's workout clothes hour. But not for long. I'm going to take advantage of the fact that no one can see me. *winking emoji*

I saw the dots moving that indicated the other person was typing.

Forget going back to my workout. I was glued to my phone.

Gabe: I want a picture.

I looked down at myself. *Hmmm... I didn't even choose my good workout clothes.*

Chapter Fifteen

Diane

Gabe: Diane?

Diane: Permission not granted.

He called me, and I answered right away.

"What permission?" he asked. His voice was low, almost a growl.

"I was teasing you. I don't like my workout clothes, and I'm a bit sweaty, so I don't want to take a picture of myself."

"Diane."

"That's a final answer." Well, not really. If he kept insisting, I might give in. But I wasn't going to share that bit of information. "Ummm... I'm actually in your living room." It didn't feel right to keep that info from him. "I hope that's okay. Doing a workout in my attic—"

"Diane, you can use the house as you like. Feel free to work in the living room, work out, whatever, okay?"

"Thanks. Are you still stressed?" I asked him.

"Yeah."

"You were so tense this morning."

"Trust me, I'm even more so now."

I was about to say that I'd love to be around and help him out, but where would that lead us? We hadn't talked about... well... *us*.

"That massage you started this morning was great. If only I had you here to do it."

I felt like my heart was about to leap out of my chest. "You'd want me there with you?"

"Fuck yes."

I swallowed hard. "You can call me anytime. I do have some de-stressing skills over the phone too," I added quickly. "Though they're nothing compared to my in-person skills."

"I might take you up on it."

"Yes, please do," I whispered. It felt like we were walking on eggshells around each other. Actually no, a better description was that we were simply in uncharted territory.

"Then I'll call you tonight. Now I'd better take care of this shit show."

"Sure," I said.

I was inexplicably excited after I finished talking to him. I put the phone down and then turned around, intending to head upstairs, before remembering that I was actually working out. Holy shit, he'd made me forget my head completely.

I dutifully did my routine for the next forty-five minutes, keeping an eye on my phone, but he didn't call again. Then my phone beeped, and I rushed to get it.

I groaned. I had a message from my ex.

Chuck: You've got my old laptop. It's not in my storage room. I'm going to need it back.

Oh for fuck's sake, really?

He could go to hell for all I cared. If he wanted a laptop, he could buy himself one. I didn't want to see him ever again.

My body didn't tighten up quite the way it had the last time he'd contacted me. Still, it didn't mean I wanted to see the idiot, even though it was his laptop. And yeah, it was at the bottom of one of the boxes I hadn't bothered to open. But considering I'd financially supported him through post-grad, he could go shove it.

The morning tutoring sessions went by quickly. As lunchtime approached, my stomach began to rumble, so I made myself a quick stir-fry.

While eating, I looked at job ads. It was my favorite pastime nowadays, but damn it, nothing appealed to me at all. After spending so much time outdoors with my tourist groups, I couldn't imagine being inside a hotel all day. If only I could find a second job with another touring agency that could pay me more money.

Then a dangerous thought infiltrated my mind. Maybe it was because I already had some experience with tutoring, but... what if I started my own tour company? It would be a one-woman show, of course, but I'd love that. The downsides were affording health insurance and such.

And yet, the more I thought about it, the more excited I became. I could set my own hours and even do the tours the way I wanted them versus how my boss, George, insisted I do them. I'd call the shots. Oh, I had so many ideas. I grabbed a pen and paper and immediately wrote them down, afraid I might forget them once I started my next tutoring lesson.

I did the afternoon sessions in the living room. They passed quicker, and I was certain it was because I couldn't wait to chat with Gabe.

I intended to wait for him to make the first move, but I lost the battle during my last session.

Diane: Hey, want to catch up before dinner?

I chastised myself after I sent it—I didn't want to seem desperate—but he answered immediately. That meant he was looking forward to it, right?

Gabe: I'm gonna have dinner first. Haven't eaten all day. I'll have a burger at the hotel restaurant.

Diane: Damn, now I'm in the mood for burgers. Okay, then let's catch up after dinner. My tutoring session finishes in forty minutes.

After that, I focused on my pupil, not wanting to be unprofessional.

I couldn't believe my luck—I had ten students now every week. I assumed it was because I charged less than other tutors, but my price seemed fair since I wasn't actually a teacher—something I specifically mentioned in the bio. I didn't want to mislead anyone because I didn't have a teacher's certificate.

"Okay, Diane. I'll see you next time," my student said.

"Next week, same time, right?" I asked.

"Yes. This is great. I'm so glad I found you."

I smiled at that. My clients were so genuine.

After closing my laptop, I got off the couch, stretching a bit. This living room was so gorgeous. I'd have a hard time staying cooped up in my attic again once Gabe was back.

I walked into the kitchen, intending to cook a quick dinner, but then the doorbell rang. I closed the fridge and dashed toward the front door. I'd ordered a number of things from Amazon and was happy they'd arrived already, although I was pretty sure the delivery date was tomorrow.

When I opened the door, I was surprised to find a vaguely familiar young man.

"Hey, Diane," he said. *Oh, he knows my name.* He was carrying a bag of food. "You don't remember me, huh? I work at Gabe's bar. In the kitchen, actually."

"Sorry. You look a bit different in broad daylight." I felt like a moron.

"I've brought you a burger. Gabe said you wanted one."

I stilled. "Oh wow. Thank you."

"You're welcome."

"How are things at the bar?" I asked.

"It's probably going to be crazy tonight. I heard someone say we were featured in a TikTok that went viral, so we expect a lot of customers. And with Gabe gone... Anyway, have a great evening. I've got to hurry before rush hour starts."

It was super early, only six o clock.

"Thanks again. Have a great evening."

I practically ran to the kitchen, grinning from ear to ear. *Hell yes*. I opened the bag and put the burger on a plate, immediately taking a bite. It was just as delicious as I remembered. After two more bites, I stopped and grabbed my phone, calling Gabe.

He'd already sent me a message.

Gabe: How's your burger?

I held the phone between my ear and my shoulder as I put the burger on a plate, then went back to the living room, sitting at the dining table.

"Hey." I could hear the smile in his voice.

"Hey. This is such a cool surprise." My heart skipped a beat. "I can't believe you sent me this!"

"Why not? I actually had my burger sent to my room so we can have dinner together, sort of."

My stomach leaped with joy. It warmed my heart at how thoughtful he was.

"The burger is delicious. I could kiss your cook."

Gabe growled.

"What was that?" I asked.

"You're not kissing Micah or anyone else."

I pressed my thighs together, shaking my hips a bit on the chair as a shudder went through me.

"It was just a figure of speech," I said.

"You will kiss *no one else* while I'm gone."

I nearly swallowed my tongue before whispering, "Okay."

I bit the inside of my cheek, unsure what else to say, then decided to switch topics. "I could use a glass of red wine."

"You're welcome to take any bottle from the fridge."

I laughed nervously. "Hmm... last time I drank red wine, things were... well, you remember. Who knows what I'll do?"

"What are you afraid of? I'm not even there."

"I can find enough ways to embarrass myself, even on the phone," I assured him.

"Now I'm intrigued."

"No red wine," I decided. "So, you still have to stay there the whole week?" I double-checked before taking another mouthful of the burger, swallowing it quickly.

He sighed. "Yes. We've managed to make a lot of headway today, but some things can't be rushed, unfortunately. And the team appreciates me being here."

"I bet they do."

We spoke a while longer, and after we finished, I noticed I had a message from my sister.

Celia: Hey, girl, are you free tonight?

Diane: Sure. You need me at the bar?

Celia: It would be amazing if you could drop by. We're swamped thanks to a viral TikTok, and Gabe is on a business trip, as you probably already know.

Diane: I'll be there in around twenty minutes.

I changed quickly, suddenly fueled by energy. I was looking forward to spending the evening with my sister and helping Gabe at the same time, even though I wouldn't see the man himself. But maybe that was for the best—I didn't think Gabe and I could be so close to each other and not give ourselves away.

I felt guilty for not telling Celia the truth, but I wanted to talk to Gabe first. This was too messy, though I didn't feel bad at all. I had no idea where it would lead. I was just super happy that I'd gotten a burger and a few orgasms last night. As a plus, Gabe made me swoon today.

To say the place was full was an understatement. I could barely make my way to the bar. Once I was behind the counter, I took a deep breath, then went straight to Celia.

"All right," I said, clapping my hands and looking at the three other bartenders. "Put me to work."

The pace was insane, nothing like the other time I helped. And I'd thought it was busy back then too.

Everyone was asking for a specific type of cocktail. That's probably what the viral TikTok was about. My phone went off with messages several times while I was helping out, but I didn't even have a few seconds time to check them. I knew it couldn't be anything bad or urgent, though, or the sender would have called.

We were completely swamped right until we closed at two o'clock in the morning.

"I'm exhausted," Celia declared. The guys agreed in unison.

I yawned. "This is insane. I mean, it's good for the business, but you guys definitely need more support."

"Gabe said when he gets home, he'll hire three more full-time bartenders, even though we don't need them most of the time, because this cannot go on."

"That's great," I said. I liked that he was a considerate boss who didn't want to overwork his employees.

"Oh, I think someone named Cal is here for us," Celia said, pointing outside. "Gabe texted me earlier. He doesn't want us going home alone."

Holy shit, I'd forgotten about Gabe. Then I remembered the million texts and took out my phone.

Gabe: Celia said she asked you to come to the bar. I really appreciate it, but you don't have to.

Gabe: Saw some pics online. You're gorgeous.

Gabe: Cal is going to take you and Celia home.

I was swooning again. Not just because he was taking care of me but because he was taking care of my sister.

"All right, boys. Let's all go," Celia said.

We all walked out at the same time. One of the guys got in his car, the other ordered an Uber, and my sister and I went with Cal.

Once inside the car, I said, "Sir, I'm so sorry that you had to stay up this late."

"Please, call me Cal. And it's not a problem. Don't worry about me. I'm going to drop you off first."

"Thank you."

We were completely silent during the drive. We were both exhausted.

"So, how's everything going? How's living with Gabe?" Celia asked in a low voice as we almost reached the house.

I tensed instantly. I was exhausted, and my defenses weren't on point. "It's good. I'm in the attic a lot. I just cook in the kitchen."

"And things aren't weird at all?" she continued.

"No," I replied, avoiding her gaze. "I mean, you know how things are when you have a housemate. You have to be careful."

"Mm-hmm. That's true. Oh, we're almost there."

"Do you want to crash with me?" I asked her.

She shook her head. "No, you know me. I need to decompress a bit."

"True." I kissed her cheek, then looked at Cal. "Thank you so much for dropping me off."

"My pleasure."

I got out of the car and headed inside the house, taking the stairs two at a time and yawning as soon as I stepped inside my bedroom. My head was pounding, but I was hoping it was simply because it was very late. Nothing a good night's sleep wouldn't solve.

I undressed and grabbed my phone to set the alarm clock as I slipped between the covers butt naked.

I had a message from Gabe.

Gabe: Cal said he's dropped you off. Call me if you can. If you're too tired, we'll talk tomorrow.

Oh, no way could I talk now. I was exhausted, but I smiled just before I closed my eyes. How could this man make me swoon so much?

Chapter Sixteen
Gabe

My motto in life was "Don't worry about something until it happens."

Worrying simply wasn't productive, unless, of course, you could proactively do something. I was good at problem-solving. Local management in Texas was grateful I'd flown down and worked overtime along with everyone else. I never asked anyone to do something I wasn't willing to do myself. That was another rule I lived by.

As a result, we got everything up and running faster than I'd initially assumed, so I returned to Boston earlier. There was another crisis here, although much smaller. We'd done a limited-edition series of aged bourbon bottles and were including a pack of playing cards. But the packaging company screwed up the measurements, and the packaging machines couldn't automatically put the cards with the bottle. They had to be fitted manually. Everyone in production was on it, but I was going to join them, too, once I finished the tasks for today.

I texted my brothers and half brothers before I boarded the plane.

Gabe: I'll be back today already.

Maddox: All good?

Gabe: In Texas, yes. In Boston, we need to manually put some promo material on 3000 bottles.

I touched down at four o'clock in the afternoon and headed straight to the office, where I had several fires to put out. At six o'clock, I went to the distillery.

I couldn't wait to go home, relax, and check on Diane. I'd messaged her twice today, but she hadn't answered. What was up with that?

There was a flurry of activity in the distillery, and to my astonishment, my half brothers were here.

"When did you arrive?" I asked them.

Maddox, Leo, and Nick had their shirt sleeves rolled up to their elbows and were packing the cards with the bottles.

"Just now."

"Did I ask you to come and I forgot?"

I wouldn't put it past me. I was exhausted from the past few days.

Nick chuckled. "No. You said you're playing catch-up, and we came to help."

"The rest of the crowd is coming too," Maddox said. "I talked to Jake earlier."

It still amazed me that Maddox and Jake had managed to form a tentative friendship. Natalie working with Maddox definitely helped. They'd barely exchanged a few words before that.

"Thanks. All right, I'll start with that stack." I pointed at a huge pile of overturned boxes. They were stuffed with bottles and promo cards, waiting to be manually sealed.

"Don't. You've been burning the candle at both ends this week. We've got this," Leo said. "And with Jake, Colton, and Cade, we'll do this quickly."

"Thanks, man. I'm dead on my feet; otherwise, I wouldn't even let you do this. Let's talk this weekend. We'll do something together so I can make it up to you." Then I reached for a box. Despite what they said, I didn't want to just leave them to do all the heavy lifting.

Nick cocked a brow. "You don't need to make up for anything. This is what family is for. And anyway, we don't have time to meet this weekend."

He exchanged a glance with Maddox and Leo.

"What are you doing this weekend that you don't want to tell me? Please don't say you're conspiring with Grandmother."

Maddox held his hands up. "Hell, no. That's where your mind went? What did we ever do to deserve that?"

"My apologies. You're right," I said.

Still, Maddox looked a bit uneasy as he glanced at our brothers.

"Mom is coming into the city," Leo explained.

"Oh, right. Well, have fun."

"Yeah. She hasn't been here in a while," Nick added.

His voice was tentative, which was so unlike him.

Maddox shrugged. "We're showing her around this weekend."

"Cool."

What, was I twelve years old? Then again, I never knew how to react when they brought up their mom. I'd never met her. Somehow it felt like I'd betray my own mother by doing so, which couldn't be further from the truth. Both women had been lied to. Their mom wasn't a homewrecker. Neither knew of the other until the end, and yet every time they brought her up, things became awkward.

I managed to seal ten boxes before Nick said, "Dude, go home. The rest of the crew is here."

I looked up to see Jake, Colton, and Cade striding toward us.

"You go. We've got this," Jake exclaimed.

"You guys are all workaholics, even more than me," I declared. "How come you're even here?"

Cade shook his head. "Don't put me in the same category as these two." He pointed one thumb at Jake and the other at Colton.

"Sorry, my bad."

"Colton and I are making huge progress," Jake said. "And besides, this is an emergency."

"You look like shit," Colton said.

"That's exactly how I feel," I replied. I felt guilty that they came here after their workday to help me out, but I was also immensely grateful.

We worked side by side for a while before taking a break. That's when I realized Leo, Maddox, and Nick had their heads together. I recognized the tight expression on Maddox's face and had an inkling that I knew what they were talking about. I made my excuses and joined them.

"You all really need to work on your poker faces because they're a dead giveaway that something's wrong."

Leo narrowed his eyes, looking at the others too. "Fuck, he's right. Stop with the sour faces."

"I meant you too!" I clarified.

He scoffed. "I don't look nearly as bad as these two bozos."

"Is this about Dad?"

All three of them went rigid.

Leo scratched his chin and nodded. "My contacts tell me he's looking for a huge property."

"What for?"

"Rumor has it," Maddox said, "that he wants to build a hotel."

"Oh, for fuck's sake."

"You were thinking about going into the hotel business, too, weren't you?" Maddox asked.

"Yes! Seems like a natural expansion from the bar business, but right now my priorities are building a bigger distillery."

I looked at the rest of our brothers and then made a split-second decision.

"There's no need to involve the others in this," I said.

"We weren't going to," Leo said.

"I don't see why we should annoy everyone with Dad's antics," Nick added. "It's not like last time with the shares. There's nothing anyone can do about this."

I didn't know how, but I wasn't going to allow Ryan Whitley to mess with our legacy. Not again.

Him coming back to Boston was out of the question. He'd done so much damage to the Whitley name over the years that we'd barely recovered. He wasn't going to tear it down again.

"When you find out what exactly he wants to buy, let me know."

"Let all of us know," Maddox said. "I'm starting to think Colton and Jake were right."

Coming from Maddox, this was shocking. Those three were on good terms now, but I never thought I'd hear Maddox say he actually agreed with them.

"About what exactly?" I asked.

"Giving him money. Feels like we gave him a prize for all the shit he's pulled. And now he has enough capital to continue messing up the name."

"He won't," I assured him. "I'll make sure of that. Now, let's get back to work before the others catch on."

An hour later, we finally finished everything.

"All right, everyone. Cocktails are on the house, but it has to be some other evening when I can join you," I said at 11:00 p.m. "I'm exhausted right now."

"I'll hold you to that, don't worry," Cade said good-naturedly. "Come on. Let's all go."

The warehouse manager was the last one out, checking everything before closing up.

I went home, and once I got inside, I remembered that Diane hadn't responded to my messages all day. That was unlike her. Not that I was an expert at communicating with women.

"Diane?" I called, looking around the living room. It was empty.

Was she not home? She would have told me if she went somewhere, right?

Then again, why should she? She didn't owe me an explanation for anything.

I was about to go to bed, but then I saw she'd left her phone on the kitchen counter. Fuck, something was really off. She wouldn't have simply left it in here. When I touched it, the screen lit up with all the messages from me.

I went back to the entrance and up the spiral staircase. Her door was open—yet another sign that something was off. I sprinted up the last steps.

"Diane?" No response. "Diane?" I asked again.

"Am I imagining this?" The faint voice came from the bedroom.

I walked straight to her. She was lying on one side, hair plastered on her face. She was a sweaty mess.

"What happened?"

"Some sort of virus. I don't even know. I feel like death."

I sat at the edge of the mattress, putting my hand on her forehead. "You have a fever. Did you take anything for it?"

"I don't even remember. I think I did, maybe a few hours ago. What time is it now?"

"It's midnight," I said.

"Oh shit."

"I tried calling you."

"Damn. I forgot my phone downstairs. I wanted to call my sister and see if she could drop by. My whole body hurts."

I sat beside her, rubbing her neck and shoulders.

"That's a bit better," she said. "How are you good at everything? Even curing flu or whatever this is. And wait a second, how come you're back?"

"I finished earlier than anticipated, and I wanted to surprise you," I admitted.

She grinned even though she was clearly not feeling well. "You came home thinking you were going to get some and instead find me looking like death."

I burst out laughing. "You never lose your sense of humor, huh?"

"No, never," she murmured. "It's what keeps me going right now. I feel so dehydrated. I wanted to make myself tea at the kitchenette earlier but couldn't even get out of bed."

I looked around and made a split-second decision. "I'm taking you to the master bedroom."

She blinked her eyes open. "Why?"

"Because I can take care of you better there and keep an eye on you. Plus, I know my way around my kitchen better than here."

She laughed. "There's no learning curve. I only have two appliances."

"I'm going to lift you in my arms."

"That would totally make my day. I've spent it lying in bed, and now I can feel up those sexy muscles."

"I'm glad to be of service," I informed her, peeling her cover away. "I'll change you first. It's bad for you to stay in these wet clothes."

"I have nightgowns in the dresser. First door, second shelf."

I got up and followed her instructions, immediately finding a nightgown.

I took three more from the same shelf. They'd come in handy if her fever didn't break.

Diane was sitting at the edge of the bed. She was shivering. She'd already peeled off her nightgown. I used it to dry her back and then slid on one of the fresh ones.

"I bet this isn't the sexy picture you had in mind," she murmured. Her voice was fainter.

I kissed one corner of her lips. "Don't you even think about it, okay? Come on, up we go. Keep these," I told her, putting the nightgowns in her lap.

"Good thinking."

I lifted her, putting one arm under her knee and the other at her back. She laid her head on my shoulder.

"Oh, this is good," she said. She nudged my neck with her nose and then nuzzled it with her lips.

I barely suppressed a groan. Now was not the time to get turned on. She was sick. I wanted to take care of her.

"Behave so I can focus on the stairs," I admonished.

"Oops, yep. I promise I will. The last thing we need is to tumble down the stairs."

I walked slowly, and she kept her promise...until we were in my bedroom.

My cock clenched in my pants. "Diane, fuck."

"Oops. I know I was supposed to behave, but you smell so delicious."

"Really? Because I had a long-ass day and spent the last few hours doing physical labor."

"Oh my God," she said as I lowered her onto the bed. "You have to sleep."

"I'm going to take care of you first."

"You don't have to do that. You can't even do much."

"I have one of those powders that are supposed to help the immune system when you have a cold," I told her. "Want me to make you one?"

"Sure."

I kissed her forehead. "I'll be back in a few minutes."

I massaged the back of my neck on the way to the kitchen, noticing how tense I was. I couldn't believe Diane had been on her own all day. But I was home now, and I was going to look after her.

I mixed the powder with boiling water, then added some cold water in it, too, so she could drink it right away.

When I came back to the bedroom, she was asleep, so I put it on her side of the nightstand. If she woke up and was thirsty, she'd drink it. Although it tasted like shit when it was cold. Not that being hot made it much better.

I slid into bed on the other side.

Diane immediately turned onto her side and scooted closer to me, putting her head on my chest. "Mm, that's better," she murmured, clearly still asleep.

I smiled, kissing the top of her head. If she wanted to use me as a pillow, I had nothing against it.

Chapter Seventeen
Diane

I felt terrible. My head was pounding, and my body felt weak and stiff at the same time. At least I hadn't sweated through my nightgown again.

I shifted on the bed. *Wait a second. What the hell kind of pillow do I have?* It wasn't soft and fluffy; it was hard.

I opened one eye. It wasn't a pillow. I opened the other one too. No, this was for sure no pillow. It was a defined male chest.

I lifted my head abruptly, which turned out to be a big mistake. My eyes watered, but I still saw Gabe clearly, sleeping in my bed.

No, hang on. This isn't my room.

I was in his bed.

After a split second of panic, last night's memories rushed in. I'd been sick as a dog in my room, and he'd carried me here and even tried to give me medicine, but I couldn't remember drinking it.

I turned onto my other side, looking at the nightstand. There was a glass. It was only half full. Maybe I'd drunk it in the night and couldn't remember.

My phone was right next to the glass. It was seven o'clock. I slid back under the covers, curling onto one side and putting my head on the pillow this time. But I couldn't find a position I liked. I molded it into a shape I thought would be better, but still, I hated it. No, I had to go back and use Gabe's chest as a pillow.

Carefully placing my head on his skin so I didn't wake him up, I drew in a deep breath. I felt so good here. I couldn't explain it, but I was completely at peace.

I dozed off and only came to myself sometime later. I felt a light touch down my back. Gabe's chest was moving up and down quicker. Even in my hazy, sleepy state, I realized he was probably awake. I moved my head slowly, placing my hand between my chin and his chest. His eyes were wide open.

"Good morning, beautiful. How are you feeling?" he asked.

I swallowed hard. "Not good. My head is swimming. But I'm better than yesterday."

"I'll take care of you today," he announced.

"Nooo, I don't want to get you sick."

"My immune system is great. Don't worry about that."

"But you said you have a lot of things to do."

"My team has got it handled. Besides, we dealt with the crisis last night, so I have some leeway today." He kissed my forehead. "Stay here in bed while I make breakfast for both of us."

I bit the inside of my cheek as I slid down and put my head on my palm. "I could come and help out," I said half-heartedly. On one hand, I absolutely didn't feel capable of getting out of bed, but on the other, I was a bit afraid of leaving him alone in the kitchen.

"No. I'll take care of everything. You just rest," he said.

My heart grew in size. I touched his chest and then his back as he got out of bed.

"Don't tempt me already."

I grinned. "You're right. Silly me. You need your coffee first."

He looked at me over his shoulder, then took my hand, kissing it.

I was so immensely happy even though I felt like shit. I wanted to take a shower, too, as I was sticky from all the sweat. But I just couldn't muster the energy to get there.

I grabbed my phone by reflex, checking my emails. When I fell ill yesterday, I'd emailed all my tutoring students and had to cancel the appointments today too. I also had a tour booked today, and I regretfully informed my boss that I couldn't make it.

I was a warrior and liked to push through, but even I had my limits. I'd apologized to my students and offered to reschedule at their convenience.

I also messaged Celia, since I was supposed to meet her tonight for drinks.

Diane: Hey! I've got a cold. It's pretty bad. Let's meet another evening, okay?

Celia: OMG. Do you have everything you need? I can stop by after the morning shift.

Diane: No, I don't want to get you sick. And I have a lot of medicine. Don't worry about me.

Celia: Are you sure?

Diane: Yes. I'll be super mad if you show up.

Celia: Got it, boss!

I opened the Netflix app on my phone, thinking I'd watch something, but five minutes later, my head began to swim. I was in even bigger trouble than I thought.

I put it down, closing my eyes. I had no idea how long I stayed like that, but I only opened them when I heard footsteps, and then I saw Gabe carrying a tray. I instantly grinned, pushing myself up into a sitting position. My eyesight blurred.

Oh, Diane. Come on, get your shit together. A sexy man is taking care of you. You can't miss any details of this. You have to commit it to memory.

"A glass of orange juice, of course, and two boiled eggs, along with toast." He'd put a slice of butter on the plate and some sort of orange jam in a small bowl.

"Wow, this looks so professional."

He laughed. "I did my best."

Since this wasn't an actual bed tray, I had to take care not to spill any crumbs. He'd brought a plate for himself, although his was far less organized than mine. I started with the eggs. The second I swallowed the first bite, I realized this was my first meal in twenty-four hours. I was starving. Maybe that was why I was so light-headed.

"Gabe, thanks so much. God, I needed this breakfast."

I spread butter on my toast and then put jam on it afterward, munching it quickly. "Mmm, apricot jam."

"Thought you'd like something sweet."

"Oh, you're definitely a great guy."

"How do you figure that?" Gabe asked.

I sucked in my breath. "Well, you know, you carried me here. You brought me breakfast. You're basically a knight in shining armor. You're good at relationships—not that I mean to imply anything."

Gabe looked at me intently. "I've never been in a relationship. Except if you count high school, which I don't. And a two-month fling a few years back."

"You've never had a relationship?" My voice sounded like a cry.

"No. Why is that such a surprise?"

"I don't know. I thought... Never mind, it's none of my business." I looked at my plate intently. "Really, I was just paying you a compliment."

I felt him slide closer to me on the mattress. He nuzzled the tip of his nose against my cheek, then brought his mouth to my ear.

"I feel closer to you than I've ever felt to anyone." He put a hand on my waist and kissed down my neck before bringing his mouth back to my ear.

The next second, my entire body relaxed. I wasn't even aware that I was so tense before, but it was as if hearing those words released something inside me.

"I feel the same."

He straightened up, looking right at me. "So stop being so surprised that I'm bringing you breakfast and looking after you. I always give the very best in everything I do."

I started laughing. "That sounds like a business pitch."

He kissed my forehead before capturing my mouth. The kiss was slow but not tentative. He was exploring me. I shuddered and then began to tremble in earnest. How could he affect me so much with just a kiss?

He pulled back, and I protested. "No, why did you stop?"

"Because I don't want to turn either of us on."

"Wait a second. Your voice is low and raw and a bit grouchy, so..."

He cocked a brow. I looked down in his lap. He was sporting morning wood.

I grinned. "No comment."

Was I feeling like shit? Yes.

Was I also extremely proud? Hell yes. But right now, I wanted to simply stay in bed and hydrate a lot.

"I've spoken to a family friend who's a doctor. He advised that you limit effort and drink as much as possible. If you still have a fever after four days, you should go to the hospital and see if it's not something bacterial that they can treat with antibiotics."

"You've called a friend of yours?"

"I actually wanted him to come see you right away, but he said it's not necessary."

I hadn't felt so cared for since I was a kid. Chuck would never have done this for me.

"Gabe, thanks." My voice was uneven. I was sure he could tell.

"I'm at your service today. I don't need to go to the office."

"I'm probably going to sleep," I said honestly. "I'll talk to Celia, too, and let her know I'm feeling better."

"You can tell her to drop by, if you want," Gabe said.

"Well...I mean, I haven't told her about us."

"True." He trapped me with his gaze.

"So maybe I'll tell her to come another day. I just want to be in better shape when we talk to her."

"You think she'll take it badly?" Gabe asked.

"I think so," I admitted. "You're her boss, and..." I didn't voice the rest of my fears because they weren't my sister's. They were mine.

What if this was a silly mistake? What if it ended as soon as it started, and then not only would I have to move out, but I'd also have made work incredibly uncomfortable for Celia? I would hate for that to happen.

"Then we'll tell her another time," Gabe said. "Now, you said you want to sleep, right?"

"Yes."

"Scoot over." He picked up the plates and set them on his nightstand.

"Why?"

"Because you went out like a light on my chest, so I'm offering it up as tribute."

Chapter Eighteen
Diane

Three days later, I finally woke up without even a trace of a headache. In fact, I seemed to be in top shape. I hadn't sweated my nightshirt through, and even after I pushed myself into a sitting position quite quickly, I didn't feel light-headed.

I glanced over my shoulder at Gabe, who was sleeping soundly. I couldn't believe I'd spent the past three days in bed with this handsome man. He'd worked from home but was at my side whenever I needed help. I'd never been treated so well.

Since I felt great, I decided to surprise Gabe for once. He'd brought me breakfast for the past three days. Actually, he'd fed me every meal. After attempting to prepare lunch once, he simply started to order in.

I knew he loved guacamole, though it was a strange choice for breakfast. We had everything necessary in the fridge, so I chopped tomatoes and the avocado and mixed it with salt and lemon. It was more of a salsa than guac, but it was delicious.

As I put bread in the toaster, I yelped as I felt an arm around my waist.

Gabe spoke in my ear. "What are you doing up?"

I plastered my back against him. He slept in pajama pants but nothing on top. This was one of those moments when I wished my nightgown was backless. "I'm feeling perfect, and I wanted to spoil you as a thank-you."

The bread popped out of the toaster.

"But you shouldn't get out of bed."

"I feel perfectly well. You know that moment when you can tell that an illness went away?" I turned around, glancing at him. His gaze was cast down to me, laced with suspicion. "Well, I do. My mind's clear. My body's full of energy." I tilted my head to the left and the right, then pressed myself against his pajama pants. "You've got morning wood. I didn't feel it before."

"It was definitely here."

"Hmmm... you should have pointed it out."

He chuckled. "What do you want me to do? Say 'I've got a hard-on' instead of 'Good morning'?"

I closed one eye, looking at him with the other one. "So funny. Let me spread that guac on the bread."

We both ate standing at the kitchen counter.

"This is so much better than mine," Gabe said.

I barely held back laughter. His usually added far too many tomatoes, so it was a bit watery, but the man had made me breakfast for three days and took care of me, so I wasn't about to critique his cooking skills.

"Do you have plans for today?" he asked. "You said something about your tutoring clients."

I sighed. "I actually have three of them tomorrow, but none of them wanted to do a makeup session today."

Saturday was usually a busy day for tutoring, but not today. And my boss didn't have any tours for me. Understandably, he'd assigned all of them to the other guides, not knowing when I'd be available.

Gabe put two fingers under my chin. "So you're free today?"

I nodded. "Why?"

"I was thinking we could go out for a bit."

"Really? And do what?"

"Go on a date."

I nearly swallowed my tongue. "I'm on board with that." I rose on my tiptoes, kissing one corner of his mouth. I liked pressing myself against his chest. I still couldn't believe it was so strong and muscular. Gabe was the whole package.

"All right," he said. "How much time do you need before we leave?"

"I haven't had a shower in a million years."

He glowered at me. "You showered yesterday, against my wishes."

"Because requesting someone not to take a bath when they're sick is *so* normal."

"That's what my mom always said when we were little. We shouldn't wash until the fever broke."

That was cute, and I completely lost my sass. I smiled. "How about half an hour?"

"That works," Gabe said.

I did not, in fact, only need half an hour; it was closer to an hour, but Gabe was great about it. He was on the phone when I came downstairs, and the second he noticed me, he straightened up, eyes fixed me on me. "We'll talk Monday morning." He lowered his phone. "You look stunning."

"I know, right? The miracle of showering." I'd applied more makeup than usual. I wasn't even subtle about it. This wasn't exactly morning makeup, but I wanted to highlight my best features. I'd put on a dress too—one that showed my boobs and was very tight around my waist. It was my favorite color: bright yellow, like a daisy.

"Diane." His voice was a bit rough as he came closer. "This is what you want to wear today?"

I nodded. "Yeah."

As I took a step back and turned around, he said, "Woman, I want to romance you, not tear your clothes off."

Oh wow. "I trust you can do both. First be romantic and then take my clothes off."

He feathered his lips over the tip of my nose and the corner of my mouth. Then he went into a straight line to my earlobe. "You make it so damn difficult, but I'll do my best."

I was looking forward to spending the day out of the house with him. I loved the building, but I had a bit of cabin fever. "So, what are we doing?"

"First I need to drop by Maddox's house to pick up something."

"Okay."

"And after that, we'll play it by ear."

"Do we need to stop by your new house too?"

"No. I've been a few times while you were asleep. Construction's going well."

My eyes widened. "Wow. Talk about being out of it."

He frowned. "You really were sick. I'd feel better if you went to the doctor, just in case."

I shook my head. "You worry too much."

"Just about you. I'm not usually a worrier, but I do everything differently with you."

I squirmed in my spot, putting a hand on my stomach. His words were like balm to my soul.

"I'll think about it," I promised him. Although I didn't really have time to go to a doctor, and I wasn't even sure my insurance would cover it. I'd lost some benefits when they cut back my hours. But that was another story altogether.

We drove in silence for the first part, and then I chatted his ear off about anything and everything under the sun. I was usually chatty, but I couldn't lie to myself. I was a bit nervous.

"So, where does Maddox live?" I asked him.

"In the North End, although I think he wants to move," Gabe said.

"Is Maddox older than you?"

"Yeah. Everyone's older than me," Gabe replied with a laugh.

"And what exactly do they do? I totally forgot."

"Maddox has a company that provides organization and design to office spaces, Nick has fitness clubs, and Leo is into real estate."

"Do you see each other at work often?"

"Not really. Even though Whitley Industries is an entity, we each do our own thing. We do try to support each other as much as possible in business, though. For example, when I opened the bar, Spencer ran ads in all his magazines. He didn't even charge me, which I'm still not too happy about."

"How come?" I asked.

"Because that was prime ad space. But I'll find a way to pay him back somehow. Babysitting comes to mind."

My heart melted at that. "What gave you that idea?"

"He likes for the baby to bond with the family. I haven't really spent that much time with him, although I've wanted to. But when Ben was a baby, he looked so breakable that I was afraid to even hold him." He looked at me abruptly. "Don't ever tell him that or he won't trust me."

The corner of my mouth tipped up. "I won't say a word. But honestly, I think your fears are legitimate. I haven't been around babies too much. They're adorable, but yes, they look extremely breakable. Especially when they're super small and you have to pay attention to support their head and stuff. So no one in the family babysits?"

"Oh no, my grandparents often spend time with him, sometimes even overnight."

"Wait. Didn't you tell me that they're ninety? Although, your grandmother does look pretty spry."

"They're both in great shape for their age, but Spencer insists his regular babysitter be present, too, when Ben spends the night there."

We arrived in front of a gorgeous home a few seconds later.

"This is the one?" I asked when Gabe parked the car.

"Yeah."

It was a modern house with a lot of windows. "Why would he even want to move away?"

"I think he said something about it being too small."

My mouth formed an O. This looked huge to me, but then again, I'd been living in shoeboxes most of my life.

We walked to the front door and knocked several times, but no one answered.

"I'm hearing laughter. Is it possible they're outside somewhere?" I said, taking a step back.

Gabe nodded. "You're right. They're in the back. That's why they aren't hearing us. Let's go around the house."

As we walked, I kept admiring the construction. It truly was a thing of beauty. I liked the garden too; it was simple, with some sort of shrub around the perimeter.

Once we stepped into the backyard, I saw Nick, Leo, and Maddox. There was also a woman. Next to me, Gabe tensed, and I stared at him questioningly.

Maddox noticed us and practically jumped up from his chair. "Gabe, hi. Did you knock? I didn't hear it. Did you tell me you were coming?"

Gabe cleared his throat. "No, I just decided to this morning because I wanted to get those weights I loaned you."

"Hi! Nice to see you all again," I said.

He looked from me to Gabe but didn't say anything. Nick, Leo, and the older woman at the table rose too. "Diane, Gabe, this is my mother, Helen." Helen's eyes were fixed on Gabe.

"How do you do, Helen?" Gabe said, stretching his hand. "It's good to meet you. I forgot you were in the city this weekend."

"Nice to meet you, Gabe. I've always heard a lot about you from my boys."

"Diane and I aren't going to stay too long. We don't want to keep you."

"I'll bring your weights," Maddox said before disappearing into the house.

"Can't believe you two are using home training equipment when I own gyms," Nick said. Even though his tone was teasing, there was no mistaking the underlying tension.

Gabe shrugged. "I like to blow off steam at home too."

"Do you want a coffee, or something to eat? I baked some cupcakes," Helen offered.

"No, we're good," Gabe said. "But thank you."

"Sit down, then. Maddox isn't the most organized, so who knows how long it'll take him to find what you loaned him."

Gabe chuckled as we sat down, but it wasn't as naturally lighthearted as usual. An uncomfortable silence settled around the table.

"So, Helen, where do you live?" I asked.

"In Montana," she replied, "though I lived in Maine for many years."

Was it my imagination, or did Gabe stiffen even more at the mention of Maine? I knew their history, so presumably that was where his father raised his secret family. The whole situation was hard to grasp. It seemed so unreal.

"What are your plans this weekend?" I asked her. I wasn't sure what to do except make light chitchat. Clearly, everyone at the table was uncomfortable, but she was making an effort, and so was I.

"Oh, a little of this, a little of that," Helen said. Got it, she didn't want to go into detail. "The boys set up a few places for me to visit." She smiled at her sons, and I could see their family connection was solid.

"All right. Found it," Maddox said, coming out of the house.

I swear I felt everyone at the table relax.

Gabe immediately rose to his feet, and I did the same. "Thanks, man. We'll be on our way."

Maddox glanced at Gabe, then fixed me with his gaze. "Great. Have a fantastic day, you two."

Gabe and I walked back the same way we came. Once we reached the car, I asked, "Do you want to talk? Things seemed off back there."

"You picked up on that, huh?"

"It would have been hard not to. I don't know who wanted to be there less, you or Helen. Or Nick, Leo and Maddox."

"Helen is their mother."

I nodded. "Yeah, I got that."

"I'd never met her until today. My half brothers and I avoid talking about her. Or my mother, for that matter. I could have handled it better, but I was just so surprised to see her."

"Gabe," I said slowly, "I think you handled it fine. Don't be so hard on yourself."

I put my hand on his neck. He seemed to relax beneath my touch, though the veins and muscles of his neck were corded. But they softened the longer I kept my hands there.

"I know this is crazy, but it feels a bit like betraying my mom."

"Gabe," I murmured. I was hurting for him. "Sometimes pain is irrational."

"Yeah, I guess it is." He closed his eyes, tilting his head back.

I rose on my toes and tried to kiss his Adam's apple, but the man was far too tall to do that, so I jumped a bit, managed to kiss him, and then landed on his foot.

"Aah!" he yelled.

I jumped back and nearly lost my balance.

He put a hand on my arm, steadying me. His face was still contorted with discomfort.

"I'm so sorry. I just wanted to kiss your neck, and, well, coordination's not my forte."

"Obviously," he snorted, then burst out laughing. He was back to being happy again, so that was a win. "Come on. Let's go."

Once we got in the car, I realized we didn't have a plan. "So? What's on the agenda for today?" I asked.

"How would you feel about going to a cooking course together?"

I clapped my hands together. "That would be so fun."

He nodded. "I thought so." He took his phone from his pocket and opened a browser. The Google search read "Top things to do with your girlfriend in Boston." He'd *researched* this.

"Class starts in about an hour, but there's no way to make reservations online."

He'd clicked on some Michelin-type cooking for foodies. I suspected this might be above Gabe's skill level, but it sounded like fun.

"There's the phone number," he said triumphantly, grinning at me and quickly bringing the phone to his ear.

"Hello?" he said. "This is Gabe Whitley. I'm interested in one of your cooking courses. The one that starts in one hour, actually. Do you still have spots available, for two?"

A woman's voice sounded on the other end, but I couldn't gather what she was saying.

"Two people, yes. I'm sure you can make an exception. I'll pay double the price of the ticket."

I opened my mouth to contradict him, but then he said, "Excellent. Thank you. We'll see you right away."

After he hung up, I was too stunned to say anything.

"We've got our cooking course," he said.

"You offered to pay double, just like that?"

"I figured it would sweeten the deal. She admitted that the course wasn't actually full. She probably just didn't want to deal with the hassle of adding two more to her paperwork."

"What paperwork?" I asked.

"She mentioned something about insurance."

I couldn't imagine what it was like to go through life getting what you wanted simply by being able to pay more.

"Wow," I said.

He looked at me intently. "You're uncomfortable."

"I'm just not used to handling money like this. I usually have to save every penny, so paying double wouldn't even have occurred to me." I was panicking a little on the inside because I frankly couldn't afford to pay double. I could barely afford the regular entry price, but I couldn't tell him that.

"It wasn't a big deal. She said to pay on the website. I'll do that right now."

"I'll give you my card too," I said, continuing to panic.

He stared at me. "What are you talking about?"

"For the course."

"Diane, this is a date."

"No, come on. It's an activity we do together. I don't want to take advantage of you."

"Diane!" He cupped my face, drawing his thumb over my lips. "You're mine. You're spending time with me. Call it whatever you want—date, activity, whatever—but I pay, always. I take care of you, always. I'm not negotiating this."

"I'm not used to this, Gabe," I said, pulling back a bit because I couldn't entirely focus when he was touching my mouth. Come to think of it, I couldn't focus properly even when he was just looking at me like that, so I averted my gaze. "I'm a modern woman, you know? I want to split costs, and, you know, I wouldn't be one to expect my husband to financially support me. Though I would expect him to do half the housework."

There was a pause, and then I almost face-palmed myself.

"I meant generally. Don't worry, I'm not fantasizing about you putting a ring on my finger."

"I'm betting my grandmother will," he teased. "Especially after Maddox tells her about today."

"What do you mean?" I asked quickly, happy for the distraction from my faux pas.

"Let's just say what you saw this morning isn't how I usually am with my brothers. We give one another shit about everything. Grandmother is obviously trying to matchmake us. And I'm telling you, all three of those bozos are happy as clams that I showed up with you today."

"How come?"

"Because it would mean our grandmother is occupied with me."

"And that's a good thing? I'm not following."

He laughed. "I think the joke's on them because if Grandmother gets wind, she'll think her job here is done and focus on them."

"Ooooh, now I'm getting it," I said and started to laugh too.

I never knew family dynamics could be like this. My sister and I were close, but we didn't, as Gabe put it, "give each other shit." About dating, anyway. Must be a guy thing. I had no idea.

"Let's drive straight there, but we'll be a bit early," he said.

"Maybe we should make a pit stop and grab something to eat, just in case."

He frowned. "But we're cooking."

"I went to a cooking class a few years ago, and it takes a while till everything's ready, so we shouldn't go in there starving. It's going to be torture."

"You're right. What are you in the mood for?" he asked.

"Do you like burritos?"

"Sure."

"I found this truck that I love. I swear they do the best burrito."

"Where is it?"

"Near the Isabella Stewart Gardner Museum."

"Let's head there."

During the drive, my stomach growled. "Hah, see? It's a good idea to eat before the course."

"I'm not doubting it," Gabe said.

Finding a parking spot was ridiculous. I rarely had to worry about it because I used public transportation when I came downtown, but Gabe and I drove up and down the side streets of the museum a few times, and he was getting impatient.

Eventually I threw in the towel. "Let's just go to a drive-through or something."

"No, we'll find a spot," he said. "We just have to persevere."

I grinned. "That's your motto?"

"One of them."

I crossed the fingers on both of my hands, holding them up theatrically and closing my eyes. "Here's to finding a parking spot."

"Found it," Gabe said a split second later.

I opened my eyes. "Holy shit. It worked."

"The car parked there just left." He pointed at the BMW driving off in front of us.

"Huh, I have to give this 'manifest what you want' credo more credit," I said.

After Gabe parked, I practically jumped out of the car, excited for the cooking course and to get something to eat. I was hungry.

"Where's your food truck?" he asked.

"At the back of the museum. I'll lead the way," I said.

Gabe took my hand as we walked together on the sidewalk. He threaded our fingers and then looked at me. "Thanks for earlier."

"About what?" I asked, genuinely confused.

"Just being there with me. Listening, not being judgmental."

"Gabe," I said, melting into him as he let go of my hand and put it around my back, pulling me even closer to him. "Why would I judge you?"

"Why not? I'm judging myself."

"For feeling what you feel?" I asked, looking up at him.

"Kind of, yeah."

"Don't do that. But if you do, I'm here to make you forget about it."

He growled into my ear. "Don't say that again or we might be late for the cooking course."

I looked back. "You would seduce me right here in the middle of the city?"

"Fuck yes," he said.

I narrowed my eyes. "Huh, really? And you think you'd get away with it?"

My smile faded; he was dead serious.

"Yes, I do believe that."

He continued to stare at me. I stared back. He didn't break eye contact even though it was a bit awkward to walk and look at each other.

"All right, stop it. You're going to start with that manifesting thing again, and maybe you'll be successful."

"Well...," he said.

I shook my head and pointed at the food truck in front of us. "We're eating that burrito first."

Gabe kissed the side of my head and let me go.

Florence, the vendor, knew me well because I often stopped by with tourists at the end of my tour. I wasn't taking commission or anything, I simply loved her food, and I recommended it to everyone who asked me for street food.

"Diane, hi. Just you and...?" She looked at Gabe.

"And Gabe today. I'm not here with a group. I came because I'm in the mood for your burrito."

"You want the usual filling?" she asked me.

I nodded vigorously. "Yes." I glanced at Gabe. "How about you?"

"I'll take whatever you have."

"You trust me that much?"

"Implicitly," he replied.

"You're a brave man," Florence said.

"I am."

Ha, he'd hesitated a bit.

"Look, I like mine super spicy." I decided to fess up because maybe he was one of those people who only liked a bit of pepper or chili, and I liked a whole lot of it.

"Like Florence said, I'm brave," Gabe replied.

"Okay."

Florence was truly a whiz. It always amazed me how quick she was, and everything tasted fresh. She'd once confessed that she had so many orders a day that she had to redo everything every few hours. She had slow cookers for the beans and the pulled pork. It was her own personal blend, and I loved it.

"This is amazing," Gabe said after his first bite. We'd moved a few feet away from the food truck. Sometimes I ate right at the counter, but a line had formed behind us, and I didn't want us to encroach on Florence's space.

"I know. It's really the best I've ever had."

I glanced around, imagining how I'd construct the route if I ever gave tours on my own.

"What are you thinking about?"

"Starting my own touring company instead of working in a hotel," I blurted.

Gabe trained his eyes on me. "I think that's a great idea."

My heart soared. "You do? How come?"

"You've managed to book tutoring clients in a very short time, and you have good discipline working on your own. That's very important when owning a business. And you don't mind putting in the work. As investment, you'd just need a website—"

"Not even that," I replied, loving that he was treating this seriously—like a business. Chuck never thought I'd had the sense to do anything, and Gabe supporting me was something I wasn't used to. "I can set up profiles on Tripadvisor. And then I can look into making something easy on WordPress."

"Honestly, I think you should give it a go."

"I needed to hear that. Thank you for believing in me."

"You're amazing. Of course I believe in you."

I was used to Mom and Celia championing me, and I believed in myself. But Chuck never had. He'd belittled me every chance he got. I was starting to think he simply wanted to put me down to make himself feel better.

"I'm going to set things up as soon as possible, maybe talk to my boss too."

We both fell silent as we ate our burritos.

He blew out a breath. "This was huge. We could have probably split one."

I averted my gaze. "Yeah, we could have, but I thought, 'Why not go all out?'" It was obvious that we were hungry, though, considering we'd each eaten the whole thing. I patted my belly. "I could probably sleep now."

Gabe pierced me with his gaze, "You feel faint again? Maybe we shouldn't go to the course after all."

After he'd paid double? Hilarious. I'd have to be half dead to miss it.

"No, I mean the food. We ate a lot. Don't worry, I'm in top shape, and I can't wait for our Michelin-star experience."

I thought it was a very cool idea for a date, and I was still impressed that he'd looked at activities to do together. We didn't have too much time until the course started, so we headed straight there. It was only ten minutes away by car. It was a typical Bostonian redbrick building with white window trim. At the entrance, the course company was listed at door number one.

We knocked, and the door swung open, revealing a tall redhead.

"Hi, you must be Gabe Whitley," she said, looking at him. "And you are?"

"Diane," I replied.

"Good, come on in. Everyone else is already here."

We walked into an enormous kitchen. There were four other couples.

"Hi, everyone. This is Gabe and Diane. They're joining us today. That will be your station." She pointed at two empty spots between two of the couples. "I figured I would start everyone with a glass of wine. We're going to cook both white and red meat today, so you can choose red or white," she said.

"Red," Gabe and I said at the same time.

Out of the corner of my eye, I peeked at him. He caught my eye, and we fought laughter.

This kitchen was absolutely amazing. There were nine chopping boards on the kitchen island and a sink on the opposite wall. There were also three ovens and three Sub-Zero refrigerators—high-end stuff. The building must have been a converted factory, because the ceilings were super tall and the space was lined with bookcases that went from floor to ceiling, filled with all types of cookbooks.

"What are you thinking about?" Gabe whispered.

"That I'd love a kitchen like this. And a place to put all the recipe books. I know most people like to look up recipes online, but I've always loved cookbooks. Seeing the pictures, feeling the pages. I've just never had enough space to put them anywhere."

"I brought a pinot noir that is a favorite. Let me know if you like it," the host said.

"You do the honors," Gabe told me, but she poured the wine into both our glasses.

We brought it to our noses. I knew from the first inhale that it was an exquisite wine. Not as great as the one we'd gotten at the restaurant that one evening, but very close. I took a sip, and it confirmed my initial assessment.

"It's perfect," I exclaimed.

"It's a great wine," Gabe said.

We both held our glasses as she poured more. I took one more sip.

"All right, I'll walk you through the menu first." She clicked on her iPad and turned it for us to see.

Gabe whispered, "Why aren't you drinking?"

I whispered back, "Because I don't want to get tipsy."

"I'll take care of you," he said in a sensual tone I hadn't expected at all. It sent a burst of heat through me.

Hell no! We're surrounded by people. Down, girl. Besides, I was sure he hadn't even meant it in a sexy way.

As we pulled back, he winked.

Okay, maybe he did mean it that way.

I focused on the host and zeroed in on the menu. It sounded delicious, but it seemed to be very difficult to prepare.

"Wait, we're supposed to cook that?" Gabe sounded affronted, and I bit back laughter.

"Yes. I promised a Michelin-star experience, and it doesn't get more Michelin than this," the host replied.

"Right," Gabe said.

"It's an advanced course," she went on, sounding a bit panicked.

"We're looking forward to it," I said quickly, barely stifling my laughter.

She first told us a few things about herself, and then everyone introduced themselves as couples. Most seemed to have been together for a long time. The group turned out to be genuine and fun, and they were all completely proficient. Gabe looked stunned as we performed each step. I had a hunch that he wasn't used to being the beginner in the room. He was a perfectionist, so this was probably weird for him.

While we were preparing the appetizer, the man next to us said, "Damn, we should have eaten something first. I'm starving."

"I have some spring rolls I made with the morning group. Do you want some?" the host offered.

There was a murmur of agreement around the kitchen island, so she immediately took a bowl out of the fridge and put it in one of the ovens. "It'll be warm in a few minutes."

Gabe and I exchanged a conspiratorial glance, having just filled our stomachs.

The afternoon slid by easily. Gabe was a surprisingly fast learner. He was good at following instructions, I realized; he could probably cook a lot of things if he followed a recipe step by step.

The host had a clever strategy, having us eat every course right after we made it versus doing everything and then eating at the end. After cooking one course, we set the table and ate it immediately, making small talk with the other couples. I took advantage of the fact that Gabe liked to talk more than me and stole some of his food from time to time. Everything was delicious, and I didn't feel guilty that I'd snatched away one of his shellfish—he'd had four left, and he didn't seem to be eating them all.

He finished talking about the distillery and looked down at his plate before focusing on me. "So, what happened to my fourth shellfish?"

I felt my eyes widen. "You counted them?"

"Babe, I've been counting everything since we sat down with the appetizer."

I covered my mouth. The whole table laughed, and Gabe kissed the side of my head.

"And you all noticed?" I asked, lowering my hand.

"Yeah, it was pretty obvious. But he was putting on a solid show," one of the guys said, nodding at Gabe.

"I'm just not very hungry," he said. "And I like to choose my battles."

"Oh, you two are so sweet. How long have you been together?" the guy's wife asked.

"Not long," I said vaguely because I felt a bit embarrassed to tell them the truth.

"I always say it's a great mark for longevity and predicting that a couple will get along long term if they can laugh together like you two do."

"And if you know how to conspire with each other. Like you did earlier when you covered up for how bad Gabe was in the kitchen by doing the more complex tasks," one of the other attendees said.

Gabe jerked his head back. "I didn't even notice that."

I grinned at him. "Hey, we're a team. I've got your back."

"You remind me of us when we were younger," the oldest couple said, and something shifted inside me.

"Really?" These happy couples all thought we had what was needed for something long term? How could they tell?

But then my enthusiasm deflated quickly, like someone had popped a balloon. You could never judge a book by its cover. They only saw this playful interaction, but I bet they'd change their opinions if they knew I was basically living in his house. Gabe wasn't someone who wanted to commit, and neither was I. At least not at this point in my life, especially after what I'd been through.

After the way things ended with Chuck, I needed another decade or so to pass before I would even consider settling down. Trusting someone again and building a relationship like I *thought* I had with my ex took a lot out of me.

I needed some recovery time.

For the rest of the courses, I only ate my portion. Not just because everyone had caught on to my tactic but also because I was super full. The host kept filling us with wine on top of all the fantastic food.

She'd premade the dessert for us because it needed to stay in the fridge overnight. It was a delicious cheesecake, and it was creamier than anything I'd ever tasted.

Once we all finished it, she said, "Well, that concludes today's session. I'm really happy that we had such a great time. If you want, please leave a review."

"I most certainly will," I said. As someone who depended on reviews, I knew just how important they were, and I never passed an opportunity to leave one. Though if I had a bad experience, I preferred to withhold my opinion because everything was subjective. Maybe I caught someone on a bad day. I didn't want to ruin their business.

We bid everyone goodbye, and we were the first to leave. Once we stepped out, Gabe practically attacked me, kissing me as he walked us backward to the car.

Ladies and gentlemen, this was definitely the hottest kiss Gabe Whitley had ever given me. A little desperate, a lot hot, and I responded in kind.

He finally pulled back, face a bit flushed. "Fuck, I wanted to do that the whole time."

"Really? I couldn't tell."

"You have no idea how many times I fought the impulse to make up an excuse to pull you into the hallway and just kiss you. But I knew I'd make a spectacle of us."

"I have an idea, then," I said.

"Mmm?" he murmured, feathering his lips up and down my neck.

"Let's go home."

"That's the best thing I've heard all day."

Chapter Nineteen

Gabe

I rarely lost my head, but right now all I could focus on was getting Diane somewhere alone. Home sounded like the best idea.

We barely spoke during the ride; I was too focused on driving, knowing if I didn't hurry, I'd just pull over in a secluded spot and have her right here in the car.

I couldn't understand why I needed her so much, so badly. It wasn't only about sexual satisfaction; it was something different, something I'd never felt before.

We both got out of the car quickly. Diane walked in front of me, and now that we were alone, I had free rein to touch her, so I cupped her ass with both hands.

She looked at me over her shoulder. "You're an ass man, huh? You seem quite obsessed with it."

"Yours is gorgeous. Deserves to be the object of my obsession."

When we stepped inside the house, I twirled her around, keeping her against me. "But just in case you were wondering, I obsess about every single part of you."

"Hmm, want to prove it?"

"Gladly."

I moved one hand from her shoulder down the side of her body, cupping her breast over the bra as I pressed my thumb right over the base of the fabric where I knew her nipple was. She arched her back and hissed at the contact. Instead of kissing her, I pulled my head back just a few inches, watching her. She was exquisite. I cared as much about her pleasure as I did about mine. These past few days had been torture, being next to her and not being able to touch her. The few times she did attempt to climb over me, I didn't take her up on it because she'd been somewhere between delirious and exhausted. Now she was healthy and so damn sexy that I could barely focus on all the things I wanted to do to her.

One step at a time.

I pulled the elastic band from her hair. I liked her hair cascading around her back. It was thick and so damn soft. I sank my fingers into it, gently tugging.

"You smell amazing," I said.

She laughed nervously. "Probably like all the food we cooked."

"No, like cherries."

"Ah, my shampoo." Her voice was tight.

Looking her straight in the eyes, I put my finger at one corner of her mouth, then moved it slowly over her upper lip to the other corner. "You're tense. What's wrong?"

She licked her lips, and her eyes widened. "I don't know. I'm a bit nervous, I guess."

I dropped my hand from her face, putting both palms on her shoulders. "I can tell. But why?"

"I'm not even sure. I guess because the first time we were together, it was kind of by accident."

"No, it was fucking *not* by accident. I've wanted you since I saw you at the bar that first night."

She snapped her gaze back up at me. "Gabe..."

I nodded. "Then I realized you were Celia's sister. She wouldn't look kindly on me seducing you."

She grinned. "Your plans went that far, huh?"

"You have no idea. Then, when I came by her apartment, I figured we were both grown-ups, and we could do this."

I was touching her neck now. I couldn't keep my hands to myself.

"And once you moved in, I realized I'm in a ton of trouble."

"Oh my God. I thought it was just me."

I smirked. "No, it wasn't. And I can't believe my grandmother picked up on it."

"She's really good, huh?" Diane asked loudly.

"She saw something, I'm sure of it. She'll probably eventually tell me what. She has a sixth sense about these things. But... let's focus on us, Diane. You don't need to be nervous about anything."

"Why are you so charming?" she asked, batting her eyelashes. "And you were so gallant the whole day, treating me to lunch and the cooking class."

Somewhere in the back of my mind, her words registered.

Treating? That was nothing. It was less than nothing. It was basically the minimum requirement for a date.

"I enjoyed every single moment of the afternoon, but not more than I'll enjoy this," I said, walking her backward.

"Hmm, I wonder what it's going to be."

"I'll give you a few hints." I bunched her dress up, touching her legs. "I've been dreaming about these wrapped around me all day. That kitchen counter looked so good for fucking."

"You thought about that even though we were surrounded by people?"

"Fuck yes. Honestly, I barely noticed anyone else. I liked watching you. Enjoying you."

Inching her dress farther up until I reached her panties, I drew my fingers up the front of her thighs and then tried to push her dress up even more, but it wouldn't budge. Then I remembered there was a zipper at the back and pulled it down in one move.

I kissed her while I dragged the dress down from her shoulders to her feet. She carefully stepped out of it, and I looked down at her. She was wearing white underwear. It had to be silk or something because it was very soft and shiny.

"You're damn sexy."

"What was that? I didn't catch it."

I looked up at her, narrowing my eyes. "I said you're sexy."

She laughed, her whole face lighting up. "I surmised that much from the delicious growl, but it doesn't hurt to hear the confirmation. I sort of wanted to flash you when we were in the car, so you'd know what was waiting for you, but—"

"Diane, never do that. I can promise that no matter where we are, no matter what we're doing, I *will* have you."

"Yeah, I figured that might be a risk, so that's why I behaved."

"Then again, now I know you like sexy underwear, so even if you don't flash me, I'll imagine it."

I kissed her temple, then a straight line down her cheek and neck as I walked her even deeper into the house. Finally stopping, I tugged down her panties, lowering myself onto my haunches. I pushed her against the wall leading to the kitchen and nudged her to step out of her panties. She sucked in her breath, and her eyes darkened.

I didn't give her any warning before I flattened my tongue against her opening, positioning the base on her clit and the tip as far down as I could reach. She moaned, gripping my head with both hands, my nose pressed against her pelvis. She put the back of her knee over my shoulder, giving me even better access.

I licked and licked until she rose on her toes on the one foot she still had on the floor and nearly toppled over me. She was close, but we had to go upstairs. I didn't have any condoms here.

I moved my mouth back up, and she undid her bra and threw it away. I lost my train of thought at the sight. Then I stood, first cupping her breasts and then taking each nipple into my mouth in turn, twirling my tongue around it.

I felt her fingers at my zipper, and I didn't stop her. I was treading a fine line, but I needed her touch. She dipped her hand into my boxers and squeezed my cock as she pressed her palm on the crown. A shock of pleasure ricocheted through me, so unexpected that it nearly brought me to my knees.

How can she undo me with one single touch? How does she have that much power over me?

She tried to push down my jeans but barely managed to get them past my ass. I lifted her off the floor, and she immediately wrapped her legs around me, resting one hand around the back of my neck and running the other one through my hair. I kissed her, tangling our tongues, my cock pressed along the length of her pussy. She was completely wet. We had to move now or I wasn't going to make it without sinking inside her.

She moved her ass up and down, only a few inches, but the friction was driving me crazy. Fuck, it was an exercise in self-restraint.

She brought her mouth to my ear and asked, "Gabe, are you clean? Because I'm on birth control, and all my tests are good."

"I get tested regularly. I'm perfectly healthy," I said.

She let out a shaky breath. "Then we don't need to use a condom."

I kissed her hard and deep, then got rid of all my clothes right there on the staircase. After, I positioned my cock at her entrance and gave her the tip. She closed her inner muscles tight around me and then lowered herself onto my cock at her own pace.

It was an out-of-body experience. The pleasure, the intimacy, the strength of this bond that had formed between us without my realizing it. Today, it had grown even more.

She dug her heels into the backs of my legs. I knew this couldn't be too comfortable for her. She tried to push herself up and down, but that wouldn't do, so I sat down on the staircase, pulling her on top of me.

She was completely naked in my arms. I rested my elbows two steps above the one where I'd planted my ass and dug my feet firmly on one below. I was so damn ready. I knew just how to rock her world. She pushed herself up and down, putting her hands on my chest and closing her eyes. I held her ass with one hand and used the other to circle her clit.

I moved my hips in a rolling motion, and she gasped. Bringing her pleasure filled me with immense satisfaction. She was wild, and I loved that. It was insane how much I'd missed this.

I'd only had her once before, yet I felt as if I'd been missing her for months. She needed to come. Her entire body was already on edge. Her muscles were taut, and her pussy was so damn tight.

I drew in a deep breath, choosing not to focus on my own desire but on the way she succumbed to me.

When her inner muscles tightened even more around my cock, I knew just what she needed to send her over the cliff. I pressed my thumb on her clit and circled her nipple with my other thumb.

I'd never been privy to something so beautiful in my entire life. The way she climaxed was unreal. She hunched her shoulders before pushing her chest out and dropped her head back. Then she arched her back and dipped her head forward.

She laid her forehead on my shoulder, shuddering as she came down from the wave. But I didn't give her any reprieve before I secured her in my arms and then rose to my feet. She moaned slowly but didn't say anything. Then she moved her arms and pressed herself against me.

I went up the stairs, intending to head to the bedroom with her. But then she squeezed my erection, and I was done for.

"Diane," I said through gritted teeth, pressing her against the wall. "What are you doing?"

"Nothing less than what you did to me. I want to rock your world," she said.

I pressed my fingers to her pussy. Looking down between us, I leisurely circled her clit. She instantly started shaking.

"Gabe," she said, "What are you doing?"

"Punishing you."

"For what?" Her voice was weak.

"Tempting me like that."

"Is this your idea of punishment?" She furrowed her brow and tilted the corners of her mouth downward.

I pressed her back to the wall and continued my delicious torture.

She started panting and whimpered, "How is this even possible?"

"Come around my cock, Diane."

She climaxed the next second. While the first one took over her entire body, this orgasm was completely different. She dug her fingers into my arms, her head dropping to one side.

Her loud moans triggered my own pleasure. I didn't even have enough control left to move away from the wall. I kept one hand under her ass, wedging my thumb between her and the wall, and splayed the other one along her spine. Then I fucked her so hard that I could barely breathe. I'd never needed a release so fast.

I kissed her neck, then rested my forehead against her while I moved. The only thing I could focus on was chasing my release. But even through my haze, I still knew I wanted one other thing.

"I want you to come with me." My voice was so damn gruff that I wasn't even sure she could understand me.

But then she said, "Yes, I'm already coming."

I exploded inside her the second she started crying out my name. Orgasming at the same time was an entirely different experience. I was surrounded by her pleasure while I gave in to mine.

Since she had come three times, her pussy was even tighter than before. I rocked in and out of her until we were both spent and satisfied, and then I carried her to the bathroom. I didn't put her down, just stepped into the walk-in shower.

She looked around with a curious expression. "You're even bringing me into the shower? It's full service with you, isn't it?"

"You bet it is." I started the water, turning it hot, and stood to one side for a few seconds.

"Why aren't we under it?" she asked.

"Because it takes a while for the water to turn warm in this ancient house."

When I was satisfied it was a pleasant temperature, I put her down, and we walked under the spray of water. She grinned up at me as her hair turned wet.

I laughed. "What's with the grin?"

"I'm not sure how to put it into words, but I hope this expresses everything I'm feeling."

I kissed the tip of her nose. "It does, don't worry."

We cleaned up quickly, and I shut off the water before grabbing a couple towels for us. After wrapping one around herself, she asked for my blow-dryer. I had one that I used once in a blue moon, mostly in the winter if it was freezing outside. While she dried her hair, she looked at everything I had on the counter.

"Why is this completely unused?" she asked, pointing to a bottle of body lotion.

"I don't like body lotion. It just came in the same set as my shower gel."

"Can I use it?"

"Sure. In fact, I'll put it on you. You keep doing what you're doing."

She gave me a sassy smile while I squirted lotion into my palms and then started with her free arm.

"We're not going to need this," I said, undoing her towel and letting it drop to the floor. I liked the idea of her using this lotion.

"Now you're going to smell like me," I said. "And everyone will know you're off-limits."

"Interesting way of marking your territory."

"Fuck yes," I said as she put the blow-dryer down. Her hair was still a bit damp. "I don't want anyone even looking at you." Let alone coming within sniffing distance of her.

"Gabe."

I put one hand on her stomach, splaying my fingers wide to reach as much of her as I could.

"Do you understand?" I said, looking at her in the mirror. "No one."

"But that means you won't see anyone else either, right?"

"Obviously."

She hesitated. "It's *not* obvious. I've heard through the grapevine that you don't really do this."

"I don't," I clarified. "I've never wanted to or felt the need to."

And yet with her, neither of those things was true. Even though we'd just satisfied each other, the need to be closer to her was even stronger than before. I wasn't chasing yet another climax. I wasn't chasing anything. I simply relished this closeness and wanted more of it.

She turned around to face me. "You want to continue putting lotion on me? You're very good at it."

"Your wish is my command."

I'd finished with her back, and now I applied it to her breasts and belly before going down her legs. The only spot I left untouched was her pussy. Then I rose to my feet and kissed her, hungry but gentle at the same time. I felt the need to do things differently with her than anyone before. I simply felt the need to *be* different and change my ways for her. That was something I'd never planned on happening.

After I finished slathering on lotion, we went to the kitchen. I put on clothes, but she was wearing a robe because her dress got wrinkled, and her clothes were in the attic. That was an inconvenience. I didn't want her to trudge up and down that godawful spiral staircase for every little thing she needed.

I was about to ask her if she wanted to bring down a few things when the doorbell rang.

"I'll get it since I'm dressed."

"And I'm going to hide," she said.

I unlocked the front door and opened it quickly, determined to get rid of whoever it was. Probably a salesman or a delivery guy.

"Hi, Celia!" I exclaimed. Shit! This was the one person I couldn't just send away and from whom Diane couldn't hide.

Celia held up a brown take-out bag. "Hey, Gabe. I'm just going to head upstairs to check on my sister. She's been out of it all week."

"Sure, come in."

"Are you okay?"

I nodded.

"I've heard you haven't been at the office all week. Did she give you her bug or something?" She looked worried.

"No, nothing like that," I said. "Sometimes I prefer to work from home after a trip."

"I'll go straight upstairs. I don't want to keep you."

"She isn't upstairs."

Celia cocked a brow. "Right. She did tell me she's using the kitchen."

My mind raced. I saw no possible way out of this. Diane was down here wearing a robe. It wouldn't take a genius to put two and two together.

"I'm here," Diane said. She sounded uncertain as she stepped out of the kitchen.

Celia jerked her head back, then looked from her sister to me.

"How are you feeling?" she asked Diane. From her tone of voice, I knew what she actually wanted to ask was *"What the hell is going on?"*

"I'll leave the two of you to talk." I glanced at Diane. "Unless you want me to stay?"

Diane closed her eyes, took a deep breath, then opened them and looked straight at her sister. "Celia... this isn't how I wanted you to find out, but Gabe and I are dating."

Celia frowned and didn't speak right away. I suspected she was trying to rein herself in because I was her boss.

"How long has this been going on?" she asked Diane.

"Not long. The night before Gabe left for Texas."

"So you lied when I asked you how things are going with Gabe?" Celia said.

"I didn't want to tell you like that. Ideally, I wanted to take you out for coffee or something."

"How would that be any better?" she clipped.

"Celia," I said in a measured tone, "I know you care about your sister and only want what's best for her, but I won't accept that tone of voice."

"Excuse me for not reacting better, I just... Never mind." She put the bag she'd been holding on the coffee table and said, "I brought you some food. Figured you might need company, but I don't want to be in the way."

"Celia, come on," Diane said. "I know you're upset."

"I'm upset that you kept this from me. I mean, I'm happy for you because Gabe is a good guy. But he's also my boss, and things could get awkward." She sighed heavily. "Sorry, I don't want to be a Debbie Downer. I just need to process this. We'll talk later, okay?"

"Sure."

Celia marched back to the door. Diane made to go after her but then stopped.

Once her sister was out of the house, she dropped her head in her palms. "This isn't how I wanted her to find out."

I moved to stand in front of her, touching the side of her head and kissing her forehead. "She'll come around."

"I don't know. She doesn't like it when I keep things from her."

"I'll talk to her."

She whipped her head up immediately. "No, no." She put her hands on my shoulders. "Please promise me you won't do that. You're her boss. She's right about that."

"All right. I don't want to get between you and your sister. But I think I know what Celia is afraid of. She knows about my reputation. I never kept that a secret. Mostly because I figured if people knew, the word would spread, and it would be to my benefit."

She started to laugh. "Wait, you actually had a strategy around this?"

I cleared my throat. "It wasn't intentional at first, and that's all I'm going to say about it."

"Noooo, I want to know."

"Why? It's not an interesting subject, and it's not who I am right now."

"We're always a product of who we were and how we've evolved. So, spill the beans. If anything, it's a nice piece of gossip, and I'm all for that."

I groaned. "Fine."

"But while we do, I want an orange juice."

"So demanding," I teased, taking her hand and pulling her to the kitchen. "Once, I made some sort of joke with my bartenders. Then at the end of that evening, a woman approached me and basically told me she'd heard that I wasn't looking for anything serious and neither was she. Now I feel like a jackass."

"Aha," she said. "I can see how that could be useful, yes."

"Are you disgusted?" I peeled oranges, putting them in the juicer.

"No."

"Why not?"

"I don't think we have to be ashamed of anything we did if we didn't hurt anyone. That's my outlook in life."

"It's a very healthy one," I replied. Once the juice was ready, I handed her the glass.

"Aren't you going to have one?"

"No, it's just for you."

"Thank you." Her entire face lit up.

From this small gesture? I needed to find out more things she liked. If she rewarded me with that smile, nothing was going to be too hard or too complicated. I suspected that not many men had given her a reason to smile, and I wanted to change that.

I heard a beeping sound in the living room.

"That's my phone," I said. I'd left it somewhere on the couch. I didn't even remember putting it there.

Diane came behind me, and we both sat down as I grabbed my phone.

"I have a missed call from Maddox," I said.

She put the half-empty glass of orange juice on the coffee table and slid closer. "Want to return it?"

"Not right now. I need to apologize for the awkward way I behaved." I leaned on the backrest, dropping my head on it.

Diane kissed the front of my neck, making me laugh.

"How do you feel about having met Helen today?" she asked.

"There was a time when I thought I could never possibly do it. Now that I did meet her... it wasn't too bad."

"I think that's true for most things in life," Diane said, "although this is an exceptionally delicate situation."

"It's just that for so long we thought of her as the antagonist. It was unfair. If Helen hadn't been in Dad's life, he would have found someone else. It was just the way he was. I'm going to talk to Maddox and the rest. Not sure what I'll tell them yet, but I'll lead with an apology."

"Holy shit. You really are hard on yourself. Nothing I say will change your mind, will it?"

I smiled at her. "You can try."

"Hm, want to give me a hint?" She moved her shoulders playfully.

"Only after you tell me what you have in mind."

"That's not fair. It means I have to come up with some ideas in the first place."

"Yeah, but they're usually great," I assured her. "Then again, I think I'll like whatever you come up with."

Diane straddled me. She seemed to feel that I needed her closer. I liked this woman more with every passing second.

"Now *that* is proof of trust," she murmured.

"You have my trust completely."

Personal relationships and trust weren't something that even belonged in the same sentence in my experience. Not unless said relationship was with my family. But things were shifting faster than I realized, and I was looking forward to whatever came next.

Chapter Twenty

Diane

Tuesday was a big day. First, I wanted to talk to my sister, so I woke up early, baked muffins, and headed straight to her apartment. I also took muffins for the afternoon, when I was going to have a conversation with my boss. I'd told Celia yesterday that I was dropping by this morning because I didn't want to arrive at a bad moment, so she was expecting me.

She opened the door the second I knocked. I held the bag of muffins up and gave her a huge grin. She smiled, but it was a bit uneasy.

"Come in."

"You slept in," I said.

She nodded. "I did. Don't know what's gotten into me. What did you bring? Smells like muffins."

"You're right," I replied as I put four on a plate.

We sat down in the kitchen, and she stared at the bag. "How many more do you have in there?"

"A few, but they're not all for you. I'm going to talk to my boss today."

"How come?"

"Let's go over that later," I said, biting the inside of my cheek. "Look, I know you said you need some time to process, but I'm on pins and needles. We need to talk about Gabe."

Celia sighed. "I'm sorry I gave you two such a hard time. It wasn't my place to say anything, or to react in any way. You're adults, and what you do doesn't concern me."

She sounded as if she'd rehearsed this.

"You're disappointed in me, aren't you?" I asked. My stomach twisted.

"No, I could never be disappointed in you." She reached over the table, grabbing my hand and squeezing it lightly. "I'm just worried about you, that's all. I know Gabe is a good person. I just don't know if he's, you know, a good partner or if he'll break your heart."

I shook my head vehemently. "There's no risk of that. Believe me, I don't have any fantasies of this going anywhere, and besides, with everything that happened with Chuck, I'm in no hurry to be in a committed relationship. So... are we good?"

Celia nodded. Her smile was a bit tight, and I knew she was still feeling uneasy about it, but I was happy that at least she didn't seem to be upset anymore.

"Now, what's that with George?"

"Oh, yeah. That's going to be another tough one. I'm thinking of opening my own touring company."

Celia bit into a muffin, nodding thoughtfully. "I didn't see this coming."

"I only thought about it recently, but I like the idea of doing this on my own terms. "

"I think that's super brave and very, very smart. But health insurance and all that stuff will be a hassle."

"Yeah, I thought about that too. I'll manage somehow." I grinned at her. "I could use a partner in crime, if you want in further down the road."

"I'll think about it. Do you think your boss will be annoyed?"

"I'm not sure how he'll take it, honestly. I don't have any noncompete clause or anything, so that should help."

"And the muffins," Celia said.

"And the muffins."

"You'll do great, Diane."

We chatted for a bit longer, and then it was time to continue on with my day. After I left my sister's house, I went to see my boss before my tour started. I didn't want to carry the muffins around for a few more hours because they'd get all squishy, so I thought it best to see him first.

He greeted me with a smile. "Sit down, Diane. What brings you here? Ah, muffins. Must be a special occasion."

I usually used my baking skills for bribing. "So, listen, George. You know I love working as a tour guide."

"You're one of our best."

My chest filled with pride. There was no way to soften the blow. It was on the tip of my tongue to ask him, *"Why did you cut my hours, then?"* But it was none of my business.

"I want to do this on my own," I said.

He frowned at the muffin he'd just taken out. It was filled with blueberries, which he loved. "What do you mean?"

Come on, take a bite. Maybe that will soften the blow.

He didn't take a bite. Instead, he stared me down.

"I want to start my own touring company."

He jerked his head back. "Your own company? But why?"

"I'd like a bit more autonomy in my tours, and I need more hours."

"We can talk about that."

"And more money," I continued, and he pressed his lips together. "You probably figured out I'd be gone sooner or later after you cut my hours."

"I figured you were going to go back to one of those fancy hotels, not be my competition," he said, obviously hurt by my decision.

"Look, it really wouldn't be competition." I talked very fast so he wouldn't get any weird ideas. "My tours will be structured very differently, and they'd follow a theme. Most of your tours are general ones showcasing the top attractions."

"I don't feel good about this," he grumbled. "You're still doing your tour today, aren't you?" George said rather briskly.

"Yes, of course. I wouldn't bail like that."

"Hm," he said.

"And I'm going to honor all the tours I've already booked, of course."

He looked up at me briefly. "No. If you want to leave, it's effective immediately. Starting tomorrow."

I felt like he'd slapped me. This was not what I'd expected at all. "But what about the other tours?" I'd been counting on that money.

"No, I want a clean break. You said you want to start on your own, and I respect that. I will simply assign your other tours to the other guides."

"George, I didn't think today would be my last day. I simply wanted to let you know so you have time to look for a replacement."

"No need for that. The others will be happy to take over."

Crap. "Well, then, that's it, I guess, George."

"It is."

I headed straight to the meeting point with my group, feeling like everything was crashing down around my ears. Why was I so stupid? I thought I was doing an honorable thing, letting him know ahead of time. Truthfully, we didn't have any clause in the contract that told us to give advanced notice.

It was the first time since I'd started doing tours that I couldn't muster too much enthusiasm, and that was reflected in the tips.

Great! Am I about to embark on another spiral downward?

No, no. I just started on the wrong foot, that was all.

After the tour was over, I walked down the Freedom Trail lost in thought, already trying to make a plan. I still had enough of my tutoring sessions booked this week to make rent. And I had a bit of a nest egg that I'd built up since I'd started tutoring. I was sure it would all work out.

I arrived at the house at six o'clock. Gabe's car was already here. Oh God, I could imagine how this conversation would go.

I opened the door and momentarily forgot all my troubles, watching my sexy man walking barefoot through the living room.

He looked over his shoulder. "Hey. You're late."

"I had a long day. I'm a bit exhausted."

"Good thing you don't have to do anything except relax tonight."

That's when I started to sniff the air. "You ordered takeout?"

He grinned. "Even better. I cooked."

"How? What did you cook?" It didn't smell like burned food, so that was a plus.

He rolled his eyes. "Have a bit of confidence in me, would you? I followed a recipe this time."

"I'm curious."

"What's wrong?" he asked and tilted my head upward. "This is more than just tired. Something happened. Tell me. I need to know."

"Um... well, I told my boss today that I intend to start my own company."

"How did he take it?"

"Said there was no need for me to turn up for the rest of the tours I've been booked for."

"Fuck."

"I just don't know why I told him."

Gabe stepped closer to me. "Because you're honest and you wanted to give him a shot to find someone to replace you."

"Yes, exactly."

He kissed my forehead. "Right. Change of plans. My dinner is no compensation."

I looked up at him, inhaling deeply. His scent calmed my senses. Feeling the heat of his body grounded me. "What do you mean?"

"Clearly you need something to lift your mood, and my stir-fry won't cut it."

"You made stir-fry? I love it."

"Yeah, but as I remember—" He pressed a thumb against the corner of my mouth. "—it's not comfort food, is it?"

"No, it's not. But I'll enjoy it anyway. You're not mad?" I asked him cautiously.

"What would I be mad about?" He furrowed his brow.

"Because I essentially blew it."

"This isn't your fault. Sometimes things just don't work out."

I laughed nervously.

"Diane?" He stepped closer again, cupping my face with both hands.

"Nothing, I'm just... My ex would have thrown a fit. Said I couldn't even get this one thing right." *Why did I even say that?*

"What the fuck?" He skimmed his hands down my shoulders and arms, resting them on my waist. "I would never treat you like that. Putting each other down isn't the answer."

I nodded, unsure what to really say. This concept of lifting each other up was a bit alien for me. I'd tried to do that constantly with my ex whenever he hit a roadblock, but the reverse wasn't ever true. I'd never really felt like he was in my corner when something went wrong. He always managed to make me feel even worse about it.

"All right, then. Let's see what you think about my stir-fry."

It was surprisingly delicious. "Hey, this is really good."

Gabe smiled smugly. I laughed, realizing this was truly a victory for him. He also poured us white wine, and let me tell you, that was elevating the whole meal to comfort food. I felt more relaxed, and it wasn't because of the alcohol. Being around Gabe had that effect on me.

Once we finished dinner, he led me to the couch and poured more wine. "Tell me what I can do to make this evening better."

"You're off to a fantastic start," I said, taking a sip.

He set his glass down on the coffee table and then put one hand at the back of my neck, drawing his thumb from my hairline downward until it disappeared into my shirt.

"Hmm, we could watch a romantic movie," I suggested.

"Sure. You pick."

I turned around. "What's your take on Christmas movies?"

His mouth dropped. "It's not December."

"No, but they'll lift my mood. What do you think about watching *Love Actually*?"

"Why not? I've never seen it."

My eyes bulged. "That's not possible."

He laughed. "I haven't."

"Then you will totally enjoy this evening."

I was happy to share this with him. And I got to curl up next to Gabe. That was all I needed.

I kept my eyes glued on the screen the entire time. "Oh, this is my favorite part," I said when Mark came to Juliet's door and started playing carols, asking her not to tell her husband that it was him, then proceeded to tell her how he felt about her on huge posterboards.

"What exactly do you like about it? The guy's a creep. She's married to his best friend," Gabe said.

"It is pretty messed-up. But I don't know, I think it's so romantic. You know, the notes and everything."

"Only because the guy's too much of a coward to actually tell her all that."

I pushed at his shoulder playfully. "Don't be such a grinch. I still think it's romantic."

He shook his head but didn't say anything else, just pulled me even closer to him.

"How many times have you seen this movie? Ten?"

"More like forty, I think."

"How is that even possible?"

"I watch it every year for Christmas, and I also watch it once or twice during the year when I feel low."

He turned to me, kissing one corner of my mouth and then the other. "I'm here. You can tell me when you need to be cheered up, and I'll do it."

"Huh, you think you can replace *Love Actually*? That is some heavy lifting."

"I'm very confident."

I smirked. "That you are. Now stop distracting me. I don't want to miss the rest."

"Of course," he said sardonically.

"Come on, tell me the truth. You don't even like it one bit?"

"It's not too bad," he admitted.

"Ha. I knew it."

His phone pinged toward the end of the movie.

"My interior designer sent me some proposals. I'll look at them after we finish," he said, putting it down and focusing on the screen again.

I was giddy that he stayed with me to enjoy it until the end. He was becoming my best friend and partner. I had to be careful so I wouldn't get hurt.

My body and mind were so relaxed. It wasn't just the feel-good movie but the sexy man next to me too.

I paused the TV once the credits rolled. He took out his phone and opened what looked like a PDF with some interior renderings.

"This looks so realistic and professional," I said. The designer had chosen a mix of white and gold and light greens for the living room. She'd done a rendering of every room, even the gym. She was a pro.

"This looks good," Gabe said. "But she wasted that alcove by the brick wall."

There was nothing there.

I blushed violently, and he wiggled his eyebrows.

"I'd do a reading corner there," I told him. "It's perfect."

"No natural light. It's far away from the window."

"Who cares? I mostly read on my Kindle anyway."

He stared at me. "So then why do you have all those books?"

"I buy my favorites as a paperback and collect them."

"Your brain is fascinating."

"I know, right? I'd put a shelf there for all of my books. Oh, and a reading chair." Taking out my phone, I pulled up my favorite furniture website. I'd bookmarked the perfect reading chair. I held the phone in front of Gabe.

"It looks comfortable," he said.

"I bet it is."

I pursed my lips together. *Crap, what am I doing? This isn't my house.*

Gabe nodded, scrolling farther down on his phone.

"So, do you have an estimated date for when the house will be ready?" I asked, trying to keep my voice as neutral as possible.

"A lot of things are still up in the air, but Mateo said he thinks two months is doable."

"Two months? Wow, I, uh, thought something like four," I said, stumbling over my words.

He shrugged. "Honestly, the faster, the better."

A knot of panic rose in my throat. Where did that leave me?

It was on the tip of my tongue to ask what he intended to do about the lease, but I didn't know how to bring up that topic without making it sound like I wanted to move in with him. So I didn't.

Two months.

I really had to kick ass with my new tour business.

I put my head on his chest, considering replaying the movie just to calm down.

Oh come on, Diane. Everything will work out fine. Don't ruin this great evening. You watched Love Actually *with this handsome man who cooked you stir-fry and is currently massaging the back of your neck. What more could you want?*

Oh, just happily ever after...

Chapter Twenty-One
Diane

The next morning, I hit the ground running. I woke up feeling surprisingly refreshed. I also had a healthy dose of adrenaline coursing through my veins.

Over the next week, I had my hands full. I set up a profile on several websites for tourists and guides. Drawing on my experience from the tutoring lessons, I set my pricing lower than average, hoping I could make it up from tips. The main goal at the beginning was to gather reviews. I couldn't use the ones I'd received before because the guides weren't listed with the tours they did, only the company name.

I was going to start my first tour in four days. I was so impatient that I'd almost selected the date as tomorrow, but that was silly. No way would I have time to gather a group so fast.

I was restless the whole day. It didn't help that I only had three tutoring sessions.

After I finished them later that afternoon, I glanced at my phone. Gabe had sent me a message.

Gabe: How's your day?

I smiled, texting back quickly.

Diane: I've finished tutoring, and now I'm restless.
Gabe: Why don't you go for a walk to clear your head?
Diane: Great idea.

Gabe: When's your first tour?

Diane: On Saturday morning.

I even sent him the link. God, I was so excited.

Diane: Oh look, one person already signed up. I need seven. It's my superstition and lucky number.

Gabe: You're going to kick ass, Diane. I have a great feeling about it. And I'm rarely wrong.

Diane: Hmmm... But you did think living together was a good idea.

Gabe: And clearly it was.

I laughed. I couldn't argue with his logic. And I liked that he checked in on me. Maybe he'd had a sixth sense about the fact that I was a complete basket case today.

I grabbed my tote bag and descended the steps, heading outside. I didn't have any grand plans, just wanted to explore the neighborhood. I hadn't had the opportunity until now, but I had so much free time on my hands, it was unnerving.

As I perused the streets, I got a notification that someone had booked another tutoring session in the evening. This day was getting better and better.

My feet brought me in front of Gabe's house at the end of the walk. It was stunning. There were five workers here today, not just three. Maybe that was why the house was going to be ready sooner. I didn't go in because the whole yard was a mess, and I didn't want to get in their way.

A few minutes later, I decided to head home to prep for the unexpected tutoring session. Gabe's car was in the driveway, which was odd. He usually wasn't home so early.

A bout of joy coursed through me. This was just what the man did to me. It didn't matter what state of mind I was in; when I knew he was near, my entire body relaxed.

"Gabe?" I asked the second I entered the house.

When I didn't get an answer, I went looking for him. He wasn't in the gym. Maybe he was somewhere upstairs. I made to go up the staircase when I heard noises from the entrance. Frowning, I turned back, listening intently. It was a screeching noise coming from the attic. I headed upstairs, wondering why Gabe was at my place.

I walked up quickly, pushing the door open, and then my jaw dropped.

"Gabe," I whispered.

He turned around abruptly, asking, "What are you doing home already?"

"I've got another tutoring session. Oh my gosh! You bought my chair."

"Yes."

I put a hand on my stomach. "But how? When?"

"When you showed it to me, your face lit up, and I thought, 'Why not?'"

It was huge, maybe a bit too big for this place, but honestly, I didn't care. He set it right under the window.

"Although," he said, "I think it would be better if it was in the living room or something. It's taking up a lot of space here."

"No, it's perfect. I can't believe you bought this for me. Thank you."

"Consider it a gift for starting a new venture."

"How did you even bring it up here by yourself?" I walked up to it, touching the fluffy backrest.

Gabe put an arm around my waist and kissed the side of my neck. "I wasn't alone. I roped Maddox and Cade into helping me. But they couldn't stay, so I put it together on my own."

"Your brothers dropped everything just like that in the middle of the day?"

"Yes."

I turned around. "That's why you talked me into taking a walk."

"Obviously I needed an excuse so you wouldn't be here. I should have planned this better, maybe asked the girls to take you somewhere."

My God, I loved this man. There was no denying it. I rose on my toes, kissing his neck as I undid the top button on his shirt.

He treated me like I was special, like I was his to please, and it all felt so right.

I lingered there with my lips, fighting to balance myself on my toes, and then pushed the tip of my tongue forward. He groaned, and I moved back on my heels, looking up at him and grinning.

He put his hands on my hips. "You're going to make me lose my head."

"And that's a problem?"

"You've got a tutoring session, remember?"

"No, I didn't remember. You bad, charming man. You made me forget myself."

He laughed. "You should decide. Am I bad or am I charming? The two don't go together."

"Hm," I said, stepping backward. "How are your brothers?"

"Good. Leo says he might actually have a lead on a property I'd asked him to look for," Gabe said.

"For a house?" Maybe he wanted a vacation home or something.

"No. I want to build a second distillery."

"Really? You didn't tell me that."

"I can talk your ear off about all my plans for the distillery, but I can think of a better way to spend our time."

"No, I want to know." I moved his hands from my hips to my waist. "Keep them here. We don't have that much time, remember?"

"No. I literally just forgot."

I giggled. "Good to know I affect you the same way."

"You have no idea," he growled. "You affect me in every way possible."

I licked my lips, sighing. How was he so swoonworthy today?

"So... you want to expand?"

"I want to take over the world. I'm just in the process of choosing locations, and I've got my eye on Stockbridge."

"That's an interesting choice."

"I have a lot of fond memories there. My brothers and I vacationed there as kids with Mom." Warmth spread in my chest. "It was one of her favorite places, and mine. She always said it helped her disconnect because the hotel was surrounded by nature. Although she never did take a break from writing."

"I didn't know she was a writer."

"She wrote for Whitley Publishing. Ran it, actually."

"With five boys? Wow."

He nodded. "I know, but she did it so effortlessly. So, ideally, I would also build a hotel next to the distillery. It's something Mom always wanted to do. This is the first time I'm saying this out loud to anyone. I mean, Leo knows about the hotel, but not about the why. I want to build on her legacy."

"That's very inspirational."

He frowned.

"What's wrong?" I asked.

"I hope Dad doesn't fuck up things again."

"What do you mean?"

"Leo got wind that he wants to buy a property around Boston. Maddox says he wants to start a new business."

"Oh. And that's bad?"

"It's out of the question. I won't allow him to ruin the family name again."

"So what do you plan to do?"

"Stop him. I don't know how yet, but I will." He caressed my jaw with his thumb. "I'm not used to talking about this with anyone outside my family. I'm enjoying it."

He tilted forward, brushing his lips against mine.

Will you look at that? His other hand had gone down to my hip again.

"Gabe," I whispered and stepped back.

"I can't stop thinking about you," he said. "I think of you at work, at home, when I'm with you, when I'm not. Especially when I'm not with you. I'm not used to it."

His shoulders tensed for a brief second, and my breath caught. "But you like it?"

"So much."

He moved his hand even farther down, fondling my ass.

I grinned, taking a large step back this time.

"Right, I'm going to wait for you downstairs."

"We still have a few minutes."

"No." He shook his head. "It's safer if I go now."

I giggled. "I think you're right."

Chapter Twenty-Two
Gabe

Grandfather's birthday was always a very subdued affair. Most years he didn't celebrate it at all. We always stopped by his home to drop off a gift, but he never wanted a big dinner or anything. So I was surprised when he called a few weeks ago to say he was inviting all of his grandkids over for a dinner on his birthday.

"Sure," I said. "How big is the party going to be?"

"It's just us family, and that's already a lot of people. Your grandmother is planning the menu."

I stopped in the act of opening an email on my laptop. "Tell me she's not planning to cook herself."

"That's not a battle I'm willing to engage in." But I was. I respected Grandfather for choosing his battles, but I hadn't reached that point yet.

"Gabe, I can tell you're up to something."

"The less you know the better, Grandfather."

"All right. Whatever I don't know can't hurt me or your grandmother."

That made me laugh. He was exceptionally skilled at delegating things like that. I supposed it was one of the reasons why he'd been such a successful businessman.

"Oh, and bring that girl of yours," he added.

"I was going to anyway," I said.

As soon as I hung up, I wrote in the group chat with my brothers.

Gabe: Hey, you already got the invite for Grandfather's birthday, I guess?

Jake: Yeah.

Gabe: So what are we doing about convincing Grandmother to use a catering company?

Colton: We're on it. The girls are planning something.

My brothers were good at this. For some reason, Grandmother treated their better halves differently than she treated us. She actually took their advice instead of brushing them off and accepted more coddling from them.

I was fiercely protective of our grandparents, and that had always been the case. Once, soon after the scandal broke, a teacher at school made a comment that my grandparents had to have done something really bad for my father to turn out that way. I'd gotten into a shouting match with him. It was the first and only time I got suspended. My protective instincts grew stronger over the years, especially in these past few months when we've had health scares with both grandparents.

I got out of the family chat and noticed a message from Diane.

Diane: Wish me luck. One of the families in the tour canceled, so I only have three tourists, but fingers crossed they enjoy it.

Three? That wasn't even enough people to actually consider it a group. She'd put four different types of smiley faces, and I knew exactly what that meant—she was trying to see the positive in this. But I knew she was worrying.

I went back to the family group, but instead of sending a message, I accidentally hit Colton's number. I was about to disconnect, but he answered.

"Hey," he said.

"I called by mistake. I wanted to write in the family chat."

"Everything all right? You sound off."

"You picked up on that?" I teased. "My, my, you *are* getting more in tune with the family."

"Don't be a jackass."

"Sorry, you're right. So, Diane is now starting to offer tours on her own. It's her own business, and I'm damn proud of her. Long story short, she's got her first one today, and a big group canceled. She's only got three people."

"It's always rougher in the beginning," Colton said reasonably.

"I know. But it's going to make her worry. I wonder if... No, that's stupid."

"Go on."

"Maybe I can just pay people to join the group without her knowing."

There was a pause, and then Colton said, "That sounds something like Jake would do, not you."

I sighed. "I don't even know why my mind went there. Spending time with you is rubbing off on me." But then I had an idea. "I just thought of something better."

"What, paying off a group of kids? Jesus, Gabe."

"No. I'll write in the family group."

"All right, I'm curious now."

After hanging up, I immediately typed a message.

Gabe: It's short notice, but do any of you have time today at 5:00 for a walking tour of the city? As a surprise for Diane.

I'd barely blinked and already five had replied with **I'm in.**

I could just imagine Diane's expression when she saw us. I was grateful that everyone had rallied around me.

I wrote separately in the group I had with my half brothers. We had one where we were all together but rarely wrote in there, mostly because there were so many people that it made it hard to keep track of anything. They also agreed to join us.

This is going to be fantastic.

I put the phone down afterward and got to work.

Only one person was missing—Celia.

We hadn't spoken too much since she showed up at the house. Diane had asked me not to interfere, and I'd kept my word. But I knew Diane would be happy about this, so I went down to the bar in the afternoon. There was only one hour left until the tour started, so there wasn't much time.

"Celia, I need a word with you," I said.

"All right."

She put down the glass she was polishing as I motioned for her to come to the very end of the counter. The other two guys were gathered near the wine fridge, so they wouldn't hear us.

"Listen, Diane has her first tour today."

She nodded. "Yep. She texted that a family canceled."

"I know, and I prepared a surprise for her because... well... you know her superstition."

Celia's jaw dropped. "Wait, she told you about that?"

"Yes. My family is joining me on the tour, but I think she'd be very happy to see you."

Celia was quiet for a few seconds, just staring at me. It was bizarre.

"All right. If the boss allows me to take time off."

"The boss agrees."

"Then I will. And thank you. This means a lot to my sister. And... I didn't get the chance to apologize to you for acting that way at your house. I spoke to Diane about it but never with you."

I held up a hand. "No need to apologize. Sneaking around you wasn't our best idea."

"I mean, clearly I'd misjudged you. I might have listened a bit too closely to gossip."

I rearranged my cuff links.

Celia cleared her throat. "All right, when are we going, and who's going to cover the shift?"

"I'll call one of the guys we have on standby."

"I still can't believe we actually hire bartenders to be on standby."

"You never know when we'll have another of those crazy nights again, and it's totally worth it. Now come on, let's go."

At 4:55 p.m., we headed toward the meeting point at the museum. I'd parked a few streets away so Diane wouldn't accidentally see the car, as I wanted to surprise her. I was damn proud of her, and I wanted to make sure she knew it. She was following her passion and taking a risk, and I admired her for it.

I saw her immediately, standing at the foot of the steps. She didn't notice me at all, as she was engrossed in conversation with the three people who'd signed up. She was carrying a yellow umbrella that said Walking Tour so other people could join.

As I stepped closer, her eyes widened at me and Celia. Then she looked over my shoulder and jerked her head back.

I followed her gaze. The rest of the family was coming, and they'd clearly arrived together. The group was complete. Only our grandparents and Ben were missing. Maddox, Leo, and Nick joined from the opposite direction. Diane was too stunned to notice them.

But then Maddox asked, "Could we join the tour?"

She whipped her head in his direction, mouth hanging open. "Yes, sure." She looked from them to me again and flashed me a heartfelt smile. "All right, I'm going to give you the itinerary, and in case anyone wants to see something different, let me know."

"Sounds good," I replied.

For the next two hours, we were on our best behavior. We wanted her to offer the actual tourists a good experience.

"Hey, I've lived in Boston my whole life. Never knew so much stuff," Meredith said.

"Same for me," Cade agreed.

"You're an excellent guide," Natalie said, smiling from ear to ear.

"Yeah, you truly are. I'm going to leave a review for sure," one of the actual tourists added.

By the time the tour ended, it was seven o'clock. "Thank you very much," the tourists said, giving her tips. She immediately pocketed them.

After the trio left, Diane threw her arms around my neck, kissing my cheek, and then focused on the rest of the group. "This was an awesome surprise. Thank you all for coming. Sis, you're amazing."

"It was all Gabe's idea."

"Nooo," she replied with a cheeky grin.

"He messaged us all this morning," Spencer began, "asking who could spare some time, and turns out we all could."

I knew for a fact that wasn't exactly true. At the very least, Colton and Jake usually had meetings scheduled until 6:00 p.m., but I'd appreciated that they made the effort.

Colton grinned. "I've got to tell her."

I groaned. "Man, when did you get a sense of humor?"

Zoey perked up. "I think I might have something to do with it."

"Nah," Maddox said. "I vote it's on us." He pointed at himself, Leo, and Nick. "Ever since he's been hanging around us, his sense of humor has improved massively."

Colton glared at him, determined to prove the opposite, but Maddox wasn't entirely wrong. Then he looked at Diane. "I spoke to Gabe first. He was actually thinking of hiring people to pose as tourists."

Diane's mouth hung open. "That's... I'm not even sure what to say."

"It was just a fleeting thought," I defended.

"He was channeling me," Jake said.

"I won't even argue with that. Clearly I wasn't being myself," I replied.

Celia smiled broadly. "Dear sis, you always say you're too awkward. But Gabe is all on board. He even remembered your superstition."

Fuck yes, I was. There was nothing awkward about her. Every part was simply amazing.

As Diane spoke with Colton, Zoey, and Celia, I went to my half brothers. "Thank you for joining us, guys. This means a great deal to Diane."

"We couldn't miss it," Nick said on a chuckle. "One of the things I never thought would happen was you being in a relationship with someone."

"Or not wincing when the word *relationship* comes up!" Leo added.

"We couldn't miss your big gesture," Maddox said, playing right off them.

"This is the big gesture?" I asked.

Maddox patted my shoulder. "You're doing good. Don't sabotage yourself."

Leo cleared his throat. "But there's another reason that I was actually glad we have the chance to meet up. It's about Dad."

The mood between the four of us instantly shifted. By the surprise on Maddox's and Nick's faces, it was news to them too.

"For fuck's sake. We need to find a better way to get these updates about that," Nick said. "Otherwise, the rest will guess, and we said we didn't want to alarm everyone."

"Let's hear it," Maddox said.

Leo sighed. "He's looking at a property in Essex. It's huge."

"How huge?" I asked.

As he gave me the specs, I did a quick calculation in my mind.

"It would be big enough for the distillery," I said.

Leo cocked a brow. "You had me looking at Stockbridge."

"Yeah, but I'm flexible. Essex is fine, and the property is actually big enough for a distillery and a hotel," I said more to myself than to my brothers. "How's the permit situation?"

"I'll look into it. As far as I know, he's checking the same thing right now too. I should have news at Grandpa's birthday party."

"All right." I nodded. "Looking forward to hearing it."

"Now, why don't you focus on Diane?" Leo suggested. "Or your grand gesture will end up being a bust."

Diane

I couldn't believe it. This afternoon was magic. I'd had a huge group, and everyone had fun. Yes, I knew that technically it was cheating, but I was taking it as a good omen nonetheless.

"Ice cream, my treat," I announced, pointing across the street at one of my favorite shops.

"Babe," Gabe said. "You don't want to spend all your tips."

"I insist."

"Fine." Gabe looked at the group. "It'll give us all a chance to talk about how we're going to convince Grandmother to use a catering company for Grandfather's birthday."

He then looked at me. "Want to join me and this crazy group in a few weeks for the celebration?"

I felt like my chest was expanding even more, although I didn't think that was possible. "Of course. Now, what's that about catering?"

"Leave things to us," Penny said.

Meredith nodded. "We'll talk her into it."

"That's our role," Zoey clarified.

"And we're damn good at it," Natalie added.

Jake kissed her cheek. "You are."

I smiled as we walked toward the ice cream shop. "Each of you has a role?" I asked Gabe.

"Yes. At least it's true of us guys. Not sure how they roped Natalie, Penny, Zoey and Meredith into it."

"Because we're opportunistic," Cade said. "We realized they're much better at talking Grandmother into... well, letting us make life easier for her."

"We have to be careful, though," Penny said, "because she might catch on."

Gabe laughed in my ear as we stepped inside the ice cream shop. "Knowing Grandmother, she already has, but she wants to indulge you."

Once inside, everyone went to look at the display freezer, inspecting the flavors. I already knew what I wanted, so I stayed to one side. I was immediately flanked by Meredith and Natalie.

"So... we couldn't help overhearing that you'll be at the party," Natalie said.

I grinned. "I'm excited. Anything I should know? What's his name?"

"Abe. He doesn't want us to make a fuss—according to the guys," Meredith replied.

"Any advice? I appreciate the insider info."

"Honestly, Jeannie already met you, and you've got her approval," Zoey said.

I was sure I looked stunned. "I do?"

"Oh yeah, definitely. Between you and me, I think she's got serious plans for you and Gabe," Natalie said.

I laughed nervously. "Look, he and I... I mean, we're not making any long-term plans."

Meredith blinked. "Really? Hmm."

Natalie frowned, looking at Meredith. "Right."

Zoey didn't reply at all.

I shrugged. "I mean, construction on Gabe's house will eventually finish and he'll move out, so..."

Zoey nodded. "I see."

"I've known from the beginning that he's not into long-term relationships, so it's not like I'm expecting it or anything."

"If you're sure...," Zoey said.

Natalie and Meredith exchanged a glance but didn't say anything else.

"Don't you want ice cream?" I asked them.

"Sure we do. We're just letting everyone else choose first," Meredith replied.

The two of them walked to the counter, and I looked inside it too. Gabe put a hand around my waist, kissing my cheek. I leaned into him, absorbing the strength and heat of his body. I didn't even care that we were in public. Not that we were indecent or anything.

"You were amazing back there," he murmured.

"Thank you for this day. It's wonderful."

"I wanted to do something special to celebrate this milestone with you."

"You're my favorite person right now," I said with a smile.

He brought his mouth to my ear. "That was exactly my plan."

Chapter Twenty-Three
Gabe

On Grandfather's birthday, we headed to their place for lunch.

"This is so cozy. Is it the same house they've always lived in?" Diane asked as we went up the steps to the porch.

"Yeah, for as long as I can remember." I put a hand on the small of her back. "I have a lot of memories on this porch. They made some changes in the meantime, because back then they had bedrooms for us. But now they've converted all of them. They've got a study for Grandfather, a reading corner, and a room where Grandmother can stay with her friends. I'm not too sure what the rest are."

"Wow. The house doesn't look that big."

They'd put a sign on the front door that said Unlocked. I opened it and heard voices inside resounding through the living room and entrance area. We went straight to the living room. Cade and Meredith were already here, as well as Jake and Natalie. The rest hadn't arrived yet.

"Excellent. You came just in time for the debate. The more the merrier," Cade exclaimed. "Hey, Diane."

"Hi! What are you debating?" I asked.

"How long everyone else will take."

I rolled my eyes at my brother.

Diane looked at Grandfather. "Happy birthday. Thank you so much for inviting me."

"Happy birthday, Grandfather," I added.

After I shook his hand, he focused on Diane. "I'm very happy that you've joined us."

Then he glanced at Grandmother. "You know, when you started with your matchmaking project, I thought it would be a disaster, but it's turned out to be quite the opposite."

She scoffed. "Really, Abe? That's how little trust you have in me?"

"No, but our boys are headstrong, and I didn't think anything would come of it. If anything, I suspected you'd clash, but you've done well."

He kissed Diane's hand, and she laughed nervously.

"All right," I said, looking around. "Are the snacks in the kitchen?"

Grandmother huffed. "The catering company is going to be ten minutes late, so no."

How the fuck were they late? I was certain that this would be the last event Grandmother would agree to have catered. I carefully avoided looking at Jake and Cade or we would burst out laughing.

"I know you boys plotted today and tried to fool me," Grandmother said. "But Gabe came with Diane, so we'll forgive him for now."

"What's one thing got to do with the other?" Jake asked. "Just so we know for future reference."

Grandmother shook her head. "You boys will always give me headaches."

Meredith and Natalie laughed.

"Yes, they will. We're sure of that," Meredith said.

Cade put an arm around her shoulders. "Babe, don't side with Grandmother. It's a slippery slope."

"I'm on that slope, and I'm very happy," Grandfather declared.

Then he focused on Diane, who was staring with her mouth open at everyone. Maybe I should have given her a 101 on how things worked in our family, but it didn't occur to me.

"Jeannie's usually on her best behavior when someone new joins the family. I don't know what got into her today," Grandfather said, and Diane stiffened.

"Grandfather! Way to put her on the spot." I should have warned her that no one had a filter.

And yet he was right. Diane felt like a member of the family, like she'd always been here, part of the group.

Part of *me*.

The front door opened, and Zoey and Colton came in. Then Maddox, Nick, and Leo. Helen had already left town, although my brothers said she'd never just pop up for a birthday party.

"Ah, everyone's here except Penny, Spencer, and Ben," Maddox declared.

They all congratulated Grandfather and then quickly turned to Diane. I swear to God, it was almost comical. Maddox, Leo, and Nick were grinning but also theatrically each running a finger over their necks in a throat-cutting motion.

Colton shook her hand and said, "Diane, don't pay attention to these losers." He pointed at our half brothers. "They like you but are afraid of the fact that Grandmother had yet another successful matchmaking outcome. And what that means for them now."

Maddox stared at Colton. "Yeah, exactly what he said. Even I couldn't explain it that well."

"You have a gift, man," Nick said.

Leo ran a hand through his hair. "You know, him voicing it doesn't make this less dangerous."

Diane grinned. "Well, I think your grandmother is on to something."

Maddox turned to me. "Gabe, you didn't explain to Diane how things work in the family?"

"No," I admitted. "Didn't think it was necessary."

Nick groaned. "We're toast anyway, Maddox."

"I'm glad everyone is so amused," Grandmother huffed.

The door opened again. "Hello?" called a voice we didn't know. It was definitely not Penny.

"The catering company must be here," Grandmother said, walking with quick steps.

After she disappeared into the hallway, there were more voices and the sounds of dishes being moved in and out.

Colton and Maddox started to get up. "Need our help?"

"No, no," the same female voice replied.

"It's best if all of you stay out of it," Grandmother said. "They know what they're doing."

They set up a few folding tables with chafing dishes in the living room. I noticed my grandparents had rearranged some of the furniture to make space for us all.

Everything was ready in less than twenty minutes. The entire team left and promised to be here to clean up as soon as Grandmother gave them the green light.

"That was efficient," Grandmother said.

Once again, I exchanged a glance with Cade. If she could get used to this, it was a win.

The door opened again, and we all knew Spencer and Penny had arrived because Ben was giggling.

Diane smiled. "I love this family gathering," she said.

"How come?" I asked.

"I don't know. Everything's just so loud, and all of you are saying—"

"What's on our minds without any filter whatsoever," I finished for her. "You find that appealing?"

"I think it's awesome that you don't tiptoe around and just give one another the business."

"You're not wrong."

When the trio came into sight, I felt Diane melt against me. "Oh, he's so cute today."

"You like kids?" I asked her.

"You know I do. I think they're adorable, not that I've been around too many. Oh, just look at Ben. He's so precious."

"Hey, Diane," Penny said after wishing Grandfather a happy birthday. Spencer was carrying Ben, and Diane's gaze was glued to him.

"Can I take over the world's most spoiled nephew?" I asked.

"Sure."

I took him easily from Spencer. Diane was right at my side, cooing at him and smiling, then kissing his head. I liked seeing her with him. She was so at ease, already showering him with affection as if it was the most natural thing in the world.

"All right, let's get the party started," Grandmother said.

As everyone went to load their plates, Leo nodded at me. Maddox and Nick were next to him. I instantly knew Leo had news and joined them right away.

"What's this about?" I asked.

"Dad. The property is cleared to be used as a hotel," Leo informed me.

"I want to see it," I said immediately.

"Why?" Maddox asked.

"Because I want to buy it. And build the distillery and the hotel there."

Maddox looked at me intently. "I have an idea. It's been percolating in my mind for a while. You don't have to decide now, just keep it in mind."

"I'm all ears."

"Let's go into business together. I'd handle the hotel, and you can focus on the distillery."

I didn't see that coming. It had never occurred to me before. We'd always focused on our respective businesses, but the idea instantly took root in my mind.

"I'd like that." The more I thought about it, the more I wanted him as my partner.

"Besides," Maddox said with a smirk, "you're already starting to resemble Colton a bit too much when it comes to being a workaholic."

I grunted. "Will everyone give it a rest? The bar is new. It needs more of my attention."

"Exactly. I've got more time to spare than you do," Maddox said. In a more serious tone, he added, "And I've always liked the idea of adding something new to the Whitley legacy."

Leo nodded. "I'll make arrangements. It might take a while because the owner communicates at a slug's pace, but I'll let you know once everything is in motion."

"Thanks," I said. "Now, I'm starving."

"Yeah, let's get food or everyone will be suspicious if we keep talking," Nick agreed.

I filled my plate as I balanced Ben in one arm. The chafing dishes kept everything piping hot. It was a good thing Ben was too small to walk around on his own; it could be very unsafe for him wandering around these scalding pans.

"Do you want to put him down?" Spencer asked him.

"No, I can multitask," I said, putting some mashed potatoes on my plate with gravy and roast beef.

As we sat down at the table, I held him firmly with my left arm and ate with the right. When I took my third spoonful, Ben's sounds changed. I looked down at him. The poor guy was salivating.

"Aw. I'm sorry. He does that ever since we introduced solids," Penny said.

"Think he wants to taste it?" I asked.

"For sure," Spencer said. "The little guy will eat anything, I swear to God."

I put mashed potatoes on the fork and held it to his lips. He licked a bit and scrunched his face but then gave me a huge smile.

Holy shit, this is amazing! He'd never smiled like this. I loved it. I switched to a spoon and fed him more of my potatoes.

"You're really good at this," Spencer said. He sounded stunned.

"I'm just as surprised as you are."

Diane smiled at me and said, "You're a great uncle. I can hold him so you can eat if you want. I've already finished with my food, and I have some mashed potatoes left." She sounded very eager, and that stirred something inside me.

"Sure," I said, and she took him, settling Ben on her lap.

She looked really good with a baby in her arms. She kissed his forehead before starting to feed him. I couldn't look away. The image spoke to a primal part of my brain that I wasn't even aware existed until now.

I forced myself to focus on my food, which wasn't too difficult since I was starving. Everyone made small talk around the table. No one brought up work and Whitley Industries. We rarely talked shop among ourselves, and it didn't make much sense anyway, since each of us was focusing on our own companies.

Once we were done, the caterer who'd stayed behind rolled the chafing dishes out of sight on the porch and brought in trays with dessert.

"I can't believe you didn't want cake," Maddox exclaimed.

"That's like the best part of a birthday party," Leo added.

"What are you guys, four?" I asked them, but I kind of agreed. It didn't feel like a birthday party without a cake.

Grandfather chuckled. "What can I say? Not a fan of cake."

There was a good assortment of sweets, and everyone circulated around the room while eating the dessert. Spencer took Ben back from Diane, who was now chatting with Penny.

Meredith and Natalie had their heads together, looking at me. At first I thought it was a coincidence, but I kept glancing at them while I filled my plate with macarons and figured they were definitely talking about me. I headed over to them.

"Gabe," Natalie said, sounding a bit on edge.

"So, you two were clearly gossiping about me. Why don't you fill me in?"

Meredith's cheek hollowed like she bit it from the inside. Natalie looked at her feet, hesitating.

"What's wrong? Jake or Cade need help with anything, or you two? Or do you know anything about our grandparents that—"

"No, no," Natalie said quickly.

Meredith sighed. "Dammit, we do need to tell him because now he's going to make up stuff in his mind."

I nodded. "Exactly. And you'd better fess up fast because I'm damn good at jumping to conclusions."

"You know, Diane doesn't seem convinced that this is a long-term thing," Natalie murmured.

"She told you that?" My heart sank.

Meredith pressed her lips together. "Honestly, she told us that in confidence, so I feel bad just talking to you about it at all. I'd rather not give more details."

No way. They have to be wrong.

I waved my hand. "You probably misconstrued what she said. Diane isn't worried about anything."

It was true that she and I had never discussed anything further down the line, but we were both on the same page, I was sure of it. It was probably something Meredith and Natalie wouldn't understand since Meredith was engaged to Cade and Natalie and Jake were already married. But Diane and I didn't have to talk everything out.

I looked around for her. She was with Penny and Spencer, holding Ben again. I usually couldn't take my eyes off this woman, but right now, watching her with Ben was something else entirely. I walked straight to her, and she and my brother abruptly stopped talking.

"What's that?" I asked. "Why did you fall silent?"

"Because they were gossiping about you, obviously," Maddox said helpfully, appearing from behind us. Nick and Leo weren't too far away either.

"So everyone eavesdropped?" Diane asked.

"I mean, it wasn't that hard," Leo said. "You weren't keeping your voice down."

"There is very little respect for private conversations in this house," I informed her.

She nodded. "Right, right."

"You're holding up really well, actually," Leo said.

"You know, I thought I'd be more overwhelmed, what with all of you being here," Diane said, "but this is surprisingly fun."

I had no idea where Natalie and Meredith got the idea that Diane was worried about something. She was just like me—laid-back and taking things easy. No overthinking, no pressure, just enjoying each day as it came. It was one of the reasons why we fit together so well.

Chapter Twenty-Four
Diane

Every time I thought I'd gotten rid of Chuck, he proved me wrong. On a sunny Wednesday morning, I got a message from him right as I was heading out for a tour.

Chuck: Stop ignoring me. I want that fucking laptop back.

What the heck did he need his ancient Acer back for? Or maybe he just wanted another opportunity to insult me. Whatever.

I stared at the phone. I wanted to ignore it, but it was apparent that he'd keep insisting, and I wanted to get this over with.

Biting the inside of my cheek, I wondered how to organize this. I certainly didn't want to go to his new place. No, if he wanted the laptop so badly, he could come get it for all I cared.

I realized with shock that I wasn't afraid of facing him anymore.

Diane: Here's my new address. You can pick it up tomorrow between twelve and two.

Chuck: I'll come at two.

Gabe was usually at work around then, so that should be okay. The last thing I wanted was for the two to cross paths.

I didn't want Gabe to have to deal with him, or to see what an asshole he could be. Hell, I didn't even want to deal with him myself, but he was my ex; there was nothing I could do about that. And it was his laptop, after all. Besides, I felt much stronger now. I could face Chuck and not crumble afterward.

I headed straight to my meeting point for the tour. My groups were still rather small, but because I was keeping all the income, I already made more than when I worked for George. I had a great feeling about this, and not even the prospect of seeing Chuck was going to get me down.

The next day I was having second thoughts. I was a basket case, waiting for him to show up.

I didn't actually want him to step inside the house, so at two o'clock, I was waiting for him in the yard, holding the ancient laptop in my arms. He arrived ten minutes later. He was always chronically late.

I looked at him and simply felt nothing. Not even repulsion, let alone pain.

The second he stepped out of the car, he smirked, looking at the house. "Nice lodgings. Got your hands on a rich boyfriend?"

"None of your business," I said. "Why do you even need the laptop? Your fancy company can buy you another one."

"I'm starting my own business, and I don't want to waste money on buying a new laptop for an employee. This old piece of crap will do," he said. His voice was unusually tight, though he still managed to sneer the words.

"What about your job? You were so proud of it."

"It didn't work out."

"So you've been fired," I concluded.

"Don't act so superior. The job market is tough. Isn't that the excuse you always gave me? Have you finally managed to get one?"

I straightened up. "I'm running my own touring company."

He snorted. "So I was right. You clearly have a rich boyfriend to support your hobby."

"Fuck you," I bellowed. "You have never, not *once*, been supportive of me or anything I ever did even though I helped you through college."

He rolled his eyes. "How many times are you going to throw that in my face? You want me to crawl at your feet for my whole life?"

"No, just treat me with basic human decency," I replied. "Here's your laptop. There's the gate. Leave."

He yanked the laptop from me, inspecting it. "All right, no scratches."

I balled my hands into fists. "What the fuck? You're checking it for damage?"

"Obviously. I want to see if it still works."

I cocked a brow. "Excuse me?"

"Is there a plug out here?"

"No, there isn't." I didn't bother to check. I just wanted him to go.

"Then let's go inside. I need to know if it's still working."

"You're not stepping inside the house," I said incredulously. "You wanted your laptop, you've got it. That's it."

"Come on. Don't be like this. What use do I have for a laptop that doesn't work?"

"I haven't even opened it."

"Really? Then why did you take it with you?"

That was a good question.

"Probably because I knew your cheap ass would want it back at some point. Knowing you, you'd make me pay for it if I didn't have it anymore."

He pointed at me. "If this doesn't work, you'll be buying a new one."

"For fuck's sake, what's wrong with you?" I asked. "Just take your laptop and do whatever you want with it. Stop being such an ass."

He jerked his head back. "Now that you've got the rich boyfriend"—he tipped his head toward the house—"you finally have a backbone?"

I drew in a deep breath. I didn't usually raise my voice; not even during our breakup fight. He was the one shouting, whereas I was too busy trying to process what was happening.

"I've always had one. The only problem was, I was looking at you through rose-colored glasses. Now I just see you for the asshole you are. Have a nice life, Chuck. I never want to see you again. You've ceased to mean anything to me. You don't have the power to hurt me anymore."

"Really?" He smirked, then stepped closer. "You don't have any feelings left for me? You have to miss me, at least in bed."

I burst out laughing. "I really, *really* don't. You're by far not as good as you think."

He set his mouth in a straight line and help up the laptop. "If this isn't working, you're paying for it."

I snorted and pointed at the gate. "Get the fuck out."

Damn it, why did I meet him here? I should have suggested someplace downtown.

"Fine," he sneered.

As I stood here, I realized he meant absolutely nothing to me. There was a time when I didn't even think I could look at him and not crumble. Now the only thing I really felt was intense annoyance and dislike.

I didn't move until I saw him close the gate behind him, and then I went back inside the house. I was in a foul mood for the rest of the afternoon. I wasn't even sure why; giving him that crappy laptop was cathartic in a way, but still, the annoyance of talking to Chuck persisted.

Needing to get my mind off it, I decided to put something together for dinner. While I cooked, I called Mom, as I hadn't checked on her in a while.

"Hey, honey," she answered right away. "What are you doing?"

"I'm whipping up a casserole," I replied, putting her on speakerphone while I moved about the kitchen.

"Ah, I'm starting to salivate through the phone."

"Anytime you want me to come cook for you, just say so. I'm loaded right now."

Obviously I wasn't loaded, but things were going well. As soon as she gave me the green light to visit her, I would splurge.

"No, don't you worry about me. We can FaceTime."

I sighed. Yeah, that was my mom to a T; she didn't want me to spend a dollar on her even though I'd gladly do it.

We talked a bit more about everything, and then she was ready to go.

"All right, honey. Get back to cooking."

"Sure, Mom. Love you."

"Love you too."

After hanging up, I noticed I had a message from Gabe.

Gabe: Got the final date from the team. The house will be ready in one month.

I couldn't postpone my search for an apartment much longer. I was going to start later today—right now, I wanted to finish the dish.

My casserole came out exquisite. I'd added some Parmesan on top as well. That wasn't part of the recipe, but honestly, Parmesan was life. No other cheese topped it, in my opinion.

At six thirty, I heard the door open and smiled. Gabe was home. God, I was going to miss having dinner with him every evening. We should probably talk at some point about how we were going to handle things if we didn't live together anymore, but today had been hard enough already. I didn't want to tackle that too.

Gabe stepped into the kitchen and immediately came over to me. He turned me around and kissed me hard. I melted against him, returning the kiss with fervor. This was pure bliss.

He pulled back and cupped my face with both hands, pressing his thumbs on my lower lip.

"Tough day?" I asked.

"No, but I missed you." He looked down at the casserole. "This looks delicious."

"It is, but it still needs to cool a bit."

He nodded but didn't say anything.

"Are you okay?" I asked. "You seem a bit tense."

He cleared his throat. "Leo found out Dad wants to buy a property in Essex to build a hotel. Maddox and I decided to buy it instead. The new distillery and the hotel will be there."

My eyes bulged. "Holy shit! No one messes with you Whitleys, huh?"

"No. We're going to see the property next week on Tuesday, and if everything looks right, we'll make an offer."

"I'll keep my fingers crossed."

I decided on the spot to schedule apartment viewings on the same day. Then hopefully we could sort everything out that evening, after he'd put the debacle with his dad behind him.

"How was your day?" he asked, grabbing a fork. The man was impatient, as always.

"It was... okay."

"Don't sound too enthusiastic." He took a mouthful of casserole and then sucked in air to cool it as he chewed.

"Everything was fine until Chuck showed up to get his laptop. That put me in a sour mood."

Gabe put the fork back down, straightening up. "Chuck, your ex?"

I nodded. "Yes. He'd been bugging me about giving back his laptop for a while, and I kept postponing it. I told him to come get it today."

"When was he here?" Gabe asked. He had a strange look in his eyes, and his voice was a bit tight.

"Two o'clock. I wanted him to come when you weren't home. I figured middle of the day is best for that."

He stared at me. "You purposely asked him to come when I wasn't around?"

I shrugged. "He's got a penchant for annoying anyone he comes in contact with."

"Is that the only reason you didn't want me to be here?"

The hair at the back of my neck stood on end. "What other reason would I have?"

"I don't know. You tell me."

"I don't like what you're implying."

"I don't like that you asked him here at the house when you were alone."

"What exactly do you think? That I had a quickie with him before returning his shitty laptop?"

Gabe didn't say anything.

"Oh my God. You really think that?" My heart rate accelerated. "You can't be serious."

"I can't believe you wanted to meet him alone."

"So I could spare you from having to face him," I repeated slowly.

He swallowed hard, putting his hands in his pockets. He looked so sexy even when he was annoying.

"I can't believe this," I said. "I've never given you any reason not to trust me."

"You didn't tell me you were still in contact with him."

I crossed my arms over my chest. "I'm not in contact. He just wrote a few times."

"A few times?" His voice thundered.

"To ask for his laptop back."

"That was just an excuse," Gabe replied, snorting.

"You say that because you don't know Chuck. He's cheap as shit. I didn't even let him inside the house. I met him in the yard because I didn't want him to linger."

Gabe said nothing. His nostrils flared.

"You don't believe me. Right," I said, looking down at my feet and then back up. "Um, I'm just going to go."

"Where?" he asked.

"Somewhere where I'm not around you because I'm seriously going to lose my shit."

I stormed out of the kitchen.

"Diane," Gabe called after me, but I didn't stop.

I seriously needed to do something to cool off, so I went up the spiral staircase two steps at a time. Even after months, I was still winded when I got to the top.

I paced the attic up and down, then sat down in my chair, picking up my Kindle. Then I remembered Gabe got me this chair and I got up, annoyed. How the hell did he dare accuse me of cheating? He hadn't come out and said it, but it was clearly what he was suspecting. Didn't he know me at all?

I opened a window, needing some fresh air. Coming up here was a bad idea. I should have just left the house. That's what people did when they stormed off, right? Not that I'd know. But I didn't have anything with me downstairs, like my bag or my wallet. If I tried to leave now, I'd run into Gabe.

Oh, screw it. I had to go out even though I was going to have to pass Gabe. Maybe I was lucky and he wasn't in the living room anymore.

I hurried downstairs and realized I was out of luck. He was at the entrance.

Damn it.

"Diane, I was about to come upstairs. Can we talk?"

"No."

"Diane, please."

I wanted to stick to my guns, but I wasn't good at this. I hated fighting. His hair was completely disheveled, like he'd run his hand through it a million times since I saw him a few minutes ago.

He sighed. "I'm sorry."

"About what? Jumping to conclusions, or talking to me like you don't even know me, or assuming I'm a cheater?"

"All of it. I overreacted."

I scoffed. "Of course you did."

He came closer to me, but I took a step back.

"I don't know what got into me." He ran a hand through his hair again. "I heard you say his name, and it triggered something inside me, though I'm not even sure why. And then I wasn't thinking anymore. I just acted on some fucked-up instinct."

I softened. He swallowed hard, stepping toward me again. This time, I didn't step back.

"I'm sorry. I don't know what I was thinking."

I bit the inside of my cheek, staying put as he placed a hand on my neck.

"So you trust me?" I asked.

"Yes, 100 percent. Swear to God, I trust you. I really can't explain why I reacted like that."

"We all have our triggers," I murmured.

Considering the shit show that had been going on in his family, I had an inkling that this was related. I didn't say it out loud, though, because there was no point in rehashing that.

"You mean so much to me. I can't even imagine you with anyone else. It destroys me on the inside completely." He said the last word in a lower octave.

"I'm yours. Only yours, Gabe. I thought you realized that."

"You promise?"

"Yes."

"Okay. Because I couldn't stand even the possibility of anything else."

I'd never seen him like this, so raw and vulnerable in front of me, opening up completely.

"I don't—" he began, but I rose on my toes and sealed my mouth over his, wanting to show him exactly how I felt.

We all had triggers and fears, but relationships were about facing everything together, not turning on each other.

He cradled my head with both hands, pulling my entire body against his.

Gabe

I wanted to peel everything off her slowly just to watch her get more impatient. At the same time, I wanted to yank off her clothes and have her naked in front of me right now.

"What are you thinking about?" she murmured.

"All the things I want do to you. I don't even know where to start."

She grinned. "That's new. You usually seem to know everything."

It was true, but everything was different with Diane, and I was starting to accept that.

I turned her around, holding her hair in my left fist and lifting it above her head so I could kiss the back of her neck. I put my other hand on her arm, smiling against her neck when her skin turned to goose bumps. Then I lowered my hand to her belly, catching the exact moment when she pulled in her muscles, tensing like she needed to brace herself. "I like making you squirm."

"You're very good at it," she whispered.

I barely caught her words as I continued kissing up and down the back of her neck, then tugged the zipper down and trailed my mouth down her spine. Sliding my hands inside her dress, I drew my palms down the sides of her body. She moved to pull it off her shoulders.

"No. Only when I tell you to."

"Okay." She sucked in a breath.

I moved my mouth down until I reached the base of her spine, then said, "Push it down your shoulders slowly."

She took off both straps at the same time. As she lowered it, more of her ass came into view. She was wearing a thong. The way her ass hung out of it drove me crazy. I kissed down her right ass cheek and then her left one, going farther down as she lowered her dress even more.

"Drop it now," I said once it went past her ass.

I held her by the hips as she stepped out of it, then turned her around. Watching her from down here messed with my senses. Her breasts were exquisite, her bra pushing them up.

"You're so sexy." I straightened and kissed the upper part of her breasts that peeked out of the bra, then dipped my tongue between them. I lowered my hands to her buttocks, cupping both of them at the same time and pressing her pelvis into mine.

She rubbed herself against the zipper of my jeans. It was a sign that she needed friction, and I was going to satisfy her. I kept one hand splayed on her cheeks and moved the other one to her pussy, sliding my fingers inside her panties to give her skin-on-skin contact.

She rewarded me with a moan. I kissed her, wanting to feel exactly what my fingers did to her. I could read and feel her body, but the connection between us was at its most intense when we kissed.

When she pushed herself up and down, I stopped moving my hand and paused the kiss enough to say, "No. I promise I'll give you all the pleasure you crave, but I'll decide how much and when."

She swallowed hard, and I kissed her again. I felt the muscles in her ass relax. I loved feeling this change in her whenever she gave herself to me and relinquished control. She trusted me, and I was going to reward that with an amazing orgasm or two.

I didn't stop kissing her while I moved my fingers over her clit and then down the sides, over her folds. Then I dipped one finger inside her.

She whimpered. This was too much for now. I needed to ease in. She pushed her ass back, but I tilted it right at the angle I had her before. I smiled against her mouth when I felt her legs become weaker, then slid in another finger. This was going to be quick and delicious.

Her breath hitched, the first sign that the orgasm was already rolling through her. I should have pushed down my jeans or at least undone the button, as the zipper pressed painfully against my cock, but I didn't want to stop now, not when I'd brought her close to the cusp. No, her needs came first. I would satisfy her, then focus on my own pleasure.

I moved my fingers faster and then pressed my palm on her clit, gently at first. She moaned against my mouth, and I pressed even harder. She exploded the next second. I kept one hand firmly on her ass, the other at her pussy, steadying her as she rode the wave of her climax. She dug her nails into my shoulders, and I hoped she left a mark. I belonged to this woman, and I wouldn't mind a reminder of that on my skin.

Kissing her while she came was exquisite. I felt the reverberations throughout my body. I moved my hand off her clit as she calmed down; she was sopping wet and still sensitive right now, and I didn't want to overpower her senses. Not when I still had so much in store for her.

She gasped, and I pulled my head back, watching her. The contour of her mouth was completely red. My cock twitched. She looked at me through hooded eyelids and smiled. My hand was still in her panties, and she undid my jeans. Then I took off all my clothes in a blur. I didn't want anything left between us.

She took care of her own bra. Usually, I'd demand for her to only take it off when I said so, but right now, I wanted her completely naked. We were standing behind the couch, and I intended to lay her down on it. But I lost my composure way before that.

What's happening to me? I'd never needed to be inside her quite as badly as now. My body needed the connection as much as it needed breathing.

I pumped my cock up and down while I kissed down her breasts. Now that they spilled out of her bra, I couldn't hold back. I wanted to kiss all the parts of her breasts that I hadn't before. The bra had left red marks on her skin, and I traced them with my mouth. Her nipples were completely hard. I drew the tip of my tongue around them; I knew her body, and right now, they were too sensitive for me to take them into my mouth.

Straightening up, I kissed down her temple while I pressed the tip of my cock against her clit. I needed her too much to move even a foot away from this spot, but I still wanted her to be comfortable.

"Get on the couch," I said.

She immediately did exactly that. I pulled her ass toward me and positioned my cock between her thighs. I wasn't rubbing my tip against her clit anymore, just the length of my cock along her pussy. I inhaled deeply, my breaths shaky. She was so wet. She didn't need any foreplay anymore. And I couldn't stand not being inside her for one second longer.

I pushed in inch by inch, careful not to hurt or overwhelm her. She lowered herself farther toward the couch, bent her arms at the elbows, and put her palms one over the other, resting her head on her hands.

"Gabe, fuck," she whispered.

Yeah, I knew exactly what that "fuck" meant. She was overwhelmed. I kept my hands on her hips, tilting her pelvis slightly forward.

"Gabe." Her voice shook.

I loved giving her more pleasure than she thought was possible. My muscles thrummed with tension. My entire body transformed, preparing itself to go over the edge, to give Diane everything I had. She squeezed me good on every thrust. She was getting tighter and tighter, and then her legs trembled.

Fuck! I was going to come at this rate, but I wanted her to succumb first. I stilled and then pulled out.

"No!" she cried.

I rubbed my cock along her pussy. I was still desperate for every morsel of contact, but this wouldn't take me over the edge.

"What are you—oh." Her voice faded as I brought my hand to her clit. I alternated between brushing my fingers over it and nudging it with the tip of my cock.

Her breaths quickened once more, and her entire body shook lightly. She turned her head sideways. She'd closed her eyes and pressed her lips together too. I knew she was going to tip over the edge before she even opened her mouth and cried out. The second she called my name, I slid in and grunted hers in reply.

My muscles tightened even more as I fucked her relentlessly hard and then harder still. Just when she came down from the cusp, I reached my own climax. I braced both palms on the headrest to support myself or I was going to lose my balance any second now. The sensations were so strong that my vision turned black. For a few seconds, I didn't know where up and down were. I'd be hard-pressed to even remember my name right now.

Then slowly, everything came back, and I zeroed in on this insane pleasure. I rested my forehead on her shoulder blade, slowing my movements but not stopping.

Even though I'd given her all I had, I still needed this.

Chapter Twenty-Five
Diane

"Oh, it's so good to have a day together," Celia murmured.

We were both at the house, doing an indoor spa day, as I liked to call it. We put on face masks, and I even sliced cucumbers. We also made a honey mask for our feet and put on cotton socks so it soaked into our skin better.

My sister didn't have much time before her next shift, but I was happy that we could just hang out.

When she sighed loudly, I took off a cucumber, glancing at her.

"What's wrong?" I asked.

"Nothing, I'm just wondering how we got so lucky. You know, that we live in the same city and can randomly meet on a Saturday morning and do face masks."

"I'm so happy I moved to Boston even if it *was* because of Chuck."

She scoffed. I'd told her that he'd come to the house for his computer and what a jerk he was. "I still can't believe he had the nerve to ask you for that old, outdated laptop."

"It feels like he just needed a reason to meet and put me down some more. He wanted his old punching bag back so he could feel better about himself." Too bad for him he got someone completely different. *Ugh.* Seeing him that day put 100 percent closure on that whole relationship. "Although, I did do a bit of stalking. He is indeed starting a new business."

"I still don't get why you told him to come when Gabe wasn't home."

I put my hand on my chest, biting my lower lip. "I'm not sure why either."

"Gabe would have punched him into the next century. Which he deserved."

"But that's the thing. I didn't want to hide behind Gabe. I wanted to finally give him a piece of my mind, and I didn't want Gabe to have to face him. It was my issue. Somehow I felt like he would taint Gabe with his ugliness if he ever met him."

"Right, well, at least that's over, and now we know Gabe is a bit of a jealous guy."

I laughed. "Oh yeah, you could say that."

Celia removed the cucumber slices off her eyes. "Want to talk about it?"

I frowned. "Not sure. I mean, it pissed me off when it happened, but then he explained, and we made up." I blushed, not wanting to share any intimate details with my sister. "And I have to say, part of me also understands why he reacted like that. I didn't stop to think how I'd feel if the reverse were true. If I knew he'd let an ex come to the house on purpose when I wasn't here, I'd be jealous too."

"Yeah, I would *not* be chill either," Celia agreed. Then again, she was never chill.

She smiled at me. "Oh, if only I knew we'd end up here when you moved in with Gabe." She wiggled her eyebrows. "I guess that's close proximity for you, huh?"

I lifted my head. "Yeah."

She pointed at me. "You look worried."

"I just wonder what will happen after I move out."

Celia frowned, sitting up straighter on the bed. "What do you mean?"

"Well, his house is going to be ready soon, so he'll move out of here, and I'll have to find another place to live."

"Oh, I'm going to kick his ass," she said and started to stand up.

If Gabe were home, I'd jump to stop her, but he was with his half brothers this morning.

"Why?" I asked.

"Because he's asking you to move out."

"No, he's, uh... We didn't discuss it," I stammered.

"What do you mean?"

"He simply mentioned that his house was ready soon."

Celia cocked a brow, but she relaxed against the mattress. "And you didn't talk about your next steps?"

"No. He didn't mention it, and I didn't want to bring it up."

She folded her arms over her chest. "I don't get it. Why not?"

"What exactly would I say? 'Hey, Gabe, so as you know, I'm renting this attic. What's going to happen once you move out? Are we taking our relationship to the next level and moving in together, or should I move somewhere else?'" I shook my head. "I can't ask him that. What if he point-blank says he's not ready to have me move in? Or he just agrees because I ask him, but deep down doesn't want me there. I don't want to make the same mistake again."

"What are you talking about?" Celia asked. She was using one of the wet cloths I'd put in bowls between us to clean her face.

"After I broke up with Chuck, I kept trying to figure out where I went so wrong, and I think it was when I moved to Boston for him. I can't remember if he actually asked me or if I was the one who suggested it and then made all the plans."

"Diane, this isn't even remotely the same thing." She was removing her socks, wiping the mask off her feet.

"No, it's even worse. Because I'd been with Chuck for a long time, but Gabe and I are just at the beginning. So no, I won't even suggest moving in together. It needs to come from him; otherwise, I'll live in constant fear that I'm pushing too much. That's if he doesn't just outright shut me down, of course."

Celia was silent for a few moments, then spoke slowly. "Diane, I've known Gabe for quite some time. He is not like Chuck."

"I'm not implying that. Not at all. I know he's not. Chuck was a double-faced bastard." *And Gabe is everything I need.* I grabbed my cloth, too, and began wiping off my face.

"You and Chuck were together for years, and he never proposed. He never wanted to take the next step. It wasn't about you. It was about him. Gabe isn't like that. He's a decisive man."

"Precisely." He'd been so decisive with Maddox and their new property and hotel that I couldn't help but think that if he wanted to move in with me, he'd go about it the same way: straight to the point.

"Do you want me to talk to him about it?"

"God no. Why would you even ask that?"

Celia frowned. "I want to help, but I don't know how."

"Well, I made a few appointments to look at apartments on Tuesday. You want to join me?"

"Sure."

"I'd like your opinion. You know this city much better than I do."

She tilted her head, then asked, "What if you move in with me instead? I feel like this is a bad time for you to start looking for a new place, what with starting your business and all that."

Truly, it wasn't the best timing, but I didn't want to be a burden. "No, that's fine. I want my own space, especially since I'm also tutoring from home." I took off my socks too.

"Why don't you just stay here?" she asked.

"I don't want to share this space with someone else." It would feel weird after doing so with Gabe. I didn't want to room with a complete stranger.

Celia looked at me intently. "I still think you should talk to Gabe about it."

"I will, but he's got an important thing on Tuesday. I'll talk to him after we look at apartments." I wiped my feet, then looked for my sandals.

"I think he's into you. Remember how he mobilized his entire family for the tour?"

I moved next to her. Now that we'd both cleaned our faces, I could hug her. "I know. Which is why I don't want to make any wrong moves and ruin what we have."

She sighed, giving me a hug. "Damn. That motherfucking Chuck did a lot more damage than I thought. You've always been a go-getter."

"Hey, I still am!"

"And you've never been afraid to say what was on your mind."

"Not afraid," I assured her. "I'm just being cautious."

"It doesn't sound like that to me."

Chapter Twenty-Six

Gabe

"Thanks for doing this, man," I told Leo on Tuesday.

"Of course. What's the point of having one of the biggest real estate agencies in the country if not to help out family?"

"And you, too, Maddox. For wanting to invest in this with me."

"How about me? I don't get even a thanks for tagging along?" Nick asked.

Maddox and Nick were in the back seat.

"Of course you do."

"Do you have a time frame for this? A plan?" Leo asked.

I nodded. "If we like it, I want to make an offer right away."

Maddox laughed. "That sounds like my kind of plan."

"But let's see the place first," Leo replied. "Make sure it's what you need."

We arrived a short while later. The lot of land was right next to the town of Essex. There wasn't much to check out, since it was basically a field.

"And you're sure it's approved for industrial use?" I asked.

"Man, I wouldn't waste your time," Leo said.

"Just double-checking." I knew my brother was a pro.

Maddox and Nick looked around.

"It's not Stockbridge," Leo mocked, "but it'll do."

"You wanted to open a hotel in Stockbridge? How come?" Nick asked.

I shrugged. "It's a nostalgic thing. We went there a lot during the summers with Mom while growing up. But this will work. I like it."

Leo glanced between us. "Have you two discussed how a hotel and a distillery will fit together?"

"Yes," Maddox replied. "We'll make this an experience. Offer a tour of the distillery and so on."

This space was big enough, and it was close to the interstate, so all the trucks had direct access to the transportation system. Logistically, it was great.

I turned around to face them. "All right, this is legit. I vote we make an offer before Dad does."

"I agree," Maddox said.

Leo cleared his throat. "He already did, but I spoke to the seller. Asked him to wait for yours too. I might have filled him in on the kind of asshole Dad is. He agreed to wait. And if you outbid Dad by just 1 percent, he'll take your offer."

"How the fuck are they supposed to know how much Dad offered?" Nick asked.

"I found that out," Leo said smugly.

I clapped him on the shoulder. "Thanks, man. Wasn't expecting that."

"Always the best for my brothers," he said.

He told us the sum Dad had bid. Maddox and I immediately agreed to offer 5 percent more—just to make sure. Leo sent an email to the seller right away.

"All right. Let's go celebrate," I said.

As we got in the car, I checked my messages. Seeing one from Diane, I opened it quickly and got confused. She'd texted me a link. When I clicked on it, it showed me a real estate listing. Maybe she'd sent it by mistake.

"Dude, are we going or what?" Leo asked.

"Just a second."

It was a one-bedroom apartment at the end of the world. How was that even Boston anymore? I didn't get it. Why was she sending me this?

Then I saw her message.

Diane: Hey, I just found this apartment, and it's something I could afford. What do you think? I'd love an opinion. My sister says it's a dump, but I really like the rent.

I felt as if someone had punched me in the throat. *What the hell? She's been looking for apartments? Why would she do that?*

"You're angry," Maddox said when I tossed the phone in the cupholder and gunned the engine.

"You could say that," I replied through gritted teeth. "I got a message from Diane."

"She decided to dump your ass?" Nick asked.

I frowned at him in the rearview mirror.

"Oh fuck, she did, huh? Why?"

"No. She sent me a link to a shitty apartment where she thinks she can move."

"Wait, you broke up?" Leo asked. "Also, why wouldn't she ask *me* to help her look for an apartment?"

"Dude, why would she do that if she planned to dump him? Then you'd tell him," Nick reasoned.

"She isn't dumping me," I said. "She's just..."

What? I had no idea.

"The living arrangement was supposed to be temporary," I explained, trying to make sense of it.

"Yeah, but that's before you hooked up, right?" Maddox said.

"Don't you dare talk about Diane like that." What Diane and I had was more than sexual. I cared about her and wanted—no, *needed* her with me. How did she not know that?

"What's gotten into you?" Leo asked.

Maddox turned around. "Show some compassion, will you? His woman's just announced she doesn't want to live with him anymore."

That's right. My *woman. Why the fuck would she want to move?*

"I want to see the apartment," Leo declared, and I gave him the phone.

"What the fuck? This is a shithole," he said. "I can find her something much better. Wait... is that her maximum budget?"

"Probably," I said.

"Then I take it back. I can't do wonders."

"That's beside the point," Maddox said, finally getting it. He turned to me. "Why does she even want to move out?"

"That's the question, isn't it?" I was still speaking through gritted teeth. There was a knot in my throat, strangling my every breath and word. It was a completely unfamiliar sensation to me. I felt like a rug had been pulled from under me and I'd fallen into a dark hole. Why did she want to do this? It wasn't even close to downtown where she did her tours.

"You've never discussed living arrangements?" Maddox asked.

"What do you mean?" I replied. "She's living with me now."

"Right, that's now. Once you went from being roommates to—"

"Be careful," I warned.

"To being more. Damn, you're testy today. What I'm asking is, you didn't talk about what would happen further down the road?"

I shrugged. "No. Why should I? She knows we're together."

"Because that's what couples do, I'm told." That came from Nick. "Not that I'm an expert."

"Yeah, none of us are," Leo added helpfully.

"But why wouldn't you come to an agreement about how things would go? Your house is going to be ready in a few months anyway, right?" Maddox asked.

"Yeah. Two months tops," I confirmed.

"See? So it's not unreasonable for her to be looking for other spaces, knowing you'll move out. She probably doesn't want to share a space with someone else."

"That never occurred to me. We never talked about that, but I thought we had an understanding, I guess." Fuck, I was so messed-up right now.

"Should we head to the distillery?" Maddox suggested. "We can do shots."

I shook my head. "No, it's insanely busy at happy hour. We'd barely have enough space to grab a drink."

"That's a good problem to have," Nick replied.

"Then let's all gather someplace else," Maddox suggested. "You clearly need family counsel."

I pressed my head into the backrest. "No, I just need to clear my head and understand what's going on."

"Women are good at giving hints," Leo said. "I mean, I'm always oblivious, but then, when an arrangement goes to dust, one of the things I often hear is 'Oh, I gave you hints about that.' And I'm like 'What? When?' So my question is, did she give you any hints?"

I thought back to our past conversations. *Had* she given me hints? "Whenever we went by the house, she'd always tell me how much she liked it. She even mentioned how she'd decorate some of the spaces."

"See?" Maddox said. "That's a hint right there."

"Why won't she just come out and say it? I'm not good at playing games."

"Dude, what you had was casual, right?" Nick asked.

"We agreed that we're not seeing other people. That's serious, don't you think?"

"That's a committed relationship in my book," Maddox said.

"You know what? Those drinks sound good," I said. The plan was to drop off my half brothers at Maddox's. "Can we go to your place?"

Maddox hesitated. "Yes, but Mom is visiting again."

I nodded carefully. "That's great because I actually wanted to apologize to her."

There was another pause, and then Nick asked. "What for, man?"

"Last time I was not myself."

"She actually praised you for being so polite."

Fucking hell, what had she expected?

"I didn't like how I handled that," I said.

"Don't worry about it," Maddox replied.

My brothers pitched in with relationship advice and prodded me with questions all the way to Maddox's home. But I didn't have any answers.

That was the problem. They were focused on what was said or not between Diane and me, but they were missing the obvious. What if she just preferred to move out? What if she simply didn't want to live with me, and that was all there was to it? I didn't like being at a loss. All my life I knew exactly what I wanted to do next, and I went ahead and did it.

Maybe I should call the rest of the family. Since my brothers were all in relationships, they would for sure have better input than these three bozos.

Once we arrived at Maddox's place, we all got out at the same time. "How come you're still living here?" I asked. "You've been talking about moving forever."

"Because this dude keeps failing me." He jerked his thumb at Leo.

"You're my most annoying client. It's impossible to please him."

Maddox rolled his eyes. "I just know what I want."

"Why don't you build a house?" I suggested.

"I'm not getting into that," Maddox said. "No way in hell."

"See?" Leo said. "That's basically his reply to anything I come up with. It's infuriating."

I laughed, trying to put myself in Leo's shoes. Yeah, that would be annoying.

Once inside the house, Helen called out. "You boys came back early."

She stopped in the living room, and her smile dimmed when she saw me. "Gabe, hi. Nice to see you again."

"Mom, Gabe's got some personal issues he's dealing with, so we brought him here to get drunk," Maddox explained.

"I won't stand in your way, then," she said.

"I'm not intending to get drunk," I corrected. "Just a shot or something to clear my mind."

Helen frowned. "You plan to drive when you leave here?"

Leo laughed. "Mom, cut that out."

The experience was bizarre. My mom would have asked me the exact same thing.

"I'll take an Uber if I have a drink," I assured her.

"Good."

"But I'd actually like to talk to you." I looked at my brothers. "Alone."

"Sure. We'll go into the other room in the bar area," Maddox said.

"See, why the hell do you even need another house?" Nick asked. "This one is humongous."

"Are you two going to give me shit about this the whole evening?"

"Yes," Leo replied as they all left the room.

Once they were out of earshot, Helen pointed at one of the couches. "Want to sit down?"

"No, I've got too much adrenaline," I confessed. "Listen, I'll be quick. First, I just wanted to apologize for last time we met. I'd completely forgotten that Maddox told me you were here visiting. I wouldn't have interrupted your family time."

"You didn't interrupt anything. You just came by to see your brothers. I don't mind." She watched me with a kind smile.

"Second, I... well, I wasn't myself."

Her smile widened. "Maddox said you're usually very quick with a joke and very at ease with everything. Dear boy, I don't blame you for anything. It was never going to be an easy thing, meeting each other. But I have to say, I'm glad I did. I've heard so much about you and the rest of your brothers from my boys over the years and often wondered if I'd get the chance to meet any of you. Especially you because you're so close with my trio." She laughed. "I hope they haven't heard me call them that. They'd give me grief. Good God, they used to like it when they were kids."

"Thank you, Helen, for being so understanding."

"My boys told me you and Maddox are going into business together. That you're buying the lot of land your... father wanted."

My spine stiffened. "Are you in contact with him?"

She shook her head. "No. The day I found out about... well, your family... was the last time I spoke to him. I would have reached a compromise if he wanted to still be part of my boys' lives, but as you know, he never did." She took a deep breath. "I'm glad you two snatched that property from him."

"It won't stop him from trying again, but it will send a message loud and clear that Boston is off-limits." I ran a hand through my hair.

"You seem stressed."

"That obvious, huh?"

"Yes, and I don't even know you well."

"I don't know if Maddox or the others told you, but Diane and I—"

"Are in a relationship? I gathered that."

I nodded. "Anyway, she's now messaged me that she found a new place to live."

"Oh, darling, I'm so sorry. I didn't know you broke up."

"But that's it. We didn't. We just... never discussed the future. Relationships aren't my thing," I confessed. "I've always kept things very easygoing. I've never had a serious relationship. I never planned on having one. Does that make me like Father?" I asked. I hadn't even realized that I had this fear buried somewhere deep down.

Her expression instantly changed. She rolled her shoulders back, clasping her hands in front of her, and stepped closer. "Gabe, you listen to me. None of you—neither your brothers or my boys—are anything like your father. He looked all of us in the eyes for years and lied. Every word he said was a lie. Everything he did was a lie. Not wanting a relationship doesn't make you anything like him. You're all young and living your lives as you choose to. Have you ever lied to Diane?"

"No. Never. It's not what I do."

"See, that's my point exactly. You're nothing like your father. If you believe one thing, believe that."

"Thank you. I needed to hear that."

She smiled. "Now, when it comes to Diane, my understanding was that you're moving into a new house soon."

I nodded.

"Have you ever hinted that you would like for her to live with you?"

"I'm not good with hints. I'm very *in your face*. I say things like I mean them. That's the same way I process information. I don't take hints. I'm so far out of my comfort zone right now that it's actually hilarious."

"But what do you want?" she asked me.

"I don't want her to move away. I don't even want her to think about it."

"All right, so you just said you're very... direct, right?"

"Exactly."

Helen smiled again. "Sounds like you know what to do after all."

A plan started forming in my mind instantly.

"Thanks, Helen."

Turning around, I headed inside the living room, straight to the bar area where my brothers were gathered. "Guys, I'm leaving."

"How about the shots?" Maddox asked.

"Not right now. I've got an idea."

"What the hell, man!" Leo said. "We were just about to call the others."

"We can still do that. Maybe they can voice message you their advice," Nick called out.

"I don't need any. I know exactly what I want to do."

The three of them stared at me almost comically as I bid them and Helen goodbye, then left the house.

Chapter Twenty-Seven

Diane

My sister groaned, lacing her arm with mine as we walked through the apartment. Frankly, calling this an apartment was a bit of a stretch. It was more of a cubicle with two windows. It was just one room, which wouldn't be a problem. The bathroom was separate—sort of. It only had a wall. It didn't seem to have any ventilation, and I was certain there were mold issues.

"You can't move here." There were five other people here to see it, which was why Celia and I were whispering under our breaths.

"The price is great," I said.

"But the place sucks."

"Let's try to put a positive spin on it."

She cocked a brow. "The view outside is of trash cans."

She was right. It was on the ground floor, and the bins were right in front of the window.

"I can put some flowers on the windowsill, and then I won't see them."

"I bet that when you open the window, a fantastic aroma will filter in."

I nearly gagged. Shit, I didn't think about that, but she was right.

"I can use the other window too. As a plus, it has a fully equipped kitchen," I said.

"That's true," Celia conceded, "but you'll have, like, zero space to put a bed and a couch."

"I'll just buy a pullout."

"They're terrible to sleep on."

"Hey, I didn't bring you here to be a grinch."

"No, I'm just being the voice of reason," she said.

"Can you be my champion?"

She smiled, and I was certain she'd say yes, but then her smile fell. "No, because that right there is black mold, and over my dead body will you move in here."

I sighed, turning around and inspecting the crack in the ceiling she was pointing at. Yep, that was definitely black mold. "Fine. Let's go to the next appointment."

I'd texted Gabe with pictures of the earlier apartment we saw and this one, but he hadn't said a word.

"Let me know what you guys decide," the realtor said. "We've got another group coming to see the place in five minutes." His smile was polite, but his words clearly indicated he wanted us to vacate the premises.

"Sure, we'll be out of your hair," I said.

I glanced around a bit at the others looking to rent here. No one seemed impressed with the place, but I bet they were still considering it because the rent really was great.

As we stepped out, my sister said, "Hit me with what you've got."

I showed her the rest. "Two more." The next one was in the same neighborhood.

"The next place isn't far away." She pinched her nose, looking around.

"Please stop being like that."

"I'm trying, but this is a depressing neighborhood."

That's because it wasn't really a residential area, more of a commercial one with only a few units used for apartments.

"I'd only be here for a short while till I get back on my feet."

She sighed, taking my arm. We arrived at the next apartment twenty minutes later. My palms were sweaty as we walked to the front door. This one was on the ground floor too. I discovered they were the cheapest options, probably because there were always problems with the view or the lighting.

I knocked, but there was no answer. I put my ear to the door. There were no voices inside.

"The realtor isn't here yet," I said.

"Uh-huh."

I glanced at my sister. She was typing on her phone. "Shit, you need to go already?"

"No, no," she said a bit too quickly.

"Okay." I peered through the window. There wasn't much to see because there were bars on it. "From what I can tell, the place isn't too bad. I wonder if I can get the landlord to take out the bars."

"I think they're there for protection," she said, "which doesn't bode well for the neighborhood, if I'm honest. But let's see. Maybe the inside will win me over."

I smiled. "You finally decided not to be a grinch anymore."

She smiled, and it seemed almost a bit guilty. I took some more pictures and sent them to Gabe.

"I don't know why he's not answering," I said as I stood on my tiptoes, trying to make out what that huge shadow next to the fridge was. Just a trick of the light?

"Well, you did say he was busy," Celia said.

"I know."

I'd actually wanted to wait and talk about this with him tonight, but I got ahead of myself. A small part of me was hoping that I'd send him this and he'd be like "Are you crazy? We're moving in together." But he hadn't said that at all, which just reinforced my belief that I'd done a good thing by not bringing it up myself. I wasn't sure I'd recover if he told me to my face that he didn't want to move in with me.

I startled when my phone rang. I took it out, holding my breath. *This has to be Gabe.*

It wasn't.

"Oh crap. I think this is the realtor." I immediately answered. "Hello?"

"Hi. I'm so sorry I forgot to call. I've been meaning to cancel the appointment."

My stomach sank. "But we're already here."

"I'm very sorry you wasted your time. Listen, the reason I've wanted to cancel is because there's water damage. A pipe broke near the fridge, I'm told."

I groaned. "That would explain that dark shadow next to it."

"Between you and me, I wouldn't advise you to take the place right now. Let's wait and see if the landlord fixes it."

"Right," I said through gritted teeth. "Thank you for calling me."

After hanging up, I turned to my sister. She was smiling from ear to ear.

I narrowed my eyes at her. "All right. I know I told you not to be a grinch, but this is plain weird."

"Nah, I'm just happy that you don't have to live in this shithole. This is me being very, very supportive. Come on, let's go get ice cream."

I laughed. I didn't have anything else planned, so why not?

Her phone beeped again.

"Who keeps texting you?" I asked.

"No one."

I chuckled to myself. *Right.* I was betting she was seeing someone. My sister was always a bit secretive with her relationships in the beginning.

"All right, change of plans," Celia said. "I actually need to go already."

"Oh, okay. I can have ice cream by myself."

"Or... why don't you buy your favorite Ben and Jerry's and eat it at home?"

I stared at her. "Is there a reason you're trying to get me home?"

"Well, yeah. I need to get out of this neighborhood. It's depressing. And besides, I have a feeling you'll get good news soon."

"Well, I did write to a few more realtors, so maybe something will pan out."

"Exactly," Celia said, but she looked distracted. She was definitely seeing someone new.

I was thrilled for her. My sister was going on a date, and I was going to have one as well with Ben and Jerry.

Gabe

My first stop was at Target. I needed some markers and huge sheets of paper.

Thirty minutes later, I turned onto my street, parking a few feet ahead of the gate as I didn't want Diane to see me. This had to be a surprise. I'd already written on the posters in the parking lot at Target, so I had everything prepped and ready to go.

Here goes nothing.

I kept the paper rolls under my arm, and as I entered the foyer, I checked the downstairs rooms. They were empty.

She must be in the attic.

I jogged up the staircase, feeling ridiculous with the awkward posterboard.

I realized I'd been too quick to judge that dude in her favorite movie—I totally forgot the name. I'd called him a coward for writing stuff on the paper instead of telling her how he felt, but now I understood. Somehow, it was easier to write things down.

I knocked at the door, and she immediately opened it. Her jaw dropped, and then it closed again when I put my finger in front of my lips. I took the sheets of poster from under my arm and held up the first one.

It said **I love you**.

She covered her mouth with one hand.

I put that one down.

I don't want you to move away to an apartment or anywhere.

The next one said **Unless it's with me in our new home where you can...** The paper hadn't been big enough for the whole message, so I lowered it, revealing the final one.

Bring in your reading chair and anything else you want.

She put both hands on her cheeks, splaying her fingers wide as she smiled from ear to ear. I put the papers down.

"I can't believe you did this," she exclaimed.

"I can't believe you want to move away," I said, my voice almost a growl.

I stepped forward, putting an arm around her waist. She immediately laced her hands behind my neck. I loved that her instinct when I brought her closer was to pull me even closer still.

"Your house is almost ready," she murmured. "And we never..."

"I know that, but I love you, and I want you to move in with me."

She smiled before hiding her face in my neck. "I kind of got that from the posters. That was so amazing. You *did* like the movie. I will forever remember this moment."

"Good, because so will I. I wasn't kidding, Diane. I not only don't want you to move away—" I pulled back because I wanted to look at her. "—I want us to live together. I know we're not good at talking, but we'll deal with that in due course. We need to talk in detail about what we want from each other, what we expect, what we dream about. But we'll do that together."

"Together," she agreed, nodding. "Gabe, I can't believe this. I'm so in love with you, I didn't even know what to do with myself. And I tried to gauge where this was going."

"Yeah, babe. One thing about me? I'm not good with hints—picking up on them, giving them, none of that. So one of the first things," I said, taking her hand and kissing the back of it before putting it back on my neck, "is that when you want us to talk about something, don't beat around the bush."

"Be direct. Got it," she replied.

"That sounds great."

She pressed her hands into my shoulders and lifted herself onto her toes. I smiled when she brought her lips to mine, and I captured her mouth. This kiss was exactly what I needed.

She pulled back. "Oh wait, we didn't talk. How was that property you saw?"

"It was amazing, but I can fill you in later. Right now, I need you to surrender to me completely, Diane."

She bit her lower lip and sucked in her breath, then simply nodded.

I kissed her again, holding her hands behind her back with one of mine, as if she was in cuffs. But I wanted her hands all over me, so I quickly let go.

As if sensing what I craved, she brought her hands to my shirt. I paused kissing her, and she pulled my shirt over my head. She only had on some sort of pj's, and I immediately yanked off her top and then pushed her bottoms down. She wasn't wearing panties. *Perfect.* I nudged her pussy, but she swatted my hand away.

"No, I want you naked first," she said.

"Deal," I replied as she undid my belt buckle and pushed down my jeans. Then I helped her get rid of the rest of my clothes because it was faster between the two of us. When I was completely naked, I took a step back, watching her. She was absolutely exquisite, and she was mine.

I looked around, and she narrowed her eyes, laughing. "Not much of a choice, huh?"

She had a single bed. I'd forgotten that.

But the desk looked good.

I gripped her hips, walking her backward toward it, then ran my hands up to her breasts. Her nipples perked up under my thumbs. Her responsive body was driving me crazy. She was meant for me, made for me and only me forever.

I stopped when we reached the desk, perching her on top and then moving my hands farther down, parting her legs. I stroked her pussy with two fingers, rubbing them slowly up and down. She pinched her eyes closed.

"How can you turn me on so fast?"

My cock pulsed at her words.

"Because that's what we do to each other, Diane. We're made for each other."

I kissed around her breasts and down in an *S*, not a straight line, because I wanted to take her by surprise. I parted her legs even wider as

I went down, then put both her thighs on my shoulders. Her pussy was right in front of my face.

"I can never get enough of you naked," I said.

She sucked in her belly, turning completely red in her cheeks. I teased her with the tip of my tongue, running it from her clit down to her entrance. I didn't dip it in but rather slid it back up. She shuddered; I repeated the motion. She moaned, and I did it again. A groan tore through her, and she pressed her legs together against my ears. I started suckling her clit and then moved down again. She braced herself, clasping her hands at the edge of the table, probably thinking I was going to go back up again, but this time I pushed in my tongue, and she groaned even more powerfully than before. It rocked her body; I felt it deep inside my own skin.

Then I pressed the flat of my tongue on her pussy, sucked in her clit, and slid one finger inside her, making a "come here" motion. She was going to come like this; I was going to make sure of it. I watched her intently, and the second she jerked her hips forward while touching her right breast, I knew she was ready for a second finger. I pulled the one I'd already inserted out and then gave her two, doing the same motion as before, and she threw her head back, groaning loudly. I'd never heard her sound so completely unrestrained.

I needed to take her away from here. I wanted to rock her world. This desk wasn't going to do, much less her bed, but there was no way we were going to make it downstairs.

I took her legs off my shoulders and rose to my feet. Slowly, I kissed a trail up her body until I reached the base of her neck. She dropped her head back even more, giving me access. I felt her pulse under my lips as I kept moving upward.

I captured her mouth at the same time as I pulled her ass even farther to the edge of the desk. Positioning the tip of my cock at her entrance,

I nudged her clit again, and she shuddered in my arms. Instinctively, I knew I could make her come for a second time before I slid inside her. She was so sensitive that it would only take a few strokes of her clit. I moved deliberately, even as energy pulsed through me. But my need for her took over, and I entered her instead. She spasmed the next second.

Fuck yes, this is glorious.

She came wildly, squeezing me tighter and tighter until I could barely stand from the sensations. I moved in and out while she still spasmed around me. How was pleasure like this even possible?

When she calmed down, I slowed my pace and kissed her, nudging her tongue with mine. She was different after climaxing, her entire body going soft. Even her mouth felt soft.

I pulled back a bit, drawing the tip of my tongue over her lower lip and then the upper one. She squeezed her inner muscles, and I had my answer. She was still on edge. She might have come down from her climax, but her body was sensitive enough that she would have another one in no time.

Wanting to move her more freely up and down my cock, I lifted her from the desk by sliding my hands between her ass and the wood, pushing her buttocks up in the air. Fuck yes, this was going to be exquisite. She was light enough that I didn't need help supporting her. No wall, no bed. Just the two of us. I pushed her ass up and down with my hands, lowering her deeper onto my cock every time and then faster. I kissed the side of her neck, stopping in that ridge between her neck and shoulder, then back up, covering her neck and jawline with kisses.

"Your mouth. I want your mouth," I said when I was close, and she kissed me.

I let her take control of the kiss while I moved us at the pace we both needed. I loved being buried inside her like this. She pressed her heels to the sides of my body but couldn't get a good grip. She whimpered against my mouth.

"Gabe, please," she begged.

I knew what she needed. She wanted to be able to move as well. I couldn't deny her request. I wanted this to be world-shattering for her, too, not just for me. I went to that tiny one-person bed and sat down on it. With a groan, she put both hands on my shoulders. I pressed my palms into the mattress and thrust my hips up and down. We were madly chasing the high.

I knew from the first bolt of heat that went from deep in my balls to the tip of my cock that this was going to be unlike any other orgasm I'd ever had. It wasn't because of the position or because we were both so turned on. It was because of everything we'd shared before and everything we planned to share.

Her cry of relief was muffled at first, but then she took her mouth from mine, gasping for air and crying out loud, filling the room with her sounds. I drank them all up, and then I joined her, giving in to my own release. It was even more earth-shattering than I'd expected, taking over my entire body, all my senses. Every cell of my body felt alive.

I was burning for this woman, and I didn't hold back in the slightest. I wanted to make her mine for our whole lives.

Chapter Twenty-Eight
Diane

"Are you sure you want us to build it today? I mean, I can wait for the movers next week," I said, but I sounded unconvincing even to my own ears. It was our second day in the new home.

Gabe smiled. "Come on, look at your face. You're dying to see it finished, aren't you?"

I smiled sheepishly. "Yeah, so I can finally put all of my books in it."

"Then let's work on it together."

We'd turned that alcove where we first got down and dirty into a reading corner. As far as I was concerned, it was truly the perfect use for it. I'd put my reading chair here first thing, but now I pushed it to the wall so we had enough space to assemble the bookcase.

It was relatively straightforward, thank goodness. Nothing like my usual Ikea furniture; large parts of it were prebuilt. It had been delivered in a huge, heavy package, but Gabe had managed to carry it upstairs. I'd done nothing but observe that sexy ass moving up the stairs and those muscular arms bulging with the effort.

I was so giddy that I could barely focus. I'd moved with Gabe into our home, and it was amazing.

Leo had found new tenants for the lease across the road easily enough. The landlady had grumbled but eventually accepted. Gabe insisted he had no problem paying for another six months for both of us in case Leo didn't find anyone, but I put my foot down. I didn't want to take advantage of him. I liked being independent.

My business was off to a fantastic start. I was booked solidly about four days a week. I was still tutoring on the side, though, because I didn't want to let go of that income. I also kept tabs on Chuck because I couldn't help myself. And because it was easy, since he kept posting regularly on LinkedIn. His new business turned to dust before it even took off. Apparently he came up with a software idea... that infringed on another company's patent. They threatened with a lawsuit, so he had to close down. I was *trying* to be the bigger person and not rejoice, but part of me believed he simply got what he deserved. That chapter of my life was completely over, and I was looking forward to the one Gabe and I were starting now.

We worked side by side for an hour. If I was honest, he was working more than me, as this wasn't exactly a two-person kind of job. I gave him the tools when he asked for them and gladly drank up all his sexy muscles.

He looked at me with a cheeky smile when he finished. "Come on. Go get your books. I know you're dying to."

I grinned, nodding. "Yes, I am."

We'd put the boxes near the staircase, so all I had to do was open them and bring over the stacks of books. I first took out my gorgeous fantasy paperbacks, putting them in the middle row. Then my decorative candle that would separate the dark fantasy from the light fantasy, which went on the other side. I'd even bought new candles that would fit the room. I got the approval of the designer.

I put the romance section on the lowest level. I had a mix of man-chest and flower covers, and I arranged them so you couldn't see the semi-nudes unless you looked closely. I wasn't at all ashamed of them, but no need to offend anyone.

I grabbed a candle, and when I was about to put it on the shelf, I realized there was something else there already.

Huh? Is that another candle?

No, wait, it's a velvet box.

I stilled. Gabe was right in front of me.

I pointed at the small box. "Did you put that there?" I asked.

"Yes," he said. Then, before I realized what was happening, he kneeled. He opened the little box but left it on the shelf, holding both my hands.

I glanced at the ring. I loved it. It was a dark blue stone in a rhombus shape.

"Diane, I'm the luckiest man to be here with you today. I told you less than a month ago that I'm not good with hints or subtext; I say things the way I mean them."

I took the ring box, opening it even wider. In the light streaming from the window behind Gabe, the stone was even more beautiful.

"I want to ask you, here today, next to the books you love so much, in your new reading corner, to be my wife. I want to be your man for the rest of our lives, to love you and cherish you. I want to come home to you every night and enjoy our life together. Always."

I nodded. "Always. God, Gabe, I'd love that. I'd love to be your wife."

He kissed my hand but didn't slide the ring on yet. "I promise to always take care of you, to get better at pretending I don't see you stealing my food."

I giggled but covered it with my hand. I wanted to hear everything he had to say.

"And I'll pay attention to all of your superstitions. And I solemnly swear that I will never, ever cook without following a recipe. I promise to watch all your Christmas movies with you, come November and December."

I bit my lower lip and laughed nervously. "Just so you know, sometimes I start watching them in October, but I'm willing to compromise."

He laughed. "Compromise, huh?"

I smiled widely. "Well, then... how can I not marry you when you're making such a great case?"

This time he did put the ring on, then rose to his feet. I put my hands on his chest because that way I could look at both the man and the ring. I would admire the two of them until the end of time.

"I wanted to ask you here, in this place where I first realized I could never resist you. I can't wait for our life together to start."

"Hasn't it already?" I murmured.

"Okay, then I can't wait to start our life together as an engaged couple and then later husband and wife."

I smiled. "Thinking ahead already?"

"You know what I mean. I designed this place thinking I'd be here alone, but now it's the two of us. And I want you to be happy here. This is your home too. And one day, it will be the home of all our kids as well."

My heart leaped in my chest. I felt absolutely giddy.

"I can't wait for that day," I whispered.

"I can't wait either. I'll watch you in the evening, reading in your corner while I work out."

"Let's make a deal. You can only work out when I'm watching you."

He grinned. "You can talk me into a lot right now. You have no idea how happy you've made me. How deeply you've changed everything I've stood for, everything I believed in." He shook his head lightly, closing his eyes for a moment and then opening them again. "I didn't think what we have existed for anyone, except perhaps my grandparents."

"And your brothers."

He kissed both of my hands. "Seeing the others in no way prepared me for how it would feel to experience it myself. I love you so damn much."

"And I love you too," I said.

I wrapped my arms around his neck and climbed him because I wanted to jump his bones. He didn't even stumble backward. Yeah, tree was the right description for him. The man was sturdy and didn't sway. He was smiling against my lips.

"Do you think you can carry us to the bedroom?" I purred.

"Hell yes," he said.

"Thank God the stairs aren't tricky like that damn spiral staircase."

"I can't say I'm sorry about those stairs. It helped my case a lot."

He laughed and kissed my neck, jostling me up the stairs before stepping inside the master bedroom. It was huge and full of light.

"I can barely believe that I'm here with you. I want to pinch myself."

He smiled wolfishly. "I have an idea how to convince you that this is real, fiancée. It's so much better than pinching. That I promise."

Epilogue

Gabe

September

"I'm so happy you could all make it here," I said. "Welcome."

There was nothing to see on our newly acquired Essex property yet, but Maddox and I decided to show it to the family anyway. Grandmother was smiling and looking around. She'd been happy with the news that Maddox and I were starting a business together. She didn't even scoff when I informed her that I was having this picnic catered.

A team from Essex had set up everything for us already. They'd brought chairs and tables too. The entire family was here, including Celia and Kate, their mom. Diane was next to them, and I headed in their direction as everyone started to eat. Maddox and I invited Helen too—together—but she'd declined, insisting she wouldn't feel comfortable attending a family event.

"I'm so glad you came for the occasion," I told Kate, putting an arm around Diane's waist. My fiancée. *Fuck yes.*

"I couldn't miss this opportunity," she said. "And besides, we have a wedding to plan."

Diane smiled from ear to ear. I liked seeing her like this, so exuberant. "Mom had so many great ideas," she said. "I'll run them by you later."

"You don't have to. Just do whatever makes you happy."

"Oh, see, that is a fine man," Celia said.

Kate trained her gaze on me. "Gabe, are you really serious about that? Because I have some outlandish ideas at the back of my mind that I haven't even shared with Diane yet."

"Mom, what do you mean? The ones you suggested are already outlandish." Diane looked at me. "Swans might be involved."

I laughed. Okay, that was a bit more than I'd imagined, but why the hell not? It made my woman happy, and that was all that mattered.

"Come on, let's go to the table," I said. "I want to toast with everyone."

The waiters had already put flutes of champagne in front of everyone. Ben was fussing, and Penny was trying to keep him from grabbing the flute in front of her.

"He's so cute, isn't he?" Diane said, following my gaze.

"Damn right." I kissed the side of her head. "Can't wait for us to have one of our own."

She just smiled sheepishly, looking up at me. "Neither can I."

That took me by surprise, but it was a good one. "But a few weeks ago, you said—"

"I know."

I'd brought it up, asking when she'd like us to start trying, and she'd replied that she'd like to wait until her business was in a more stable place. She was doing incredibly well. Diane's tours were among the highest rated in the city, and she was constantly looking to expand, even offering day tours out of Boston to Salem. The only downside was that she was now working almost seven days a week. She'd finally agreed to drop the tutoring so she could rest in her time off. I was very proud of her.

"But if there is one thing I've learned since meeting you, it's that wanting everything to happen on a certain timeline isn't the best idea. Sometimes the best things happen unexpectedly."

"Fuck yes, they do," I said. I kissed her earlobe and then farther down her neck.

She sucked in a breath. "Gabe! Your family is here."

"I know. It's the only reason I'm not throwing you over my shoulder and taking you someplace so we can make out alone."

I couldn't wait to be a father. I'd never thought I'd feel this way, but I was so damned ready to build a life with this amazing woman.

We headed to the table and each took a flute of champagne. I tapped the side of mine with a fork and got everyone's attention. "Thank you all for coming here."

"We wouldn't miss this," Colton said.

"Today marks a new era in the Whitley family." I clinked my glass with Maddox, who winked at the group.

"We're going to continue building on the legacy," he said. "One we'll all be proud of."

"I have no doubt," Grandfather said.

"Hear, hear," Grandmother added.

"You two are a powerhouse," Colton said.

That was high praise coming from him, considering his relationship with Maddox and the rest of our half brothers wasn't always as good as now.

"And as always," Jake added, "if you're in need of any support, let us know."

"How come you all decided on Essex after all?" Natalie asked.

"Yeah, I was about to ask that too," Spencer added, taking Ben from Penny. "You mentioned something about Stockbridge at some point."

I exchanged a glance with Leo and Maddox. We hadn't told the others about the whole business with Dad. There was no point. We'd averted a crisis, and he'd fucked off back to Sydney. Maddox insisted that Dad had made no attempt whatsoever to contact him, even after finding out we'd bought the property. But I could tell that keeping an eye on him was taking a toll on my brother, so I'd offered to do it. Leo, Nick, and I were monitoring his moves in case he didn't get the message and wanted to look for other business opportunities in the Boston area.

I, for one, hoped he started something in Australia. I wanted him to do well—but away from us.

"This showed up," I replied, "and it's a great property."

"Oh, I'm so proud of you," Grandmother said. "You built a new home and found this wonderful lady."

Diane simply melted against me. I kissed the side of her head and then fake-whispered loud enough for everyone to hear. "I like how I invited everyone to celebrate a business deal, but she's proud of me for finding you."

"Oh, business comes and goes, boys," Grandmother said, "but family and relationships are what endures."

"So let me get this straight. You're only proud of him, not of me?" Maddox asked.

"Of course I'm proud of you boys continuing to grow this legacy and everything. But I'll be just as proud when you come to these events with someone on your arm."

I put a hand on his shoulder. "Dude, you did this to yourself."

"I figured you'd show me some mercy considering we're here to celebrate," Maddox told Grandmother.

Leo and Nick both laughed.

"That is not how Grandmother operates," Leo said, "and you should know it."

I held my flute up to him. "And a big thanks to Leo here, who tirelessly looked up properties."

It was true. He might not have found this one, but he had put a lot of effort into checking out Stockbridge. Maybe one day I'd open something there too. I felt invincible with Diane and my family by my side.

"You know," Natalie said, "every time Jeannie sets her eyes on one of you guys, I always think she's barking up the wrong tree. And every time I'm surprised."

Meredith put her hands over Cade's and scoffed, "Well, I don't. I trust Jeannie's instincts 100 percent. So, you know, beware."

Maddox shook his head. "Not going to happen. So why don't we focus on celebrating the happy couple and our business success today?"

Even I started to laugh. Because the fact was that even when Jeannie Whitley wasn't voicing her plans, that didn't mean she wasn't working on them.

"When are you starting construction?" Spencer asked.

My brother seemed more energetic than usual. It had to mean that Ben was sleeping better lately.

"We want to acquire the property next door, too, before we start finalizing the plan," I said.

"That adventure park?" Cade said. "I saw it in passing."

"That's the one," I added. "The owner is considering the idea, but his daughter absolutely hates it."

"You spoke to her?" Maddox asked me.

"No, just with her father, but he was adamant that she's against the sale. He won't do it if she's not on board."

Maddox waved his hand. "Oh come on. I'll meet her. I bet I can sweet-talk her into it."

Diane bit back laughter, and I cleared my throat. "Maddox, that's not going to work."

"First of all, do we even know how old his daughter is?" Cade asked.

Of course he would be the one to egg Maddox on.

"I don't know. I haven't seen her, but I'd guess she has to be somewhere around our age."

"Maybe he does have a shot," Cade said.

Maddox smirked with far too much confidence.

Diane pulled back a bit and looked up from me to him. "Wait, he's actually planning on flirting his way through a business deal?"

"Yes, he is, apparently."

Maddox wiggled his eyebrows. "Just watch a master in action."

Unable to hold back, I burst out laughing. Maddox looked very self-assured, but I had a hunch that it wasn't going to work out at all the way he imagined. Cami, the owner's daughter, was very stubborn and dead set against the idea. I could picture her and Maddox butting heads, not reaching a deal.

But I wasn't going to worry about it today.

This was a great day. I was with my future wife and surrounded by the entire family, and Maddox and I were writing a new chapter in Whitley history.

Life really couldn't get any better.

Dear Reader, this is the end of the book. For a full list of Layla Hagen's books, please visit laylahagen.com

Printed in Great Britain
by Amazon

53965789R00155

DRUIDIC RESURGENCE: THE MODERN REVIVAL OF AN ANCIENT PATH

Neo-Druidry and Eco-Spirituality: The Intersection of Past and Present

D.R. T STEPHENS

S.D.N Publishing

Copyright © 2023 S.D.N Publishing

All rights reserved

The characters and events portrayed in this book are fictitious. Any similarity to real persons, living or dead, is coincidental and not intended by the author.

No part of this book may be reproduced, or stored in a retrieval system, or transmitted in any form or by any means, electronic, mechanical, photocopying, recording, or otherwise, without express written permission of the publisher.

ISBN: 9798872802518

CONTENTS

Title Page
Copyright
General Disclaimer   1
Chapter 1: A Foray into Druidry   4
Chapter 2: Core Beliefs of Ancient Druids   9
Chapter 3: The Pantheon of Celtic Deities   15
Chapter 4: Sacred Sites and Their Significance   21
Chapter 5: Druidic Symbols and Their Meanings   26
Chapter 6: The Role of Magic in Druidry   32
Chapter 7: Tools of the Druid   38
Chapter 8: Druidry and Other Pagan Paths   43
Chapter 9: Sacred Geometry in Druidic Practices   48
Chapter 10: Druidic Herbalism   53
Chapter 11: The Energetics of Stone Circles   59
Chapter 12: Animal Totems and Spirit Guides   64
Chapter 13: Advanced Ritual Techniques   69
Chapter 14: Eco-Spirituality and Druidic Practices   75
Chapter 15: Advanced Divination Methods in Modern Druidry   80
Chapter 16: Druidic Communities and Orders   85
Chapter 17: Comparative Mythologies in Druidry   90

Chapter 18: Alchemy and Transformation in Druidic Practices	95
Chapter 19: The Philosopher's Stone: Wisdom in Druidry	100
Chapter 20: Astral Travel and Otherworldly Realms	105
Chapter 21: The Druid's Path to Self-Mastery	110
Chapter 22: Theurgy and Divine Contact	115
Chapter 23: Advanced Magical Systems and Theorems in Druidry	120
Chapter 24: Syncretism and the Global Druid	124
THE END	129

GENERAL DISCLAIMER

This book is intended to provide informative and educational material on the subject matter covered. The author(s), publisher, and any affiliated parties make no representations or warranties with respect to the accuracy, applicability, completeness, or suitability of the contents herein and specifically disclaim any implied warranties of merchantability or fitness for a particular purpose.

The information contained in this book is for general information purposes only and is not intended to serve as legal, medical, financial, or any other form of professional advice. Readers should consult with appropriate professionals before making any decisions based on the information provided. Neither the author(s) nor the publisher shall be held responsible or liable for any loss, damage, injury, claim, or otherwise, whether direct or indirect, consequential, or incidental, that may occur as a result of applying or misinterpreting the information in this book.

This book may contain references to third-party websites, products, or services. Such references do not constitute an endorsement or recommendation, and the author(s) and publisher are not responsible for any outcomes related to these third-party references.

In no event shall the author(s), publisher, or any affiliated parties be liable for any direct, indirect, punitive, special, incidental, or other consequential damages arising directly or indirectly from any use of this material, which is provided "as is," and without warranties of any kind, express or implied.

By reading this book, you acknowledge and agree that you assume all risks and responsibilities concerning the applicability and consequences of the information provided. You also agree to indemnify, defend, and hold harmless the author(s), publisher, and any affiliated parties from any and all liabilities, claims, demands, actions, and causes of action whatsoever, whether or not foreseeable, that may arise from using or misusing the information contained in this book.

Although every effort has been made to ensure the accuracy of the information in this book as of the date of publication, the landscape of the subject matter covered is continuously evolving. Therefore, the author(s) and publisher expressly disclaim responsibility for any errors or omissions and reserve the right to update, alter, or revise the content without prior notice.

By continuing to read this book, you agree to be bound by the terms and conditions stated in this disclaimer. If you do not agree with these terms, it is your responsibility to discontinue use of this book immediately.

CHAPTER 1: A FORAY INTO DRUIDRY

Welcome, dear seeker, to a realm where ancient wisdom whispers through the leaves, and echoes of a time long past still reverberate in the sacred groves of the present. This is not just a journey through the pages of history, but a voyage into the living, breathing essence of Druidry. In this inaugural chapter, we embark on a friendly foray into the world of Druids, unraveling its mysteries and understanding its relevance in our contemporary tapestry.

The Roots of Druidry

Druidry, often enshrouded in the mists of time, traces its origins back to the pre-Christian societies of Western Europe. The Druids were the learned class of the Celtic societies, revered as priests, teachers, and custodians of wisdom. However, much of what we know is pieced together from fragments—Roman accounts, archaeological findings, and the rich oral traditions that have survived the relentless march of time.

Contrary to popular belief, the ancient Druids left no written records. Theirs was an oral tradition, woven into the fabric of songs and stories, passed down through generations. This has shrouded their practices in a veil of mystery, allowing mythology to intertwine with what little history we can glean from external sources.

Druidry's Evolution and Modern Resurgence

As the wheel of time turned, the old ways seemed to fade, but they never truly vanished. They lingered in the folklore, in the whispers of the forests, and in the hearts of those who felt the call of the old paths. The 19th century saw a romantic revival of interest in Druidry, colored by the era's fascination with ancient cultures. This gave birth to what we now know as Neo-Druidry—a contemporary adaptation of these ancient practices.

Today's Druidry is not an attempt to recreate the past but rather to draw inspiration from it. It is a living tradition, growing and evolving with those who walk its path. Modern Druids come from all walks of life, each finding their unique connection to the wisdom of their ancestors.

Why Druidry Matters Today

In a world where technology reigns and the disconnection from nature grows ever more profound, Druidry offers a sanctuary —a return to simplicity, to a reverence for the Earth, and to the interconnectedness of all life. It's not just about history or spirituality; it's about living a life in harmony with the natural world and recognizing our place within it.

At its heart, Druidry is about relationship—the relationship we have with ourselves, with each other, and with the world around us. It encourages a life of creativity, of balance, and of respect for the cycles of nature. In times of ecological crisis and societal upheaval, these principles provide a beacon of hope, guiding us towards a more sustainable and fulfilling existence.

Origins of Druidry: A Brief History

The annals of history are rich with the mystique of the Druids, an enigma that has captured the imagination of scholars and spiritual seekers alike. To delve into the origins of Druidry is to embark on a journey through the mists of time, where fact and folklore intertwine, painting a tapestry of a people deeply connected to the earth, its rhythms, and its mysteries.

The Druids in Antiquity

The Druids first emerge into the light of recorded history through the writings of the classical authors, such as Julius Caesar, Pliny the Elder, and Tacitus. According to these Roman accounts, the Druids were not only the spiritual custodians of the Celtic tribes of Western Europe but also their legal advisors, healers, and arbitrators. They were the living repositories of the tribe's history, poetry, and laws, a knowledge they are said to have passed down orally, shrouding their practices in an air of secrecy that has persisted through the ages.

The Druids' world was one where the natural and the supernatural were inextricable, a cosmos filled with the spirits of the land, sky, and water. Their reverence for nature was not merely symbolic; it was a profound recognition of the interconnectedness of all life. Sacred groves, often oak, were their temples, and it was within these natural sanctuaries that they conducted their rituals, worshipped their pantheon of gods and goddesses, and sought to divine the will of the forces they believed governed the world around them.

The Celtic Connection

Understanding Druidry necessitates a foray into the wider context of Celtic culture. The Celts, a collection of tribes sharing linguistic and cultural similarities, once spanned a vast area of Europe, from the British Isles to Galatia in modern-day Turkey.

While the Druids are most commonly associated with the Celtic peoples of the British Isles and Gaul, their influence and presence were felt throughout the Celtic world.

Celtic society was intricately stratified, and the Druids stood at its apex, commanding respect that transcended tribal boundaries. Their role was not merely spiritual; they wielded considerable power in worldly matters as well. Their decisions could make or break kings, and their blessings were sought for everything from battles to harvests.

Druidry's Decline and Survival

The coming of the Roman Empire brought cataclysmic changes to the Celtic world, and with it, to the Druids. Roman expansionism and Christianity's ascent marked the beginning of a decline that would see the Druids and their practices pushed to the fringes of society and, eventually, into the shadows of history.

Yet, the essence of Druidry, its deep-rooted connection to the natural world and its cyclical patterns, survived. In the folklore and traditions of the Celtic peoples, the whispers of the ancient Druids endured, carrying the seeds of a spiritual practice that would one day find new soil in which to grow.

The Historical Tapestry

As historians sift through the layers of time, piecing together the fragments left by classical authors, archaeology, and folklore, a complex picture of the Druids and their world emerges. It is one colored by the biases of their chroniclers, the ravages of time, and the enigmatic nature of the Druids themselves, who committed little of their knowledge to writing. What remains is a tapestry woven from threads of fact, conjecture, and myth, a historical puzzle that continues to challenge and fascinate.

In the end, the origins of Druidry remain partly shrouded in mystery, a fitting beginning for a path that embraces the enigmatic and the sacred. What is undeniable, however, is the profound impact the Druids had on the cultures of their time, and the enduring legacy they have left behind, a legacy that continues to inspire and guide those who seek to walk the Druidic path in the modern world.

We conclude not with an end, but with an invitation to step deeper into the verdant grove of Druidic history and practice, where ancient roots reach into the present, and the whispers of the past guide the footsteps of those who seek the wisdom of the Druids.

CHAPTER 2: CORE BELIEFS OF ANCIENT DRUIDS

The ancient Druids, enigmatic figures shrouded in the mists of time, have long captured the imagination of historians and spiritual seekers alike. Their beliefs, intricately woven into the fabric of Celtic society, form a rich tapestry of spiritual, philosophical, and natural principles that continue to influence modern Neo-Druidry. As we delve deeper into their world, it is essential to understand the foundational beliefs that underpinned their practices and how these beliefs harmonized with the natural world they revered.

Nature and the Divine Immanence

Central to the Druidic worldview was an inextricable connection to nature. The ancient Druids saw divinity not as a distant, detached entity, but as an immanent force that permeated every aspect of the natural world. This pantheistic perspective recognized the sacredness in all things, from the mightiest oak to the smallest stream. The natural world was not merely a backdrop for human activity but a living, breathing manifestation of the divine. It was a source of wisdom, guidance, and spiritual sustenance. Through their intimate relationship with the land, the ancient Druids developed a profound understanding of the cycles of life, death, and rebirth, which were mirrored in the changing seasons and the rhythms of the natural world.

The Triad of Knowledge, Wisdom, and Truth

Druidic philosophy placed a high value on the pursuit of knowledge, wisdom, and truth. The Druids were the learned class of Celtic society, acting as advisors, jurists, and teachers. They believed that true understanding came from an amalgamation of intellectual pursuit, experiential learning, and inner reflection. Knowledge was not confined to the intellectual realm but extended to a deep, intuitive understanding of the mysteries of the universe. Wisdom, the application of knowledge, was considered essential for maintaining balance and harmony within the self and the community. Truth, an unwavering principle, was to be sought relentlessly, even when shrouded in ambiguity and paradox.

The Sanctity of Oral Tradition and Memory

In the absence of written records, the Druids relied on a rich oral tradition to pass down their lore, history, and wisdom. Memory was revered, and the power of the spoken word was paramount. Bards, a subset of the Druidic class, were the custodians of these oral traditions, using poetry, song, and story to preserve and transmit knowledge. This reverence for the spoken word elevated language to a sacred art form, believed to hold intrinsic power and magic. The meticulous memorization and recitation of lore ensured that each generation remained connected to the past, forming a continuous thread of collective memory and identity.

The Interconnectedness of All Life

The ancient Druids perceived a profound interconnectedness

between all forms of life. This belief in the unity of existence extended beyond the physical realm to encompass the spiritual and ethereal. The concept of the Otherworld, a parallel dimension intertwined with the physical world, was a testament to this interconnectedness. The Druids believed that the veil between the worlds was permeable, and significant times of the year, such as the festivals of Samhain and Beltane, provided opportunities for communication and interaction with the Otherworld. This holistic worldview fostered a deep sense of responsibility and stewardship towards the land, the community, and the cosmos.

The Ethical Framework: Honor, Courage, and Integrity

Ethical conduct was a cornerstone of Druidic belief. Honor, courage, and integrity were not mere virtues but essential components of one's character. The Druids upheld a moral code that emphasized the importance of living in harmony with others and the natural world. Honor involved maintaining one's reputation through righteous actions, courage was the strength to face adversity and uphold one's convictions, and integrity required unwavering adherence to truth and moral principles. This ethical framework guided individual behavior and societal norms, ensuring that the community functioned cohesively and justly.

As we unravel the core beliefs of the ancient Druids, we begin to understand the profound reverence they held for the natural world, the importance they placed on knowledge and wisdom, and the ethical principles that guided their lives. These foundational beliefs, though ancient, continue to resonate with modern seekers, providing a timeless framework for understanding our place in the world and our relationship with the divine. As we continue our exploration of Druidry, we carry with us the wisdom of the ancients, a wisdom that remains as relevant today as it was millennia ago.

Modern Druidry: A New Dawn

As the morning sun crests the horizon and bathes ancient stone circles in its warming glow, it also ushers in a new dawn for a tradition steeped in mystery and reverence for the natural world. Modern Druidry, a resurgence of an age-old path, is not merely a revival of ancient practices but an evolving spiritual movement that resonates deeply with the challenges and sensibilities of contemporary life.

The Roots Reimagined

Modern Druidry, often referred to as Neo-Druidry, draws its essence from the rich soil of ancient Druidic tradition, yet it is not confined by it. This modern iteration is not a rigid replica of the past but a living, breathing adaptation that respects its origins while innovatively responding to the present. One could liken it to an ancient language that has evolved over centuries, its core unchanged but its expression adapted to the modern tongue.

The ancient Druids were revered for their wisdom, spiritual insight, and deep connection with the natural world. They served as advisors, healers, and mediators, holding esteemed positions in their societies. Today's Druids aspire to emulate these roles in a contemporary context, serving as stewards of the earth, seekers of wisdom, and advocates for peace and harmony.

Diversity in Modern Druidry

The beauty of modern Druidry lies in its diversity and inclusivity. Unlike the structured hierarchies and dogmas that characterize many spiritual paths, Druidry in its current form is fluid, allowing practitioners the freedom to shape their practice according to their personal beliefs and experiences. This openness has fostered a vibrant tapestry of interpretations and expressions, from those who strictly adhere to historical reconstructions to those who blend Druidic practices with other spiritual paths, creating a rich and diverse spiritual ecosystem.

Modern Druidic organizations and orders, such as the Order of Bards, Ovates, and Druids (OBOD) and Ár nDraíocht Féin (ADF), offer structured paths of study and community for those seeking guidance and fellowship. However, many choose a solitary path, finding solace and connection in their individual practices. Whether in a grove or alone beneath the canopy of stars, the spirit of Druidry thrives in the hearts of its followers.

Embracing the Modern World

Modern Druids are not anachronisms, yearning for a return to bygone days; they are fully engaged with the world around them. They embrace modern technology and science, viewing them as tools that, when used responsibly, can enhance their understanding of the universe and aid in the stewardship of the Earth. For instance, they may use social media to connect with like-minded individuals across the globe or employ scientific knowledge in their ecological endeavors, bridging the ancient and the contemporary in a harmonious dance.

One of the most compelling aspects of modern Druidry is its emphasis on ecological responsibility and sustainability. As the world grapples with environmental challenges, the Druidic reverence for nature and its cycles offers a profound framework for understanding and addressing these issues. Modern Druids often find themselves at the forefront of ecological activism, drawing from their spiritual beliefs to advocate for the preservation and healing of the planet.

Modern Druidry is not a relic but a renaissance, a tradition reborn and reimagined for the contemporary seeker. It honors its roots while branching out to embrace the complexities and challenges of the modern world.

CHAPTER 3: THE PANTHEON OF CELTIC DEITIES

In the druidic tradition, a profound connection to the natural world is paralleled by a rich tapestry of deities, each embodying elemental forces, natural phenomena, and human endeavors. These gods and goddesses form the heart of the Celtic pantheon, revered not only for their divine might but also for their intimate intertwining with the lives of those who worship them. The druidic path often involves cultivating relationships with these deities, understanding their archetypes, and honoring their presence within the natural world and the self.

Deities of Land, Sea, and Sky

The Celtic pantheon is characterized by its variety and complexity, with gods and goddesses representing the land, sea, and sky. Among them, Danu is often revered as the primordial mother, a figure of fertility and abundance, embodying the Earth itself. Her children, the Tuatha Dé Danann, are a race of deities whose stories weave through Irish mythology, each member possessing unique attributes and responsibilities.

The sea, a domain of both bounty and mystery, is personified by Manannán mac Lir, a deity of the Otherworld who navigates the ethereal mists between realms. His is a presence felt in the pull of tides and the whispers of sea-spray, a guardian of the threshold between worlds.

In contrast, the sky is the domain of the thunderous Taranis, whose voice reverberates in the crash of thunder and whose power flashes in the strike of lightning. His is a force both destructive and life-giving, a reminder of the raw, untamed energy that suffuses the world.

The Cycle of Life and Death

The rhythm of life and death holds a central place in Celtic belief systems, embodied by deities who represent these cyclical forces. The Morrígan, a complex figure often seen as a triad of goddesses, presides over war, fate, and sovereignty. Her presence is that of the raven, the carrion bird that follows in the wake of battle, and the prophetess who foresees the threads of destiny.

Contrasting the Morrígan is Brigid, a goddess of healing, poetry, and smithcraft. She ushers in the spring, her flame a beacon of rebirth and renewal. Her dual aspect as both a nurturing mother and a fierce protector encapsulates the interplay of creation and preservation.

Guardians of Craft and Skill

Druidry also venerates deities of skill and craft, recognizing the divine in human endeavors. Lugh, known as the master of all arts, embodies excellence and versatility. His prowess is not confined to battle alone; he is a patron of craftspeople, artists, and healers alike, symbolizing the pursuit of mastery in all forms.

Similarly, Ogma, credited with the invention of the Ogham script, represents wisdom and eloquence. His is the power of the spoken word, the enchantment that lies in tales well told and knowledge carefully preserved.

Harmonizing with the Divine

Engaging with the pantheon is more than an act of reverence; it is a process of harmonizing one's own spirit with the divine. Druidic practices often involve meditation, ritual, and contemplation designed to forge connections with these deities. By aligning oneself with the attributes of a particular god or goddess, adherents seek to embody their qualities, finding guidance and inspiration in their ancient myths and stories.

These deities are not seen as distant, omnipotent figures but as accessible, relational beings whose energies pervade the natural world. In honoring them, one honors the forces they represent —the fertility of the earth, the depth of the sea, the expanse of the sky, and the intricate dance of life and death. Through ritual, celebration, and mindful living, druids seek to become attuned to these divine energies, weaving them into the fabric of their daily lives.

From the primordial energies of land, sea, and sky to the intricate dance of life and death, each deity embodies fundamental aspects of existence. As we continue our exploration of Druidry, these gods and goddesses will serve as touchstones, guiding us deeper into the heart of this ancient path.

The Wheel of the Year: Druidic Festivals

In the tapestry of modern Druidry, the Wheel of the Year holds a position of considerable reverence and significance. This cyclical calendar marks the passage of the seasons through eight festivals, each brimming with symbolic import and rich in ritual. These festivals serve not only as a homage to the natural rhythms of the Earth but also as spiritual milestones that guide the practitioner through a journey of perpetual renewal and transformation.

The Festivals of the Wheel

The Wheel of the Year is segmented into eight festivals, with each festivity embodying a unique facet of the Druidic understanding of time and nature. These festivals are not merely commemorations but are seen as living, breathing events that invite participants to immerse themselves in the ebb and flow of the natural world.

Samhain (October 31st - November 1st): Often considered the Druidic New Year, Samhain marks the end of the harvest season and the beginning of winter. It is a time of reflection, remembrance, and honoring the ancestors. The veil between worlds is believed to be thinnest on this night, facilitating communion with the spirits.

Yule (Winter Solstice, around December 21st): Celebrating the rebirth of the Sun, Yule is a festival of light in the deepest darkness of winter. It is a time of hope and renewal, as the days begin to lengthen once again.

Imbolc (February 1st - 2nd): Imbolc heralds the early signs of spring. It is a festival of purification and a celebration of the returning light and life. The goddess Brigid is often honored during this time, symbolizing fertility, healing, and poetry.

Ostara (Spring Equinox, around March 21st): The balance of day and night at the Equinox brings the promise of fertility and growth. Ostara is a celebration of this equilibrium and the burgeoning life that spring brings forth.

Beltane (May 1st): This festival ignites the fires of creativity and passion. Beltane marks the height of spring and the beginning of summer. It is a time of fertility, sensuality, and the vibrant interplay of masculine and feminine energies.

Litha (Summer Solstice, around June 21st): At the peak of the Sun's power, Litha is a celebration of light and abundance. It is a time to rejoice in the fullness of life and to acknowledge the nurturing warmth of the Sun.

Lughnasadh or Lammas (August 1st): As the first of the harvest festivals, Lughnasadh is a time of gratitude for the bounties of the Earth. It is also a time of sacrifice, as the Sun begins to wane and the days grow shorter.

Mabon (Autumn Equinox, around September 21st): The second harvest festival, Mabon, is a time of balance and reflection. As day and night hold equal sway, it is a period for giving thanks and preparing for the darker half of the year.

Rituals and Celebrations

Each festival is marked by specific rituals and customs that deepen the connection between the practitioner and the natural world. These rituals often involve elements such as fire, which symbolizes transformation and renewal, and water, which signifies purification and healing. Chants, songs, and dances are also integral, serving as means to harmonize with the rhythms of nature and to express joy, gratitude, and reverence.

At Samhain, for instance, a common ritual involves setting an extra place at the table to honor the ancestors, while at Beltane, the maypole dance weaves participants together in a tapestry of unity and festivity. Yule logs are burned to welcome the return of the Sun, and at Imbolc, candles are lit to represent the growing light.

The Wheel and the Modern Druid

In contemporary Druidry, the Wheel of the Year serves as a powerful tool for self-reflection and spiritual growth. Each festival presents an opportunity to align with the natural cycles and to draw lessons from the Earth's transformations. The cyclical nature of the Wheel teaches the importance of balance, resilience, and the beauty of impermanence.

The festivals also foster a sense of community as practitioners gather to celebrate, often in groves or other natural settings, strengthening their bond with each other and with the Earth. In an increasingly disconnected world, these celebrations offer a touchstone, grounding individuals in the rhythms of nature and the communal spirit of the Druidic path.

The Wheel of the Year forms a core component of Druidic practice, encapsulating the cyclical and interconnected nature of life. Through the observance of its festivals, modern Druids not only honor the traditions of their ancestors but also cultivate a deep, living relationship with the natural world and its ever-unfolding mysteries.

CHAPTER 4: SACRED SITES AND THEIR SIGNIFICANCE

In the verdant embrace of nature, enshrined in the quietude of forest glades and the mystical silence of stone circles, lie the sacred sites of Druidry. These are places where the veil between worlds is thin, where the ancient Druids performed rituals and sought communion with the divine. As we delve into the sanctified grounds of Druidic lore, we begin to comprehend their significance not only in ancient times but also in the contemporary revival of Druidry.

The Hallowed Groves

To understand the significance of sacred groves in Druidry, one must appreciate the Druidic worldview that perceives divinity in all forms of nature. Sacred groves, often known as 'Nemeton' in the Celtic tongue, served as the cathedrals of the Druids, where natural sanctuaries, untouched by the profanity of axes, became the epicenter of worship and ceremony. In these leafy enclosures, the Druids found solace and connection to the natural world, reinforcing their belief in the interconnectivity of all life. The groves were not merely geographical locations but portals to the spiritual realm, fostering a deeper understanding of the cycles of life, death, and rebirth, evident in the ever-changing seasons.

The Resonance of Stone Circles

As we transition from the serenity of groves to the enigmatic stone circles that punctuate the landscapes of Britain and Ireland, their purpose extends beyond mere curiosity. These megalithic structures, like the famed Stonehenge or the lesser-known but equally captivating Ring of Brodgar, function as cosmic calculators and celestial observatories. Their precise alignments with solstices, equinoxes, and specific star constellations elucidate their role in marking the Wheel of the Year, a cornerstone of Druidic practice. As the sun's rays pierce through these ancient stones on auspicious days, we are reminded of the continuity of time and the ancient wisdom that sought to harmonize human existence with the greater cosmic dance.

The Wellsprings of Wisdom

Not all sacred sites are marked by the prominence of towering stones. Springs and wells, often unassuming and tucked away in the quiet recesses of the landscape, held profound spiritual significance for the Druids. These wellsprings, viewed as the abode of deities and the source of curative powers, were frequented for healing, divination, and the veneration of water deities. The practice of 'clootie' trees, where cloths are tied to branches near sacred wells as offerings or petitions for blessings, reflects the enduring legacy of these sites in modern Druidic practice.

As we immerse ourselves in the study of these sacred sites, we uncover layers of symbology, reverence, and cosmic alignment that are integral to Druidic belief. While these sites serve as conduits to the past, their enduring legacy in modern Druidry is a testament to the unbroken thread of spirituality that connects us to our ancestors. They remind us of the sanctity of the natural world and the enduring human quest for understanding our place within it.

The sacred sites of Druidry, encompassing groves, stone circles, and wells, are more than mere points on a map. They are vibrant loci of spiritual energy and historical continuity, informing and enriching the modern Druidic path. As we explore these sanctified grounds, we tread the footsteps of the ancients, seeking wisdom and connection in the sacred embrace of the Earth.

The Bardic Tradition

In the intricately woven tapestry of Druidic culture, the bards held a position of reverence and significance. Their role transcended mere entertainment; bards were the custodians of memory and the messengers of the mystical. Their poetry and stories were not just art—they were conduits of wisdom, history, and cultural identity.

The Historical Bard

In ancient Druidic society, the bard was more than a mere poet or musician; they were the bearers of culture, the scribes of the oral tradition. The bard's task was to memorize vast compendiums of lore and history, encapsulating the struggles and triumphs of their people through epic poems and songs. Their works were not merely recitations of facts; they were imbued with allegory, metaphor, and spiritual significance, often intertwined with the cosmology and mythos of the Druids.

Training to become a bard was a rigorous and demanding journey, often taking upwards of a decade or more. Aspirants would learn not only the intricacies of language and meter but also the subtleties of performance. To be a bard was to hold a mirror to the soul of society, reflecting its deepest values, fears, and aspirations.

Bards in Modern Druidry

In contemporary Druidry, the bardic tradition has undergone a renaissance. Modern bards are still the storytellers, poets, and musicians, but their role has expanded to include various forms of artistic expression. They are painters, sculptors, and dancers, each contributing to the rich tapestry of modern Druidic life.

For modern Druids, the bardic arts are not confined to the retelling of ancient tales; they are also a means of engaging with the present. Bards create works that reflect current societal challenges, weave tales that inspire ecological stewardship, and compose music that resonates with the frequency of the natural world. They are not mere entertainers; they are catalysts for reflection, introspection, and communal unity.

The Spiritual Aspect of Bardism

At its core, the bardic tradition in Druidry is deeply spiritual. It recognizes the divine essence that permeates all forms of art. Whether it is the cadence of a well-crafted poem, the melody of a haunting tune, or the vibrant strokes of a painted landscape, each is seen as an expression of the Awen—the divine inspiration central to Druidic belief.

The Awen flows through the bard, enabling them to transform the mundane into the sublime. Their creations are not just for the pleasure of the senses; they are vehicles for spiritual awakening and growth. Through their art, bards can elicit profound emotional responses, stir the soul, and awaken a deeper connection to the natural world and the ineffable mysteries of existence.

The bardic tradition is a testament to the enduring human need for storytelling, creative expression, and the communion of shared experiences. In Druidry, this tradition is not a relic of the past but a vibrant and evolving practice. The modern bard bridges the gap between the ancient and the contemporary, between the human and the divine, weaving tales and creating art that both honors the legacy of their ancestors and speaks to the heart of the present moment.

As we journey deeper into the world of Druidry, the bardic tradition stands as a beacon, reminding us that art is not just decoration but a profound expression of the human spirit, a reflection of our deepest truths, and a portal to the divine.

CHAPTER 5: DRUIDIC SYMBOLS AND THEIR MEANINGS

Symbols serve as the shorthand of the soul, a visual lexicon capable of conveying layers of meaning and ancient wisdom in a single glance. In the realm of Druidry, symbols are not mere representations; they are conduits of power, mystery, and connection to the natural world and its rhythms. Let's delve into the mystique of Druidic symbols, unraveling their meanings, origins, and their enduring significance in the practice of modern Druidry.

The Awen: The Flow of Inspiration

Central to Druidic symbology is the Awen, often depicted as three rays of light emanating from three points of light or as three dots with rays descending from them. The term "Awen" in the Gaelic language translates to "inspiration" or "essence," capturing the core of Druidic practice — the quest for spiritual inspiration and enlightenment. The three rays represent harmony, balance, and the unity of opposites, embodying the Druidic belief in the interconnectedness of all things. They are also seen as a symbol of the triad of the mind, body, and spirit, which must be in equilibrium for one to live a fulfilling life.

The Awen is not just a symbol but a state of being, sought after in meditation and ritual. It represents the divine spark of creativity and insight that Druids strive to ignite within themselves. It is a reminder of the ever-present flow of the spirit of the universe, offering wisdom, poetic inspiration, and a deeper understanding of the natural world.

Ogham: The Mysterious Tree Alphabet

Another cornerstone of Druidic symbolism is Ogham, an ancient writing system often referred to as the "Celtic Tree Alphabet." Each character or "fid" in Ogham corresponds to a particular tree or plant, each bearing its own unique spiritual significance and essence. For example, Birch, the first tree in the Ogham, symbolizes new beginnings and purification, while Oak, the king of trees, signifies strength, stability, and nobility.

Ogham is not merely an alphabet but a sacred system of knowledge and divination. Each tree's attributes are thought to carry messages and wisdom from the natural world. Ogham is deeply entwined with the Druidic reverence for trees as living, spiritual entities. The practice of Ogham divination involves casting sticks or stones inscribed with the symbols and interpreting the patterns and relationships they form when they fall.

The Triskele: The Spiral of Continuity

The Triskele, or triple spiral, is a motif that appears frequently in Celtic and Druidic art. Its three spirals are believed to represent a variety of triads, such as land, sea, and sky; past, present, and future; or creation, preservation, and destruction. Like the Awen, it embodies the principle of threes, a sacred number in Druidry.

The Triskele is a symbol of motion, progress, and the cyclical nature of life. Its spirals evoke the continuous flow and progression of time and the seasons. It also resonates with the concept of reincarnation, a belief held by some Druids, reflecting the soul's journey through various forms and lifetimes.

The Green Man: The Face of Nature

The Green Man is an enigmatic figure found in many cultures but is particularly associated with Celtic and Druidic traditions. Typically depicted as a face surrounded by or made of leaves, the Green Man symbolizes the union of humanity and nature, the life force that flows through the natural world.

He is a reminder of the cycles of growth and decay, of the eternal rebirth of nature in the spring after the death of winter. The Green Man is both ancient and ever-new, embodying the resilience and endless creativity of nature.

Symbolism in Modern Druidry

In contemporary Druidry, these symbols and others continue to play a vital role. They adorn altars, jewelry, and ritual tools, serving as touchstones for meditation and sources of insight. They are not relics of a bygone era but living symbols, evolving and accruing new layers of meaning as Druids engage with them in their practices.

These symbols bridge the gap between ancient wisdom and modern experience, providing a means of accessing and expressing the ineffable — that which lies beyond the reach of words. In the hands of modern Druids, they are keys to unlocking the mysteries of the self and the cosmos.

Druidic symbols like the Awen, Ogham, Triskele, and the Green Man are more than mere marks or glyphs. They are potent tools for spiritual exploration and growth, weaving together the past and present, the human and the divine, the material and the ethereal. They beckon practitioners to delve deeper into the mysteries of Druidry, guiding them on a path strewn with the rich tapestry of Celtic spirituality and wisdom.

Nature and the Druidic Path

The Druidic tradition is deeply rooted in the natural world, seeing it not merely as a resource to be exploited, but as a sacred, living tapestry of which humans are an integral part. Let's delve into the symbiotic relationship between Druidry and nature, exploring how this ancient path sees the natural world, interacts with it, and draws spiritual nourishment from it.

The Living Cosmos

In the Druidic worldview, nature is not inanimate or passive. It is a dynamic, living cosmos brimming with spirits, energies, and consciousness. Trees, rivers, stones, and mountains are not seen as mere physical objects, but as living entities with spirits. This animistic perspective is fundamental to Druidic practice, which often involves communicating with and honoring these natural spirits.

For Druids, every aspect of the natural world is infused with the divine. The sun, moon, and stars are not distant celestial bodies but are imbued with spiritual significance. Celestial events like solstices and equinoxes are not just astronomical occurrences but are sacred times of power and reflection. The phases of the moon guide rituals and magical workings, acknowledging the moon's influence on the natural world and the human psyche.

Sacred Interactions

Druidic practice involves a respectful and reciprocal relationship with nature. It's not a one-sided affair where humans take what they need without giving back. Instead, Druids seek to live in harmony with the natural world, taking only what is needed and offering gratitude and blessings in return. This can involve rituals of offering, such as pouring libations onto the earth or leaving biodegradable tokens of appreciation in sacred groves.

This reciprocity extends to environmental stewardship. Modern Druids often engage in ecological activism and land conservation, seeing this as part of their spiritual duty. The health of the natural world is directly tied to the spiritual wellbeing of the Druid, and so protecting and restoring nature is a sacred task.

Nature as Teacher

In Druidry, nature is not just a place to live; it is a source of wisdom and learning. Druids believe that by observing the rhythms and patterns of nature, one can gain insights into the mysteries of life and the cosmos. The changing seasons teach about the cycles of birth, growth, decay, and rebirth. Animal behaviors provide lessons in adaptation and survival. Even the patterns of leaves and the flow of rivers can hold profound spiritual lessons for those attuned to nature's subtleties.

This aspect of Druidry involves spending time in nature, not just passively enjoying its beauty, but actively engaging with it. Walking in the woods, sitting by a stream, or simply being present in a garden can be acts of spiritual communion and learning.

The Healing Power of Nature

Druids also recognize the therapeutic benefits of nature. Modern psychology has begun to acknowledge what Druids have long known: that spending time in natural settings can have significant positive effects on mental health. This concept, often referred to as "eco-therapy" or "forest bathing" in contemporary terms, is a vital component of the Druidic path.

For Druids, the healing power of nature goes beyond stress reduction or mood enhancement. It is a form of deep, spiritual healing that involves realigning the soul with the natural rhythms of the earth. This can involve meditative practices in nature, herbalism, or energy work at sacred sites.

The relationship between Druidry and nature is profound and integral. It is a symbiotic bond that nourishes both the Druid and the natural world. By understanding and embracing this connection, one can step onto a path of harmony, wisdom, and spiritual fulfillment. In a world where the disconnection from nature is all too common, the Druidic perspective offers a healing and transformative vision, one where humans and nature exist in respectful, sacred communion.

CHAPTER 6: THE ROLE OF MAGIC IN DRUIDRY

In the realm of Druidry, the concept of magic transcends mere illusion or sleight of hand; it is a profound and intricate facet of the spiritual path. To understand Druidic magic, one must first appreciate that it is deeply rooted in a profound reverence for nature and its inherent powers. The aim is to elucidate the contours of magic within Druidry, exploring its significance, practices, and the philosophical underpinnings that render it an indispensable element of this ancient yet ever-evolving path.

The Essence of Druidic Magic

At its core, Druidic magic is about connection. It is the ethereal thread that weaves together the practitioner with the cosmos, the earth, and all living entities. This interconnectedness is foundational to Druidic belief and practice, and magic is the means by which Druids engage with these connections in a deliberate and profound way. It is a practice that honors the belief that every stone, plant, animal, and breath of wind possesses a spirit—a life force that can be interacted with and respected.

Practices and Rituals

Druidic magic is not a monolithic construct; it is a tapestry of varied practices and rituals, each resonating with the vibrations of the natural world. These practices include, but are not limited to:

Visualization and Meditation: Druids harness the power of their mind's eye to envisage outcomes, connect with spiritual entities, or attune themselves to the energies of the earth. Meditation serves as a vessel for grounding and centering, essential for any magical working.

Nature Immersion: Embracing the sanctity of nature, Druids often perform rituals in sacred groves or near ancient trees, drawing on the potent energies of these spaces. The belief is that nature is not merely a backdrop but an active participant in the magical process.

Incantation and Chanting: Words are wielded with precision and intent in Druidic magic. Chants, often in the form of poems or songs, are used to raise energy, invoke deities, or manifest desires. The vibration of sound is a potent force within Druidic practices.

Symbolic Gestures: Druidic rituals are rich with symbolic actions, such as the casting of a circle to create sacred space, or the anointing of the forehead with water from a sacred spring. Each gesture is laden with meaning and intent.

Divination: Druids engage with various forms of divination, such as reading Ogham staves or observing the flight patterns of birds, to gain insights, seek guidance, or understand the will of the divine.

Philosophical Foundations

The philosophy underpinning Druidic magic is as rich and diverse as the practices themselves. A key principle is the belief in the animistic nature of the universe—that everything has a spirit and a consciousness. This belief necessitates a respectful approach to magic, where the practitioner seeks harmony and balance rather than domination or control.

Another significant philosophical aspect is the concept of *Wyrd*, often understood as a web of fate or destiny. Druids perceive their magical workings as interactions with this web, understanding that each action can have far-reaching consequences, thus emphasizing the importance of ethical considerations in magical practice.

Magic in Druidry is not an arcane relic of the past but a vibrant and living practice that continues to evolve and adapt. It is a testament to the Druidic path's reverence for nature and its dedication to harmony and balance. Through the practices and philosophies of Druidic magic, practitioners find a profound connection to the world around them, a connection that enriches their spiritual journey and fosters a deep sense of unity with the cosmos.

Rituals and Rites of Passage

In the verdant fabric of Druidry, rituals and rites of passage stand as threads that weave the past and present into a continuous tapestry of spiritual practice. These ceremonies, rich in symbolism and steeped in tradition, are the milestones and markers of a Druid's path, guiding practitioners through the seasons of the year and the seasons of life. Let's endeavor to elucidate the quintessence of these ceremonies, unraveling their significance and the transformative power they hold in the journey of a modern Druid.

The Essence of Druidic Rituals

At the heart of Druidry, rituals are more than mere formalities; they are a profound communion with the natural world, the ancestors, and the pantheon of Celtic deities. These ceremonies, whether celebrated solitarily or communally, serve as a nexus point between the mundane and the sacred, opening portals to higher consciousness and facilitating a deepened understanding of one's place in the cosmos.

Rituals in Druidry are often conducted within the sanctity of nature, in groves that whisper ancient secrets or by standing stones that have borne witness to the passage of aeons. Here, the Druid engages in a series of symbolic acts, from the lighting of candles and the offering of libations to the chanting of invocations and the casting of circles. Each gesture is imbued with intention, transforming the ritual into an alchemical process that transmutes the spiritual seeker.

Rites of Passage: Celebrating Life's Transitions

In the undulating journey of life, Druidry recognizes and honors the pivotal transitions that shape our existence. From birth to death, these rites of passage are celebrated with reverence and ritual, each tailored to mark the significance of the milestone it represents.

Birth and Naming Ceremonies

In welcoming a new soul into the world, Druids conduct naming ceremonies, invoking the blessings of the elements and the divine to guide the child's path. These ceremonies are replete with symbols of potential and protection, often incorporating the planting of a tree or the bestowal of a namesake stone, rooting the child in the embrace of nature and the community.

Coming of Age

The transition from childhood to adulthood is a momentous occasion, marked by a rite of passage that signifies the individual's readiness to assume greater responsibilities within the community. This ceremony often involves a quest or a challenge, a symbolic journey that echoes the hero's odyssey, culminating in the recognition of the young adult's place within the circle of Druids.

Handfasting and Marriage

Handfasting, the sacred union of two souls, is celebrated with profound joy and solemnity. The ritual, often conducted in the presence of the elements, involves the literal tying of hands with a cord, symbolizing the couple's commitment to intertwining their destinies. This ancient practice, replete with blessings and vows, sanctifies the bond of love and partnership, weaving it into the fabric of the community.

Death and Passing Over Rites

In the twilight of life, Druids view death not as an end but as a transition to another realm of existence. The passing over rites are conducted with deep respect and compassion, aiding the soul's journey to the Otherworld. These ceremonies often involve a recitation of the individual's achievements, a celebration of their life, and a gentle guiding of their spirit to the ancestors and the divine, ensuring that their essence continues to resonate within the sacred grove of memory.

The Transformational Power of Ritual

Engaging in Druidic rituals and rites of passage is a transformative experience, one that transcends the boundaries of time and space. These ceremonies serve as a conduit for personal growth, facilitating a profound connection with the self, the community, and the divine. Through the rhythmic cadence of ritual, the Druid is continuously reborn, shedding old skins and embracing new vistas of spiritual understanding.

In the intricate dance of existence, rituals and rites of passage are the steps that lead the Druid through the spirals of life. They are the whispers of the ancestors, the songs of the earth, and the echoes of the divine, harmonizing the individual soul with the symphony of the cosmos. As we continue our journey through the realm of modern Druidry, these ceremonies stand as beacons, illuminating the path of the seeker and imbuing the quest with sacred significance.

CHAPTER 7: TOOLS OF THE DRUID

In the world of Druidry, tools are more than mere physical objects; they are sacred conduits of energy, symbols of the craft, and extensions of the practitioner's intentions. Let's explore the various tools that are integral to Druidic practices, their symbolism, usage, and the profound connection that Druids establish with these instruments of their ancient art.

The Wand and Staff: Symbols of Authority and Guidance

Among the most iconic tools in Druidry are the wand and the staff, each serving a distinct purpose in the Druid's journey. The wand, often crafted from wood associated with specific magical properties, is a tool of invocation and direction. It is used to channel energy, cast circles, and in the directing of spells or intentions. The wood chosen for a wand might vary depending on the purpose for which it is intended; for instance, an oak wand for strength and protection, or a willow wand for healing and emotional work.

The staff, typically longer and sturdier than the wand, is a symbol of the Druid's journey and authority. It represents the world tree, a central concept in many pagan traditions, symbolizing the axis mundi, or the connection between the heavens, earth, and underworld. The staff is a walking companion, a tool for ceremonial use, and in some traditions, a marker of one's progress through the Druidic grades.

The Cauldron: Vessel of Transformation and Rebirth

The cauldron is a potent symbol within Druidry, representing transformation, rebirth, and the womb of the Goddess. In ritual, it is used for brewing potions, scrying, or as a container for offerings. The cauldron symbolizes the transformative nature of magic, the blending of ingredients to create something new, and the mysteries of the feminine divine. It is a reminder of the ever-present potential for change, growth, and renewal.

The Druid's Altar: A Sacred Space

The altar is the Druid's sacred workspace, a focal point for rituals, and a personal sanctuary for meditation and reflection. It is often adorned with items that hold personal or spiritual significance, such as crystals, statues of deities, candles, and symbols of the elements. The altar is a microcosm of the Druid's world, reflecting their beliefs, their connection to the natural world, and their spiritual journey.

The Significance of Personalization

While there are common tools used in Druidic practice, it is the personalization of these tools that imbues them with deeper meaning. Druids are encouraged to craft or find their own tools, infusing them with personal energy and intention. This process creates a bond between the practitioner and the tool, making it a unique extension of their own spiritual essence.

Tools are often consecrated in a ritual, aligning them with the Druid's purpose and energy. This consecration is a sacred act, marking the tool's transition from a mundane object to a key instrument in the Druid's spiritual practice.

The tools of the Druid are more than mere instruments; they are sacred objects, imbued with symbolic meaning and personal significance. They serve as bridges between the physical and spiritual realms, facilitating the practitioner's interaction with the energies of the universe. In the hands of a Druid, these tools become allies in the journey of spiritual exploration, growth, and connection with the natural world.

The tools of Druidry are extensions of the practitioner's will and intention. They are symbols of the ancient path walked by Druids, and each tool holds a key to unlocking deeper layers of meaning and understanding in their spiritual practice. As we continue to explore the rich tapestry of Druidry, these tools stand as reminders of the profound connection between the physical and the spiritual, the practitioner, and the path.

The Three Grades: Bard, Ovate, and Druid

In the tapestry of modern Druidry, the path is often conceptualized as a journey through three primary grades or roles: Bard, Ovate, and Druid. These grades represent different aspects of learning, spiritual growth, and service within the Druidic tradition. Let's delve into the distinct characteristics of each grade, exploring their historical roots, their roles in contemporary Druidry, and the journey through these stages.

The Bard: The Keeper of Lore and Art

The first stage in the Druidic path is that of the Bard. Historically, Bards were the poets, musicians, and storytellers of Celtic societies, revered as keepers of lore, history, and ancestral wisdom. In modern Druidry, the Bardic grade is centered around the development of creativity, the study of mythology, folklore, and the arts, and the cultivation of the powers of observation and expression.

Bards are often seen as the custodians of culture and heritage, using their skills in art and language to connect with the ancestral past and to express the sacred in the world around them. Training in the Bardic grade typically involves learning about Celtic mythology, developing artistic skills, engaging with nature through the arts, and exploring the power of storytelling and poetry.

The Ovate: The Seer and Healer

The second grade in the Druidic path is the Ovate. Ovates are traditionally associated with divination, healing, and working with the mysteries of life and death. This grade delves deeper into the spiritual and esoteric aspects of Druidry, focusing on developing skills in areas such as divination, herbalism, and understanding the cycles of nature.

Ovates are often seen as intermediaries between the physical and spiritual realms, using their knowledge and skills to bring healing and balance. Training for an Ovate may include studying herbal lore, practicing various forms of divination (like Ogham or tarot), engaging in meditation and journeying practices, and exploring the mysteries of birth, death, and rebirth.

The Druid: The Wise One and Guide

The third and final grade is that of the Druid. This stage is associated with a deeper understanding of philosophy, teaching, counseling, and leadership within the community. Druids are often viewed as wise counselors, spiritual leaders, and keepers of sacred knowledge.

The training and development at this stage involve a deeper exploration of metaphysical concepts, ethical considerations, leadership skills, and the practice of ritual and ceremony. Druids are expected to embody the wisdom of both the Bard and the Ovate, integrating these skills into a comprehensive understanding of the self, the community, and the wider world.

The Journey Through the Grades

The journey through the grades of Bard, Ovate, and Druid is not merely a process of accumulating knowledge but a transformative spiritual and personal journey. Each grade builds upon the last, guiding the practitioner deeper into the mysteries of Druidry and their own inner landscape. It is a path of continual growth, learning, and service to both the community and the natural world.

While these grades provide a framework for training and development, the journey of each Druid is unique, influenced by their personal experiences, talents, and spiritual calling. The journey through Bard, Ovate, and Druid grades is a lifelong path of discovery, connection, and contribution to the tapestry of Druidry and the world.

The three grades of Bard, Ovate, and Druid offer a structured yet flexible path for those seeking to delve deep into the Druidic tradition. Each grade represents a vital aspect of the Druid's journey, providing a framework for learning, growth, and service within the ancient yet ever-evolving path of Druidry.

CHAPTER 8: DRUIDRY AND OTHER PAGAN PATHS

In the diverse tapestry of contemporary spirituality, Druidry often intertwines and overlaps with various other Pagan paths. Let's explore the relationship between Druidry and these paths, examining the similarities and differences, and how Druidry fits into the broader landscape of modern Paganism.

Similarities and Shared Philosophies

Druidry shares several core principles with other Pagan paths, which often leads to a harmonious coexistence and cross-pollination of ideas and practices. Some of these shared elements include:

Nature Reverence: Like many Pagan paths, Druidry places a strong emphasis on the reverence of nature. This shared belief system fosters a deep connection with the natural world, seeing it as a source of spiritual wisdom and a living entity to be honored and protected.

Polytheism and Pantheism: Most Pagan paths, including Druidry, are either polytheistic, worshiping multiple deities, or pantheistic, seeing divinity in all aspects of nature. This allows for a rich tapestry of deities and spiritual beings, often rooted in ancient mythologies and folklore.

Ritual and Celebration: Druidry shares with other Pagan paths the practice of marking the cycles of the year through rituals and celebrations. These often align with the solar and lunar cycles, such as solstices, equinoxes, and full moons, and are times for community gathering, reflection, and reverence.

Distinctions from Other Pagan Paths

While there are many similarities, Druidry also possesses unique aspects that distinguish it from other forms of Paganism:

Cultural and Historical Roots: Druidry has its roots in the ancient Celtic cultures of Britain, Ireland, and Western Europe. This specific cultural lineage differentiates it from other Pagan paths that may draw from Norse, Greek, Egyptian, or other ancient traditions.

The Role of Bards, Ovates, and Druids: The structured progression through the grades of Bard, Ovate, and Druid is a distinctive feature of many Druidic traditions, emphasizing a journey through different aspects of learning and spiritual growth.

Emphasis on Art and Creativity: While all Pagan paths value creativity, Druidry particularly emphasizes the role of the arts in spiritual practice. The Bardic tradition, with its focus on poetry, music, and storytelling, is a central aspect of Druidic practice.

Interactions and Integration

In the modern context, there is often a fluid interaction between Druidry and other Pagan paths. Practitioners may blend elements from different traditions, creating a personalized spiritual practice that resonates with their beliefs and experiences. This syncretism is often seen as a strength, allowing for a diverse and evolving spiritual practice that can adapt to the needs of contemporary seekers.

For some, Druidry may serve as a primary path, supplemented by practices from other traditions. For others, Druidic practices may be one component of a broader Pagan practice. This flexibility reflects the inclusive and adaptable nature of modern Paganism.

Druidry's place within the broader Pagan landscape is both distinct and integrative. While it maintains its unique identity through its specific cultural roots and practices, it also shares many core principles with other Pagan paths. This relationship allows for a rich exchange of ideas and practices, contributing to the vibrant diversity of modern Pagan spirituality.

In the journey of spiritual exploration, Druidry offers a path that is deeply connected to the ancient Celtic traditions while also being part of the larger tapestry of contemporary Paganism.

Ancestry and the Modern Druid

In the contemporary practice of Druidry, the concept of ancestry holds a profound significance. So let's explore the role of ancestry in modern Druidry, examining how ancestral heritage and lineage influence and enrich the Druidic path.

Understanding Ancestry in Druidry

Ancestry in Druidry goes beyond the mere tracing of biological lineage. It encompasses a spiritual connection to those who have come before, both within one's family and the wider historical lineage of Druids and Celtic ancestors.

Biological Ancestry: For many modern Druids, exploring their family heritage can be a meaningful journey. It involves understanding where they come from, the cultures and traditions of their ancestors, and how these elements contribute to their identity. This exploration often includes genealogical research and learning about the historical contexts in which their ancestors lived.

Spiritual Ancestry: In addition to biological lineage, spiritual ancestry plays a crucial role in Druidry. This concept acknowledges a connection to the ancient Druids and the Celtic ancestors, whose wisdom and traditions form the bedrock of modern practices. Engaging with spiritual ancestry involves studying ancient texts, myths, and practices, and seeking to embody the wisdom of these spiritual forebears.

Honoring the Ancestors

Honoring the ancestors is a fundamental aspect of Druidic practice. This can be done through various rituals and ceremonies, which serve as a way to remember, honor, and invoke the presence of the ancestors.

Ancestor Altars: Many Druids create ancestor altars, which may include photographs, heirlooms, or symbols representing their ancestors. These altars become focal points for remembering and honoring the lineage and can be especially significant during festivals like Samhain, which is traditionally a time for honoring those who have passed.

Storytelling and Oral Traditions: Sharing stories about ancestors, whether family stories or ancient myths, is a way to keep their memory alive. This practice not only honors the ancestors but also preserves cultural and family heritage.

Ancestry and Personal Identity

For modern Druids, exploring ancestry is also a journey of personal identity and growth. Understanding one's roots can provide a sense of belonging and grounding, particularly in a spiritual path that values connection to the past.

Personal Growth: Delving into one's ancestry can lead to personal revelations and growth. It may bring to light family patterns, traits, and stories that shape one's identity and life path.

Cultural Appreciation: For those whose biological ancestry is not Celtic, engaging with Druidry involves an appreciation and respect for Celtic culture and traditions. This inclusive approach recognizes that one does not need Celtic blood to honor and learn from Celtic wisdom.

In modern Druidry, ancestry is a tapestry woven from threads of biological lineage, spiritual heritage, and cultural learning. It forms an integral part of the Druid's identity, grounding them in a lineage that stretches back through time. By honoring their ancestors, modern Druids create a bridge between the past and the present, ensuring that the wisdom, traditions, and stories of their forebears continue to enrich and inform their spiritual journey.

CHAPTER 9: SACRED GEOMETRY IN DRUIDIC PRACTICES

In the realm of Druidry, sacred geometry is not merely a collection of shapes but a profound language that speaks of the patterns and principles underlying the natural world. Let's investigate the significance of sacred geometry in Druidic practices, exploring its role in understanding the universe, rituals, and symbolism.

The Essence of Sacred Geometry

Sacred geometry is the study of geometric shapes and proportions that are considered sacred, reflecting the patterns of creation and the fundamental structures of the universe. In Druidry, it is seen as a key to unlocking the mysteries of nature's designs, from the spirals of galaxies to the symmetry of flowers.

Patterns of Creation: Sacred geometry is observed in the natural world, where its principles manifest in the arrangement of leaves, the structure of crystals, and the patterns of animal markings. Druids believe these patterns are a reflection of the divine blueprint of creation.

Cosmic Harmony: Sacred geometry is also seen as a representation of the harmonious relationships between all things. It reflects the interconnectedness of the universe and the cycles of growth, decay, and rebirth.

Sacred Geometry in Rituals and Symbolism

In Druidic rituals and symbolism, sacred geometry is used to align with the energies of the natural world and the cosmos.

Creating Sacred Spaces: When Druids create sacred spaces, such as groves or altars, they often use principles of sacred geometry. The circle, a fundamental shape, represents wholeness and infinity. Aligning ritual spaces with the cardinal points and celestial bodies, Druids reflect the geometric order of the heavens.

Symbols and Tools: Many Druidic symbols incorporate aspects of sacred geometry. For instance, the Awen symbol, with its three rays, represents balance and the flow of energy. The use of wands and staffs can also be seen as aligning with the line, a basic component of geometry, symbolizing direction and connection between two points.

Sacred Geometry in Personal Practice

For the modern Druid, integrating sacred geometry into personal practice can enhance their connection to the natural world and the spiritual realm.

Meditation and Visualization: Meditating on geometric shapes can be a way to tap into deeper levels of consciousness and the universal patterns they represent. Visualization of shapes like spirals, circles, and triangles can aid in focusing energy and intention.

Learning from Nature: By observing and studying the geometry present in nature, Druids can gain insights into the workings of the natural world and how to live in harmony with it. This practice can be as simple as observing the patterns in leaves or the arrangement of petals in a flower.

Sacred geometry is a key element in the tapestry of Druidic practice, offering a way to understand and align with the fundamental patterns of the universe. Whether through ritual, symbolism, or personal study, engaging with sacred geometry allows Druids to deepen their connection to the natural world and the intricate patterns that weave through all of existence. In this way, sacred geometry serves as both a tool for spiritual growth and a reminder of the beautiful complexity of the cosmos.

The Esoteric Traditions of Druidry

Let's investigate the esoteric traditions of Druidry, a facet that often remains shrouded in mystery. These traditions encompass the deeper, more mystical aspects of Druidic practice, offering insight into the spiritual and metaphysical dimensions of this ancient path.

The Veil of Mystery in Druidic Esotericism

Esoteric Druidry refers to the aspects of Druidic practice that are typically hidden or reserved for the more dedicated practitioner. These elements often require deeper study and a more profound understanding of the Druidic path.

Historical Context: The esoteric aspects of Druidry have their roots in the ancient Druidic traditions, where knowledge was passed down orally and reserved for initiates. This secrecy was partly due to the sacredness of the knowledge and partly as a response to historical challenges, particularly during times when Druidic practices were suppressed.

Modern Interpretations: In contemporary Druidry, esoteric traditions are often interpreted through a modern lens. This involves a blend of historical understanding, personal insight, and adaptation to current contexts, making the esoteric traditions both dynamic and evolving.

Core Esoteric Practices

Esoteric Druidry encompasses a range of practices that aim to deepen the spiritual journey and connect with the divine.

Meditation and Visualization: These practices are central to esoteric Druidry, used as tools for inner journeying, connecting with the divine, and accessing deeper wisdom. Visualization techniques often involve journeying to the Otherworld, a realm in Druidic cosmology that is home to deities, ancestors, and spirit guides.

Divination and Prophecy: Druids historically were known for their skills in divination and prophecy. Modern esoteric practices include the use of Ogham staves, tarot cards, or scrying to gain insights into the past, present, and future.

The Mystical Path of Druidry

Esoteric Druidry is deeply intertwined with the mystical pursuit of understanding the nature of reality and one's place within it.

Connection with the Natural World: At its core, esoteric Druidry maintains a profound connection with the natural world. This connection is not just physical but deeply spiritual, viewing nature as a manifestation of the divine.

The Quest for Inner Knowledge: Esoteric Druidry places great emphasis on the inner journey, seeking knowledge and enlightenment. This path involves exploring the depths of one's consciousness and understanding the subtle energies that govern the universe.

The esoteric traditions of Druidry offer a pathway to deeper spiritual understanding and a more profound connection with the natural and divine realms. These practices, while often shrouded in mystery, provide a rich and nuanced perspective on the Druidic path, inviting practitioners to explore the depths of their spirituality and the mysteries of the universe. Through meditation, divination, and a deep connection with nature, esoteric Druidry continues to be a vital and evolving aspect of the modern Druidic practice.

CHAPTER 10: DRUIDIC HERBALISM

Let's explore the green heart of Druidry and the intermediate aspects of Druidic herbalism and uncover the rich tradition of plant knowledge and its applications in modern Druidic practices, blending ancient lore with contemporary understanding.

The Roots of Druidic Herbalism

Druidic herbalism is deeply entwined with the Druidic reverence for nature. It encompasses a holistic approach to plants, viewing them not just as physical entities but as spiritual beings with their own energies and spirits.

Historical Perspectives: The ancient Druids were renowned for their extensive knowledge of plants and their properties. They used this knowledge for healing, rituals, and creating sacred spaces. Although much of the specific plant lore has been lost over time, contemporary Druids draw on historical texts, folklore, and intuitive practices to reconnect with this tradition.

Modern Adaptations: In the modern context, Druidic herbalism often intersects with other herbal traditions. It emphasizes a sustainable and respectful approach to plant use, focusing on local flora and the ethical harvesting of plants. This practice is not just about using herbs for physical healing but also for spiritual and energetic purposes.

Druidic Herbal Practices

Druidic herbalism is as much an art as it is a science, involving both practical knowledge and intuitive understanding.

Medicinal and Ritual Use: Herbs in Druidry are used for healing the body, mind, and spirit. This includes creating herbal remedies, teas, and tinctures for physical ailments, as well as using herbs in rituals and ceremonies for spiritual healing and protection. The choice of herbs is often guided by both their medicinal properties and their symbolic meanings within Druidic lore.

Connecting with Plant Spirits: An essential aspect of Druidic herbalism is developing a relationship with the spirit of the plants. This involves understanding the essence and energy of each herb, and how it can be used in harmony with the practitioner's intentions. Meditation, communication, and offering gratitude to the plants are key practices in this process.

Herbal Magic and Divination: Druidic herbalism also extends to magical practices, where herbs are used in spellwork, amulets, and divination. The properties of herbs are harnessed to amplify intentions, protect, or attract certain energies. This practice requires a deep understanding of the symbolic and energetic properties of different plants.

Herbal Wisdom in Druidry

This section delves deeper into the wisdom and knowledge embedded in Druidic herbalism, highlighting its significance in the broader context of Druidic practices.

The Wheel of the Year and Herbalism: The use of herbs is closely tied to the Druidic Wheel of the Year. Certain herbs are associated with specific festivals and seasons, reflecting their natural cycles and the energies of the time. For instance, mistletoe is particularly revered during the Winter Solstice, while Beltane might focus on the vitality of spring herbs.

Educational and Preservation Efforts: Modern Druids are often involved in educational initiatives to share knowledge about herbs and their uses. This includes workshops, written resources, and community gardens. There is also a focus on the conservation of plant species and the preservation of natural habitats, reflecting the Druidic commitment to ecological stewardship.

Integrating Herbalism into Daily Life: Practical advice on integrating Druidic herbalism into daily life includes creating a personal herb garden, ethically foraging for wild herbs, and incorporating herbal practices in daily rituals and self-care routines.

Druidic Herbalism presents a pathway to connect deeply with the natural world, tapping into the ancient wisdom of plants for healing, spiritual growth, and ecological harmony. It's a practice that encourages respect for nature, self-awareness, and a sustainable lifestyle, resonating with the core values of modern Druidry.

Celestial Bodies and Druidic Cosmology

Let's investigate the fascinating interplay between Druidry and celestial bodies, exploring how the movements and energies of the moon, stars, and other celestial phenomena are integral to Druidic belief systems and practices. We can bridge ancient wisdom with contemporary understandings of the cosmos, providing a comprehensive guide to celestial Druidry.

Understanding Celestial Influence in Druidry

The celestial bodies have always held a profound significance in Druidic cosmology. They are not only seen as physical entities but also as spiritual symbols and guides.

The Moon's Phases and Druidry: The lunar cycle plays a crucial role in Druidic practices. Each phase of the moon, from the new moon to the full moon, symbolizes different energies and aspects of life. For instance, the new moon is often associated with new beginnings and the full moon with culmination and clarity. Druidic rituals and ceremonies are often aligned with these lunar phases to maximize their spiritual potency.

The Stars and Constellations: Druids have traditionally paid close attention to the stars and constellations, using them for navigation, divination, and as a calendar. The positioning of certain stars and constellations at different times of the year signals the shifting of seasons and is often used to time festivals and rituals. The study of celestial patterns also offers insights into the deeper workings of the universe from a Druidic perspective.

Solar Cycles and Druidic Festivals: The sun's journey across the sky and the changing seasons are closely observed and celebrated in Druidry. Festivals such as the solstices and equinoxes mark key points in the solar cycle, each bearing its own spiritual significance and rituals. These festivals help Druids attune to the natural rhythm of the earth and the sun, fostering a deeper connection with the natural world.

Celestial Symbolism and Mythology

Druidic cosmology is rich in symbolism and mythology related to celestial bodies, offering a metaphysical understanding of the universe.

Mythological Representations: Many Celtic myths and legends involve celestial themes, with gods and goddesses often embodying astronomical phenomena. For example, the moon goddesses in Celtic mythology are associated with intuition, wisdom, and the feminine divine, reflecting the moon's influence in Druidic spirituality.

Astrological Interpretations: While not astrology in the conventional sense, Druids often interpret celestial patterns and alignments as omens or messages from the divine. This involves a more intuitive and symbolic approach, focusing on the spiritual and energetic implications of celestial events.

The Cosmic Dance: Druids view the movements of celestial bodies as part of a cosmic dance or cycle, which reflects the interconnectedness of all things. This perspective encourages a holistic understanding of one's place in the universe, emphasizing harmony with the celestial rhythms.

Practical Applications in Modern Druidry

Incorporating celestial elements into modern Druidic practice can be both meaningful and enriching.

Observation and Meditation: Regular observation of the moon, stars, and sun fosters a deeper appreciation of the celestial cycles. Combined with meditation, this practice can lead to profound spiritual insights and a sense of cosmic connectedness.

Rituals and Ceremonies: Celestial phenomena can be integrated into Druidic rituals and ceremonies. This might include moon rituals, star gazing sessions, and celebrations of solar festivals, each designed to align with and draw upon the energies of these celestial bodies.

Learning and Teaching: For those interested in deepening their understanding, studying celestial phenomena from a Druidic perspective can be a rewarding pursuit. Sharing this knowledge through teaching and community gatherings helps keep the tradition alive and evolving.

Celestial bodies play a significant role in Druidic cosmology and practice. By understanding and aligning with these celestial patterns, modern Druids can deepen their spiritual practice and connection to the universe, continuing a tradition that has been a pillar of Druidry since ancient times.

CHAPTER 11: THE ENERGETICS OF STONE CIRCLES

It's time to explore the spiritual and energetic significance of ancient stone circles within Druidic practices. These ancient structures, often shrouded in mystery, have been central to various spiritual traditions, including Druidry. Their significance lies not just in their historical and archaeological value but also in their profound energetic and symbolic meanings.

Understanding Stone Circles in Druidic Context

Stone circles have been a source of fascination and reverence throughout history. In Druidry, they are seen as more than just arrangements of rocks; they are viewed as sacred spaces where the boundaries between the physical and spiritual worlds become thin.

Historical Significance: Many stone circles date back to the Neolithic and Bronze Age periods. Their precise purpose remains largely unknown, but they are thought to have been used for astronomical observations, rituals, and as places of gathering for ancient communities. In Druidry, these sites are respected as connections to ancestors and ancient wisdom.

Energetic Hotspots: It is believed that stone circles were intentionally built at places where the Earth's energy is particularly strong. These sites are often located at ley lines or Earth's energy lines, making them powerful spots for spiritual practices. Druids harness these energies in their rituals, meditation, and healing work.

Symbolic Representations: Each stone circle has its unique configuration and energy, which can symbolize various aspects of life, death, and rebirth. The circular layout represents the cycle of life, continuity, and connection to the universe. They serve as reminders of the interconnectedness of all things.

Experiencing Stone Circles in Modern Druidry

Incorporating stone circles into modern Druidic practice offers a unique way to connect with the Earth's energy and ancient traditions.

Visiting and Connecting with Stone Circles: Visiting these ancient sites can be a profound experience. Druids often perform rituals, meditate, or simply sit in silence within these circles, feeling the energy and listening to the whispers of ancient times. It is an opportunity to connect with the ancestors and the natural world in a deeply spiritual way.

Rituals and Ceremonies: Many modern Druids use stone circles for seasonal ceremonies, particularly during solstices and equinoxes. These ancient sites provide a powerful backdrop for rituals that honor the natural cycles of the Earth and the cosmos.

Personal and Collective Healing: The energetic properties of stone circles are believed to facilitate healing. Druids may use these sites to perform healing rituals or to meditate for personal and collective healing, tapping into the Earth's energy for restoration and balance.

The Role of Stone Circles in Eco-Spirituality

The reverence for stone circles in Druidry also highlights a deep ecological understanding and respect for the Earth.

Sacred Geography: Understanding the sacredness of the land and its features, like stone circles, encourages a respectful and sustainable relationship with the Earth. It fosters an eco-spiritual awareness, recognizing the Earth as a living, sacred being.

Preservation and Protection: Druidic interest in stone circles goes hand in hand with efforts to preserve these ancient sites. Modern Druids often advocate for the protection and respectful treatment of these and other sacred sites, emphasizing the importance of heritage and the Earth's sanctity.

Connecting with the Land: Engaging with stone circles is a way to deepen one's connection with the land and its history. It provides a tangible link to the past and a reminder of humanity's enduring relationship with nature.

Stone circles play a significant role in the Druidic tradition, serving as portals to the past, energetic hotspots, and symbols of life's cyclical nature. They are a testament to the ancient wisdom that continues to inspire and guide modern Druidry, embedding a deep sense of respect and reverence for the natural world and its mysterious history.

Runes and Ogham: Written Mysteries

Let's delve into the mystical realms of runes and Ogham within the context of Druidry, offering a more advanced look at these ancient systems of writing and their magical applications. These symbolic scripts are not just tools of communication but are imbued with deep spiritual meanings and are integral to the practice of Druidic magic and divination.

The Mystique of Runes in Druidic Practice

Origins and Evolution: Originating from the ancient Germanic tribes, runes are an alphabet where each character holds specific meanings and energies. Over the centuries, their use has evolved from mundane writing to powerful symbols in divination and spellwork. Although not originally part of the Celtic Druid tradition, they have been adopted and adapted due to their profound spiritual resonance.

Runes as Magical Symbols: In Druidry, each rune is believed to encapsulate the essence of the forces it represents, from natural elements to abstract concepts. They are used in magical work for their power to influence and manifest change. For instance, the rune *Fehu*, representing wealth, might be used in rituals to attract abundance.

Divinatory Practices: Runes are also powerful tools for divination. Casting runes allows a Druid to gain insights into the present and potential futures, guiding them to understand the path ahead. This practice involves not only interpretation based on the symbolism of the runes but also an intuitive understanding of their deeper messages.

Exploring Ogham: The Druidic Tree Alphabet

Ogham's Celtic Roots: Unlike runes, Ogham is a script that originated within Celtic society and is closely associated with Druidic traditions. Known as the tree alphabet, each character corresponds to a specific tree or plant, reflecting the Druids' deep reverence for nature.

Ogham in Ritual and Divination: Ogham staves, made of wood or stone, are used in divinatory practices. Each stave's connection to a particular tree or plant imbues it with unique energies and meanings. For example, the *Birch* stave, known as *Beith* in Ogham, is often associated with new beginnings and purification.

A Tool for Meditation and Magic: Beyond divination, Ogham is used in meditation and magical workings. Contemplating a specific Ogham stave can help a Druid connect with the attributes of the corresponding tree, fostering a deeper bond with the natural world and enhancing their spiritual and magical practices.

Integrating Runes and Ogham into Modern Druidry

Personalized Practices: Modern Druids often develop their unique relationship with runes and Ogham. Some might use them in combination, while others may prefer to specialize in one. Their use is highly personal and reflective of each Druid's path and connection with these ancient scripts.

Educational and Spiritual Journey: Learning and working with runes and Ogham is a journey of both education and spiritual exploration. It involves studying the historical and cultural backgrounds of these scripts, as well as developing an intuitive understanding of their deeper meanings.

Creating Sacred Space: Many Druids create sacred spaces with runes and Ogham, using them to mark the boundaries of ritual circles or to adorn altars. This not only adds a layer of magical protection but also enhances the spiritual potency of the ritual space.

We have uncovered the rich and mystical world of runes and Ogham in Druidry, offering insights into their historical backgrounds, spiritual meanings, and practical applications. These ancient scripts are more than mere alphabets; they are keys to unlocking deeper magical and spiritual knowledge, serving as vital tools for divination, meditation, and magical workings in the modern Druidic path.

CHAPTER 12: ANIMAL TOTEMS AND SPIRIT GUIDES

Now we turn to the mystical connection between Druidry and the animal kingdom, focusing on the significance of animal totems and spirit guides as we explore the deep symbiotic relationship between Druids and various animal energies, unraveling the spiritual and symbolic meanings of these connections.

Understanding Animal Totems in Druidic Tradition

The Concept of Animal Totems: In Druidry, an animal totem is not just a symbol but a spiritual entity that represents certain qualities, strengths, and insights. These totems are believed to guide, protect, and communicate wisdom to the practitioner. They are more than mere symbols or metaphors; they are revered as spiritual allies.

Identifying Personal Totems: Discovering one's animal totem is a journey of self-exploration and spiritual awakening. It often involves meditation, observation, and reflection. The process is highly personal and intuitive, with many Druids believing that a totem chooses the individual, revealing itself in dreams, visions, or through recurring encounters in the natural world.

Working with Animal Totems: Once identified, Druids work with their animal totems in various ways. This can include invoking the totem in rituals, meditating on its qualities, or seeking guidance from it during challenging times. Each totem brings unique insights and strengths, aiding the Druid in their spiritual journey and everyday life.

The Role of Spirit Guides

Spirit Guides in Druidic Practices: Spirit guides in Druidry are often perceived as manifestations of animal spirits but can also encompass ancestors, mythical beings, or even elemental forces. They serve as intermediaries between the physical and spiritual worlds, offering guidance, protection, and wisdom.

Communicating with Spirit Guides: Interaction with spirit guides is a key component of Druidic practice. It often occurs during meditative states, rituals, or through divination practices. The communication is not always verbal; it can be symbolic or through intuitive understanding.

Spirit Guides and Personal Growth: Engaging with spirit guides can be transformative. They often challenge individuals to grow, heal, and understand deeper truths about themselves and the world around them. This relationship is dynamic and evolves as the Druid progresses on their spiritual path.

Integrating Animal Energies into Druidic Practices

Rituals and Ceremonies: Animals and their symbolic meanings play a crucial role in Druidic rituals and ceremonies. For instance, a Druid may call upon the energy of a hawk for clarity of vision during a ritual, or a bear for strength and protection.

Ecological Connection and Respect: The Druidic path emphasizes a harmonious relationship with nature. Working with animal totems and spirit guides reinforces this connection, fostering a deeper respect for the natural world and its inhabitants.

Personal and Collective Insights: Animal totems and spirit guides provide not just personal insights but also collective wisdom. They are seen as links to the ancestral past and the collective unconscious, offering guidance that transcends individual experiences.

Elemental Forces and the Four Directions

The mystical world of elemental forces and the four cardinal directions are central to many Druidic rituals and practices. Let's explore how these elemental forces and directions are understood, respected, and integrated into Druidic life and spirituality.

Understanding the Elemental Forces

The Quintessence of Elements: In Druidry, the elements – Earth, Air, Fire, Water, and Spirit – are seen as fundamental forces of nature and the universe. Each element represents specific aspects of life and the natural world, playing a vital role in maintaining balance and harmony.

Earth - Stability and Grounding: Earth symbolizes stability, grounding, and fertility. It is associated with the physical world, nature, and the body. In rituals, invoking the Earth element is about connecting with the physical realm and seeking grounding and stability.

Air - Intellect and Communication: Air represents intellect, communication, and knowledge. It is linked to the mental realm, thoughts, and wisdom. Druidic practices involving Air focus on the pursuit of knowledge, clarity of thought, and effective communication.

Fire - Transformation and Energy: Fire symbolizes transformation, energy, and passion. It is associated with change, inspiration, and courage. Rituals invoking Fire often seek to harness its transformative power for personal growth and spiritual awakening.

Water - Emotion and Intuition: Water represents emotion, intuition, and the subconscious. It is linked to feelings, dreams, and psychic abilities. In Druidic practices, Water is invoked for emotional healing, enhancing intuition, and exploring the subconscious.

Spirit - The Unifying Force: Spirit, often seen as the fifth element, represents the unifying force of the universe, connecting all things. It is associated with the divine, the soul, and the unseen energies that permeate all existence.

The Four Directions and Druidic Rituals

Significance of the Four Directions: The four cardinal directions – North, East, South, and West – are integral to Druidic rituals. Each direction is aligned with specific elements and energies, offering unique attributes and powers to rituals and ceremonies.

Aligning with the Directions: Druidic practices often involve aligning with the four directions during rituals to harness their energies. This alignment is both a physical act, such as facing a specific direction, and a spiritual one, involving meditation and invocation.

Creating Sacred Space: In Druidry, casting a circle or creating sacred space often involves calling upon the four directions. This act acknowledges and invites the energies of each direction, creating a balanced and protected space for rituals and spiritual work.

Integrating Elemental and Directional Energies

Personal and Ecological Balance: Working with elements and directions is not only about personal spiritual practice but also about recognizing and maintaining ecological balance. Druids see themselves as part of the natural world, and these practices reinforce their connection to the Earth and its cycles.

Rituals and Daily Practices: Elemental and directional energies are incorporated into various Druidic rituals, from seasonal celebrations to rites of passage. In daily practices, Druids might meditate on a specific element or direction to bring balance to an aspect of their life.

Healing and Divination: Elements and directions are also used in Druidic healing practices and divination. For example, a Druid might use stones or crystals representing different elements for healing purposes or use the directions as a guide in divinatory readings.

It is important to encourage a deeper understanding and respect for these primal energies, inviting Druids to harmonize with the natural world and its elemental powers.

CHAPTER 13: ADVANCED RITUAL TECHNIQUES

As we delve into the deeper aspects of Druidic practice, we look to provide an in-depth understanding of the sophisticated rituals that form the backbone of advanced Druidic practice. These rituals, evolved and refined over centuries, are not just mere ceremonies but are considered powerful tools for transformation, connection with the natural world, and spiritual enlightenment.

The Evolution of Ritual in Druidry

To appreciate the complexity and depth of advanced Druidic rituals, it's essential to understand their evolution. Initially, Druidic rituals were simple, focusing on the cycles of nature and the basic elements of earth, air, fire, and water. As Druidry evolved, these rituals became more elaborate, integrating aspects of celestial movements, sacred geometry, and deep esoteric knowledge.

This evolution reflects a growing understanding of the universe and the Druid's place within it. The rituals thus transformed from straightforward seasonal celebrations to intricate ceremonies that involve detailed preparations, specific invocations, and the use of complex symbols and tools.

Components of Advanced Rituals

Advanced Druidic rituals are multifaceted and can vary significantly in their composition and purpose. However, certain elements are commonly found in these practices:

Preparation and Purification: Preparation is crucial in advanced rituals. This can involve fasting, meditation, and purification practices such as bathing in natural waters or using sacred herbs like sage for smudging. The purification of the ritual space is also essential, often done with elements like water and fire to cleanse and consecrate the area.

Sacred Geometry and Alignment: Many advanced rituals incorporate the principles of sacred geometry, aligning the ritual space with specific patterns like the Flower of Life or the Celtic Spiral. These patterns are believed to resonate with cosmic energies and help align the participants with the natural order of the universe.

Celestial Timing: The alignment of rituals with celestial events - such as solstices, equinoxes, lunar phases, and specific astrological configurations - is a common practice. These timings are chosen for their powerful energetic influences and their symbolic meanings.

Invocation and Chanting: Advanced rituals often involve the invocation of deities, ancestral spirits, or natural forces. This is typically done through chanting, singing, or reciting specific verses or mantras that are believed to have vibrational powers.

Use of Advanced Tools: While basic tools like wands and staffs are common in Druidry, advanced rituals may include more specialized items. These can range from intricately carved stones and crystals to specially crafted ritual garments and uniquely designed altars.

The Purpose and Power of Advanced Rituals

Advanced rituals in Druidry are not merely ceremonial but serve multiple purposes:

Transformation and Healing: Many advanced rituals are designed for personal transformation and healing, aiding participants in their spiritual journey and personal growth.

Connection with the Divine: These rituals often aim to establish a profound connection with the divine forces of nature, the ancestors, or the Celtic pantheon of gods and goddesses.

Eco-Spiritual Work: Reflecting Druidry's deep connection with nature, some advanced rituals focus on healing the Earth, aligning with its energy lines, and working towards ecological balance.

Advanced ritual techniques in Druidry are a testament to the tradition's depth and its continuous evolution. These practices, steeped in ancient wisdom and adapted to modern understanding, offer a pathway to profound spiritual experiences. They serve not only as a bridge to the past but also as a relevant and powerful tool for personal and collective transformation in the contemporary world.

In embracing these advanced rituals, modern Druids continue a rich legacy, adapting and evolving the ancient ways to find harmony and wisdom in the complexities of the modern era.

Druidry and the Modern World

Druidry, with its deep roots in ancient Celtic traditions, has seen a significant resurgence in the modern era. So let's explore the ways in which Druidry interacts with, influences, and is influenced by contemporary societal and environmental issues. The focus is on three main areas: the role of Druidry in environmental activism, its integration with modern lifestyles, and the challenges and opportunities faced by Druids in today's world.

Druidry as a Force for Environmental Advocacy

One of the most prominent aspects of modern Druidry is its strong emphasis on environmental protection and activism. Druids, with their deep reverence for nature and belief in the sacredness of the Earth, are often found at the forefront of ecological movements. They bring a unique spiritual perspective to environmental issues, viewing the protection of the natural world not just as a practical necessity but as a sacred duty. This belief system aligns closely with many contemporary concerns about climate change, biodiversity loss, and environmental degradation.

Druidic practices, rituals, and teachings often emphasize the interconnectedness of all life, a concept that resonates powerfully in the context of ecological sustainability. Modern Druids use their gatherings, such as those during the Wheel of the Year festivals, to raise awareness about environmental issues and to foster a sense of community around shared ecological values. They also engage in practical actions, from tree planting and conservation efforts to participating in environmental protests and policy advocacy.

Integrating Druidry with Contemporary Lifestyles

Another aspect of Druidry's modern resurgence is its adaptability to contemporary lifestyles. In a world dominated by technology and rapid change, Druidry offers a way to reconnect with nature and find balance. Modern Druids come from all walks of life and incorporate their beliefs and practices into their daily routines in various ways. This can range from simple mindfulness practices and nature walks to elaborate rituals and celebrations.

The challenge for many modern Druids is finding ways to practice their faith authentically within the constraints of a busy, technology-driven world. Some have turned to online communities and digital platforms to share knowledge, connect with other Druids, and organize events. Others focus on integrating Druidic principles into their professional lives, advocating for sustainable practices and ethical decision-making in their workplaces.

Challenges and Opportunities in the 21st Century

As Druidry continues to evolve, it faces both challenges and opportunities. One significant challenge is the risk of commercialization and dilution of Druidic practices. As interest in spirituality and nature-based religions grows, there is a danger that the core principles and traditions of Druidry could be co-opted or misrepresented. This requires a careful balance between preserving ancient traditions and adapting to contemporary contexts.

On the other hand, the modern era presents unique opportunities for Druidry. The global environmental crisis has led to a widespread reawakening of interest in earth-centered spirituality. Druidry's message of reverence for nature and ecological responsibility resonates strongly with many people seeking a more sustainable and balanced way of life. Additionally, the increasing interconnectedness of the world provides opportunities for Druidic communities to network and collaborate on a global scale, spreading their message and influencing larger societal and environmental changes.

The resurgence of Druidry in the modern world is a testament to its enduring relevance and adaptability. As a spiritual path deeply rooted in the reverence for nature, Druidry offers valuable perspectives and practices for addressing some of the most pressing challenges of our time. Its integration into contemporary lifestyles and its role in environmental advocacy highlight the dynamic and evolving nature of this ancient path.

CHAPTER 14: ECO-SPIRITUALITY AND DRUIDIC PRACTICES

In the tapestry of modern Druidry, eco-spirituality stands out as a vibrant thread, intertwining the ancient wisdom of Druidic practices with contemporary environmental consciousness. Let's explore the essence of eco-spirituality within Druidry, its manifestation in modern practices, and the broader implications for our relationship with the natural world.

The Essence of Eco-Spirituality in Druidry

Eco-spirituality in Druidry is rooted in the profound reverence for the Earth and all its inhabitants. This perspective sees the natural world not as a resource to be exploited but as a sacred, living entity deserving respect and protection. The Druidic belief in the interconnectedness of all life forms the foundation of eco-spirituality, emphasizing that human well-being is intrinsically linked to the health of the Earth.

Modern Druids express this connection through various practices that honor the Earth, such as seasonal celebrations that align with the cycles of nature, rituals that invoke the spirits of land, sea, and sky, and meditations that foster a deep sense of oneness with the natural world. These practices are not only spiritual expressions but also serve to remind practitioners of their duty to protect and preserve the environment.

Eco-Spirituality in Practice

In practical terms, eco-spirituality in Druidry manifests in several ways. Many Druids engage in environmental activism, advocating for policies and actions that safeguard the natural world. This activism can take the form of participating in protests, supporting conservation efforts, and promoting sustainable living.

Another important aspect is the use of natural spaces for spiritual practices. Sacred groves, stone circles, and bodies of water are often the settings for Druidic rituals and gatherings, highlighting the significance of these natural sites. The protection and maintenance of these spaces become a form of spiritual stewardship for many Druids.

Furthermore, eco-spirituality is reflected in the everyday choices and lifestyles of modern Druids. This might include adopting a more sustainable lifestyle, engaging in practices like permaculture or organic gardening, and making conscious choices to reduce one's environmental footprint.

Broader Implications for Humanity and Nature

The eco-spiritual approach of Druidry offers broader lessons for humanity's relationship with nature. It challenges the dominant paradigm of viewing nature as merely a resource and advocates for a more harmonious, respectful relationship with the Earth. This shift in perspective is crucial in addressing the environmental crises facing the planet, such as climate change, biodiversity loss, and pollution.

By integrating ancient wisdom with modern environmental ethics, Druidry's eco-spirituality provides a powerful framework for rethinking how we interact with our environment. It encourages a move away from exploitative practices towards a more sustainable, balanced way of living that honors the Earth as a sacred, living system.

The integration of eco-spirituality into modern Druidic practices represents a vital and transformative aspect of this ancient spiritual path. It not only enriches the spiritual lives of its practitioners but also contributes to the broader movement towards a more sustainable and harmonious relationship with the natural world. Through its teachings and practices, Druidry offers valuable insights and tools for fostering a deeper connection with the Earth and advocating for its protection and preservation.

The Druid in the Digital Age

In the evolving landscape of the 21st century, the ancient path of Druidry finds itself intersecting with the digital age. Let's explore how technology influences and shapes modern Druidic practice, from the way Druids connect and learn to the integration of digital tools in spiritual practices.

Digital Connectivity and Community Building

One of the most significant impacts of technology on modern Druidry is in the realm of community building and connectivity. With the advent of the internet and social media, Druids from around the world can connect, share knowledge, and participate in discussions regardless of geographical boundaries. Online forums, social media groups, and websites dedicated to Druidry have become vibrant hubs of activity where practitioners can exchange ideas, find support, and deepen their understanding of Druidic principles.

These digital platforms have also enabled the creation of virtual gatherings, rituals, and celebrations. Especially in times when physical gatherings are not possible, these online spaces provide an invaluable means for maintaining community connections and continuing spiritual practices. They offer a way for those who may be isolated due to location or other circumstances to participate in the Druidic community.

Technology in Spiritual Practice

The integration of technology into spiritual practice is another area where the digital age intersects with Druidry. While the core of Druidic practice remains rooted in nature and personal experience, technology can enhance these experiences in various ways. For instance, mobile apps for meditation, guided imagery, and nature sounds can aid in creating a conducive environment for spiritual practices, especially for those living in urban areas.

Additionally, technology has made a wealth of resources readily available for those seeking to learn about Druidry. E-books, online courses, podcasts, and video tutorials have made it easier than ever to access information about Druidic history, philosophy, and practices. This democratization of knowledge has played a significant role in the resurgence and spread of Druidry in the modern world.

Balancing Technology and Tradition

Despite the benefits, the integration of technology into Druidic practice is not without its challenges. One of the key concerns is maintaining a balance between embracing useful technological tools and preserving the essential nature-based and experiential aspects of Druidry. There is a delicate balance to be struck between using technology as a tool to enhance practice and allowing it to overshadow the fundamental principles of connection with nature, personal introspection, and experiential learning.

Druids in the digital age are tasked with navigating this balance, finding ways to use technology that support and enhance their practice without detracting from the core values of Druidry. This may involve setting boundaries around technology use, consciously choosing when and how to engage with digital tools, and always prioritizing direct experience and connection with the natural world.

The intersection of Druidry and the digital age offers both opportunities and challenges. Technology has played a crucial role in the spread and evolution of modern Druidry, offering new ways to connect, learn, and practice. However, maintaining the essence of Druidry in an increasingly digital world requires a conscious effort to balance the use of technology with the traditional, nature-centered focus of the path. As Druidry continues to evolve, this balance will be key to preserving its integrity and relevance in the modern world.

CHAPTER 15: ADVANCED DIVINATION METHODS IN MODERN DRUIDRY

Divination, the practice of seeking knowledge of the future or the unknown by supernatural means, has been a cornerstone of Druidic practices since ancient times. In modern Druidry, advanced divination methods have evolved, integrating traditional techniques with contemporary insights. Let's explore these advanced methods, their significance, and their application in the modern Druidic path.

The Evolution of Druidic Divination

Historically, Druids were known for their skill in divination, which was used for guidance, decision-making, and understanding the will of the divine. Ancient methods included augury (interpreting the flight patterns of birds), omens, and the casting of lots using objects like stones or bones. Over time, these practices have evolved, incorporating elements from various cultural and spiritual traditions.

In modern Druidry, divination is not seen as mere fortune-telling but as a deep and meaningful practice that connects the practitioner with the natural world and the deeper currents of life.

It involves interpreting signs and symbols not just to predict the future, but to gain insight into the present and to understand the interplay of various forces and energies at work.

Contemporary Techniques in Druidic Divination

Modern Druids employ a variety of advanced divination methods, each with its unique symbolism and methodology. Some of the most prominent techniques include:

Ogham Divination: Ogham is an ancient alphabet, where each character is associated with a specific tree or plant. Modern Druids use Ogham for divination by carving or drawing these characters on pieces of wood or stone, casting them, and interpreting their arrangement and orientation.

Geomancy: This method involves interpreting patterns formed by tossed handfuls of soil, rocks, or sand. In a contemporary setting, this can also be done using specially marked dice or randomly generated dots on paper.

Tarot and Oracle Cards: While not originally part of ancient Druidic practices, many modern Druids use Tarot and oracle cards, often with imagery and themes resonant with Celtic mythology and Druidic symbolism.

Astrology: Celtic astrology, based on lunar cycles and the Celtic Tree Calendar, is another tool for divination. It involves interpreting the positions of celestial bodies to provide guidance and insights.

Nature-Based Divination: This includes observing natural phenomena such as weather patterns, animal behavior, and the growth patterns of plants. Modern Druids often see these as messages from the natural world or the divine.

Application and Interpretation in Modern Contexts

The application of these divination methods in modern Druidry extends beyond personal guidance. It is also used in community decision-making, spiritual development, and understanding ecological and social patterns.

The interpretation of divinatory signs in Druidry is a skill that requires intuition, knowledge, and a deep connection with the spiritual and natural worlds. Modern Druids often spend years honing their skills in divination, learning to understand the complex interplay of symbolism, intuition, and observation.

Moreover, divination in Druidry is approached with a sense of responsibility. It is understood that the insights gained are not deterministic but offer potential pathways and perspectives. The emphasis is on empowering the individual or community to make informed choices rather than prescribing a fixed course of action.

Advanced divination methods in modern Druidry represent a rich and complex blend of ancient traditions and contemporary insights. These practices provide a means for Druids to engage deeply with the spiritual and natural worlds, offering guidance, wisdom, and a deeper understanding of the intricate tapestry of life. As a part of the modern Druidic path, they embody a living tradition that evolves and adapts to the needs and understandings of each generation.

Sacred Journeys: Pilgrimages and Quests in Modern Druidry

The concept of a sacred journey, a pilgrimage or quest, holds a special place in the Druidic tradition. These spiritual journeys, whether physical or metaphorical, are central to the Druidic pursuit of wisdom, connection with the natural world, and personal transformation. In modern Druidry, these journeys have adapted to contemporary contexts while retaining their profound spiritual significance.

The Nature of Sacred Journeys in Druidry

Sacred journeys in Druidry can take various forms, ranging from physical pilgrimages to specific natural or historical sites, to inner quests for knowledge and spiritual growth. These journeys are seen as opportunities for deepening one's connection with the Earth, the ancestors, and the divine. They are times of reflection, learning, and significant life transitions.

Physical Pilgrimages: These involve traveling to places of historical or spiritual significance to the Druid path. Sites like ancient stone circles, sacred groves, and wells are common pilgrimage destinations. Modern Druids may travel to these places to perform rituals, meditate, and connect with the energy and history of the land.

Spiritual Quests: Apart from physical travel, sacred journeys also encompass personal quests for wisdom and understanding. These can involve deep meditation, study, and engaging in practices that challenge and expand one's spiritual boundaries.

Contemporary Expressions of Druidic Pilgrimages

In the modern context, Druidic pilgrimages have adapted to fit contemporary lifestyles and circumstances, yet they retain their core purpose of spiritual exploration and growth.

Group Pilgrimages: Organized pilgrimages where groups of Druids travel together are common. These group journeys offer a sense of community and shared experience, allowing participants to learn from each other and deepen their collective understanding of Druidic traditions.

Solo Journeys: Many modern Druids also undertake solo pilgrimages, seeking personal reflection and a deeper connection with the natural world. These journeys are often times of significant personal transformation and spiritual insight.

Virtual Pilgrimages: With the advent of digital technology, virtual pilgrimages have become a way for those unable to travel to experience sacred sites. Through online tours and interactive experiences, modern Druids can remotely connect with these significant places.

The Impact of Sacred Journeys

The impact of sacred journeys in Druidry extends beyond the duration of the journey itself. These experiences often lead to profound personal growth, a deeper understanding of the interconnectedness of all life, and a renewed commitment to the Druid path.

Personal Transformation: Pilgrimages and quests often act as catalysts for personal change, helping individuals overcome challenges, gain new perspectives, and grow spiritually.

Cultural and Historical Connection: By visiting ancient sites and engaging in traditional practices, modern Druids forge a tangible connection with the past, enriching their understanding of Druidic history and culture.

Ecological Awareness: Through the deep connection with nature experienced during these journeys, many Druids develop a stronger commitment to ecological preservation and environmental activism.

Sacred journeys, whether physical pilgrimages or inner quests, are a vital aspect of modern Druidry, providing pathways for spiritual exploration, personal growth, and a deeper connection with the natural and spiritual worlds. These journeys, adapting to the needs and realities of the modern world, continue to be a cornerstone of the Druidic path, offering profound experiences of transformation and insight.

CHAPTER 16: DRUIDIC COMMUNITIES AND ORDERS

In the tapestry of modern Druidry, communities and orders play a pivotal role in preserving traditions, fostering learning, and building a sense of kinship among practitioners. We examine the diverse landscape of Druidic communities and orders, including their structures, functions, and the unique roles they play in the contemporary Druidic movement.

The Structure and Diversity of Druidic Communities

Druidic communities and orders vary widely in their structure, practices, and philosophies. Some are tightly-knit groups that focus on specific traditions or practices, while others are more eclectic, embracing a range of beliefs and rituals. The structure of these communities can be formal, with defined roles and hierarchies, or more fluid and egalitarian.

Key types of Druidic communities include:

Groves: These are local groups that often gather for rituals, celebrations, and learning. Groves may be affiliated with larger Druidic orders or operate independently, focusing on the needs and interests of their members.

Orders: These are larger organizations that often have a national or international presence. They provide a framework for Druidic practice, offering training programs, organizing events, and publishing materials on Druidry.

Online Communities: With the advent of the internet, virtual communities have become an integral part of modern Druidry. These platforms allow for the sharing of resources, discussion, and even virtual rituals, connecting Druids from all over the world.

Functions and Activities of Druidic Communities

Druidic communities and orders serve several vital functions in the modern Druidic movement:

Preservation and Transmission of Knowledge: They are custodians of Druidic knowledge, preserving ancient wisdom and adapting it for contemporary practice. Through training programs, mentorship, and publications, they ensure that the teachings of Druidry are passed on to new generations.

Spiritual and Ritual Practice: Communities provide a space for collective rituals and celebrations, which are central to Druidic practice. These gatherings reinforce the communal bond and allow members to experience the power of group rituals.

Support and Fellowship: Druidic communities offer a sense of belonging and support. For many practitioners, these communities are a spiritual family where they can share experiences, learn from each other, and grow together in their spiritual paths.

Challenges and Opportunities

Modern Druidic communities and orders face various challenges and opportunities in the 21st century:

Inclusivity and Diversity: As Druidry attracts a more diverse following, communities are challenged to be inclusive and accommodating of different perspectives and practices. This diversity can enrich the tradition, bringing in new ideas and approaches.

Adapting to Change: In a rapidly changing world, Druidic communities must find ways to stay relevant and accessible. This includes embracing technology, addressing contemporary issues, and evolving their practices while staying true to core principles.

Environmental and Social Activism: Many Druidic communities are actively involved in environmental and social causes, reflecting the Druidic reverence for nature and commitment to societal well-being. This activism is an expression of their spiritual values in action.

Druidic communities and orders are essential to the vitality and continuity of modern Druidry. They provide a framework for practice, a repository of knowledge, and a supportive network for practitioners. As they navigate the challenges of the modern world, these communities play a crucial role in shaping the future of the Druidic path, ensuring its relevance and vibrancy for generations to come.

The Psychology of Druidic Rituals

The practice of Druidry, rich in rituals and ceremonies, is not only a spiritual journey but also a psychological one. We delve into the psychological aspects of Druidic rituals, exploring how they impact mental states, foster personal growth, and facilitate a deeper connection with the self and the natural world.

Influence on Mental and Emotional States

Druidic rituals are designed to engage participants on multiple levels – physical, emotional, mental, and spiritual. This holistic engagement has profound psychological effects:

Inducing Altered States of Consciousness: Many Druidic rituals involve elements like rhythmic drumming, chanting, or meditative practices that can lead to altered states of consciousness. These states enable practitioners to transcend ordinary perception, accessing deeper levels of awareness and intuition.

Emotional Catharsis: Rituals often provide a safe space for the expression of emotions, allowing participants to process feelings like grief, joy, or gratitude more fully. This emotional release can be healing and transformative.

Cognitive Reappraisal: Engaging in rituals allows practitioners to reframe their perspectives on life events, fostering a sense of empowerment and resilience. Rituals often symbolize the cycle of life, death, and rebirth, offering new ways to understand and cope with change and loss.

Personal Growth and Self-Reflection

Druidic rituals serve as catalysts for personal growth and self-reflection:

Enhancing Self-Awareness: The introspective nature of many Druidic practices encourages individuals to look inward, fostering greater self-awareness and understanding of one's thoughts, emotions, and behaviors.

Promoting Mindfulness and Presence: Druidry places a strong emphasis on being present in the moment, particularly in rituals that involve interaction with nature. This mindfulness practice enhances mental clarity, reduces stress, and improves overall well-being.

Encouraging Integration of the Self: Druidic rituals often involve symbolically traversing the realms of land, sea, and sky, or engaging with archetypal figures. These experiences can help individuals integrate different aspects of the self, leading to a more cohesive and balanced identity.

Social and Collective Dimensions

Druidic rituals also have a significant social and collective dimension:

Fostering Community and Belonging: Participating in group rituals strengthens the sense of community and belonging. This social connection is crucial for mental health, providing support, validation, and a sense of shared purpose.

Collective Effervescence: Engaging in rituals with others can lead to a sense of collective effervescence – a shared euphoria that reinforces social bonds and communal identity. This experience is deeply rewarding and can enhance one's sense of interconnectedness with others and the world.

Rituals as a Mode of Teaching and Learning: In a communal setting, rituals serve as a powerful medium for transmitting values, traditions, and wisdom. This shared learning experience is not only educational but also builds a collective repository of knowledge and understanding.

The psychology of Druidic rituals is a complex and multifaceted area, interweaving the individual and the collective, the emotional and the cognitive, the spiritual and the mundane. These practices offer a rich tapestry of experiences that can profoundly impact mental and emotional well-being, personal growth, and social connectedness. By engaging in these rituals, modern Druids continue a tradition that nourishes the human psyche in ways that are as relevant today as they were in ancient times.

CHAPTER 17: COMPARATIVE MYTHOLOGIES IN DRUIDRY

The exploration of mythology is a fundamental aspect of Druidic study, offering rich insights into the beliefs, values, and worldviews of ancient cultures. In this advanced exploration, we delve into the comparative analysis of Druidic mythology, examining its similarities and differences with other world mythologies, and the insights this comparison offers into the universal themes of human experience.

Intersecting Themes in World Mythologies

Druidic mythology, deeply rooted in Celtic culture, shares several common themes with other mythological traditions:

Creation and Cosmology: Just as in many other cultures, Druidic myths often explore the origins of the world and the forces that shape it. Comparative study reveals similarities in how different cultures understand the cosmos, time, and the role of chaos and order in creation.

Heroic Journeys and Quests: The motif of the hero's journey, central in Celtic and Druidic tales, is also found in various other mythologies. These narratives often involve quests for knowledge, battles with formidable foes, and journeys to otherworldly realms, reflecting universal human experiences of struggle, growth, and transformation.

Nature and the Divine: Many mythologies, including the Druidic, personify natural elements as deities or spirits. This anthropomorphism highlights a shared human tendency to view nature as imbued with spiritual significance and reflects common beliefs about the interconnectedness of all life.

Druidic Mythology in Comparative Perspective

When placed alongside other mythologies, certain unique aspects of Druidic mythology become apparent:

Celtic Cycles of Myth: Unlike the linear narratives seen in some cultures, Celtic myths often depict cyclical time, emphasizing regeneration and the interconnectedness of events. This perspective offers a unique understanding of time and existence.

Emphasis on Otherworldly Realms: Druidic myths frequently explore the concept of otherworldly realms, which are closely intertwined with the physical world. This contrasts with mythologies that depict a more distinct separation between the divine or spiritual realms and the earthly plane.

Fluidity of Characters and Forms: Celtic deities and mythological figures often display shape-shifting abilities and ambiguous qualities, reflecting a worldview that embraces complexity, transformation, and the blurring of boundaries.

Insights from Comparative Mythology

Studying Druidic mythology in comparison with other traditions yields several insights:

Cultural Exchange and Influence: Comparative mythology

highlights the exchanges and influences between different cultures over time. For instance, similarities between Celtic and Norse mythologies can be traced back to historical interactions between these cultures.

Universal Human Questions and Themes: At their core, all mythologies grapple with the same fundamental human questions about creation, existence, morality, and the afterlife. This shared inquiry underscores the commonality of human experience across cultures and epochs.

Adaptation and Evolution of Myths: Understanding how Druidic myths compare with others also sheds light on how myths evolve and adapt over time, influenced by social, environmental, and historical contexts.

The comparative study of Druidic mythology offers a window into the rich tapestry of human belief and imagination. By exploring the similarities and differences with other mythological traditions, we gain a deeper appreciation of the universal themes that connect us and the unique perspectives that enrich our understanding of the world. This exploration not only deepens our knowledge of Druidry but also fosters a greater appreciation for the diversity and complexity of human cultural expression.

Metaphysics and Druidry

In the advanced stages of Druidic study, metaphysics – the branch of philosophy that examines the fundamental nature of reality – plays a crucial role. We delve into the metaphysical principles underlying Druidic beliefs, exploring how these principles inform the Druidic understanding of the universe, life, and the interconnectedness of all things.

Understanding the Druidic View of Reality

Druidic metaphysics is deeply rooted in a holistic view of the universe, where everything is interconnected and interdependent. This perspective is characterized by several key concepts:

Immanence and Transcendence: Druidry holds that the divine is both immanent, existing within all things, and transcendent, beyond the physical world. This dual aspect of the divine reflects a belief in the sacredness of the natural world as well as the existence of other realms or dimensions.

Cycles of Nature and Existence: A fundamental principle in Druidic thought is the cyclical nature of existence, mirrored in the changing seasons, life cycles, and even cosmic cycles. This perspective emphasizes the importance of balance, harmony, and the acceptance of change and transformation as natural processes.

Interconnectivity of All Life: Central to Druidic metaphysics is the idea that all life forms, including humans, animals, plants, and even inanimate objects, are connected in a complex web of relationships. This interconnectedness is seen as both physical and spiritual, with actions in one part of the web affecting the whole.

Metaphysical Practices in Druidry

Druidic metaphysical concepts are not only theoretical but are also reflected in various practices:

Meditation and Visualization: Druids use meditation and visualization techniques to explore different levels of reality, connect with the natural world, and tap into deeper levels of consciousness.

Ritual and Ceremony: Druidic rituals often symbolize metaphysical concepts, such as the unity of the physical and spiritual, the cycle of birth, death, and rebirth, and the interconnectedness of all beings.

Nature-based Practices: Engaging with the natural world is a form of metaphysical practice in Druidry, helping to ground the abstract concepts of metaphysics in tangible experiences.

The Implications of Druidic Metaphysics

The metaphysical principles of Druidry have profound implications for how Druids view and interact with the world:

Ethical Considerations: The belief in the sacredness of all life and the interconnectedness of all things informs Druidic ethical perspectives, emphasizing respect for nature, sustainability, and the importance of living in harmony with the earth.

Spiritual Insight and Growth: The metaphysical framework of Druidry offers a path for spiritual insight and growth, encouraging practitioners to explore the deeper mysteries of existence and their place in the universe.

Healing and Restoration: By understanding and aligning with the natural cycles and interconnected nature of reality, Druids engage in practices aimed at healing themselves, their communities, and the planet.

Metaphysics in Druidry provides a rich and complex framework for understanding the nature of reality and our place within it. These principles inform not just the philosophical aspects of Druidry but also its practical and ethical dimensions, guiding Druids in their pursuit of wisdom, harmony, and balance with the natural world.

CHAPTER 18: ALCHEMY AND TRANSFORMATION IN DRUIDIC PRACTICES

Alchemy, traditionally known for the transmutation of base metals into gold, in Druidry, is understood in a more metaphysical and spiritual sense. Let's delve into the advanced concepts of spiritual alchemy and transformation within Druidic practices, exploring how these principles are applied for personal and collective growth.

The Spiritual Alchemy in Druidry

In Druidry, alchemy is viewed as a transformative process of the self, where the practitioner undergoes a metaphorical journey from a base state to a more enlightened and refined existence. This process involves several stages:

Purification and Preparation: Similar to the alchemical concept of calcination, this stage involves the burning away of the ego and impurities, leading to a state of humility and readiness for transformation.

Dissolution and Discovery: In this phase, akin to alchemical dissolution, there is a breaking down of old structures and beliefs, allowing for the emergence of new insights and the discovery of inner truths.

Reintegration and Rebirth: Resembling alchemical coagulation, this stage represents the reintegration of these insights and truths into the individual's life, resulting in a rebirth of the self into a more harmonized and enlightened state.

Transformation Through Druidic Rituals

Druidic rituals often symbolize and facilitate this alchemical transformation process:

Seasonal Celebrations: The eight festivals of the Druidic Wheel of the Year mark the cyclical nature of life and its constant state of flux and renewal, echoing the transformative journey of the soul.

Rites of Passage: These rituals, such as initiations into different grades (Bard, Ovate, and Druid), symbolize the stages of spiritual growth and the transformation of the practitioner's identity and role within the Druidic community.

Nature-based Practices: Engaging with the natural world in Druidry is seen as a way to connect with the cycles of growth, decay, and renewal, mirroring the inner alchemical process of the individual.

Alchemy, Wisdom, and Enlightenment

The ultimate goal of spiritual alchemy in Druidry is to attain wisdom and enlightenment:

Integration of Opposites: The alchemical journey involves balancing and integrating opposing forces within the self, such as light and dark, masculine and feminine, physical and spiritual. This integration leads to a state of inner harmony and understanding.

Attainment of Wisdom: Through this transformative process, practitioners gain deeper wisdom, not just intellectually but also experientially, understanding the deeper truths of existence and their interconnectedness with all life.

Service to the Community and the Earth: The enlightened state in Druidic alchemy is not just for personal salvation but is also seen as a means to serve the community and the Earth. The wisdom gained is used to guide, heal, and nurture both society and the natural world.

Alchemy in Druidry represents a profound and intricate journey of spiritual transformation. It is a metaphorical process that involves purifying, discovering, and reintegrating aspects of the self, leading to a state of wisdom and enlightenment. This transformative path is central to the Druidic pursuit of personal growth and the harmonious balance with the natural world. Through this process, Druids seek not only personal fulfillment but also to contribute to the greater good of their community and the Earth.

The Quantum Druid: Exploring the Intersection of Druidry and Quantum Physics

The intriguing intersection with quantum physics offers a contemporary perspective on ancient wisdom. Concepts from quantum physics resonate with Druidic teachings and practices, providing a deeper understanding of the nature of reality and our place within it.

Quantum Concepts in Druidic Context

Quantum physics, with its focus on the behavior of the smallest particles in the universe, reveals a world that is profoundly interconnected and not entirely predictable, resonating deeply with Druidic views of nature and existence.

Interconnectedness: Quantum entanglement, where particles remain connected regardless of distance, echoes the Druidic principle of interconnectedness of all things in the universe. This concept underscores the belief that every action has an impact on the whole, a foundational idea in Druidic ethics and environmental consciousness.

Observer Effect: In quantum physics, the observer effect suggests that the act of observation influences the outcome of experiments. This parallels the Druidic idea that human consciousness interacts with and shapes the world around us, emphasizing the power of intention and perception in shaping reality.

Potentiality and Manifestation: Quantum physics introduces the concept of potentiality, where particles exist in multiple states simultaneously until observed. This aligns with Druidic beliefs in the power of potential and the manifestation of reality through intention, visualization, and ritual.

Druidry in the Quantum Age

The alignment of quantum physics and Druidic principles offers a modern framework for understanding ancient wisdom:

Redefining Magic: The seemingly magical phenomena in quantum physics, such as particles being in two places at once, provide a scientific basis for reinterpreting what might be considered magical in Druidry. It allows a modern Druid to view magic as the interaction with the deeper, quantum level of reality.

Ethical Implications: Understanding the universe as an interconnected web, as both quantum physics and Druidry suggest, has profound ethical implications. It fosters a worldview that emphasizes responsibility for our actions and their impacts on the broader ecosystem.

Ritual and Practice: The parallels between quantum mechanics and Druidic practice can enrich ritual work, infusing it with a deeper understanding of how intention and consciousness might interact with the fabric of reality.

Challenges and Opportunities

Integrating quantum physics into Druidic practice is not without challenges, yet it offers exciting opportunities:

Complexity and Mystery: Quantum physics is inherently complex and often counterintuitive, mirroring the mysteries at the heart of Druidic practice. Embracing this complexity can deepen the sense of awe and wonder in Druidic practice.

Dialogue Between Science and Spirituality: This intersection opens up a dialogue between science and spirituality, challenging and expanding our understanding of both fields. It invites a more holistic view of the world that harmonizes scientific understanding with spiritual wisdom.

Personal and Collective Growth: Incorporating insights from quantum physics into Druidry can aid personal growth and development, offering new perspectives on the nature of reality, consciousness, and our potential to effect change.

The intersection of Druidry and quantum physics offers a rich and fertile ground for exploration. It bridges ancient wisdom with modern science, providing a unique perspective on the mysteries of the universe and our role within it. This convergence invites Druids to explore new dimensions of understanding, ethics, and practice, fostering a deeper connection with the natural world and the unseen forces that shape our reality.

CHAPTER 19: THE PHILOSOPHER'S STONE: WISDOM IN DRUIDRY

Let's explore the concept of the Philosopher's Stone, not as a literal substance for transmuting base metals into gold, but as a metaphor for wisdom and enlightenment in Druidic practices. This advanced exploration delves into the transformative journey towards wisdom, the role of nature in this process, and the application of this wisdom in daily life.

The Transformative Journey to Wisdom

In Druidry, the quest for the Philosopher's Stone is akin to the pursuit of deep, spiritual wisdom. This journey involves several key aspects:

Self-Discovery and Inner Alchemy: Just as the alchemist seeks to transform lead into gold, the Druid seeks to transform the self. This involves introspection, meditation, and confronting one's shadows, leading to personal growth and spiritual awakening.

Integration of Knowledge and Experience: True wisdom in Druidry comes from the integration of intellectual knowledge with personal experience. It is about understanding the cycles of nature, the flow of the seasons, and the rhythms of life, and incorporating this understanding into one's worldview.

Ethical Living and Wisdom: Druidic wisdom is not only about personal enlightenment but also involves ethical living. It teaches balance, harmony with nature, and responsibility for one's actions, reflecting a deep understanding of the interconnectedness of all things.

The Role of Nature in Attaining Wisdom

Nature plays a central role in the Druidic path to wisdom:

Learning from the Natural World: Druids believe that nature is a teacher and a guide. The patterns and cycles of nature offer insights into the nature of existence and our place within the larger web of life.

Rituals and Ceremonies: Druidic rituals, often conducted in natural settings, are designed to align practitioners with the natural world, opening pathways to deeper understanding and wisdom.

The Healing Power of Nature: Engaging with nature is also seen as a healing process, helping to restore balance and clarity, which are essential for the development of wisdom.

Application of Wisdom in Daily Life

Druidic wisdom is not meant to be esoteric or detached from everyday life. Instead, it has practical applications:

Living in Harmony with Nature: Wisdom in Druidry encourages sustainable living, respecting and protecting the environment, and understanding our role as stewards of the Earth.

Community and Relationships: Wisdom extends to understanding and nurturing relationships, recognizing the importance of community, and practicing compassion and empathy.

Personal Fulfillment and Service: The ultimate goal of attaining wisdom in Druidry is to achieve personal fulfillment and to serve others. It is about using one's knowledge and experience to contribute to the well-being of others and the world.

The pursuit of the Philosopher's Stone in Druidry symbolizes the journey to wisdom and enlightenment. This wisdom is deeply rooted in understanding and living in harmony with nature, integrating knowledge and experience, and applying these insights in ethical and meaningful ways. It is a journey of transformation, not just of the self but also of the world around us, embodying the true essence of Druidic spirituality.

Sacred Sound and Vibrational Healing

Let's explore the concepts of sacred sound and vibrational healing in Druidry by delving into the ancient and modern understanding of sound's power in healing practices, the role of music and chant in Druidic rituals, and the integration of these practices into contemporary Druidic spirituality.

The Power of Sound in Druidic Practices

Sound has always been an integral part of Druidic rituals and practices, believed to possess profound healing properties and the ability to connect the physical and spiritual realms.

Vibrational Nature of Sound: Druids understand that sound is vibration and that these vibrations can interact with the energetic fields of living beings. This interaction can bring about changes in physical, emotional, and spiritual well-being.

Use of Chants and Songs: Traditional Druidic chants and songs are more than mere words set to melody; they are considered tools for transformation. These sounds are thought to resonate with specific energies of nature and the cosmos, harmonizing the individual's energy with these larger forces.

Instruments in Rituals: Instruments such as drums, flutes, and harps are often used in Druidic rituals. The rhythmic beating of a drum, for example, is used to induce trance states, facilitate meditation, and connect with the deeper rhythms of nature.

Integration of Sound Healing in Modern Druidry

As Druidry evolves, the use of sound and vibrational healing has adapted to incorporate contemporary understanding and techniques:

Sound Baths and Healing Sessions: Modern Druids may conduct sound baths, where participants are immersed in the sounds of gongs, singing bowls, and other instruments, facilitating deep relaxation and healing.

Chanting and Mantra Meditation: The use of chanting, drawing from both traditional Druidic and other spiritual traditions, has become a common practice. Chanting mantras can help focus the mind, elevate the spirit, and harness personal and universal energies.

Nature Sounds for Healing: Recognizing the restorative power of nature's sounds, such as the rustling of leaves, flowing water, or bird calls, modern Druids often integrate these sounds into meditation and healing practices.

The Role of Sound in Spiritual Growth and Community

The use of sound and vibrational healing extends beyond personal well-being and plays a significant role in Druidic spiritual growth and community bonding:

Enhancing Spiritual Experiences: Sacred sound is used to deepen spiritual experiences, facilitate journeying to other realms, and connect with deities or ancestral spirits in rituals and ceremonies.

Community Building: Group singing and music-making in Druidic gatherings are not just for enjoyment; they are essential for building community bonds and creating a shared energetic space.

Ecological Connection: Sound practices in Druidry also foster a deeper connection with the natural world. Listening to and creating sounds that reflect nature's rhythms encourages a harmonious relationship with the environment.

Sacred sound and vibrational healing are key components of advanced Druidic practices. These practices offer profound healing benefits, enhance spiritual experiences, and strengthen the bonds within the Druidic community and with the natural world. By integrating traditional wisdom with modern techniques, Druids continue to explore and experience the transformative power of sound.

CHAPTER 20: ASTRAL TRAVEL AND OTHERWORLDLY REALMS

We will investigate the advanced Druidic practices of astral travel and the exploration of otherworldly realms, including the concepts and techniques for navigating these spiritual journeys, the significance of otherworldly experiences in Druidic tradition, and the integration of these experiences into personal spiritual growth.

Understanding Astral Travel in Druidry

Astral travel, or astral projection, is a practice where the consciousness separates from the physical body to journey in the astral plane. In Druidry, this practice is deeply rooted in the belief in otherworldly realms and the interconnectedness of all existence.

Techniques and Preparation: Successful astral travel in Druidic practice often involves deep meditation, visualization, and ritual preparation. Techniques may include focusing on specific symbols, rhythmic breathing, and the use of chants or mantras to achieve the necessary state of consciousness.

Safety and Grounding: Emphasis is placed on the importance of grounding and protecting oneself before attempting astral travel. This includes practices for energy shielding and methods for ensuring a safe return to the physical body.

Ethical Considerations: Druidic teachings stress the ethical implications of astral travel, emphasizing respect for all beings encountered and the integrity of one's actions in the astral realm.

Exploring Otherworldly Realms

The concept of otherworldly realms is central to Druidic cosmology, with these realms being seen as places of deep wisdom, learning, and connection with the divine.

The Nature of the Realms: Druidic tradition describes various realms, each with its unique characteristics and inhabitants. These include realms of ancestors, spirit guides, and deities, as well as elemental and nature spirits.

Learning and Guidance: Journeys to these realms are often sought for wisdom, healing, and spiritual guidance. Interactions with otherworldly beings can provide insights into personal challenges, spiritual development, and deeper universal truths.

Integration of Experiences: Experiences in these realms are believed to offer profound personal transformations. Druids seek to integrate these experiences into their daily lives, using the insights gained to enhance their understanding, compassion, and connection to the natural world.

The Role of Astral Travel in Modern Druidry

In contemporary Druidic practice, astral travel continues to be a vital aspect of spiritual exploration and growth.

Personal Development: Astral travel is seen as a tool for personal growth, self-discovery, and the expansion of one's consciousness beyond the physical realm.

Community and Teaching: Experiences in astral travel are often shared within the Druidic community, contributing to a collective understanding and the passing down of wisdom.

Adapting Ancient Practices to Modern Times: Modern Druids adapt ancient techniques of astral travel to contemporary practices, blending traditional wisdom with new insights and understandings.

Astral travel and the exploration of otherworldly realms are advanced practices in Druidry that offer profound spiritual experiences. These journeys allow practitioners to transcend the physical world, gain wisdom and guidance from other realms, and integrate these experiences into their spiritual path. By engaging in these practices, modern Druids continue a tradition of exploration and connection that is as relevant today as it was in ancient times.

The Ethics and Morality of Modern Druidry

We will explore how Druids today interpret and apply ancient principles to contemporary ethical dilemmas, the role of nature-centric ethics, and the importance of personal responsibility and community in moral decision-making.

Contemporary Interpretation of Ancient Principles

Modern Druidry, while rooted in ancient traditions, faces new ethical challenges in today's world. The adaptation of ancient Druidic principles to contemporary issues is a key aspect of ethical practice in modern Druidry.

Relevance of Ancient Wisdom: Druids look to their ancient past for guidance on living ethically, interpreting age-old wisdom in the context of modern societal and environmental challenges.

The Druidic Virtues: Principles such as truth, honor, and integrity, which were esteemed in ancient Druidry, are adapted to guide behavior in areas like environmental stewardship, social justice, and personal conduct.

Balancing Tradition and Modernity: The challenge for modern Druids lies in balancing reverence for tradition with the need to address current global issues, from climate change to social inequality.

Nature-Centric Ethics in Druidry

At the heart of Druidic ethics is a profound respect for nature, which informs moral decision-making and actions.

Environmental Stewardship: Druidry advocates for living in harmony with the Earth, encouraging sustainable practices and environmental activism.

Interconnectedness and Responsibility: Recognizing the interconnectedness of all life, Druids feel a moral responsibility to protect ecosystems and biodiversity.

Learning from Nature: Druids believe that observing natural systems can offer insights into ethical living, such as the importance of balance, diversity, and symbiosis.

Personal Responsibility and Community

Druidic ethics emphasize both personal responsibility and the role of community in cultivating a moral society.

Individual Ethics: Each Druid is encouraged to develop a personal code of ethics, reflecting on how their actions align with Druidic principles and affect the broader world.

Community and Cultural Ethics: Druidic communities often engage in discussions about ethics, providing a space for collective reflection, learning, and support in ethical practices.

Service to Others: Druidry teaches that ethical living includes service to others, fostering a sense of community, kinship, and mutual aid.

Challenges in Ethical Druidry

Modern Druids face unique challenges in applying their ethics in a complex world.

Navigating Modern Dilemmas: Issues such as technology use, political involvement, and global economics require Druids to constantly reassess and redefine their ethical stances.

Diversity within Druidry: As a diverse and evolving spiritual path, Druidry encompasses a wide range of perspectives, leading to rich but sometimes challenging ethical debates within the community.

Global and Local Action: Druids are called to act ethically on both global and local scales, balancing immediate community needs with broader environmental and societal concerns.

The ethics and morality of modern Druidry are dynamic and evolving, rooted in ancient wisdom but responsive to contemporary challenges. Through a deep connection with nature, a commitment to personal and communal responsibility, and an ongoing dialogue within the community, Druids seek to live ethically and contribute positively to the world. This chapter underscores the importance of ethical living as a cornerstone of Druidic practice and its relevance in today's increasingly complex world.

CHAPTER 21: THE DRUID'S PATH TO SELF-MASTERY

Let's examine the concept of self-mastery within the context of modern Druidry. It explores how Druids cultivate personal growth, self-awareness, and mastery over their internal and external environments through spiritual practices, ethical living, and a deep connection with nature.

Cultivating Personal Growth and Self-Awareness

In Druidry, the journey towards self-mastery is a lifelong process of personal development that involves understanding and harmonizing the self with the natural world and the wider community.

Self-Reflection and Meditation: Integral to self-mastery in Druidry is the practice of self-reflection and meditation. These practices aid in understanding one's thoughts, emotions, and actions, leading to greater self-awareness and mindfulness.

Balancing the Inner and Outer Worlds: Druids strive to achieve balance between their inner selves and the external world. This includes harmonizing personal desires and ambitions with the needs of the community and the environment.

Continuous Learning and Adaptation: Self-mastery involves an ongoing commitment to learning, growing, and adapting. Druids view life as a continuous journey of discovery, where each experience provides an opportunity for personal development.

Ethical Living as a Path to Self-Mastery

Ethical conduct is a cornerstone of the Druidic path to self-mastery. Living in accordance with Druidic values and principles is seen as essential to personal growth and spiritual fulfillment.

Living in Harmony with Nature: Druids believe that ethical living involves a deep respect for and harmony with nature. This includes sustainable living, environmental stewardship, and recognizing the interconnectedness of all life.

Community Involvement and Service: Engaging with and serving one's community is viewed as a vital part of self-mastery. Druids often participate in community service, social justice initiatives, and efforts to support and uplift others.

Personal Responsibility and Integrity: Druidry teaches that personal responsibility and integrity are key to self-mastery. This means being accountable for one's actions, living truthfully, and upholding one's commitments and responsibilities.

Practices for Self-Mastery in Modern Druidry

Modern Druidry offers a range of practices and rituals that support the journey to self-mastery.

Ritual and Ceremony: Regular participation in Druidic rituals and ceremonies helps to reinforce personal commitment to the path of self-mastery. These rituals often involve affirmations of intention, gratitude, and the celebration of personal growth.

Nature Connection: Spending time in nature and engaging in practices such as forest bathing, wildlife observation, and gardening are seen as vital for grounding and connecting with the

Earth, which is central to self-mastery in Druidry.

Creative Expression: Many Druids use creative expression, such as writing, art, and music, as tools for self-discovery and personal growth. These creative practices are avenues for exploring and expressing the inner self.

The Druid's path to self-mastery is a multifaceted journey that encompasses personal growth, ethical living, and a deep connection with nature. Through self-reflection, community engagement, and spiritual practice, modern Druids strive to master themselves and in doing so, contribute positively to their communities and the natural world. This underscores the importance of self-mastery in Druidic spirituality and its relevance in today's world.

Shamanic Practices in Modern Druidry

Let's delve into the integration and adaptation of shamanic practices within modern Druidry and explore the historical connections between Druidry and shamanism, the incorporation of shamanic elements into contemporary Druidic practices, and the role of these practices in personal and communal spiritual development.

Historical Connections and Contemporary Perspectives

Shamanic elements have been intertwined with Druidic practices historically, both sharing a deep reverence for nature and the use of altered states of consciousness for spiritual exploration.

Historical Overlap: Ancient Druids, like shamans, were seen as mediators between the physical and spiritual worlds. They used trance, divination, and ritual to gain insights and guide their communities.

Modern Adaptation: Contemporary Druids often draw on

shamanic techniques such as journeying, animal totems, and drumming, adapting them within a Druidic framework to enhance spiritual practice.

Respecting Cultural Origins: Modern Druids are mindful of the cultural origins of shamanic practices, approaching them with respect and acknowledging their diverse global sources.

Shamanic Elements in Druidic Rituals

Shamanic practices are incorporated into Druidic rituals to deepen the connection with the natural world and the spiritual realm.

Drumming and Trance Work: Drumming is commonly used in Druidic rituals to induce trance states, facilitating journeys to otherworldly realms and deepening meditation practices.

Animal Spirits and Totems: Many Druids work with animal spirits as guides and protectors, seeing them as messengers and teachers that offer wisdom and insight.

Nature Connection: Shamanic practices emphasize a profound connection with nature, encouraging Druids to engage deeply with the land, plants, and animals as part of their spiritual path.

Personal and Communal Development Through Shamanic Practices

Shamanic elements in Druidry contribute to both personal growth and the strengthening of community bonds.

Personal Transformation: Shamanic journeying and meditation offer pathways for self-discovery, healing, and personal transformation, allowing individuals to explore their subconscious and spiritual dimensions.

Community Healing and Support: Shamanic practices in

Druidry often include group rituals and ceremonies that foster community healing, support, and a shared sense of spiritual purpose.

Ecological Awareness: Engaging with shamanic practices heightens ecological awareness and responsibility, aligning with the Druidic emphasis on environmental stewardship and sustainability.

Challenges and Ethical Considerations

Integrating shamanic practices into modern Druidry also presents certain challenges and ethical considerations.

Cultural Sensitivity: Druids are aware of the need for cultural sensitivity and avoiding appropriation when incorporating shamanic practices from other traditions.

Balancing Tradition and Innovation: Finding a balance between traditional Druidic practices and the incorporation of shamanic elements can be challenging, requiring a thoughtful approach that respects the integrity of both paths.

Accessibility and Inclusivity: Ensuring that shamanic-influenced practices are accessible and inclusive to all members of the Druid community is a key consideration, promoting diversity and understanding within the tradition.

This highlights the valuable role of shamanic practices in modern Druidry, contributing to the richness and depth of Druidic spiritual practice. By incorporating shamanic elements, modern Druids embrace a holistic approach to spirituality that honors their ancestral roots while adapting to the needs and understandings of the contemporary world.

CHAPTER 22: THEURGY AND DIVINE CONTACT

We will explore the advanced practice of Theurgy within modern Druidry, focusing on establishing contact with divine energies and being whilst exploring the nature of Theurgy, methods to connect with the divine, and the role of divine contact in Druidic practices.

Understanding Theurgy in Modern Druidry

Theurgy in Druidry is the practice of invoking the presence of divine forces or deities for spiritual development and transformation.

Concept of Theurgy: Theurgy in Druidry is understood as a sacred process of aligning with divine energies to enhance spiritual growth and understanding. It goes beyond mere ritual to create a profound connection with the spiritual realm.

Divine as a Source of Inspiration and Wisdom: Druids view divine contact not as a means for material gain but as a pathway to gain wisdom, inspiration, and insight. This contact is sought to deepen one's spiritual practice and understanding of the universe.

Integrating Theurgy with Druidic Beliefs: Theurgy in Druidry is seamlessly integrated with its core beliefs, such as reverence for nature, the sanctity of life, and the interconnectedness of all things.

Methods of Establishing Divine Contact

Druids use various methods to establish contact with divine energies, each tailored to individual beliefs and experiences.

Ritual and Ceremony: Specialized rituals and ceremonies are conducted to invoke divine presences. These often involve specific chants, offerings, and symbolic actions designed to align the practitioner with the energies being invoked.

Meditation and Visualization: Meditation and visualization are key practices in Theurgy. Druids meditate to reach a state of consciousness where they can perceive and interact with divine energies.

Nature-Based Practices: As Druidry is deeply connected with nature, many Druids find divine contact through interactions with the natural world, seeing the divine in every aspect of the natural environment.

The Role of Divine Contact in Druidic Practice

Divine contact plays a significant role in the spiritual lives of Druids, influencing both their personal practices and their contributions to their communities.

Personal Transformation: Engaging with divine energies is seen as a catalyst for personal transformation and spiritual enlightenment. It is a deeply personal journey that varies from one individual to another.

Community and Cultural Impact: Divine contact also influences the way Druids interact with their communities. Insights gained from these experiences often guide Druids in their roles as healers, teachers, and leaders.

Ethical Considerations and Challenges: The practice of Theurgy comes with its ethical considerations. Druids approach these practices with humility and respect, acknowledging the limits of human understanding in the face of the divine.

Theurgy and divine contact in modern Druidry represent a profound and complex aspect of the Druidic spiritual path. This practice allows Druids to explore the deeper realms of spirituality, providing insights and experiences that enrich their understanding of the universe and their place within it. Through Theurgy, Druids seek not only personal enlightenment but also to contribute to the greater good of their communities and the world at large.

Sacred Sexuality in Druidry

Let's investigate the complex and profound subject of sacred sexuality within Druidry and examine the historical context, the spiritual significance, and the contemporary practices of sacred sexuality in the Druidic tradition.

Historical Context and Evolution

Sacred sexuality in Druidry has ancient roots, intertwining with Celtic myths and rituals. Historically, sexuality was revered as a potent force of nature and creation.

Ancient Beliefs: In ancient Druidic culture, sexuality was often linked with fertility rites and the natural cycles of the Earth. It was a means to honor the divine and the life-giving forces of nature.

Evolution Over Centuries: Over time, the interpretation and practice of sacred sexuality have evolved. Modern Druidry reinterprets these ancient practices with a contemporary understanding of sexuality, consent, and spiritual connection.

Spiritual Significance

In Druidry, sexuality is not merely a physical act but a profound spiritual experience that connects individuals to the divine and the natural world.

Connection with Nature: Sexual union is seen as a mirror of the natural processes of creation and regeneration, symbolizing the interconnectedness of all life.

Energetic Exchange: Sacred sexuality is considered an exchange of energy that can lead to heightened spiritual awareness and deeper understanding of one's own divine nature.

Tool for Personal and Spiritual Growth: It is also a path for personal growth and spiritual development, allowing individuals to explore the depths of their being and their connection to the universe.

Contemporary Practices and Ethics

Modern Druidic practitioners approach sacred sexuality with mindfulness, emphasizing consent, respect, and spiritual intention.

Consensual and Respectful Practices: Modern Druids advocate for consensual and respectful expressions of sexuality, with a strong emphasis on the physical, emotional, and spiritual well-being of all participants.

Ritual and Ceremony: Sacred sexuality is often incorporated into rituals and ceremonies, creating a sacred space where sexuality is expressed as a form of divine worship and connection.

Integration with Other Spiritual Practices: It is integrated with meditation, energy work, and other spiritual practices to create a holistic approach to spirituality that honors the sacredness of the sexual self.

In Druidry, sacred sexuality is a profound and integral part of the spiritual path. It is a practice that honors the divine within and around us, connecting deeply with the rhythms of nature and the universe. By embracing the sacredness of sexuality, Druids explore the depths of their spirituality and forge a stronger connection with the natural world and the divine.

CHAPTER 23: ADVANCED MAGICAL SYSTEMS AND THEOREMS IN DRUIDRY

Next, we explore the intricate and advanced magical systems and theorems that form a part of contemporary Druidic practice and provide an insight into the complex mathematical and theoretical frameworks that underpin the mystical practices within Druidry.

Theoretical Foundations of Druidic Magic

In Druidry, magical practices are not only seen as rituals but also as sophisticated systems with deep theoretical underpinnings.

Mathematical Symbolism: Numbers and geometric patterns are seen as fundamental to understanding the universe. Druidic magic often incorporates these elements to create symbolic representations of natural laws and cosmic order.

Theoretical Constructs: Concepts such as the interconnectedness of all beings, the flow of energy in the universe, and the impact of intention on reality are central to Druidic magical theory. These constructs provide a framework for understanding how magic operates within the natural world.

Advanced Magical Systems

Druidry includes a variety of advanced magical systems, each with its own unique practices and philosophical basis.

Ogham-Based Magic: Building upon the ancient Druidic alphabet, Ogham, this system uses symbolic language to interact with the natural world and the energies it contains.

Astronomical Alignments: Druids study and utilize the alignments of celestial bodies for timing and enhancing their magical workings, believing that these alignments have profound effects on energy flow and consciousness.

Elemental Magic: Advanced elemental practices involve not only the four traditional elements (earth, air, fire, water) but also consider the quintessence or spirit, delving into the deeper metaphysical aspects of each element.

Integration of Magic and Science

Modern Druidry often seeks to integrate magical practice with scientific understanding, seeing them as complementary rather than contradictory.

Quantum Theories: Some Druidic practitioners explore parallels between quantum physics and magical practice, particularly in concepts such as the observer effect, interconnectedness, and the nature of reality.

Eco-Magic: This approach combines ecological science with magical practice, using ritual to positively influence the environment and promote ecological balance and sustainability.

Advanced magical systems in Druidry represent a harmonious blend of ancient wisdom and modern understanding. These systems are deeply rooted in the natural world, reflecting a profound respect for the universe and its laws. By studying and applying these advanced systems and theorems, Druids engage in a continuous process of learning and spiritual growth, contributing to their journey towards wisdom and enlightenment.

The Future of Druidry

Let's embark on an explorative journey into the potential future pathways and evolutions of Druidry by delving into the prospective trends, challenges, and advancements that might shape the Druidic path in the years to come.

Technological Integration and Evolution

As we move further into the digital age, Druidry, like many other spiritual paths, faces the challenge and opportunity of integrating technology into its practices.

Digital Ritual Spaces: The potential for virtual gatherings and rituals through advanced technology, allowing practitioners from all over the world to participate in ceremonies and sacred observances.

Eco-Technological Synergy: The growing importance of eco-friendly technologies in Druidic practice, emphasizing the harmonious relationship between nature and technology to promote environmental sustainability.

Societal Influence and Growth

Druidry's role within the broader societal context is likely to expand, addressing contemporary global challenges.

Environmental Advocacy: Druids are expected to take on more significant roles as advocates for environmental protection and sustainability, leveraging their spiritual connection to nature to drive ecological initiatives.

Cultural Influence: As interest in spiritual and earth-centered practices grows, Druidry may influence various aspects of culture, from art and music to community building and social activism.

Theoretical and Philosophical Expansions

Druidic philosophy and its theoretical framework are anticipated to evolve, integrating new insights and discoveries from various fields.

Quantum Mysticism: The interplay between Druidic practices and quantum physics could lead to new understandings of reality and spirituality, offering a unique perspective on the interconnectedness of all existence.

Global Druidic Synthesis: The potential for synthesizing Druidic wisdom with other spiritual traditions from around the world, leading to a more inclusive and diverse spiritual practice.

As we look to the future of Druidry, it is clear that the path is dynamic and evolving. While staying true to its roots in nature and ancient wisdom, Druidry is poised to adapt and grow in response to the changing world. The future of Druidry is not just about preserving the past but also about forging new pathways and integrating new insights for a sustainable, harmonious, and spiritually fulfilling future.

CHAPTER 24: SYNCRETISM AND THE GLOBAL DRUID

As the sun sets on the horizon of our comprehensive exploration of Druidry, we arrive at a compelling facet of this ancient path: its syncretism and global influence. Let's delve into how Druidry, while deeply rooted in its Celtic origins, has embraced and integrated elements from various spiritual paths and cultures, evolving into a truly global phenomenon.

The Interweaving of Traditions

Druidry, traditionally seen through the lens of ancient Celtic spirituality, has always been a fluid and adaptable path. In the modern era, this adaptability has allowed it to intersect with diverse spiritual practices and philosophies. This syncretism is not a dilution of its essence but an enrichment that brings a more holistic and inclusive approach to spirituality.

Integration with Eastern Philosophies: The modern Druid path has shown a remarkable affinity for integrating concepts from Eastern philosophies such as Buddhism and Hinduism. Concepts like mindfulness, meditation, and a deeper understanding of the self and the universe have found resonance within Druidic practices.

Influence of Western Esotericism: Elements of Western esoteric traditions, including Kabbalah and Hermeticism, have also woven their way into Druidry, offering new dimensions of mystical understanding and magical practice.

Embracing Indigenous Wisdom: There's been a growing appreciation and incorporation of indigenous wisdom from around the world, recognizing the shared reverence for nature and the wisdom of ancestors.

Druidry in a Global Context

The expansion of Druidry beyond its Celtic roots into a global movement has been a journey of both challenges and opportunities. This global spread has brought about a cross-pollination of ideas, practices, and perspectives, enriching the path for all who walk it.

Cultural Sensitivity and Adaptation: As Druidry spreads, it faces the challenge of respectfully integrating practices from various cultures. This requires a deep sensitivity and understanding to avoid cultural appropriation and to honor the origins and contexts of these practices.

Building Global Communities: The digital age has facilitated the growth of international Druidic communities. These online platforms have become spaces for shared learning, support, and the celebration of the diversity within the Druidic world.

Eco-Spirituality as a Universal Language: The environmental focus of Druidry has found a universal appeal. As our planet faces ecological crises, the Druidic emphasis on living in harmony with nature resonates across cultures, making it a truly global concern and connecting point.

The Path Ahead: Syncretism as Evolution

The journey of Druidry into the future is marked by its continued evolution through syncretism. This evolutionary process is not about losing its identity but about enriching its tapestry with diverse threads of human spiritual experience.

Honoring the Roots, Embracing the New: As Druidry grows, it continues to honor its Celtic roots while also embracing new influences. This balance is key to maintaining its integrity and relevance.

A Living Tradition: Druidry, as a living tradition, adapts and evolves with time. This dynamism ensures that it remains a vibrant and meaningful path for seekers in the modern world.

Unity in Diversity: The syncretism of Druidry is a testament to its underlying philosophy of unity in diversity. It acknowledges that while paths may differ, the quest for understanding, connection, and harmony with the natural world is a shared human endeavor.

As Druidry stands at the crossroads of the ancient and the modern, the local and the global, it continues to offer a rich, diverse, and evolving path of spiritual practice. Its journey is a beacon of hope and unity, demonstrating that wisdom and reverence for nature transcend cultural and geographical boundaries.

In the serene embrace of ancient woods, under the watchful gaze of the moon, and in the harmonious chorus of nature, we find the spirit of Druidry alive and thriving. As we draw this book to a close, let us reflect on the journey we have traversed together, exploring the depths of Druidic resurgence and its manifestation in the modern world.

The Timeless Tapestry of Druidry

Druidry, an ancient path, steeped in mystery and wisdom, has shown us the importance of living in harmony with nature.

It has taught us to revere the Earth, honor the cycles of the Wheel of the Year, and to find spiritual connection in the land, our ancestors, and the cosmos. This journey through the chapters has been a testament to the enduring relevance of these principles. We've rediscovered how the old ways, though ancient, resonate profoundly in our contemporary lives, offering solace, understanding, and a deep, abiding connection to all that is.

The Evolution of Modern Druidry

The modern Druidic movement, a vibrant tapestry of diverse threads, has been a story of rebirth and adaptation. From the misty hills of ancient Celtic lands to the digital forums of the internet age, Druidry has evolved to embrace a global community. We've witnessed its journey from a localized tradition to a worldwide spiritual path, open to all who seek its wisdom. This evolution is not just a change in numbers but a profound expansion in perspectives, practices, and interpretations.

Embracing Diversity: Druidry today celebrates the multitude of voices within its fold. It's a path where different cultures, beliefs, and practices converge, each adding their unique hue to the Druidic spectrum.

Eco-Spiritual Awakening: Amidst the environmental challenges of our time, Druidry has emerged as a beacon of eco-consciousness. We have seen how its principles inspire a deeper ecological understanding and an active engagement in environmental stewardship.

Communal Bonds: The essence of community in Druidry, both in physical groves and online sanctuaries, has been a source of strength and inspiration. These communal bonds have fostered a sense of belonging, shared learning, and collective celebration.

Envisioning the Future Path

As we look towards the horizon, the future of Druidry shimmers with potential. It invites us to continue exploring, adapting, and growing within this ancient yet ever-new tradition.

The Journey Continues: The path of Druidry is endless, with each step offering deeper insights and more profound experiences. We are encouraged to keep learning, practicing, and evolving on this spiritual journey.

Innovation and Tradition: As Druidry walks into the future, it balances the preservation of ancient wisdom with the incorporation of new ideas and technologies. This dynamic equilibrium ensures that the path remains relevant and vibrant.

Heritage and Progress: The commitment to preserving the core traditions of Druidry while embracing the changes of the modern era is paramount. This delicate balance ensures that the essence of Druidry, its heart, and soul, is passed on to future generations intact yet enriched.

Final Reflections

As we conclude this exploration, let us carry forward the wisdom, experiences, and connections we have forged. Druidry, a path of harmony, wisdom, and deep ecological insight, offers a unique lens through which to view our world and our place within it. It is a journey of continuous discovery, a path that weaves together the past, present, and future into a tapestry of spiritual fulfillment.

In the spirit of Druidry, let us walk forth with reverence for nature, a thirst for knowledge, and a heart full of gratitude for the journey. The path is ever-unfolding, and each of us is a pilgrim on this sacred journey of rediscovery and resurgence.

THE END

Printed in Dunstable, United Kingdom